Y0-CAS-373

Murder Has Consequences

Giacomo Giammatteo

Other books by Giacomo Giammatteo:

Murder Takes Time
Friendship and Honor Series, Book 1

A Bullet for Carlos
Blood Flows South, Book 1

FRIENDSHIP AND HONOR SERIES BOOK 2

Murder Has Consequences

GIACOMO GIAMMATTEO

INFERNO PUBLISHING COMPANY

MURDER HAS CONSEQUENCES
by Giacomo Giammatteo

© Copyright 2013 Giacomo Giammatteo

All rights reserved. No part of this book may be reproduced or transmitted in any form or by any means, electronic or mechanical, including photocopying, recording or by any information storage and retrieval system, without written permission from the author, except for the inclusion of brief quotations in a review.

INFERNO PUBLISHING COMPANY

For more information about this book, visit
www.giacomogiammatteo.com

Print ISBN 978-0-9850302-6-1
Electronic ISBN 978-0-9850302-5-4

This book is a work of fiction. Names, characters, places, and events herein are either the product of the author's imagination or are used fictitiously. Any resemblance to actual persons, living or dead, is entirely coincidental.

A note to readers

I write these stories with one thought in mind—what makes for the best read. Most of my stories are told in a combination of third person and first person point of view. You will notice the bullet image when it is first person and the gun image when it is third person. If a change in POV occurs within the same chapter, you will notice a series of 3 asterisks, like this: ***

I bring this up because a few people got confused in the last book. I hope you don't find this a distraction, as I believe telling the stories this way makes for a better reading experience.

Thanks, and I hope you enjoy the book.

Giacomo

"Oaths are something you swear to when you're young, and wish you hadn't when you get old."

– Nicky Fusco

INTRODUCTION

Wilmington, Delaware

Actions have consequences. I learned that long ago.

- I learned it when I was five years old and got caught stealing ciga-rettes.
- I learned it when Mikey "The Face" Fagullo beat our asses for not giving him a cut of the smokes we stole from a boxcar.
- I learned it when Father Tom caught us playing cards instead of attending mass.
- Mostly I learned it when I shot Freddy Campisi. That lesson cost me ten years in prison.

Different actions yield different consequences. Do something wrong—get sent to prison. That's one kind of consequence. But that's the easy one. If you go to prison, you do your time and get out. It's over. Done with.

But there is another, far worse, consequence—the one you have to live with day in and day out. The kind of consequence you beat yourself up over. The kind that won't go away. I did my time for killing Freddy Campisi. The other things I've done I have to live with. Those are between me and God. They are my cross on earth.

Nicky Fusco

CHAPTER 1

RESTRAINT

Wilmington, Delaware

I looked out my window toward Front Street, then lifted my head until I caught sight of the steeple of St. Elizabeth's Church. On a good day, when my window was open, I could hear the bells ringing. All I heard today was traffic. I picked up the phone and dialed Angie; she'd be expecting me for dinner. Adapting to my new life had been tough. I had traded excitement and danger for the routine of a family and a steady job. All in all a good trade, but at times I still itched to do something. Angie answered on the fifth ring. I always counted because I hung up if no one answered after ring five.

"Hello."

Angie had the best voice in the world. Strong and forceful, but… gentle too.

"Hey, babe, I've got to check a job tonight, so I'll be a little late. You and Rosa eat without me."

"I'll wait for you," she said. "Rosa's eating with a friend."

"Okay, if you don't mind. I'll see you later."

I grabbed my briefcase, a thin black leather one Angie gave me for my birthday, put the blueprints inside and headed for the door. "Sheila, tell Joe I'm going to check that new site."

"Which one?"

"The new condos."

"Okay, see you tomorrow."

I hated lying to Sheila. Hated lying to Angie even more, but this was something that had to be done. I checked my watch as I started the car— 4:45. That should give me plenty of time to get there before Marty Ferris left work. He was Rosa's scum-sucking ex-stepfather who needed to be taught a lesson. This meant I'd have to get up early to check those condos before work tomorrow, but that would be all right. I liked seeing the site, making sure there were no surprises. It wasn't just the bricks and mortar I needed to calculate, but also how much scaffolding and how many planks and braces we'd need. All of that mattered.

I was thinking about how lucky I was to have this job when I suddenly realized Union Street was coming up. I put on the blinker, turned left, and headed south, pulling into a parking spot just north of Sixth Street by my favorite water-ice stand. After checking the time again, I got out and grabbed a drink then got back in the car. Marty Ferris would be out soon. He was going to pay for what he did to Rosa. It had been more than six months now, and I had abided by all the rules my old hit-man mentor, Johnny Muck, had taught me. No matter what I had promised Angie, it was time for Marty to learn a lesson.

***

MARTY FERRIS CAME OUT of the bathroom, washed his hands twice, dried them, and tossed the paper towels into the bin. It was almost time to quit, and not much made him happier than that. Another day hacking at slabs of meat with a cleaver had earned him enough for his weekly bills and a few beers at Teddy's. Not nearly what he deserved for putting up with all the assholes who came in demanding special cuts, or trimming of fat, but it was the best he could do considering the economy. At times he felt like taking one of the knives and cutting some fat off a few of the customers, especially Mrs. Mariano. What a pain in the ass she was. That woman was never satisfied. She came into the shop every Thursday, walking as if she had a t-bone stuck up her ass.

'Don't forget to cut off all the fat, Marty. All of it.'

Her nagging voice grated on his nerves, staying with him long after she left. Stupid bitch should realize it was the fat that made the meat taste good, but he'd never tell her that.

Marty finished wrapping a few chops for the customer he was waiting on, and cleaned his knives as he waited for the day to end. The clock chimed—it was five-thirty, the first thing since lunch that put a smile on Marty's face. He untied his apron and headed for the back room. "Time for me to go, Sal. See you tomorrow."

"See you, Marty."

After scrubbing his hands he exited the building, got in his car and headed south on Union Street. He wanted to go home and shower, but he hadn't had a beer since Tuesday night, and he was itching for one. He thought about stopping at the bar, but then remembered it was Thursday, his day for subs at Casapulla's.

***

I SAT IN THE car a block north of where Marty worked, still sipping on my water ice to cool off. There wasn't much better than water ice on a hot day. As I thought that, I marveled at the genius of combining sugar, ice, and lemon into a drink that is damn near addictive, tasted good, and actually quenched your thirst. Water ice was one of the things I had missed most when I lived in New York, and missed even more in prison. I hadn't been all over the country yet, but so far I hadn't found anyplace that had water ice like Wilmington. For such a little city it had a lot of special things, particularly when it came to food.

Someone I didn't recognize was walking north on Union Street. I could tell he knew me by the way he stared, leaning down a little to get a better look at who sat behind the wheel. His face was familiar, but I couldn't put a name to it for the life of me. Frankie was always the best at that. I don't think there was anyone Frankie forgot once he met them. Even ten years later he could instantly spit out a name. I always wanted to be able to do that, but never could. I sighed as the guy headed toward me. There was no way I was coming up with his name in time.

The guy stooped over, leaned toward the car and smiled. "Hey, Nicky. Good to see you again."

I reached my hand out and shook his, then started to fake a forgotten-name moment, but I ended up doing what I always did when faced with this situation. "I know I should remember your name, but I don't."

The guy laughed, probably to cover up the embarrassment that he was forgotten. If only people knew it wasn't them, just a common thing.

"It's Howard. Remember, ninth grade, Sister Louise?"

I thought a second, then shook my head. "I don't, Howard. I'm sorry. I barely remember Sister Louise."

He smiled, laughed some more. "That's okay. Good to see you anyway. Take care."

"Yeah, take care, Howard."

As he walked up the street, I repeated the name in my head, hoping to remember it in case we ran into each other again. Within a few seconds I started looking for Marty again, focusing on the cars going south on Union Street. A minute later I saw his car, letting it pass before pulling out and falling in a few blocks behind him. We went past Front Street, past the park, past the street where he lived and over the bridge into Elsemere. As soon as he headed over the bridge I knew where he was going; on Thursdays Marty usually treated himself to a cheesesteak at Casapulla's. Most people thought Philly had the best cheesesteaks, but little old Wilmington, Delaware, made the best subs and steaks, bar none, and Casapulla's was king. Had been for more than fifty years.

Originally I'd planned on torturing Marty, but something inside of me wouldn't let me do that, so while I waited in the car, I decided I'd just have a talk with him. If that didn't work, I'd shoot him to get it over with. I had planned on doing it before he got his food, but despite how much I hated the guy, I couldn't justify killing him on an empty stomach. Everyone deserved a good last meal.

Rather than risk being seen, I turned around, deciding to wait for him by his house. I went back across the bridge and was lured in by a McDonald's sign boasting the billions they'd sold. It flashed at me on the left, so I turned into the parking lot and waited. Marty lived in Canby Park, just across the street, and from here I could see him coming. If he kept to his routine, he'd go home to shower then go out for a few beers. Perfect. I'd wait for him to leave the bar and take him then.

After half an hour, I began to worry. It shouldn't have taken him that long to get a sandwich, not even if they were busy. I waited ten more minutes then started the car and drove to Casapulla's. Marty's car wasn't there.

Shit. How did I miss him? I turned and drove back past Marty's house. Not there, either. Maybe it wasn't meant to be. I never thought stuff like that, so perhaps it was an omen. Angie had been after me with constant reminders not to do anything illegal, and while I promised her I wouldn't, this was one thing I'd promised myself long before that so it didn't count.

Maybe she was right, though. Even guys like Marty deserved a second consideration. I pulled to the curb, put the car in park, and took a quarter from the change slot under the radio.

Tails.

I flipped the coin, a toss to determine Marty's fate.

Heads.

I nodded. All right, Marty lives. I popped the car in gear and headed home, a good feeling in my gut. Sister Mary Thomas would be proud. As I drove home I wondered what I would have done if the coin had landed on tails.

It took less than five minutes to get home. Angie and I had moved into a single-family home on Beech Street. It was only a few blocks from where we grew up, but the houses were nicer and still within the St. Elizabeth's school district. It also put me a few blocks closer to where the guys hung out and played cards. Doggs was still around, and still running games, and Patsy the Whale and Charlie Knuckles were there too. Mikey the Face was serving time, and Pockets had gotten killed in an armed robbery. Some of the others had just moved on.

I parked the car, threw the bag in the trunk, and headed up the sidewalk to the house, then climbed the steps to the stoop two at a time. When I reached the top, I pushed open the front door. Angie stood in the center of the room, hugging Rosa. They were crying.

I nearly ran to them. "What happened? Are you all right?"

"It's Marty," Angie said. "Rosa met him for subs and they got into an argument. He hit her."

My body tensed. Fists clenched. *That fuckin' prick is gonna pay.*

Rosa broke away from her mother and grabbed me, hugging. "Dad, don't do anything. I'm okay. Nothing's wrong. Don't hurt him, okay?"

I held her close. Patted her back. All I could think of was what Mamma Rosa used to say to me when things got bad. "*Non ti preoccupare, Rosa.*"

"English!" she hollered. "Speak English."

"All I said was don't worry." Inside though, things churned. Thoughts of what I'd do to Marty when I got him, and how much I'd make him suffer. I thought of nails and screws and hammers and acid…

Then I felt her pinch me. "Dad. *Dad*, are you listening?"

I looked down at her and rubbed the back of her head. "What?"

"Did you hear me when I said don't hurt him? I meant it."

Her eyes were red from crying and her cheeks were tear-stained, but her face was that of an angel. How could I refuse. "All right, Rosa. But I swear…"

"Don't worry. It will never happen again. I'm through with seeing him for good."

I pulled her to me. Hugged her. *You're right, Rosa. It will never happen again.*

CHAPTER 2

HOMECOMING

Brooklyn, New York

Tom Jackson figured he'd been a killer all his life. *Born a killer,* as his daddy used to say about Beau, one of their hunting dogs. Tom remembered crying when Beau killed his favorite chicken, but when Tom told Daddy, his father did what he always did—taught him a lesson. He went to the kitchen, brought back a butcher knife and handed it to Tom.

"Do what you've got to do, boy," he said, and nodded toward Beau.

When Tom cut Beau, the dog let out a sickly yelp that made Tom cry more, and that sent his father to the shed. When his daddy came back with the whipping stick, Tom dried his tears quickly—around the Jackson house, the more you cried, the more you got whipped.

His father beat Tom something fierce that day—the kind of beating his daddy gave the dogs if they disobeyed, the kind that drew blood and hurt for days. Tom learned his lesson. Years later, after his mama died, Tom used that same knife to slit his father's throat, but he didn't cry when he killed his father. Afterwards, Tom buried him beside Beau, settled all the accounts on the farm, then packed what little he had and headed out.

Thinking back on that day Tom wondered if killing Beau was what set him down his path in life. It was either killing Beau or the army. If it *had been* the army they'd done a good job of it. Tom liked killing more than anything, even sex.

The thought of sex made him wonder about his wife, Lisa. Images came to mind of her soft curves and the tiny bit of plumpness around her belly. Tom hated women who were too skinny. Half of them nowadays were nothing but bones. It reminded him of eating a chicken wing. Lisa had just enough meat, and he liked to wrap his arms around her at night and feel that little jiggle.

A throb of pain in Tom's leg caused him to stir. He rubbed the spot around the wound where the bullet had struck. It had mostly healed, but a slight limp remained. The doctor said it might stay with him for as long as a year, though Tom doubted that. He'd always been a fast healer. Even when his daddy beat him real bad, the bruises faded in a day or so. He guessed that's why his daddy hit Tom on Friday nights mostly—that, or the drinking.

A bump in the road shook Tom, igniting more pain. He stared out the window of the cab at all of the people, crowding each other, all in a hurry. And the cars, crammed together, horns beeping. It had been a long time since he'd seen something like this. "How much farther?" he asked the cabbie.

"About fifteen minutes."

Tom reached into his knapsack and pulled out his discharge papers. *Dishonorable.* What the fuck were they thinking? After all he'd done for them. Worse part of it was that they discharged him for killing what they called a *holy man.* Those sons of bitches didn't have any holy men. *All fuckin' heathens.* He should have shot the whole village, kids and all. Then there would have been nobody to tell about what Tom had done. That's what he'd do if he could do it over—kill them all.

He hadn't realized how much he'd tensed up until another sharp pain raced up his leg. He breathed deeply, relaxed, let his mind drift. He was supposed to think about calming things, but his mind kept going to Lisa. But thoughts of her made him anxious, and stiff. He wanted nothing more than to grab her and throw her in bed, but he worried that she'd be ashamed of him. She'd been so proud of what he'd done in the army, even suggested he re-enlist if they let him.

The cabbie pulled up to his building, got out and helped Tom to the door with his bags. Tom paid the fare, tipping him good, then took the elevator to the fourth floor and made his way to #412. He knocked, but didn't expect to find her home; it was still early. When she didn't answer he sat on the floor against the wall, dreaming of the night they'd have together, but worrying about telling her what had happened. As he thought about all of the issues with starting over, he remembered she kept a spare key hidden in the laundry room.

Minutes later, he returned with the key and opened the door, tossing his bags on the floor. He got a drink of water, then headed into the bedroom to shower. The bedroom was small, but it had a nice closet, big enough for both of them to hang their clothes, though neither of them were clothes hounds. As he stripped off his shirt, he went to the closet, wanting to smell her scent. It had been so long.

Tom stopped dead, staring. Not believing what he saw. Hanging next to her clothes were several suits, shirts, and ties. And on the floor, three pair of men's shoes.

"What the fuck…"

He put his shirt back on, not bothering to shower, then he punched himself in the face, hard. Then again. After that he sat on the edge of the tub and cried. For nearly ten minutes he wondered what he'd done wrong, what drove her to do this. With no answers, he stood and walked to the living room, locked the door, then got his bags and put them in the bedroom closet. He grabbed his knife and gun and sat on the bed to wait.

A cat meandered in, a small black cat with a tiny voice. It rubbed against Tom's leg and meowed, but so softly he barely heard it. Tom picked it up, set it on the bed, and stroked its head. He rubbed it gently at first, then his muscles tensed. He wondered if the cat belonged to the man. Tom's hand tightened around its neck, but just as he was about to squeeze the life from it, another soft meow emerged. The cat looked up at him with innocent eyes.

"Who do you belong to?" Tom asked, and relaxed his grip. He'd wait and see. No need to do it now.

An hour later the front door opened. The sound of a woman's laughter rolled down the hallway. It was Lisa; he'd know that laugh anywhere. Tom smiled, but only for an instant. Hot on the trail of her laughter was a man's voice. Tom's fist clenched around the handle of the knife, the veins in his hands bulging. It took all of his training to restrain himself, to keep from rushing down the hall and slitting the man's throat. Tom's patience held for almost fifteen more minutes, suffering while they laughed and chatted about shared experiences that he knew nothing about. He forced himself to take measured breaths. Slow, easy, measured breaths, following the path of the qi.

"I'm taking a shower," Lisa said.

"Not without me," the man said. "And just think—I've got a whole week off. Any ideas of what to do with all that time?"

Tom closed his eyes, tensing.

When the bedroom door opened, he grabbed Lisa's arm and yanked her to the side. He stepped forward, into the movements of the man, and shoved the knife into his gut. Lisa screamed, but Tom pushed the blade all the way under the ribs and into the lungs. The man clutched at his wound, gasped as he collapsed. He'd be dead in a few minutes.

Tom turned to Lisa, placed the knife against her face. "One more noise and I'll kill you."

She must have finally recognized him. She caught her breath and her hands flew to her mouth. "Tom! Oh my God. What have you done?"

He wanted to cut her. His hand twitched, started to move, but he kept his control. Pushed her onto the bed. "Quiet."

The man on the floor gasped a few last breaths. A spittle of blood dripped from his mouth.

"My God, you killed him." Lisa moved toward the man, but Tom held her back.

"What did you expect me to do?"

"What are you doing here? Why—"

Tom's fist tightened around the knife. "I'll ask the questions." He grabbed her throat, pressed the knife to her pulsing neck. "Is there any reason why I shouldn't kill you?"

He wanted to hit her, but he didn't much take to hitting girls, leastwise, as long as they did him right. That's what his daddy always taught him, but that was just before Tom's daddy beat his mama right into her grave. Beat her so bad her head swelled up like a rotten melon. Couple of weeks later she keeled over. Daddy had Tom get the shovel that day and start digging.

"Got to be deep," Daddy told Tom. "Real deep. Don't want no coyotes gettin' to her."

No sir. Tom didn't take to hitting females. If a woman was a target, he'd shoot her with a fifty caliber, blow half her head clean off, but there was no sense in striking a woman. He'd seen his daddy do enough of that.

"Calm down, Lisa. Stop crying."

Her cries went from uncontrolled bawling to sobbing, then to sniffles. Finally, she sat on the bed, shaking.

Tom walked to her, blood covering his hand and arm and the front of his clothes. "I didn't mean to upset you, but…well, he had to die. You understand that don't you?"

Lisa nodded, wiping her eyes with the sleeve of her blouse.

Finish the job. The phrase rang in his head, a reminder of his training. But he wouldn't do it—couldn't do it. *No way* he was going to kill Lisa. He pulled her to him, the blood from his shirt smearing her forehead. She trembled. He felt her resistance but held her in place. "You'll have to be brave. I won't hurt you as long as you do what I say."

She sobbed louder. "Okay."

"Good, because we're going to have to clean up this mess, and it's important that we clean up real good."

"Okay," slipped out between sobs.

"Grab his feet and help me get him in the tub."

Lisa cried all the way to the bathroom. She kept her head turned, refusing to look at the body, but she made it without puking—that was good. He took the shower curtains off so they wouldn't get messy then ran water before placing the body in the tub. Lisa stood next to Tom, shaking, and staring at her bloody hands.

"I need to wash," she said.

"Not yet," Tom said. "Get the hacksaw."

TOM REMOVED THE HEAD, but he made Lisa do the feet and hands. And the dick, of course. She threw up several times and passed out once for a few seconds, but she got through it. They placed the body parts in separate plastic bags. He triple-wrapped the bags, placed them both inside of suitcases and covered them with more plastic bags. The last thing Tom wanted was leakage. He carved something into the back of one of the hands just before he put both of the man's hands and the dick into a different bag.

Tom turned to Lisa. "Get all those clothes out of the closet, and be thankful I don't stuff you in one of these bags."

When she finished, Lisa ran to the sink and started scrubbing.

"Not yet," Tom said. "You need to clean that tub. It's going to take a lot of scrubbing."

Tom cut out the carpet where the blood had stained it. He stuffed the pieces into more bags, which he placed alongside the others. Then he made Lisa scrub the floors, and then the tub five times with bleach. When she finished, he told her to get in the tub.

Fear filled her eyes. She cried.

"I'm not going to hurt you," he said. "Scrub yourself."

As she did, her eyes never left him. After the third time, she rinsed and reached to turn off the shower. He stopped her.

"You aren't clean yet. Keep scrubbing."

She stood naked, arms wrapped around her breasts, shivering. "I'm clean."

He shook his head. "Not yet."

She washed herself five more times before Tom allowed her to stop. He placed his knife against her skin, above her pubic hair. "This won't hurt," he said, and slid the blade across her, drawing a thin line of blood.

Lisa stifled a scream.

"That is to cleanse you," he said. "Blood cleans the soul."

Lisa shook so hard it looked as if she might break apart.

Blood trickled down the front of her, mixing with her hair. When he thought enough had come out he threw her a clean washcloth. "Scrub yourself with that. Make sure it goes inside of you. I want you pure."

She cleaned herself for fifteen minutes, crying the entire time. Afterward, he cleaned the cut, put a bandage on her then made her dress in a nightgown as they watched TV.

"I have to call someone. Tell them I'm not coming to work tomorrow."

"Bullshit," he said. "You have to go to work. Can't miss work for something like this." He flipped through a few channels and looked at her. "On second thought, maybe you better call. I'll need help with these suitcases. I've decided to put them somewhere to draw attention."

"Maybe I *should* go in," Lisa said. "They might wonder—"

"You're coming with me." Tom's voice had taken on a hard tone. "Call and leave a message. And hurry up. I want to watch a show."

Lisa made the call, then went back to sit on the couch with Tom. She sat at the end, as far from him as she could. He motioned her closer. She slid half a cushion toward him.

"Who does the cat belong to?"

Lisa gasped and ran toward the bedroom. "Buster! Buster, where are you?"

"I didn't hurt him," Tom said. "I asked who he belonged to."

Lisa came back with the cat nestled in her arm. "I found him on the streets." She cast a quick glance toward the door, then back at Tom.

He smiled. "If you want to keep Buster alive, you'll do everything I say." Tom's voice got that hard tone again, and he said, "And if you even look at that door again, you'll end up like your boyfriend. I'll cut you up myself and feed you to Buster."

Lisa got on her knees in front of him, tears flowing. "I'll do anything you want, Tom. Please don't hurt Buster. He didn't do anything."

Tom took the cat from her arms and placed him on the sofa. "Do what I say and nothing bad will happen."

They watched television for almost two hours, before Tom said he wanted to go to bed. When they got to the bedroom, Lisa took off her nightgown and grabbed a pair of green pajamas from her drawer. They were sprinkled with little white kittens.

"Sleep naked," Tom said. "I like us sleeping naked."

She nodded and silently climbed into bed, fear tainting every movement. As she pulled the covers around her, Tom draped his legs over her and hugged her from behind. "I miss that little belly you used to have. You've gone and gotten skinny on me."

"I've been working out," Lisa said, her voice tremulous.

Tom was silent for a while, though he kept rubbing her stomach, careful not to touch the cut. He thought about what had happened to his life, and about what that man had done to her. She'd been a good girl when he married her. And now this. "Who else fucked you?"

Lisa made a noise like a gasp, and she squeezed her legs together. Tom looked over her shoulder. Her eyes were closed tight, as if she was trying to hide.

"Who?" He demanded. "I want the names of every one of them."

She started crying. "There wasn't anyone else. I swear. Only…him." She had almost said his name. That would have been a mistake.

Silence fell over them while Tom thought. He had learned a lot while he was away, especially what made a woman dirty and unclean. He thought about her betrayals. He knew what needed to be done. "I didn't mean just while I was away. I meant ever."

CHAPTER 3

A BEAUTIFUL MORNING

Brooklyn, New York

Frankie Donovan stretched as he opened his eyes, but then he quickly shut them. The sun blaring through the window promised another beautiful day in Brooklyn. Despite that, Frankie made a note to shut the blinds. No sense in waking up too happy.

He turned towards the warm body beside him, ready to tease Kate into waking. But instead of Kate's crop of Irish-red hair, he found himself looking at Shawna. He had almost called her Kate. *Mother of God. What a mistake* that *would have been.*

Frankie leaned over, lifted the covers and ran an appreciative eye down the curve of Shawna's back to the round firmness of her ass. He leaned forward and kissed her cheek—the one on her face. "You want coffee?"

She popped up, a worried expression on her face. "What time is it?"

"Early, don't worry."

"What time?" Panic filled Shawna's voice as she slipped her panties on.

"Six-thirty. You've got time."

"Six-thirty? You sure?"

"I'm looking at the clock."

Hearing that, she relaxed. "Sorry. I can't afford to be late. Those assholes are looking for any excuse to fire me."

"Tell them you were sleeping with Detective First Class Frankie Donovan, hero of Brooklyn. They'll forgive you."

"Or laugh in my face."

"There's always that possibility," Frankie said, and wrapped his arms around her waist. "Have I told you how sweet you are?"

"Not everyone thinks so." Shawna leaned back and kissed him. "Sorry for being grumpy. I get nervous."

Frankie rubbed the bottom of her back. "I can cure nervous."

Shawna stood, slipping her panties off again. "No thanks on your *cure*, but since you're in a generous mood, I'll take coffee. I'm grabbing a quick shower."

"Want a bagel?"

"Half of one," she said, then, "You should consider getting a bigger apartment. Or at least one in a better neighborhood."

"I like the company here. These are real people," Frankie said, but the door to the bathroom was already closing.

Frankie went to the kitchen, started the coffee, cleaned up a few things, and popped a bagel into the toaster. The phone rang while he was pouring coffee. "Donovan."

"Frankie, it's Carol. You've got a body, or something like it, not far from home. Mazzetti's on the way."

"'A body or something like it.' What the hell is that supposed to mean?"

"I just repeat what I'm told," Carol said.

"Give me the address." Frankie scribbled it on a piece of paper he ripped from the front of the refrigerator. "Uh huh. Okay. I'm all over it."

Shawna stood beside him, wrapped in a towel. She perked up as she looked at the address. Frankie sniffed her hair and kissed her. "Hate to do this, but I've got to go."

"Was that a body-call?"

"Yeah, and it sounds like it could be a nasty one."

She picked up her cell and started dialing, but Frankie grabbed her phone. "Whoa. No way. You're not calling it in from here. I don't mind giving you a heads up and helping out, but I can't let you have a story because you were in my bed when I got the call."

"That's bullshit and you know it." She took her phone back and started punching in the numbers. "I'm getting a camera crew."

"I swear, Shawna, don't do it. You get there before anyone else and I'll crucify you."

"So you won't give me a *break* because I was here, but you're willing to punish me and make me arrive last to the scene?"

Frankie shook his head, cursing. "Goddamnit." He thought for a minute. "All right, here's the deal. You can sit around the corner and wait till another station shows. As soon as you see them you can come in, but not a minute earlier. How's that?"

Shawna smiled. "Fair as shit. Thanks." She kissed him and rubbed his ass.

"All right, maybe a few minutes earlier," Frankie said, and rushed off. "Lock the door when you leave."

It took Frankie twenty-five minutes to get to the scene because of traffic. Mazzetti was sitting on the stoop of a run-down apartment building, waiting for Frankie, smoke leaking from the side of his mouth. A couple of young kids were squeezing through a hole in a chain-link fence, leading in from a patch of broken concrete they'd made into a makeshift basketball court.

"You guys live here?" Frankie asked.

"Who wants to know?" the tallest one said.

Frankie showed him the badge. "We *might* have a stiff upstairs. Know anything about it?"

The short one bounced the ball from hand to hand, shaking his head. The older one said, "Wouldn't be the first time."

"You didn't answer me. You live here?"

They both said no almost at the same time.

"All right, let us know if you hear anything, will ya'? Help me out and I'll get you a pass on something. Not drugs, but something."

A light seemed to go off in their eyes. "You got a card?"

"I got two," Frankie said, and pulled a couple out of his shirt pocket.

"Dressed a little *fly* for a cop," the little guy said. First time, he'd spoken except for the 'no.'

Frankie smiled. "You worry about getting me a lead. I got the rest covered."

Little Guy bumped fists with Frankie. "Keep a line open, dude. I might call."

"Do that," Frankie said. He kicked a few bottles aside as he made his way to the steps. "Hey, Lou. How's it going?"

"From here it's fine." He lifted his head toward the top of the building. "Up there, I don't know."

"They got no elevator?"

Lou struggled to stand, hand placed on his leg as he pushed up. "They got an elevator but it's broken. How's that for a place, huh?" He got to his feet with some effort, and walked toward the front door. "Tell you what, if it's the super that's dead, close the case. I don't blame someone for killing him."

"So what, you want me to carry you up?"

"I'd die first."

"You're right about that." Frankie got to the bottom of the stairs and looked up. It seemed like an endless climb. "What floor?"

"Sixth, which might as well be the fiftieth. I ain't gonna make it."

Frankie crushed out his cigarette in the grass next to the sidewalk. No sense in making the climb more difficult. He grabbed Lou by the arm and started up the first flight, avoiding any contact with the railing. God knows what germs were on it.

A few remnants of green paint clung to the sides of the stair treads, but they were so worn in the middle there weren't even any splinters. The walls were covered with graffiti, and though some was the same old raunchy stuff that had been decorating walls for decades, other parts were funny. Frankie found himself smiling. It wasn't much different than his own building.

A few minutes later they hit the top of the steps, Mazzetti panting as if he were dying. "Donovan, we better solve this case quick, because I'm not coming back up here."

Frankie nodded to the two uniforms standing in the hallway. About ten feet from them sat what appeared to be two large suitcases wrapped in plastic garbage bags. "What have we got?"

"Not sure yet," one of them said. "One of the kids found this when they came out this morning. There's a note on it that says 'more bodies coming' and there appears to be blood on it."

Frankie made his way over, with Lou right behind him. "You didn't open them?"

"Hell no. Could be a bomb in there. I called it in and they told me to wait for you."

Mazzetti brushed a hand in the air. "Nobody's setting off a bomb in this place."

"Open it up," Frankie said.

"Kate's on her way," Lou said. "We should wait for her."

Just the mention of Kate's name made Frankie uncomfortable. She had resisted all of his attempts to get back together even though they hung out a lot and had gotten to be damn good friends. He looked around, then addressed one of the uniforms. "You talk to any neighbors yet?"

"No answer at three of them. The others swear they heard nothing."

The sound of footsteps climbing the stairs got Frankie's attention. "That you, Kate?"

"It's me. Ask Mazzetti to come give me a hand."

"You know what you can do with that hand," Lou said. "Hurry and get up here."

A few minutes later Kate and her team stood in front of the suitcases. She nodded to Donovan. "I see Shawna Pavic's team got here early."

"Yeah, I saw that," he said.

Kate grabbed his arm and pulled him aside. "I don't get you, Donovan. You go out of your way to attract women, but you don't let anyone in. If it's just sex you want, get a prostitute. You're doing yourself and Shawna both an injustice by pretending."

Frankie clenched his teeth. He wanted to say *bullshit*, and a few other things…but she was right. "That hit below the belt, Kate."

"That's where I aimed," she said, and joined her crew.

Her cameraman took pictures, and another member of her team cut the plastic and pulled out the first suitcase. Tentative, he unzipped it.

"Whoa, we got a body," he said and stepped back.

Kate moved in, studying it. "No head. No hands or feet." She rolled the torso to the side. "And no male organ. I'm guessing the rest of him is in the other suitcase."

Mazzetti covered his mouth with his handkerchief and stepped closer. "They cut his dick off? The least they could have done was give us a whole body to work with."

"If we don't get lucky, this one will be a John Doe for a long time," Frankie said.

"Unless there's a wallet with a license stuffed up his ass," Lou said.

Kate turned and glanced at Mazzetti. "You want to take a look?"

"That's your department," Lou said. "I just catch killers."

Frankie's phone rang and he answered it. "Donovan."

"Frankie, it's Donna. Mom needs you to come home."

She sounded upset. Frankie stepped a few feet away. "What's the matter? She sick?"

"No, she's…just come home, all right."

"Donna, I can't just pick up and leave. I'm in the middle of a case. What's going on?" Irritation started to set in, like it always did when Frankie spoke with his sisters, especially Donna.

He waited through a long silence, trying to listen to what Kate was telling Lou, then Donna spoke again, but through a lot of sobbing and tears. "It's *Dad*, Frankie. He's dead."

Dead! "What happened? When?" Frankie put one hand to his head and began walking in circles. "Holy shit."

"It happened this morning," Donna said. Frankie could barely understand her through all the tears. "He had…a…heart attack."

Frankie stopped walking and took a deep breath. "Okay, Donna. Okay, take it easy. I'll be down as fast as I can. Is Mom okay? Are you okay?"

Her crying had gotten out of control. "Just get down here fast. Mom needs you…we all do."

"I'm leaving right now. Take me about two, probably two and a half hours to get there. Tell Mom I'm on my way."

He put the phone in his pocket and headed toward Mazzetti.

Lou must have sensed something was wrong. "Who was that? Everything okay?" When Frankie didn't answer, Lou walked over to him. "Donovan, you okay?"

Frankie shook his head. "My dad died."

"Goddamn. I'm sorry. Shit!" Lou grabbed hold of Frankie and hugged him. "Are you all right?"

Frankie nodded. "Tell Kate, will you? I gotta go."

"Go on. Get out of here," Lou said. "I got this covered."

Frankie looked around the scene, as if there were something he was still supposed to do. "Yeah, I gotta go. I'll call you later." He ran all the way down the steps, and to his car. He stopped at his apartment, grabbed a suit and other clothes, then bounded down the steps. Within fifteen minutes he was heading across the Verazzano Bridge on I-278. Soon he would connect with I-95 and be on his way south to Wilmington. The problem was, Frankie didn't want to go home. Not even for a funeral.

CHAPTER 4

A LONG RIDE

It didn't take long for Frankie's mind to start drifting, Donna's words playing over and over in his head like an old 45 record stuck in a groove.

It's Dad, Frankie. He's dead.

Frankie hit the steering wheel with the palm of his hand. "Goddamn." He stepped on the gas at the same time, kicking the speedometer up a notch to eighty-five. Donna sounded bad, and he knew his mom would be a basket case. His other sisters, too.

A nagging, dull pain simmered in his gut. He didn't know if his body wanted to throw up or...he just didn't know. As his mind drifted, he wondered if this was how Nicky felt when his pops died. Frankie remembered that funeral as if it were yesterday. Now that he knew what it felt like to lose a father, Frankie wished he'd done more to console Nicky. Come to think of it there were a lot of things Frankie wished. Like that he'd called his father more often. He couldn't remember the last time he called his father just to talk. Frankie searched his memory, but kept coming up blank.

Was it Dad's birthday? Did I even call him on his birthday? No, I didn't. It was Christmas. What a fuckin' loser I am.

He wiped a tear from his eye, took out a smoke and lit it, sucking hard. Had he argued with his dad the last time they talked? He usually did.

When was the last time he told his dad he loved him? He flicked the cigarette out the window, getting no comfort from smoking it. "You're a piece of shit, Bugs Donovan. A goddamn rotten piece of shit."

He tried getting his mind off that line of thinking, searching for anything that would take him away from thoughts of funerals and death. From the corner of his eye he saw the sign for New Brunswick, bringing back a memory of a girl he dated, although not for long. She didn't like Brooklyn, and Frankie wasn't about to leave it. Even that thought brought bad memories, and thoughts of the girl made him think of his mother.

Marriage is forever, she always said, and she lived her life that way, at least on the surface.

Frankie grew up thinking his dad was an ass, always keeping tabs on his mother, never letting her out on her own, demanding to know where she was going or where she'd been. Frankie wondered how, and why, his mother put up with it, and he ended up hating his father for the way he treated her. It wasn't until years later that Frankie found out his mother had trouble keeping to one man. He refused to believe the rumors for years. By the time he knew the truth, his relationship with his father was gone.

The idea of marriage made Frankie think of his own twisted life. He'd been through more relationships than he cared to admit, and most of the break-ups were his fault. In fact, he seemed to avoid *any* relationship that held promise for marriage, sticking to married women, or ones otherwise involved. Shawna popped into his head, and he made a mental note to tell her what was going on with his father.

He liked thinking about the good old days of his childhood, but he was wise enough now to realize they never were that good. *Maybe it's time to start a new life.*

Frankie wished he could go *way* back. Back to when things were simple, when he and his friends ruled the streets. As he thought about how much he missed those days, he wondered where Paulie was, and how Nicky was doing. He hadn't talked to Nicky since the incident in Brooklyn six months ago, but Nicky *had* sent a letter. He'd found Angela and they got married. If Frankie remembered right, they lived on Beech Street, not far from where they all grew up.

Then Frankie thought about Bobby, Donna's husband, which brought back memories of the old days, specifically of the gang fight that sent Nicky away, the one where Nicky killed Bobby's brother. Both of them being at his father's wake wouldn't be good, but Frankie didn't know what to do about it. Bobby had to be there, and Nicky would show up out of respect. It's the way he was. As he worried about what might happen, he pushed the thoughts aside.

Guess I'll find out soon enough.

CHAPTER 5

REUNION

Wilmington, Delaware

I got up early, went for my morning run, had coffee with Angie, and then headed off to work. What I wanted to do was kill Marty Ferris but that would have to wait. Even though I promised Rosa I wouldn't hurt Marty, a burning desire to punish him churned in my gut.

What kind of cowardly fuck hits a kid?

When I got to Front Street I took a right and had to immediately lower the visor to keep out the morning sun, which promised a nice day. Traffic was already bad. When I stopped for the light at the corner of Front and Clayton I looked over at the spot where a barber shop used to be when we were kids. We walked there once a month to get haircuts and sit and listen to the old guys tell stories.

My dreams were interrupted by the sound of a horn beeping behind me. I'd been sitting at the traffic light for probably half a second after it turned green. *Impatient bastard.* Everybody was in a hurry. I stayed on Front Street, passing by other old memories, continuing in a half stupor all the way to downtown, then turned in by the river where the new construction was going on. After spreading the prints across the hood of the car, I took a closer look at the building site. We'd be sending half the damn company here in a week or so, and the boss sure as shit didn't want a delay once the project got started.

It took me almost an hour to finish, forcing myself to double-check the numbers. Every time I did something like this I thought of Tony and how much faster he could have done this, but with those thoughts came the memory of what he did to Angie. I never understood how any man could do that to a woman. I hated him for what he did, but I hated him almost as much for tainting my memories. Now I couldn't think of old times without that popping into my head. I rolled up the prints, put everything in the front seat and headed to the office. Before I got two blocks the phone rang. It was Angie.

"Hello?"

"Nicky, I just got a call from Mary Ellen Donovan. Frankie's father died."

"What? Goddamn. When?"

"This morning. He had a heart attack."

"Holy shit. Poor Mrs. D."

Somebody swerved in front of me, forcing me to hit the brakes. *Stupid fuck.*

"When's the wake?" There was no need to ask where. Everybody still got buried at Jimmy Maldonaddo's, though they had moved to better facilities. Burying people was a good business, good enough to support four brothers and their families and let them all drive Caddies.

"Probably tomorrow night. I'll call later. And would you stop calling it a wake. People say 'viewing' now."

"Guess I'm old fashioned. We are still supposed to stay up and watch aren't we?"

"Stay up eating and drinking is more like it, and telling tales." She paused. "Are you going over tonight?"

"I'll have to think about it."

I hadn't talked to Bugs since New York. He had been pissed at me—more than pissed—especially after what happened to Tony. Not for the first time I wondered if the relationship with Bugs had survived. We hadn't talked in six months and I was more than apprehensive. With Tony dead, and Paulie gone…somewhere, Bugs was the only connection I had to the old memories, the ones that got more important with every year that passed.

Angie broke the silence. "I don't care what you do, Nicky, I'm going to the house. I'll get Rosa to help make meatballs and ziti. There will be a lot of people; they'll need food."

Angie had her *it's-the-right-thing-to-do* voice working. I knew there was no point in arguing. "Whatever you think, but warn Rosa so she doesn't throw a fit at the last minute."

"She'll be fine. I raised that girl to know her duties; besides, she loves cooking for people."

"I wonder who she got that from?" I turned onto the street where our office was, parked and got out. "All right, listen. I'll try to get off early so I can clean up and we can get there at a decent time. If it just happened this morning, I doubt Bugs is even here yet. They'll need time alone."

"Okay, I'll see you tonight," she said, then before hanging up, "Nicky… have you and Bugs talked since you were in New York?"

"No. I sent him a letter, that's all."

"Is that going to be uncomfortable?"

"I guess, but his father died. That takes precedence."

***

DRIVING PROVIDED SOME SANITY for Frankie, and for a minute he wished the drive were longer. He was in no hurry to get caught up in the drama that surrounded his family, especially under these circumstances.

And Nicky.

He presented another problem, one the shrinks at the department would love to analyze, not to mention Internal Affairs. Frankie was a cop and he had let a killer go. Sure Nicky was his best friend and had saved Frankie's life, but Frankie was a cop, and the fact remained that he let a killer walk.

So here he was, driving through New Jersey's Pine Barrens, wondering why he was afraid of relationships and dreading a reunion with his screwed-up family and his killer friend. It was going to bring everything to the surface again, after it had taken him so long to bury it. He shook his head and focused on the drive while restraining a laugh. If a shrink got hold of him now, he'd crack like a bad egg. *God give me the strength*, he thought, and let off the gas. No sense in getting there too early.

An hour later Frankie pulled off I-95 and within fifteen minutes he was turning onto Clayton Street. In some ways the area looked the same as it had thirty years ago. The cars parked out front were newer models, and the streets weren't as full of kids playing stick ball or the best-of-all game—Relievio—but the houses hadn't changed and the feel of the neighborhood hadn't either.

He turned onto Banning Street and parked by the school, knowing there wouldn't be a space by his house. Or was it because he needed the time to himself before he got there. Enough tears had been shed on his way from Brooklyn, but he knew more were coming, especially after he saw his mom. Halfway down the block he braced himself, determined not to let his emotions get the best of him.

Suck it up, Bugs.

If he owed his dad anything, it was the strength to be strong for his mother and sisters. Frankie found extra willpower and wished it into the rest of his body as he climbed the steps to the house. Several people were on the stoop, smoking. One of them stood, rushing to greet him as he approached. It was Mary Ellen, his youngest sister.

"Frankie!" She threw her arms around him and the bawling began. "I'm so glad you're here. Mom is a mess. She needs you."

Frankie held her close, rubbing her back. "It's all right, Mary. How are *you* holding up?"

"I'm okay, but Mom and Donna are the worst. Even Uncle Donnie can't calm her down. She keeps asking for you."

"I better get inside," Frankie said. He slid his arm over her shoulder and started up the steps, nodding to one of the neighbors who waved.

He reinforced his will before entering the house, then he opened the front door and stepped into the living room. The house was the same. A braided throw rug—frayed around the edges—covered most of the room. Hardwood floors which hadn't been polished in twenty years took up the rest of the space. There wasn't room for a coffee table, only a sofa, one end table, and two small chairs that flanked an old TV.

His mother occupied the honorary spot on the sofa, her sisters on each side. Frankie didn't make it five feet into the living room before his mother jumped up and ran to him, handkerchief in one hand and a rosary in the other.

"Frankie! God bless you for coming so soon."

She threw her arms around him and let herself fall into his embrace. If she had been crying before, it had been nothing to compare with her tears now.

"He's gone, Frankie. What will I do without him?"

Frankie rubbed her back, kissed the top of her head. "You'll be okay, Mom. We'll take care of you."

As he comforted his mother, his sisters, Donna and Marie, ran to him, tears flowing. They wrapped themselves around him and their mother in a huge ball of tears. Emotion ripped Frankie's gut apart but he held to his conviction to remain tough for them. There would be plenty of time to cry later. "It's okay. I'm here now."

When he finally escaped their embrace, Frankie headed toward the kitchen to get something to drink. It only took three steps to get through the dining room. He forgot how small this house was. A big guy in a brown suit held out his hand to Frankie as he passed. "Sorry about your dad."

Frankie almost didn't recognize him; it was Donna's husband. "Bobby, I didn't see you there." He shook Bobby's hand and they embraced, not like family, but acquaintances. "Donna doing okay?"

Bobby shook his head. "She hasn't stopped crying since it happened."

"Yeah, I think it'll be a long night, Bobby. You doin' okay? How's work?"

Bobby shrugged. "We'll talk later. I gotta worry about Donna now."

Frankie didn't like that answer, but he let it go. He had plenty to keep his mind occupied without having to worry about his degenerate brother-in-law. "Sounds good. I'll catch up with you another time," Frankie said, and headed into the kitchen. He thought Bobby's eyes looked a little funny, but that could've been explained by crying—if he had. If not, it could've been explained by drugs, and if Frankie had a c-note to bet he'd place it on the drugs. Anyway, that was Donna's problem.

Relatives kept pouring in all day. The ones who still lived in Wilmington got there early, but by late afternoon people were arriving from Jersey and Philly. By five o'clock the house was jammed. So was the back yard. Frankie looked around and smiled. With all these people and only one bathroom, it could have been a disaster, but neighbors on both sides opened up their houses, letting people use their bathrooms. That's the way people were here—real neighbors.

Angie walked in the front door, arms loaded with food. A young girl was right behind her. Frankie walked over and hugged Angie, a brief smile lighting his face. "Damn it's good to see you. Thanks for coming."

"I'm so sorry about your father, Frankie." She kissed his cheek. "I figured you could use the food."

"We can use it, and we really appreciate it," Frankie said, and he took a quick glance of the room, tension building. "Is Nicky here?"

"Dad's parking the car," Rosa said. "There wasn't any place for two blocks."

Frankie stared at her for a moment, then shook his head. "Dad? My God, is this…" He turned to Angie, a question on his face.

She blushed. "I forgot you never met Rosa." She placed Rosa between herself and Frankie. "Rosa, I know you've heard your dad talk about him, but this is Frankie Donovan. Mr. Donovan to you."

"I can't believe it," Frankie said. "And we'll have none of that Mr. Donovan shit around here. Call me Bugs or Frankie. I feel old enough as it is."

Rosa smiled, but she leaned in and whispered, "I have strict orders."

Frankie winked, and then reached for the food in Angie's hands. "Let me help," he said, and grabbed the bowl then started toward the kitchen. He inhaled deeply, the aroma bringing back memories. "Is this what I think it is? Mamma Rosa's meatballs?"

Angie's laughter was full of pride. "Just call them 'Little Rosa's' meatballs now. And they're just as good."

"Little Rosa…I still can't believe it."

Rosa set her food on the table and gave a bashful smile as she extended her hand. "I'm very sorry about your father, Mr. Donovan."

Frankie grabbed her and hugged.

"She's as pretty as her mother isn't she, Bugs?"

Frankie spun to see Nicky standing behind him, another bowl of food in his hands. Frankie waited until Nicky set it down then grabbed him in a warm embrace. "Goddamn it's good to see you, Rat." He squeezed him hard, fighting back tears. He wasn't going to cry, had made a vow on that. "Thanks for coming. I appreciate it."

Nicky patted his back. "Didn't know if you'd want me or not, but Angie had her mind made up."

Frankie pushed back, looking Nicky up and down. "I'm glad she did," he said, then grabbed Rosa and pulled her to him. "And you. Look how beautiful you are!"

"Where's your mom, Bugs?"

"On the sofa," Frankie said. "You'll need to break through the wall of relatives, but she's there." He grabbed Nicky's arm. "Come on. She'll be happy to see you." He turned to Angie. "You too, Angie, and Rosa. Come on."

As they offered condolences to his mother, Frankie noticed something going on between Donna and Bobby. Frankie made his way closer, hoping to forestall any embarrassment. By the time he got there Bobby's voice had already gotten too loud.

"What the fuck is *he* doing here?"

Frankie took two quick steps and grabbed Bobby's arm, squeezing hard. He leaned in and whispered. "I don't know what's going on, but you better keep it down. Have some *goddamn* respect." He let go of Bobby's arm but continued glaring at him and then at Donna.

"Keep out of it, Frankie. It's none of your business," she said.

"It sure as hell *is* my business. If you can't control your emotions, go outside."

"No need for *us* to leave. Just tell your killer friend to."

So *that* was it. *I should have known.* "Leave Nicky out of this. He came to pay his respect."

Bobby pushed close to Frankie. "Like he did that night in Woodside when he killed my brother?"

Frankie had to look up at Bobby; he was a big guy. "Nicky did his time for that."

Bobby scoffed. "Ten years for my brother's life seem fair to you?"

Frankie glared harder. "Let it go."

"I'll let it go for now, but—"

Frankie grabbed hold of his shirt. "Listen, forget the fact that your brother killed our friend, or that he was trying to kill me. This is for your own sake—leave Nicky alone. You don't know who you're fucking with. I know you're a big man, Bobby, and I know you're tough, but trust me, you don't want any part of Nicky Fusco."

Bobby shook him off, took Donna's hand, and led her into the dining room.

Nicky was standing there when Frankie turned around. "Trouble, Bugs?"

"Just my sister and her husband. They're upset, is all."

"Got anything to do with me?"

"Nothing, Nicky. Forget about it, okay?"

Nicky said, "Yeah, no problem, Bugs," but he stared at Bobby as he said it, and Bobby stared back.

CHAPTER 6

LOU GETS A PARTNER

Brooklyn, New York

Sherri Miller wasn't even born when the phrase "black is beautiful" became popular, but she embraced it, embodied it, and lived it every minute of her life. She was a billboard for it, and drew whistles, stares, and even lewd remarks whenever she walked down the streets—certain streets anyway. Most of all she was proud of it, which showed with every one of her many smiles and the frequent laughter that accompanied those smiles.

As the door closed behind her on Lieutenant Morreau's office, she walked past Carol's desk, out the door, and started down the steps. The lieutenant's words played in her memory like a recording, and, from the description he gave her, the guy she needed to talk to was coming up the steps. Sherri stopped halfway down.

"Lieutenant Morreau said to find the grumpiest, nastiest, most foul-mouthed cop in the station. That you?"

Lou Mazzetti stopped, one hand on the rail and one on his knee for support. "Getting bad when I'm panting like this and I'm only halfway there, but be careful what you say—I might get a second wind and kick your ass."

Sherri reached out and took hold of his arm, offering one of her smiles as she did. "Sherri Miller, your new partner."

"I should've known Morreau would screw me," Lou said. "I asked for an Italian partner."

"*Buon giorno, Signore.*"

Mazzetti looked at her as if she came from Mars.

"My mother was Sicilian," Sherri said.

Lou took her hand and started back up the long climb. When they reached the top of the stairs, he looked her over. "Lucky day for me. I finally got a partner I like to look at, *and* you're half Italian." He reached to shake her hand. "Lou Mazzetti. Tired, grumpy, half-dead dago cop."

Sherri laughed. "Nice to meet you, Lou."

"Same here, and before we get started, let's get coffee."

"I already started a fresh pot for you."

"I'd normally kiss you for that, but they'd probably charge me with harassment, so I'll just say thanks."

"You're as goofy as Carol said."

"Yeah, that's me." Lou turned the corner into the coffee room and grabbed two cups. "How do you take it?"

"Little bit of cream. No sugar."

Lou brought the coffee over and sat next to her. "What strings did you pull to get partnered with me?"

"I had to go all the way to the mayor's office, but I got what I wanted."

Lou took a sip of his coffee and smiled. "What got you into homicide?"

"Lots of things."

"Yeah?"

Sherri stared at him over the rim of the Styrofoam cup. She tried to make the sip last forever, but it didn't work, so she set the cup down. "Is this going to be one of those deals where you keep asking me until I tell you?"

"Probably. I like to know a little something about my partners."

Sherri drained the rest of her coffee and tossed the cup into the trash basket in the corner.

Lou nodded. "Good shot."

"Yeah, well, environment and all that. Anyway, as far as what got me into Homicide… I was heavy into drugs and halfway to prostitution when a cop saved my ass. Actually, he busted my ass, but I guess he felt sorry for me or something. Instead of taking me in, he hooked me up with a rehab center. Took me almost two years, but I finally got off everything. During the process I figured out I liked helping people, so I went back to school and then to the academy." She lowered her head, looking like she might tear up. "I wish my dad could have seen me graduate. He would have been proud."

Lou waved a hand. "Don't be too sure. My old man said the only reason I became a cop was because I was too stupid to be a mobster."

Sherri cocked her head and gave Lou a skeptical look. "Get out."

"It's true. No shit." Lou pulled out a smoke but didn't light it, though he fidgeted as if he was going to. "By the way, what you told me—anybody else know about it?"

"A couple of people."

"It'll be a couple plus one now, but no more than that." Lou pushed his chair back and stood, heading for the door. "Come on, Miller. I'll show you what we have so far." He turned right down the hall and took another right into a room with a conference table in the center. "We call this the chart room. I used to solve cases just by following leads, but now Donovan has got me using charts and actually thinking."

Sherri walked over and stood before the chart hanging on the back wall. "There's not much here."

Lou came up beside her. "You got in at the beginning of a case. We'll be learning as we go on this one. For now, all we know is what you see here: suitcases covered in plastic found in hallway; chopped up body parts inside; no head, hands, feet, or member."

"You mean his dick was cut off?"

"I didn't want to get crude, but yeah, his dick was cut off. Not his balls though."

Sherri shook her head. "There are some sick bastards out there." She flipped through the papers in the folder Lou had on the table. "And there are no witnesses to any of it?"

"No one saw anything. Or heard anything."

"So why was the body left there? Any connections to unusual things in the building?"

"I'm with you on that. Why that building? Why that floor? Could have left the body anywhere—a dump, a dumpster, an alley…"

Sherri nodded. "I'd like to look at the scene if you don't mind. I know you've been—"

"No, I need another look anyway, except I'm not climbing the steps. You can do that alone. I do want to check out the area though, maybe talk to a few more people."

"Fair enough. Let's go."

"You drive," Mazzetti said. "I hate driving."

"Is there anything you like to do?"

"Shoot people. I *love* to shoot people. That's why I joined the force."

Sherri turned her head. "How many people have you shot?"

"None yet, but I hope to remedy that on this case."

"I didn't know Homicide was going to be so much fun," Sherri said.

"Fun? Wait till Donovan gets back; he's a real barrel of laughs."

Sherri got the car and picked Lou up at the curb. She pulled out and headed toward Prospect Park. "Mazzetti, I really do like you."

"That makes one."

THE CRIME SCENE LOOKED the same from the outside: same ten-story apartment building, same concrete stoop with the edges worn, and the same overflowing dumpsters reeking of last week's garbage on the side.

"This is it," Lou said. "Sixth floor. And the elevator's broken, so it's a hike."

"I'll go up. You take the side." Sherri half jogged to the front door, her butt straining to get out of her pants as she bounced up the steps with the energy of a teenager.

"Don't stop till you hit the sixth floor," Lou yelled as he walked toward the dumpsters.

The area around them had already been checked, and they had been emptied and inspected, but in the two days since he'd been here they were already full again. Lou didn't expect to find anything new, but he wanted to check the scene, see if anything jumped out at him. Trash hung over the rim, and garbage lay strewn on the ground surrounding the area. A couple of suitcases with a body in it could easily get lost in that mess—maybe that's what the killer didn't want. Maybe the killer *wanted* the publicity and that's why he put the suitcases in the hallway. Lou lit a cigarette and shook his head. *Sick fuck.*

He went back to the front door, stood beside the stoop, and questioned everyone who passed. They had all been interviewed already, and Lou got nothing new. An older black man came in with his wife. Lou showed them his badge. "How long has that elevator been busted?"

"About a week, maybe ten days."

"Ten days is more like it," the wife said. "I know, because I called the super."

"You see anything unusual in the last couple of weeks? Any strangers hanging around? Anybody having troubles?"

The old guy laughed. "Detective, everybody in this building's got troubles, but as far as strangers, I haven't seen any. And I can tell you, whoever dragged that body up those six flights of stairs is a younger man than me."

Lou thanked them and thought about what the man said. The guy was right. Carrying a body, even one missing the head and hands and feet, was a formidable task. He took out his notepad and wrote it down.

Guy must be in good shape, he wrote.

He was still adding more thoughts when Sherri returned, coming down the stairs.

"You find anything?" she asked.

He looked at her with raised brows. "Did you run up and down those steps?"

"About halfway up, and all the way down. I need to build steps into my workout."

"Me, too."

"I assume the crime scene guys printed the railings and walls and all of that," Sherri said.

"Yeah, and as you might guess, we got a truckload of prints. Cleared most of them with tenants, but that still left too many to be of much use. I got two guys trying to narrow them down, and another one matching against known offenders, but I'm not waiting for a payday."

Lou took out another smoke. "I talked to a couple who said the elevator's been broken about ten days. Likely means the guy knew it was out. So what, do you think it's someone who knew I would draw the case and they wanted to kill me in some fancy way, making me climb these steps?"

Sherri pointed her finger at him. "That's exactly how I see it."

A cell phone rang, and Lou reached for it. "Mazzetti."

"It's Kate."

"Spit it out."

"Not much. A knife wound in the gut is what killed him. They cut him up afterwards."

"They?"

"You heard me right. *They* used a hacksaw, standard variety found at a hardware store, but whoever did the head didn't do the hands, feet or private part."

"So we got two sick fucks out there?"

"I can't swear to it, but that's what it looks like."

"Goddamn, that's all I need. All right, see you later, Kate." He hung up and turned to Sherri. "In case you didn't hear, we got two assholes to catch now."

"We need to get busy then," Sherri said.

"Hey, Miller. The way I figure this is that one of them has got to be a woman. We're probably looking for a pair of crazies. Maybe drugged-up psychos."

"Why a woman?"

"No way a guy is cutting another guy's dick off. Just doesn't work that way."

Sherri laughed. "That's one theory the profilers probably don't have in their playbook. So, yeah, we got nothing else going we might as well run with that. How about we start with missing persons, though. See if we can turn up someone who cares about this dude."

* * *

TOM JACKSON SAT ON the edge of the sofa and watched the news on each channel to see how they reported on his masterpiece. He didn't like two of the journalists but the third was a cute young blonde—perky and full of life. After a few minutes of watching, he chose her.

"Lisa, get me the number for whatever station Cindy Ellis works for."

Lisa was in the kitchen fixing tea when he called to her. She ran in, panicked. "What?"

"Cindy Ellis. Find out where she works and get me a phone number."

"What for?"

He turned to Lisa, slowly stood and headed toward the kitchen. "Did you make tea for me?"

She hurried ahead of him. "No, but I'll get you some—"

He punched her in the back so hard she fell forward, gasping. She reached for her back with one hand while trying to break her fall with the other. Before she got her balance, Tom hit her again, this time in the neck. She collapsed in a heap on the floor. He stepped over her and got the tea kettle. For a moment he held it above her, tilted, almost letting the boiling water drip onto her face, but then he decided not to. He still had to look at that face—for a while anyway. He gritted his teeth and closed his eyes. Already he'd broken one of his cardinal rules—a man doesn't hit a woman. And now she'd made him go and do it. He breathed deeply, calming himself.

"Get up and get that number now, will you?" His voice was calm and pleasant.

She struggled to get to her feet. "I'll get it right away."

Tom went back to the sofa with his tea and waited for her to return. When she brought him the number, he pulled out his disposable cell phone and called. "I need to speak with Cindy Ellis."

"I'm sorry but Ms. Ellis is not available. Would you like her voicemail?"

"Yes, please," Tom said, and when he got her recording, his message was brief. "I wanted to let you know that there *will* be more bodies. Soon."

CHAPTER 7

A LONG WAKE

Wilmington, Delaware

After the incident with Bobby, I got Angie and Rosa and told them we were leaving. We offered condolences again to Mrs. Donovan, then Angie and Rosa kissed Bugs goodnight.

"You coming to the wake?" Bugs asked.

"You know I'll be there." I hugged him. "Really sorry about your dad. It's been a while since Pops died, but I'll never forget how it made me feel."

"Thanks. And don't worry about Donna and her husband, they're—"

"I've already forgotten. See you tomorrow."

Angie sat in the passenger seat and Rosa got in the back. We rode home in silence, but as soon as we got in the door Rosa asked if she could go to her friend's house.

"It's just down the street, Dad."

I looked at the clock. "It's already ten."

"How about for one hour? I'll be home by eleven."

Angie shook her head. "You heard your father. Go upstairs and make sure you have something to wear for tomorrow night."

"Do I *have* to go?"

"You *know* you do," Angie said. "Frankie is your father's best friend."

Rosa looked at me but I gave her no encouragement. Angie was right; Rosa needed to go.

She bolted up the hardwood steps, feet stamping with a little too much defiance. "I'm calling Jennie, so don't come busting into my room."

Angie looked as if she might say something but I tapped her arm. "Why don't you change clothes. I'll pour wine, and we'll sit on the stoop and talk."

"That sounds good," Angie said, and disappeared up the steps.

I opened the wine, let it sit on the counter, and started toward the bedroom. Angie was already on her way back down. "Nobody changes clothes as fast as you," I said.

She opened her robe to reveal nothing but a pair of panties. "Keep that in mind when considering other women," she said, and smacked me on the butt. "I'll be outside, so hurry up."

It took me almost ten minutes, but I was meticulous about hanging up my clothes and putting shoe trees in my shoes. Angie was already on the stoop. As I sat next to her, she handed me the wine glass.

"What was that all about with Bobby?"

"Nothing."

"It looked like something to me," she said.

I thought about how to answer. I didn't like lying to my wife. After an uncomfortable moment of silence, I decided. "The guy I shot that night at Woodside was Bobby's brother."

Angie took a big sip of wine. "I never knew that. A lot of bad blood then?"

"A lot."

Angie sipped her wine. "Rosa brought it up."

I nodded. "She's getting to that age. Kids notice everything, and then the questions start."

"She's trying to get leverage," Angie said. "And the best way for her to do that is to find something we do wrong."

"Yeah, well she's got an edge there. Lot of material to work with."

Angie kissed me on the cheek. "You've changed. No one can complain about you now."

I kissed her back, on the lips. "Thanks. I need that now and then." I didn't tell her I needed it more than occasionally, and I didn't mention how much it helped, but knowing Angie, I'm sure she knew. We sat and talked for a few more minutes, finished our wine, then watched TV and went to bed.

I WOKE TO THE smell of Angie's red sauce simmering on the stove, and of meatballs cooking—perhaps two of the most wonderful aromas in the world. Many nights in prison, I closed my eyes and recalled that sensation, let it fill my mind until I could almost taste the red sauce and meatballs. I swear on some of those nights, some of the more desperate ones, it actually sated my hunger.

After dressing I went downstairs, stole a few of the not-yet-ready meatballs while deftly dodging Angie's spoon, then kissed her goodbye and headed to work.

"Take an umbrella," Angie hollered from the kitchen. "It's supposed to rain."

I frowned, but grabbed an umbrella from the closet before heading out. As the door closed behind me I heard an angelic voice say,

"Bye, Dad. Love you."

Those few words, hollered from an upstairs bedroom, brightened my day. Suddenly the prospect of rain didn't seem so bad.

I HAD A HELL of a lot to do at work, and the day raced. For a while I even forgot about my problems with Marty. And despite my aversion to wakes, as the day came to a close, I found myself in a good mood though I hated viewings. I swore long ago that I'd never go to another one, other than my own, but this was different; Bugs was my best friend, and he had been there for me when my father died. Besides being the right thing to do, I owed him.

Angie was dressed and ready to go before Rosa and I were. I could always count on her to be on time and wearing a smile. When I came down the steps and saw her, I whistled. "Looking good tonight, lady."

"Tonight?"

"Yeah, tonight. The rest of the time you look terrible."

She laughed, but still, I was glad her wooden spoon wasn't within reach.

Rosa rushed past me, grabbed her mother's arm, and said, "Lock the door, Dad," as she raced down the sidewalk. Both of them were laughing. I felt strange being in such a good mood before going to a wake, but sometimes that was best. It made it easier to deal with the emotions that were sure to come. I started the car and reminded Rosa of the names of Frankie's sisters. "Donna's the oldest, then Marie, and—"

"I know them, Dad. I met them all last night."

"Okay," I said, and pulled away from the house.

As I turned on Dupont Street, Rosa said, "Do I call him *Mr. Donovan* or *Frankie*?"

"*Mr.* Donovan," Angie said.

"So what's Uncle Frankie like, Mom?"

"He's great," I said.

Angie turned to face Rosa. "Frankie is a lot like your father, but if I had to explain the difference I'd say…your father remembers the day everybody was born; Frankie remembers the day they died."

Rosa just said, "Oh."

I laughed.

IT WAS A SHORT drive to the funeral home. Ten minutes later we pulled into the lot at Jimmy Maldonaddo's, early enough to have our pick of spots. I parked in the back, saving the close spaces for the older people.

"Christ's sake, Dad, why are you parking back here?"

I gritted teeth and slammed the car into park, afraid if I spoke now I'd be too harsh. Rosa had gotten into a habit of saying that particular phrase—*Christ's sake*—just like Tony did, and it pissed me off. Raised the hackles on the back of my neck. *Goddamn, is it genetic or something?* But how can a curse be genetic? Neither Angie nor I used that expression, and Rosa never knew Tony. *Go figure.*

"Cut the shit. If I hear that come from your mouth again, it will be bad."

We entered the funeral home through big double doors. A man at the front pointed us toward the Donovan room. Angie signed the book for all of us, her handwriting being the best. We were the fourth ones there. After signing, Angie walked into the room where the services were being held and took a seat near the back, second row from the last.

I looked around. "I'm going to find a restroom."

Rosa pointed toward the back. "Right over there," she said, then, "I'm going to catch a smoke."

I gritted my teeth yet again. I hated her smoking, but I encouraged her to be open with me, and she took full advantage of that.

Angie grabbed her arm before she left. "Stay away from the front door. There's no need to show other people you smoke at your age." Angie shook her head and huffed. "Fifteen years old and smoking…"

"Don't worry, Mom. No one will see me. And Thanks." She smiled at me as she left, knowing I'd been the one who broke that barrier for her. All in all, this had been a good year for us. Not without trying times, but good.

I headed back to the rest room and by the time I returned the place was filling up—must have been twenty-five or thirty people with more coming every few minutes. I said hi to Mr. Chinski, telling him how sorry I was to hear of Eddy's passing, then I nodded to Patti McDermott, stand-ing across the room talking to someone I couldn't place. Patti was the girl we all dreamed about as kids, and right now she looked better than ever. I had to fight the urge to keep from staring.

I let a few people pay their respects, and then Angie, Rosa and I got in line. I walked up, hands folded before me, head bowed. I didn't want to look at anyone; recognition brought smiles and I didn't want to smile. I dreaded looking at Bugs, still remembering how I felt when my father and Mamma Rosa passed away. I remembered, too, how Bugs helped me, stayed out all night walking the streets with Mick. That thought hurt too. Goddamn Mick. Him gone as well.

Angie knelt and said her prayers, Rosa alongside her. I followed them, placing a small ceramic frog in the coffin with Mr. Donovan. Sounds like a stupid thing, but he always liked it when I caught frogs as a little kid. At least he said he did, and knowing Mr. Donovan, I doubt he'd lie about it. Way I figure it, maybe he liked frogs, so I thought I'd bring him one last one. There weren't many things in his coffin. That's the way it was with traditions—either people bought into them or they didn't. Most people had long-since abandoned the tradition of placing favorite things in the coffin, but I kept firm to it. Mamma Rosa had taught it to me and I figured if the tradition was important to her, how could I do less.

Angie kept to it too. She told me she placed a picture of us in her dad's coffin. That created a big stink with her husband, Marty. *He* looked *at what she put in there!* That was against all the rules. He accused her of being lots of things that night and none of them nice. One more reason to hate Marty Ferris.

Bugs embraced me as I passed by him on my way to offer condolences to his mother. I didn't want to go, not with Donna and Bobby sitting next to her, but it had to be done. I leaned down and hugged her. "You know how sorry I am, Mrs. Donovan."

An already-damp handkerchief wiped a steady flow of tears from her eyes. "I know, Nicky. Thank you for coming. You were always such a nice boy."

I moved to Donna, leaning in to hug her, but she glared at me and threw out a warning. "Don't touch me."

I wanted to smack her, but held myself in check. This was Frankie's sister and it was her father's wake. Respect was due no matter what. I straightened. "I'm sorry for your loss, Donna." I looked to her husband. "You too, Bobby." After that, I quickly consoled the other sisters then went back to give Bugs a last hug.

As I embraced him and patted his back, he whispered, "I don't mean to sound irreverent or anything, but I just saw Patti McDermott, and I'd still do her right in the middle of church."

"Easter Sunday?"

"Yep."

It was difficult not to smile at that, but I managed it, or I thought I had. When I got back to the pew and slid in next to Angie, she leaned over and whispered.

"I see you two had your mandatory discussion about Patti."

I gulped. Talk about sweating it out. I didn't want to be this close to a funeral home if Angie had Patti McDermott on her mind. That was a deposit on a ticket to the next room.

***

THE CROWD WAS BUILDING, and, with each person that passed, Frankie felt more tears welling up inside of him, but he wasn't letting them out. If he did it would be like a dam bursting, and that plain wasn't happening. Not now. Not ever. Frankie looked at the people in line, searching for those he recognized. Several of Patti McDermott's brothers were there, and Mr. Chinski followed by the DiNardo family. He hoped the DiNardos didn't bring any roaches with them, though he figured they came for the food that would be served afterward. Frankie greeted all of them with a fake smile and a warm hug—even Jack McDermott, Mick's older brother, who had busted their balls a dozen times when they were younger. After Bonnie DiNardo passed, he was surprised to see Sister Mary Thomas, her habit dusting the floor and seeming to propel her across the room. She hugged him and used her handkerchief to wipe tears from his eyes.

"Frankie, I haven't seen you in so long. It's a shame for it to be under these circumstances."

He hugged her back. "Say a prayer for him, Sister. Please?"

"I already have. And I'll get all of the sisters to join in tomorrow. Father Tom will dedicate a mass on Sunday."

Frankie smiled, a genuine one. "Thank you, Sister. We appreciate it."

Sister Thomas left, heading toward the back where Nicky and Angie sat with Rosa. Frankie focused on the remainder of the people in line. The crowd wasn't huge, not like Nicky's dad or Mamma Rosa, but a decent number of people had showed up. Frankie was disappointed that nobody from the smoke shop came, but he hadn't really expected them. They never knew his dad, and Frankie had been gone a long time.

The crowd soon dwindled to nothing. Frankie and his sisters got in line to pay the final respects. He waited to go last. After Donna took their mom to her seat, Bugs blessed himself and knelt in front of the coffin, staring at the man he hated for so many years. His father had stuck by him, though, and from what he could tell, loved his son, even if he didn't show it much.

Frankie blessed himself again, said the Trinitarian formula, and reached into his pocket and pulled out a badge. It was the first one he got when he became a cop. He laid it on his father's chest, tucked under his left hand. "I love you, Dad," he whispered, and kissed his cheek. As he stood to leave, he said, "Take care of him, God."

***

BUGS INSISTED WE COME to his house after the wake. Even though I didn't want to, Angie gave me the glare—the one that promised retribution, lameness, death, and worst of all, withholding of sexual favors, all with one look. With a look like that she could have made a good nun. Having no option, I agreed, so we left the funeral home early. Angie and Rosa had made more food, which we stopped to pick up on the way to Bugs' house to prepare for the onslaught of people. When we got to Bugs' house Angie took over, issuing orders to everyone, even the relatives, as to who should do what.

Before long they all arrived, Mrs. Donovan's sister and her husband ushering her in, followed by Bugs and his younger sisters. Donna and Bobby came in last.

She shot me a look, then whispered to Bugs, although it wasn't much of a whisper. I heard her from halfway across the room. "What's he doing here?"

Bugs was responding to her when I stepped up. I didn't want to cause him any trouble. "I was just leaving."

He grabbed my shoulder. "No need for you to go, Nicky. She's—"

"There is a need for him to go," Donna said. "I don't want him here."

I started for the door, but she continued her ranting.

"And take that slut wife of yours with you."

I froze. Spun around and grabbed her by the arm. Despite my anger I was able to keep my tone at a respectable level. "Maybe this is all an act for your husband, or maybe you think I forgot what really happened that night. In either case, you seem to be counting on me to keep quiet; I wouldn't count on that holding up for long."

Donna turned to go, but I yanked her back "I didn't forget that it was you who begged me to save Bugs. That night cost me ten years of my life and I don't forget shit like that." I nodded to Bobby, who was standing to the side, staring at us. I started to walk away but turned back. "One more thing. I'm cutting you some slack because of your father, but you better not cause trouble for Angie or Rosa."

Bobby yanked her to the side, grilling her. He looked pissed.

I said goodbye to Mrs. Donovan and Frankie's other sisters, then found Angie and explained the situation to her. "Call when you're ready and I'll pick you up."

"No need to. We'll get a ride. Are you going home?"

Rosa poked her head into our conversation. "Drop me off at Abbie's, please?"

"You can stay here and help," Angie said.

I shook my head. "No need for her to stay. I'll drop her off. I might go play cards or stop by Teddy's. Either way, I won't be too late."

Angie kissed me. "Night, babe."

I smiled. She hadn't called me that in a long time, but whenever she did it brought a smile to my face, reminding me of our younger days. Angie always worked magic with me.

I leaned in and kissed her again. "Night, babe," I said back to her then headed for the door.

CHAPTER 8

DRINKS AT THE BAR

Wilmington, Delaware

Bobby Campisi had hold of Donna's shoulders, shaking her. "What did he mean by that? He said you begged him to go. Go where? When?"

Frankie came up behind them and tore Bobby away from his sister. "Cut the shit! Both of you." He stared at Donna. "What the hell is wrong with you? Mom's on the couch crying, and you're over here fighting." He got close to Donna. "If you can't act civil, leave." He turned to Bobby. "That goes for you, too. Straighten up or get out."

"That's an easy decision for me," Bobby said. He didn't slam the door when he left, but he closed it hard.

Donna acted as if she would go for him, but Frankie stopped her. "Let him go. He'll be back."

She wiped her eyes with a handkerchief. "I'm sorry, Frankie. You know how he gets."

"That's no excuse for your behavior. And trust me, you don't want him to get crosswise with Nicky."

"Bobby can take care of himself."

Frankie shook his head. "Not with Nicky."

By ten thirty Bobby hadn't returned and Donna's worry showed each moment. She pestered Frankie for the third time since Bobby left. "Find him, Frankie. He should have been home by now."

"Yeah, and I shouldn't have to go find him. That asshole is your problem."

"Just tonight, okay. I need him."

Frankie looked at his watch and sighed. "Where does he normally go."

"There are a couple of places, but when he wants company he usually goes to Teddy's."

Frankie pointed at her before heading for the door. "Take care of Mom while I'm gone."

***

I THOUGHT ABOUT GOING home, but that didn't sit well, and I didn't feel like playing cards, so I drove by to see if Marty Ferris was at Teddy's. He went there a lot during the week to catch a game and down a few beers. The parking lot was full, but I saw Marty's car. I parked across the street and went inside. A couple of guys said hi as I made my way across the old hardwood floors to a seat at the bar, two down from where Marty Ferris sat. Jack McDermott was at the other end. I nodded to him, hadn't spoken to him since prison. I never liked Jack much, but he helped me a few times in the joint, and he was the Mick's brother.

Fred was working this end. I signaled for him to bring me a beer, motioning at the same time to buy one for Marty. He delivered mine, set one in front of Marty and told him where it came from.

Marty looked down at me, a smile on his face until he saw who it was, then he shoved it aside. "I don't need your beer, Fusco."

I moved a seat up so I was sitting next to him. "No need for us to be hostile. I'm buying you a drink is all."

"Don't try playing your games. You don't scare me."

"I'm not trying to scare you, Marty. Just reason with you. I'm Rosa's father and she doesn't want you around anymore."

Marty downed a shot then a half a mug of beer, wiped his mouth and smiled. "How's it feel to be gettin' seconds of everything? I was your daughter's father before you, and I was banging Angela while you were in prison." He laughed and then drained the mug.

I gripped the edge of the bar. The things I could do to him raced through my mind, but this was neither the place nor the time. "There's no reason to talk like that. I don't want any trouble."

"I know you don't want trouble from me. You caught me by surprise that day in the park. That won't happen again."

I reached into my pocket and pulled out a ten, set it on the bar for Fred. "All I'm saying is, think about it. You might reconsider." I walked out then, alert in case he tried something. By the time I reached the door a plan was formulating. It wasn't going to be pretty for Marty.

I sat in the car and played an anagram game on my phone while I waited for Marty to come out. Teddy's was popular tonight. I must have seen eight or ten guys I knew going in, including that asshole husband of Donna's, Bobby Campisi. I wondered what he was doing here; he should have been at Bugs' house. I thought about going over and kicking his ass, but put it off. That could wait for another day, too.

After playing a few more games I saw Bugs park his car and go inside. *What the hell is going on?*

Bugs being here ruined my plans for Marty, but it gave me a new idea, one Marty would like even less than what I originally planned.

After leaving Teddy's I borrowed a truck from one of the job sites and put a large metal toolbox in the back. I drove to the canal banks and found a remote spot, then dug a nice deep hole. Very deep. Didn't want animals digging things up. I set the toolbox in the hole and covered it up with brush and then returned the truck and went home. I went to sleep on the couch so I didn't wake Angie.

***

FRANKIE STORMED INTO TEDDY's place, making no attempt to hide his displeasure. Bobby was sitting next to Jack McDermott, both of them with a shot and a beer. Frankie had a strong urge to smack Bobby, but he managed to calm himself before he got to the bar.

"Hey, Bobby, what's going on?"

Bobby turned on the stool, staring at Frankie. "Donna send you?"

"You know she did."

"I figured as much." Bobby threw down a shot, signaled Fred for a refill, and motioned for Frankie to sit. "Don't get me wrong, Frankie, I love your sister, but she can be a ball-buster."

Frankie let out a small don't-I-know type chuckle. "Bobby, no need to tell me about women. My marriage lasted eight months."

Fred came over with another shot for Bobby, nodded to Frankie. "You drinkin'?"

Reaching for money, Bobby said, "Fred, this is my brother-in-law, Frankie Donovan. Get him whatever he wants."

A smile lit Fred's face. "Frankie! No shit. I ain't seen you since you were a kid."

Frankie laughed. "If I remember that's when you and Teddy were chasing me and Tony Sannullo down Fourth Street."

Fred seemed to go back in time, eyes in a trance. "The good old days, huh." Then he got serious. "But hey, I heard about your dad. I'm sorry."

"Thanks, Fred. It was a surprise to all of us."

"I heard about Tony, too. I don't know if that requires a condolence, but if so…"

"Not necessary. Tony got what he deserved."

Fred nodded as he wiped the counter. "So what'll you have? It's on me."

"You got any cello?"

"Limoncello? You bet. Frozen glasses, or on ice?"

"Frozen, and make it two. They go down easy."

Bobby set his mug on the counter. "All this booze goes down easy. That's the problem. But I'm gonna fix that, along with everything else."

"How's that?" Frankie asked.

"I'm going to take care of Donna and the baby, and I'll make your mother proud of *me*." He sipped on his beer again. "All the old man ever talked about was Frankie, the hero cop."

Frankie's eyes went wide. "My old man?"

Bobby looked at him. "What, you never knew?"

"We didn't talk much."

Bobby took a long gulp of beer and signaled for a refill. "Your family is so fucked up."

"I know that, but there's no sense in making yours that way. Donna needs you, and—"

Bobby turned in his seat, facing Frankie. "Don't come down here from New York and tell me how to run *my* family. You sit up there and don't do shit for years on end, leaving me to deal with Donna and your wacko mother and then—"

"Go easy, Bobby. Don't talk about my mother like that."

"I'm the one that's been dealing with your father and your sister and the rest of your loony family, so don't preach to me."

"I'm not preaching, just asking you not to talk that way about my family."

"I'm telling you, your mother and Donna are cut from the same cloth. They're both nuts."

The words hurt, but the truth usually did. Frankie poked his finger into Bobby's chest. "Shut-up about my family."

"Get the fuck out of here. This ain't your goddamn bar.

"It sure as shit ain't *your* bar."

"It's gonna be, and before too long."

"What? Donna says you don't have a pot to piss in."

"She's a whore anyway, just like her mother."

Frankie grabbed Bobby's mug of beer and smashed it against his head, knocking him off the stool. Hunched over and swaying, Bobby came at Frankie. Frankie hit him in the face with a solid right, then followed up with a knee to the groin. Bobby fell to his knees, hands supporting him from the floor. Frankie kicked him in the side, sprawling him out, sunny side up.

Bobby lay there, bleeding from the head and nose. He wasn't getting up. Frankie leaned over top of him. "You ever say anything about my mother again and I'll kill you." He tossed a twenty on the counter, downed the cellos Fred had set there, grabbed his smokes and left.

Frankie slammed the door as he walked out of the bar. He got into the car and started for home, deciding at the last minute to see if Nicky was around. It would be nice to have someone to talk to before he went back to all the grief and bullshit that waited for him, especially from Donna. She'd been a pain in the ass all of his life.

Frankie turned onto Beech Street, recalling the address from the letter Nicky sent, and parked in front of the house. His car wasn't there, but Frankie didn't know if he had walked or driven home. He rang the doorbell, then knocked, but no answer. He thought about going home, but decided to check the smoke shop. When he didn't find Nicky, he decided to call it a night. A few minutes later, he walked through his mother's front door.

Donna ran up to him. "Did you find him?"

"I found him but he didn't come home with me."

She looked down at Frankie's hands, blood still staining them. Anger flared in her eyes. "What did you do? Is Bobby all right?"

"You want to baby him? Go scoop him off the floor at Teddy's. All I did was give Bobby what he's needed for years. I should have done it long ago, at Woodside."

Donna looked around, then threw out an angry whisper. "You *killed* his brother. Wasn't that enough?"

Frankie got as close as he could to her ear. "I'm through with this conversation. In case you forgot, our father's dead, and Mom needs us." As he finished talking he looked to the side and saw Angie approaching.

"Frankie, did you see Nicky? I've been trying to call him and I get no answer."

"I didn't see him, but maybe he went to the smoke shop to play cards. If you need a ride, I'll drive you."

Angie shrugged. "I hate to ask you…"

"Don't mention it," he said, and grabbed her arm. "Get Rosa. I'll get the food."

"Rosa went to a friend's house," she said. "And I'm leaving the food here. I'll come tomorrow to clean. I'll have more food for the funeral, too."

Frankie kissed her cheek. "You're the best, Angie. I don't know how to thank you."

"There's no need for thanks. You know that."

***

Fred and two other patrons helped Bobby Campisi clean himself up. He refused hospital treatment, saying he'd be all right by morning. Jack McDermott watched it all then picked up his drink and moved about five seats up the bar, plopping down next to Marty Ferris.

Marty glared at him as if he were intruding. "Plenty of empty seats."

"Yeah, I know, but call me a concerned citizen."

"Concerned about what?"

"Not about you, if that's the confusing part. I saw the way you talked to Nicky. Not real smart."

"What business is it of yours?"

"I don't want him going back to jail over some asshole like you."

"I'm not worried. You saw him leave. I don't guess he wants trouble from me." Marty flexed the muscles on his forearms. "These butcher arms will teach him a thing or two."

"I don't think you understand, Marty. Nicky didn't leave because he was afraid of you. He left so he didn't kill you in front of everyone." Jack looked around, eyes darting to the corners of the bar. "If I were you, I'd be careful going home, and even more careful once you got there."

Marty brushed it off. "I told you, I ain't scared of him."

"Yeah, well that's mistake number one. Mistake number two would be leaving here alone." Jack finished his beer then stood. "I'm heading out. See you around, Marty."

***

DONNA PACED THE LIVING room floor, her eyes darting to the door at the slightest sound. She walked over, pulled the curtains aside and looked up and down the street, then continued her ritual.

"What's wrong, dear?" her mother asked from the sofa.

"Nothing, Mom. I'm upset about Dad, that's all."

"Where's Bobby?"

"He drove some people home. He'll be back soon."

Mrs. Donovan nodded her head and went back to the almost catatonic state she'd been in, her hands folded in her lap and eyes staring at the wall opposite her. Donna walked toward the kitchen, brushing past several people as she made her way through the dining room. Frankie was out back catching a smoke. When he came inside, Donna cornered him.

"Bobby's not back yet, and Mom's asking about him. What happened at Teddy's?"

"I kicked his ass. That's what happened."

Donna chewed on fingernails that had already been gnawed to stubs. "I'll bet Nicky did something to him. I'm calling the cops."

Frankie grabbed her arm. "You're not calling anybody. And Nicky wasn't even there."

Donna yanked her arm away. "Something's wrong. Bobby wouldn't stay away like this."

He clenched his teeth and shook his head. "All right, I'll go back to the bar, but call me if he comes home while I'm gone. The last goddamn thing I want to be doing is searching bars for your asshole husband." He slammed his hand against the wall, then headed out the back door and down the walk.

Frankie went back to Teddy's but nobody had seen Bobby since the fight, so Frankie hit a few other bars, with no success. *I wonder where he is?* After a few more stops at local hangouts, Frankie headed home.

Donna met him on the sidewalk, halfway to the door. She must have been watching out the window.

"Did you find him?"

Frankie shook his head. "Nothing. I went to Teddy's, and every other bar I know. Nobody's seen him."

She buried her face in her hands and bawled. "Something's wrong. I know it."

Frankie hugged her, patting her back as he did. "I'm sure he's all right. Don't worry." He kissed her cheek. "Why don't you try to get some sleep. When you wake up, I'm sure he'll be here. We've got a big day tomorrow taking care of Mom. She's going to be a mess at the funeral."

Donna sobbed. "You're right. I should get some sleep." She started toward the house but turned and hugged Frankie. "Thanks. I'm sorry I've been so irrational."

"Don't worry. You want me to wake you when he comes home?"

"Just tell Bobby to, but tell him to be quiet."

"Okay, big sis. Goodnight."

She kissed his cheek. "*Buona notte*, Francis."

Frankie laughed. "Call me that again and I'll kick your ass."

As he walked down the steps, Frankie wondered where Bobby really was, and why he hadn't come home. *Something* was wrong, and it wasn't going to be good when Donna found out.

CHAPTER 9

ANOTHER FUNERAL

Wilmington, Delaware

Detective Jimmy Borelli woke on the first ring of the phone, got out of bed and answered before the third ring. "Borelli."

"Get dressed, Jimmy. We got a body."

"Where?"

"Canby Park, the other side of the tracks by the creek."

"Near the Lion's Den?"

"Bingo."

"See you there."

***

AT THE FIRST RAYS of sunlight Donna woke in a panic. She ran down the hall and banged on Frankie's door.

"What the hell!" Frankie got out of bed and flung the door open. "Jesus Christ, Donna. Have some respect."

Tears stained her face. "I told you something happened. He's not home. There's no way Bobby would miss Dad's funeral. No way."

Frankie furrowed his brow. He had to admit that missing the funeral would be stretching it, even for Bobby. He held her close and talked softly. "Go make coffee. I'll be right down and we'll figure this out."

"Frankie, he—"

"Coffee, Donna. Make some coffee. I'll be right there."

He got dressed in a hurry and met her in the kitchen. She had coffee brewing in an old percolator. Frankie breathed in the aroma. Maybe it was a throwback to his youth, but he still loved the smell, and taste, of percolated coffee. He grabbed two cups from the cabinet and some sugar for Donna.

"You heard nothing from him?" Frankie asked. "Did you check your phone?"

"Of course I checked my phone. And I called our house, and called our neighbors. The car's not in the driveway."

Frankie thought about it. "Okay, listen. After the funeral I'll call the local—"

"After the funeral! I can't wait until then." She pounded her fists on his chest. "Goddamn, Frankie. Don't you understand, something's wrong. Something happened to him."

Frankie grabbed hold of her arms. "Listen close, Donna. I don't give a shit about Bobby right now. All I care about is getting our father put in the ground in a respectful manner. And if you screw this up for Mom, I'll never forgive you. This isn't something we get second chances on." He gazed into her eyes. "Now here's what's going to happen. We're going to the funeral and everyone will act civilized, as if nothing is wrong. Once we get back here, I'll find Bobby."

Frankie poured the coffee and put sugar in for Donna. "One sugar, right?"

She whimpered. "And a little cream."

Before they finished their coffee, Frankie's other sisters arrived, and he was thankful for it. They could take care of Donna now. He went upstairs to finish dressing, then checked his messages and made a few calls before rejoining the family. Lou Mazzetti hadn't called, but he didn't really expect he would; Lou would never bother him at a time like this. He did wonder, though, how he was making out with the investigation. Before he realized how much time had passed his younger sister, Mary Ellen, called him to get ready for the services.

The funeral mass went fine, the biggest surprise of the day being Sister Mary Thomas showing up with Nicky, Angela, and Rosa. He didn't expect Sister Thomas to come, but was honored that she did. She nodded to him when their eyes met, and folded her hands in a signal of prayer. Before long the services were over, the trip to the cemetery come and gone, and then they were back at the house, preparing for the long road to recovery from grieving.

If only Mamma Rosa were here. She always said that a pound of laughter cured ten pounds of grief. The problem was, laughter was a scarce commodity at the Donovan house.

Sometime around two or three o'clock, one of Frankie's aunts said a man was at the front door asking for him. Frankie wondered who it could be, but his gut told him it had to do with Bobby. When he opened the door and saw those high-arched brows sitting above bright blue eyes, he knew who it was, and that meant he knew what it was about. There was no reason for Homicide Detective Jimmy Borelli to be here unless there was a body.

"Jimmy Borelli? I hope you're here for condolences."

Only a small smile lit Jimmy's face, a practiced one that Frankie had yet to master. "You got a minute, Frankie?" When Jimmy asked it, he moved away from the door and nodded toward the street, a why-don't-you-come-out-here type of look on his face.

Frankie looked back into the living room then stepped outside, closing the door behind him. "What's up?"

Jimmy was taller than Frankie by a few inches, way too tall for most Italians, but the height was something he inherited from his Polish mother, that and the blue eyes and round face. He had a face like a basketball, only with smooth pale skin. "I hate to do this, Frankie, but somebody's got to know. We just found Bobby Campisi's body."

"Shit! Where?"

"Canby Park. In the woods near the creek. You remember the Lion's Den?"

"Of course I remember. How'd it happen?"

Jimmy looked intently at Frankie as he spoke. "Beaten pretty badly, side of his head cracked open, looks like more than a casual beating to me. We got him at the M.E.'s now."

Jimmy pulled out a pack of Marlboro Lights, and tapped them against his hand to pack them tight. "We're pretty sure he wasn't killed at the scene. There wasn't much blood by the body."

Frankie took a smoke that Jimmy offered him, then the light. "I'll tell you this much, Jimmy. Bobby didn't walk there on his own. Somebody forced him there, because he was too damn big to carry." Frankie smacked the bricks by the side of the door. "Shit!"

"Was he here last night?"

Frankie nodded. "He was at the wake, then back here. Then he left again."

"All right, tell you what. I know it's a bad day, so I'm not going to take any more time, but let's talk tomorrow, okay?"

"Okay, thanks Jimmy. I appreciate it. Let me know anything you find out. I'll tell Donna."

Jimmy hesitated. "You know the drill. We're going to need her to ID the body."

Frankie asked with a suspicious glance. "What kind of shit is that? You know what Bobby looks like, and besides, don't tell me you don't have prints on him."

Jimmy shrugged.

Frankie got real close. "If you want to talk to Donna just say so, but don't try this bullshit of needing her to ID the body. She'll be going through enough."

"I'm not trying to be a ball-buster, but I need to talk to somebody."

"You should have said what you wanted, not tried to use Donna. I'll come down later. Give me a couple of hours."

Jimmy nodded. "You got it. Call me first, though. I'll meet you there."
Borelli handed Frankie a card. "Don't forget. Call me."

"I'll do it, Jimmy. Thanks."

**

Jimmy Borelli walked down the sidewalk, down the steps and got into his car. He started it up, casting a glance back to the house to see if Frankie was watching—he'd gone back inside. Jimmy took out his notepad and pen and wrote:

'He never asked if we had suspects. And he never mentioned the fight in the bar.'

He placed an asterisk next to that one.
He's a cop. Why wouldn't he mention the fight?

CHAPTER 10

DIG THE HOLES DEEP

Wilmington, Delaware

After we left the funeral we took more food to Bugs' house and then I told Angie I was leaving.

"You sure you can't come in?" she said.

I shook my head. "You know the situation with Donna. And now Bobby's missing. I don't want to cause trouble for Bugs."

She kissed me on the cheek. "All right. I'll call if I need a ride."

"See you, babe."

I GOT IN THE car and drove to Teddy's. Marty only worked half a day today, and I hoped he'd stop at Teddy's on his way home. I found a comfortable spot where I wouldn't be seen, and waited. Before long Marty showed. He parked on a quiet, side street, perfect for what I wanted to do. An hour later he came out of the bar, lit a smoke, and headed for his car. I got out quietly, set off at a fast pace to intercept him.

I knocked him out, gagged him and put him in the trunk of my car. I drove Marty's car to his house a few blocks away, went back and got mine, and headed to the canal banks.

I remembered the canal banks from when we were kids, when we used to go there to "park" with the girls. The only girl I ever took was Angela, and we had a hell of a lot of fun. On warm, clear nights we'd sit outside the car and watch for boats coming up the canal. All the while we'd be snuggling and grabbing at each other. Those were the days when we couldn't keep our hands off each other, couldn't live without each other's touch. The cold nights were the best. When the moon was out and the stars lit the sky. Bitter, dry, cold. Thinking of that made me want to go home, get Angie, and drag her out here.

I quickly shook those thoughts off and focused on what I had to do. I drove around a few times, making passes by where I had dug the grave, then onto all the connecting roads. After parking, I walked the trails looking for signs that anyone might have been there since I left. It was almost dark, but I could see good enough. Nothing seemed disturbed. I drove around one more time, then headed toward the exit, parking on a side road behind some trees. I waited almost twenty minutes, in case someone had been there, then went back. Feeling safe now, I went to the spot and took Marty out of the trunk. His hands and feet were tied and his mouth gagged but he was awake. I put my gloves on so I didn't leave prints.

"I'm going to take the gag out, Marty, but if you make any noise I'll kill you. Do you understand?"

He nodded vigorously. I blindfolded him, then removed the gag. He stood silent while I got a few things from the trunk. He kept turning his head, as if he were trying to figure out where he was, even though he couldn't see.

"If this is about Rosa, we can work that out." His voice carried a plea for mercy.

I felt like spitting on him; instead, I grabbed the cloth and gagged him again. Then I took the shovel and smashed his right knee. He tried screaming, but only a few grunts came out. He fell to his knees, then face down in the dirt, his hands still tied. "Don't say her name or I'll hit you again."

He nodded.

"I'm going to remove your gag again. Don't make me put it back in." When I was done he started begging.

"I never hurt her. I took care of her while you were in jail. I paid for her—"

"Shut the fuck up."

While he was silent I uncovered the hole, a pit four feet deep, four feet long, and maybe thirty inches wide. At the bottom was the toolbox I took from a job site. I had drilled a hole in the top with a plastic tube running through so Marty could suck air. There was plenty enough space for him to sit curled up, even stretch his legs a little. Once I got it ready, I removed his blindfold.

He blinked his eyes a few times, stared at me, then he must have seen the hole because he went blank, fear overtaking him. "What the fuck is this? What are you doing?" He tried getting up, but his feet and hands were tied.

"I'm making sure you don't ever hurt Rosa again."

He trembled and pissed himself. When he spoke his voice rattled. "Nicky, please don't do this. Oh my God, please. I'll do anything."

I grabbed his collar and dragged him closer, then stood him up and shoved him into the box. He fell awkwardly, crumbling into a heap, head on the ground. He didn't start crying until I untied his hands and feet and started to close the lid.

"Oh God no! Please? *Mother of God*, how can you do this?"

"I tried to reason with you, Marty. I asked nicely. I threatened. Nothing worked."

A semblance of hope crept into his voice. "I'll do anything. Tell me what I need to do, but for God's sake don't do this."

"I don't want to do this, Marty, but I can't trust you. People say anything when they're about to die."

His tears came in waves. In between the fits of sobbing he prayed to God, and to the Holy Mother.

"You should never have hit Rosa, and you shouldn't have said what you did about Angela. Some things are unforgivable." I went to the trunk, got two dozen bottles of water and tossed them in the box. "This will keep you alive for a while. You can go without food for a long time. The heat will be bad, but you'll be far enough under the ground that it shouldn't kill you." I looked around, checking for people. "Use that tube to breathe. With any luck you'll last a few weeks, but I doubt you'll want to. Just in case, I'm leaving you with this knife." It was a plain pocket knife. No way to trace it to me. "When you get tired of living, slice your wrist or your throat. Either one will do. Make sure you do it deep enough, though."

I closed the lid, his screams echoing in the little metal box. By the time I shoveled a foot or so of dirt on top, I could barely hear him. After that I put a couple of different sized cardboard boxes over the straw to muffle the sound so no one could hear him even if they ventured this close. Each of those had a few holes to let air in. I didn't want him to die too soon.

When I finished, I covered my tracks, walked back to the car and left. Rosa wouldn't be bothered by him again.

CHAPTER 11

QUESTIONS

Wilmington, Delaware

Jimmy Borelli left Frankie's house and made his way to Fourth Street. He parked across from Teddy's then walked inside, scanning the place for familiar faces as he made his way toward the bar. He picked a seat near the end, about as quiet a spot as he could find, then signaled for Fred, who arrived a moment later with a cold beer.

"Hey, Jimmy. Ain't seen you in a while."

"That's the way I like to keep it. Can't let my beer-drinking side get the best of me."

"Ain't that the truth," Fred said, and handed him a beer. "What can I do for you? I heard you were asking questions."

"Trying to find out what happened last night with Bobby." Borelli set his beer down and eyed Fred while pulling out his notepad. "You want to tell me about it."

Fred shook his head. "Not much to tell. Bobby came in and had a couple of beers, then Frankie showed up. They seemed friendly at first, Bobby even bought Frankie a couple of drinks. Then it turned ugly."

"What made it turn ugly?"

"I don't know. I was at the other end of the bar. I heard Frankie say something to Bobby, then Frankie picked up the mug and smashed it into Bobby's head. After that…well there ain't no better way to say it—Frankie beat the shit out of him."

Jimmy scribbled a few notes then looked up at Fred. "Who else was here?"

"From what I hear you already talked to most of them. Billy Thompson was here with his wife. Millie had her favorite spot occupied. And Tim and Russ were sitting at the corner table with two girls I don't know." Fred raised his head, thinking. "Marty Ferris was sitting at the bar, and Jack McDermott was here, too. That's all I can think of besides the ones I know for sure you already talked to."

"Anything else you can think of? Was Fusco here?"

Fred backed up a step when Borelli mentioned Nicky's name. "I don't remember him being here."

Borelli slapped his pad on the bar. "That's not what I heard."

"I must have missed him, Jimmy. You know how busy it gets in here."

Borelli let his glare linger, put his pad away, and dropped a five on the counter. "You get any memory, call me."

He stormed out of the bar, went across the street to his car, started it up and rolled down the windows. It was a nice day for windows down. He lit a smoke and scanned his list for what he hoped wasn't there. No matter what he thought of Frankie, he was a cop, but the customers at Teddy's had been unanimous—Frankie and Bobby got into a fight and Frankie beat him half to death, flooring him with a mug of beer then kicking the shit out of him before leaving. Everyone also agreed that Frankie left while Bobby was still lying on the floor bleeding, but…and this is a big one, he could have waited for him outside and finished the job later.

And he could have had help from Fusco, Jimmy thought, not forgetting that Bobby had been part of the Woodside gang, the fight that put Nicky in prison.

***

For almost ten minutes, Frankie put off telling his sister about her husband, trying to get the courage to face what he knew would be her wrath. He had his other sisters and his aunt sit down to tell his mother. Then he took Donna upstairs to a bedroom and closed the door.

Frankie's eyes must have given him away; he didn't even get the words out before she started crying.

"What's going on?" she demanded. "Why'd you bring me up here? Did something happen to Bobby? Is he all right?"

Frankie took her in his arms. "He's gone, Donna. Somebody killed him." He helped her to the bed, sitting beside her as she wailed and pounded him with fists.

"*Somebody* killed him? You *know* who it was. It was Nicky. He did it to get even for that fight."

"Calm down. There's no way Nicky did this."

Her voice raised an octave or two, loud enough to pierce his ears. "You didn't see his eyes last night when he stared at Bobby. He scared me, Frankie. He even scared Bobby." She covered her face with her hands. "I know he killed him. I *know.*"

She went on hysterically for minutes, long enough and loud enough to draw relatives upstairs to help comfort her. Once several of them got there, Frankie excused himself. "I've got to go identify Bobby. I won't be long."

That brought on a new wave of tears and continued sobbing. "Tell the cops who did it, Frankie. You tell them."

On his way out the front door, Frankie called Jimmy Borelli. He needed to get this over with.

***

Jimmy's cell rang and he picked it up. "Hello."

"Jimmy, it's Ed. Frankie Donovan said he's coming down to ID the body." Ed paused. "What the hell is that all about?"

"We need to talk to Donovan. Meet me there. I'm on my way."

It took Jimmy ten minutes to get to the morgue, huddled at the corner of Front Street and Maryland Avenue. Sometimes the traffic proved unbearable, but today it was light, like a Sunday morning. Frankie got there shortly afterwards, parked the car and walked up to meet Jimmy. Borelli flipped his cigarette into the parking lot as Frankie approached.

"Frankie, meet my partner, Ed Mrozinski."

Frankie shook his hand. "Got a brother named Paul?"

Ed smiled. "Sure do. He's in California now, married with three kids."

"Lucky bastard."

"For the kids or California."

"Both, I guess. Next time you talk to him, tell him I said hi." Frankie turned to Jimmy. "So what's the story. I know you didn't bring me here to ID him, and sure as shit not to meet your partner."

"We need to talk."

"About the fight?"

Jimmy nodded. "That, and other things, but I know you don't have much time. I just want some basics."

"You want to do it here, or go somewhere?"

Jimmy walked down the steps into the parking lot. "It won't take long, and I know you're going to be busier than ever now. It's a damn mess, isn't it?"

Frankie nodded. "They all are. It makes it worse when it's someone you know."

"Yeah, tell me about it. I went through this a few years ago with my sister's kid."

Frankie turned to him, surprised. "Ellen's kid? What happened?"

"Drugs."

"Nasty shit," Frankie said, and reached for a smoke. "So here's the rundown. We're all at my mom's house and Bobby is getting mouthy with Donna. They fight all the time. I didn't want Mom hearing that shit, so I told them to settle down or leave. Bobby left." Frankie stopped to accept a light from Ed, then continued. "After he left, Donna got worried and sent me to look for him. Teddy's was my first stop."

"So you figured he'd be there?" Ed asked. "He drink a lot?"

Frankie sucked hard on his smoke. "He was married to my sister."

Jimmy smiled. "So you found him at Teddy's?"

"Yeah, he was at the bar, spouting off about a lot of stuff. I tried being civil, but he started in on Donna, which I didn't mind too much, but then he started in on my mom." Frankie sucked the last bit of life from his cigarette, then crushed it out on the blacktop. "He called her a whore, Jimmy. I had to hit him."

Jimmy looked as if he might say something, but whatever it was, he held it in. "Then what?"

"I hit him with a mug of beer, cracked him on the side of the head, then I kicked his ass some more." Frankie got angry all over again. "But I'm telling you, he was okay when I left. Hurt, but okay. No way what I did killed him."

"He have money?"

Frankie laughed. "Who, Bobby? He didn't have a pot to piss in, a window to throw it out of, or a sidewalk for it to land on. They still live in my aunt's old house."

Borelli looked hard at him. "So where'd he get the bank account?"

"What bank account?"

Borelli nodded to Mrozinski, who pulled out his notepad. "Fifty grand in an account in his name only, and a safe deposit box we haven't accessed yet."

Frankie whistled. "Are you shitting me? Fifty grand?"

"Fifty large," Jimmy said.

"I have no fucking idea where he'd get that kind of money, but I intend to find out."

Jimmy put up a hand. "How about you let me do that. Now, getting back to the night in question, where did you go after you kicked his ass?"

"Home, to my mother's house."

"Straight home?"

Frankie shook his head. "First I went to see Nicky, but he wasn't home, so I walked the park for a few minutes."

"About how long?"

Frustration settled in. "I don't know. A few fucking minutes. Five, ten. Shit, maybe it was fifteen. What difference does it make?"

"It might make a lot of difference once we get the TOD." Jimmy scribbled some notes in his pad. "Why didn't you tell me earlier about the fight?"

"I didn't feel like it. I knew we'd talk again, and I figured you weren't going to solve the case today."

"Was Nicky there last night?"

"I already told you I went looking for him. No, he wasn't there."

"That's not what I heard."

"Bullshit! Don't try to pin this on Nicky because you think he's an easy mark. He didn't do it."

"Was he at the wake last night?"

Frankie's face twisted into a scowl. "Of course he was there. Angie and Rosa, too."

"What time did he leave?"

Frankie thought. "I don't know. Ask him."

"I plan to," Jimmy said. "I'm just getting my facts straight." He wrote a few more things on his pad. "You know about that, don't you? Getting your facts straight, I mean."

Frankie pushed him, spurring Ed to grab his arm. "Fuck you, Borelli. How about that? I'm done here." Frankie pushed Mrozinski aside and headed to his car, started it and wheeled out of the parking lot.

"I guess you pushed the right button," Mrozinski said.

Jimmy stared at the car tearing down the street. "Yeah, but which button was it? The Bobby button, or the Nicky Fusco button?"

CHAPTER 12

THE NEXT NAME

Brooklyn, New York

All day long Tom tore up carpet, cutting it into small pieces and stuffing those pieces into plastic garbage bags. He thought he'd taken care of this on day one, but then he found a spot of blood, so now everything had to go. Anyplace there'd been blood, he stripped it to the bare floor, had Lisa scrub everything with bleach several times, then, when she finished, he watched as she scrubbed herself. No matter how many times he told her, she never did it enough so he had to do it himself.

"Stop, Tom. It hurts."

"I'll stop when you're clean. You need to be clean if you're going to work tomorrow." He said it before he realized the implications, then thought about how to ensure she kept quiet. Until now he'd relied on her fear for Buster and herself, but once she got out of the house that fear would fade.

Lisa cried, probably for the fourth time since lunch. "I don't know if I can do this. I'll never be able to go to work."

He turned her around and dug the tough bristles of the brush into her ass cheeks. "Your prints are on the hacksaw. Or did you forget?"

"Why are you doing this? I said I'm sorry a million times already. I just…"

He threw the brush aside, stood and faced her. "Just what? Got tired of waiting for me? Couldn't keep your legs closed and wait for your husband?" Tom gritted his teeth. "I should kill you now and get it over with."

She stood in the tub, naked, arms wrapped about herself, lips quivering. Tom handed her the brush. "Finish scrubbing. I'm going to get a sandwich. You want one?"

"Yes, if you don't mind."

He took her phone with him and left the apartment. He went down one flight of stairs then waited. If she took the elevator, he could still beat her down, and if she took the stairs, he'd be there to greet her.

Ten minutes later Lisa opened the door and crept out, hurrying down the steps. When she reached the third floor, Tom grabbed her. "Going somewhere?"

She froze. Her hands flew to her mouth to cover it. "I was…I…"

"Save your breath. Let's go back upstairs, and if you make a sound…"

"I won't."

He shoved her into the apartment, then shoved her toward the table in the dining room. "Sit." He got clothesline from the closet in the hall and tied her to the chair, hands and feet. A dishtowel served as a gag. When he finished he turned her chair to face the wall and whispered. "If this is moved even one inch when I get home, I'll kill you."

She nodded.

"Good. I might be a while. Do you want me to bring you a sandwich?"

She shook her head.

When Tom left this time, he knew there'd be no trouble. He grabbed a burger and fries, and then he took public transportation to Long Island, where Lisa's mother lived. She was old and lived by herself, and Lisa was her only relative. The old bag had no friends; she was too damn mean for that.

It only took Tom about an hour to take care of her, one quick stab to the lungs, and then he carried her to the basement and tucked her into a corner behind a stack of boxes. It would be weeks, if not months, before anyone found her.

Tom cleaned up, grabbed the old woman's cell phone, and then took the train back to the city. He took his time, walking around town and enjoying the sights. By nine o'clock he was home.

Lisa sat in the exact position she had been in when he left. She was sitting in piss, and it had leaked to the floor but that was all right. She needed lessons in humility, and cleanliness. She needed lessons in a lot of things. He should get a whipping stick like his daddy had. That's what he should do.

Tom untied her and removed the gag. "Clean up your mess then take a bath. And do it right or I'll do it for you."

Half an hour later she came out of the bathroom and into the living room where he was watching television. Lisa knew the routine. She stood in front of him, naked, awaiting inspection. At the commercial break he muted the TV and focused on her. Her skin was red and scratched from the scrubbing, especially around her crotch and her ass.

"Is it okay?" Lisa asked, her voice tremulous.

"Turn around."

She turned slowly, and when she did, he leaned in and sniffed her. "You did a good job. Now get me some water and join me. This show is funny as hell."

"Can I get dressed?"

Tom thought for a moment, his eyes narrowing. "Panties, that's all."

They watched shows for almost two hours then went to bed. Tom crawled in beside her, snuggling up to her back and letting his hand rub her stomach. She curled up, eased closer to the edge of the bed and pretended to sleep, but he knew what she was doing. Slowly, he pulled her panties down and rubbed her, exciting himself, but not her. Thinking of the other men in her life made him agitated, made him want to hurt someone.

"I need another name," he said, and when he did, he yanked some of her pubic hair out.

She yelped like a scared pup. "There isn't any—"

He grabbed her by the throat. "A name, Lisa."

She didn't hesitate this time. "Ben Davidoff," she said, but then quickly added, "but it was only one time."

"Where does he work?"

"At my building, on the sixth floor."

Tom lay silent, which must have worried her. "Tom…you're not going to do anything there, are you? They have guards in the building. And—"

He stroked her hair gently, letting his fingers trace down her cheeks. "Not to worry. I wouldn't do anything to him where you work." He turned her over, and said, "Spread your legs."

Tom finished with her, then lay with his arms wrapped around her. "Don't even think of running away. You hear me?"

"I wouldn't try to run away. You know—"

"If you try, I'll kill you."

"You don't have to worry, Tom."

"Well, just in case, I went to see your mother today. She—"

"What?" Lisa jumped up and ran for the phone, fumbled with it, then punched in some numbers. On the third ring she heard a phone ringing in the apartment. It was coming from Tom's pants, next to the bed.

Tom reached over and pulled out a small cell phone and said, "Hello, Lisa. This is your mother." And then he laughed like hell.

Lisa ran for the door, but Tom grabbed her. He spun her to face him and narrowed his eyes. "I paid your mom a visit today. Don't worry, she's all right. For now. But if you mess up, nobody will ever find her."

"What do you mean? What did you do?"

Tom smiled. "I moved her to a safe place, a place only I know about." He leaned close, narrowed his eyes, and said, "And if you even whisper anything to the cops or anyone else, she'll rot and go to hell before I tell you where she is."

Lisa's knees buckled. She fell to the floor. "Why are you doing this?"

"Get in the bed," he said. "Time you learned a lesson."

"Why are you doing this to me? I just—"

Tom smacked her and then straddled her, his hands in a choke-hold on her neck. "You just what? Fucked half the city? Couldn't wait for your husband to get home?"

She tried breaking his grip but he was too strong. "I'm sorry," she managed to get out, then he released her. "I'm sorry," she said, through tears.

"I know you're sorry." He got off of her and sat on the edge of the bed, pulling his pants down. "Now get over here and do what you do best. Whore!"

Lisa took her time, doing everything Tom said. As she pleasured him, Tom thought about Ben Davidoff, and what he'd do to him.

CHAPTER 13

THE NEXT VICTIM

Brooklyn, New York

Tom Jackson woke early, went for a two-mile run, then did his daily routine of push-ups, sit-ups, and pull-ups before settling down to a cup of coffee. He was reading the paper when Lisa came out of the shower. "I need eggs and toast," he said, without looking up.

She pulled the towel tighter around herself. "Do you want bacon?"

"That goes without saying. And hurry up. I have places to go."

"Where are you going? I thought I was going to work today."

"You are, but that doesn't mean I can't go somewhere." He sipped his coffee and turned the page on the newspaper. "Remember, if I suspect something I'll kill you first, then Buster, and then I'll let your mother rot."

Lisa nodded. "I won't say anything."

"Good," he said. "If you see me in the building, don't even look at me."

Her hands shook as she poured her tea. "You're not going to…do anything, are you?"

He laughed then continued his meal. Before he left, he gave her instructions on what to do.

Lisa worked on the fourth floor. At ten o'clock she called Ben Davidoff and arranged to meet him in the cafeteria for lunch. Tom watched from a table nearby, close enough to get a look at Ben and be able to pick him out of the crowd. After lunch he followed Ben upstairs, saw him go into the restroom and then back to work. The way Ben so eagerly agreed to meet Lisa told Tom two things: Ben was pussy-hungry, and Lisa screwed him a lot more than once. She'd pay for that lie.

For two more days, Tom followed Ben—home at nights, into work in the morning, and back and forth to lunch. The man did everything the same. Took the same routes to and from work, and always went to the restroom after lunch, like clockwork. He was making it easy, almost too easy. All that remained was to determine where Tom wanted to do him. And *how* he wanted to do it.

Tom decided to do it at work. Ben seemed to be a proud man. Doing him at work would be the most humiliating. Tom gathered everything he needed—a small stepladder, orange cones, an out-of-order sign, disposable gloves, a baseball cap, sunglasses, and a nice ponytail wig to wear under the hat.

That day about fifteen minutes before Ben would finish lunch, Tom went to the sixth floor, careful to avoid looking into any of the cameras placed throughout the building. He exited the elevator on the sixth floor, placed the cones at the entrance to the restroom, put the out-of-order sign on the door, then got on the ladder and acted as if he were working on the lights. When Ben turned the corner to the restroom, he stopped cold.

"Oh," he said, and started to leave.

"No, you're all right," Tom said. "I was just finishing. Go on in." He stepped off the ladder and removed the sign from the door.

Ben smiled and passed by. "Excuse me."

Once he was inside, Tom put the sign back up and waited for half a minute, giving Ben enough time to get started. Tom opened the door, saw Ben's feet under the stall, smiled and drew his gun. Tom went into the stall next to Ben's, stood on the toilet and leaned over the top.

"Hello, there," he said, gun pointing at Ben. "You want to get up and step outside the stall?"

Panic showed in Ben's eyes. "What the hell—what is this about? What are you doing?"

"Step outside the stall, please. And keep your voice down. If you get too loud, I'll shoot you, and then people will come, and I'll have to shoot them."

Ben yanked his pants up, holding them with one hand while he opened the door. "If it's money you want, I can—"

Tom laughed. "I don't want your money, Ben. For God's sake, I'm not a thief."

Ben's brow furrowed, confusion replacing the panic in his eyes. "What do you want? Do I know you?"

Tom seemed to give it thought. "You don't know me, and for now, just hold your hands in front of you. You can let your pants drop. I won't look."

With awkward moves, Ben let go of his pants and held his hands out, trembling. "What are you going to do?"

"Tie you up so you can't go for help."

More confusion showed in Ben's eyes as Tom tied his hands, then put a gag in his mouth. Tom punched him hard in the right kidney, dropping Ben to his knees. Then he punched his left kidney, bringing him to all fours. "You thought you could get away with fucking another man's wife and not get caught?" Tom walked around him in circles, knelt before him and stared into his eyes. "It didn't work, Ben. I found out, and now you're going to pay."

Ben's eyes went wide, pleading. His head shook side to side.

Tom grabbed a fistful of hair and dragged him into the stall, the same one Ben had used. He brought him up to the toilet and shoved his face under the water, pressing on the back of his head with his foot. Ben fought, moving to the side and kicking, but he was easy to restrain. When Tom thought Ben might have had enough, he let the pressure off and Ben came out of the toilet bowl like a submarine breaching the surface at full speed. Desperate breaths came from his nose. He gasped and made funny sounds through his gag. He tried to stand, but Tom put the gun at the back of his head. "Stay still. I won't hurt you. I'm just having a little fun."

Scared rabbit eyes looked up at Tom, filled with pleas of mercy.

"Did you like eating my wife's pussy?"

Ben hesitated, as if wondering what the right answer would be. After a moment of indecision he opted for a shake of the head.

Tom smiled. "Liar! I'm sure you did. And I understand. When I start, I don't like to stop." His hand quivered. He almost pulled the trigger, but instead he breathed deeply, calming himself. "Why don't we pretend that the shit in that toilet is her pussy. And guess what, I'm going to let you eat all you want." Tom removed the gag, grabbed Ben by the hair, and shoved him into the tank, then used his foot to hold him down. Ben thrashed and tossed his head about, but Tom held him under the water, looking at his watch as he did. It took almost a full minute for Ben to quit kicking, then a few seconds of inactivity—perhaps while he tried to gather strength—followed by a full-blown breakout attempt. It was pitiful to watch, but pleasant enough revenge. For forty seconds longer, Tom held him under before removing his foot. Ben didn't move. Dead for sure.

Tom pulled down Ben's underwear, exposing his ass cheeks, then took out his knife and began carving. When he finished he taped a note to the stall door.

This will give those cops something to think about.

CHAPTER 14

WHERE IS MARTY FERRIS?

Wilmington, Delaware

Frankie tore out of the morgue parking lot, and called Nicky. It rang five or six times before going to voicemail. "Nicky, where are you? We need to talk. Now!"

A minute later, Frankie's phone rang. He grabbed it off the seat. "Nicky?"

"Bugs, what's going on? I heard about Bobby—"

"Where did you go after you left Teddy's?"

A long pause followed. "Not that it's any of your business, but I went to play cards."

"I went to the shop that night; you weren't there. I went to your house, too."

"Yeah, well I'm sure these questions came from Borelli, and it's none of his business."

"This is a murder investigation; it sure as hell is his business."

Nicky paused and Frankie could almost feel those hawk eyes staring him down. "Let me put it straighter, Bugs. It's none of *your* business."

"If that's the way you want it—fine. But you better get your alibi straight because Borelli will be looking hard at both of us for this."

"Did you do it?"

"Are you fucking crazy? Don't try and turn that shit on me."

"I'm hanging up. You're obviously not in the mood to talk. Sorry again about your dad. You know we all liked him." The line went dead.

Frankie felt like tromping on the gas and racing down the street, but he knew better. As bad a driver as he was, he'd probably have a goddamn accident. Besides, maybe Borelli was right. Maybe Frankie did kill Bobby after all. Until the report came in he wouldn't know shit. He did hit him with a fucking mug full of beer.

"Please don't let that be it, God. I don't need Donna hating me any more than she does now."

Frankie fielded a lot of questions when he got home, brushing them aside by telling them it was police business, but soon he got Donna upstairs, alone.

"What do you want?" she asked. "I've got to be with Mom."

"There are plenty of people with Mom. I need answers."

"About what?"

"Finances. You said you were broke, but Bobby was talking to me about buying a bar and said he had big deals coming up. You know anything about that?"

She brushed it off. "He always talked like that. All his life he wanted to own a bar. I think he figured it was the lazy man's way out. Own a bar and the money rolls in without working, just have to stand around and talk to people. Stupid fuck."

"Watch your mouth."

"He's my husband. I'll talk about him any way I like."

"Yeah, well there was more to this than that. I can tell. Besides, Borelli said there was a checking account in Bobby's name with a decent amount of money in it? You know about that?"

"Of course I knew," she said, but she said it too fast. Donna never was a good liar. "I forget how much he…we had in there, but it was pretty good."

Frankie nodded. "Borelli said there was almost three grand in there."

"I know. We've been saving for a vacation."

Frankie took her chin and lifted it, staring at her with all the compassion he could manage. "Donna, there was fifty grand in there—*fifty*—not three."

He saw the gaping eyes, the dropped jaw. This was no act.

"What?" she said.

"Where did he get it?" Frankie asked.

Donna's mind must have been racing. "Where did he get that kind of money?" Then, as if she just thought of it. "What's going to happen to it? They can't take it, can they?"

"If they can prove he got it illegally, they can."

She got off the bed, covering her face with her hands. "You've got to stop them. That's *our* money. They can't take it."

"Where did he get it?"

"I *don't know* where he got it, but if it's in our bank account, it's ours. They can't take it."

Frankie pushed her back to the bed. "Don't start spending it, because sure as shit that money's going to be confiscated." He hugged her, and held her for a moment. "I'm going down to be with Mom. Do you want me to send someone up here to be with you?"

She seemed to get a grip on herself. "No, I'll be all right. Go on."

Frankie took the steps to the living room slowly. He didn't want to face his mother's questions or her sorrow. He just wanted to be back in Brooklyn working a case with Lou.

His mother was sitting on the sofa. She had stopped crying, at least for the moment, and was surrounded by relatives offering comfort. Frankie walked up and took her hand. "You want to go for a walk, Mom?"

Her eyes lit up. She stood with a strong resolve. "A walk might do me good."

About halfway up the block, Frankie started talking. "You know how sorry I am about Dad. I wish I would have talked to him more the last few years."

"He was proud of you. He always bragged about you."

Frankie choked back a tear. She was saying all of the things he didn't want to hear. Why didn't she tell him what a prick his father had been and how he hated Frankie's guts.

"Was he a nice guy, Mom? I mean—"

"He was a gentleman, Frankie. A fine gentleman."

"You always fought. Why did you even marry him?"

She was silent for a long while. Silent as they passed the Brezlors' house, and the Gibsons', and the Schmidts'. Then she spoke, but in a very low voice. "Because I was carrying a baby in my stomach."

That shocked Frankie, but not as much as his mother probably thought it would. Things were different in her time. "Mom, that's not so bad. Remember, I had to get married too."

She squeezed his hand and cried. "But the baby wasn't his, and he knew. He knew, and he still married me."

"What?" Frankie didn't mean to sound so shocked, but he realized it too late.

His mother seemed to stumble on the sidewalk. "That's right. Donna is not his child."

Frankie's throat tightened. He felt a sharp pain in his gut. He didn't want to ask this question, but he *had* to. "And me?"

His mother stopped, hand going to her heart. Her tears came easily now. "I don't know. I wish I did." She fell into his arms and let her tears fly.

Frankie hugged her and patted her back, but inside he seethed. He'd heard rumors when he was a kid, but had refused to think they were true. When he met Alex last year, it was the first time he let himself believe the rumors *might* be true, but he still didn't know. Not for sure.

No wonder his father questioned her when she went out and demanded to know where she'd been. No wonder he treated Donna and Frankie like shit. All of these years Frankie had looked at his mother as a saint for putting up with his father. Now he realized neither one of them was a saint.

Goddamnit, Mom, why did you tell me this?

***

Jimmy Borelli went through the checklist of people he had talked to so far. Only a few remained to be interviewed—the two women with Tim and Russ; Nicky Fusco; and Marty Ferris. Of all of them, Marty was the one Jimmy wanted to talk to the most. He left a message on Marty's answering machine but got no response. His work said they hadn't seen him. *So where is Marty? Is he dead?* Jimmy lit a smoke and savored the first drag, the best one. *There's only one person I know of who wants Marty Ferris dead—and that's Nicky Fusco.*

CHAPTER 15

SISTER THOMAS'S RULES

Wilmington, Delaware

They held Bobby's wake two days later at Maldonaddo's. Most of the people there showed up to offer condolences; Jimmy Borelli came armed with questions. He got there early, paid his respects to Frankie and Donna, then sat in the back, taking notes on who was and wasn't in attendance. Prominent on the "wasn't" list was Nicky Fusco, though Borelli didn't expect him to come, not with Donna ranting and telling anyone who would listen that Nicky was the one who killed her husband. Jimmy made note of it, but took the accusation with a grain of salt; Donna had nothing but suspicions to fuel her rage.

Jimmy got up when Jack McDermott came in and slid down the pew so Jack could sit next to him. "Hey, Jack," he whispered. "How's it going?"

Jack gave him a skewed look. He had hung out with Jimmy's older brother, but he and Jimmy had never been friends. "All right, I guess. Came to pay respect."

"Yeah, some shit, huh? First Frankie's father, now Bobby. Bad luck, bad timing. All of it."

"I guess so," Jack said, but kept his focus on the front.

Borelli leaned close to him. "Jack, you seen Marty Ferris around?"

"I hardly know Marty."

"Is that so?" Borelli sat silent for a moment. Donna was crying something terrible up near the casket. When she slowed down Borelli again leaned in close. "I only asked because I heard you were talking to him at Teddy's the night Bobby got killed."

Jack shot him a look to kill. "Just two drunks talking, that's all."

"What about you, Jack? I know you wanted Bobby dead."

Jack's face twisted into a crooked smile. He leaned close to Borelli and whispered, "I wanted Campisi dead more than anybody, except maybe Fusco, but you're gonna have to get new suspects, because neither one of us did it." Jack poked Borelli's chest with his finger. "And maybe you should keep your questions to the proper place. This ain't it."

Borelli must have realized he wasn't getting any more from Jack, so he moved to the next pew. He asked a few more questions of people, but every time he did he noticed Frankie fuming from his spot at the front.

About midway through the viewing, Frankie motioned for Borelli to join him outside. Jimmy got up and followed. Frankie had a smoke lit by the time Jimmy got out the front door.

"What the fuck is the matter with you, Borelli?" Frankie pushed him, taking him off balance.

Jimmy held his hands up, but he took a stance as if he was ready to fight. "Go easy, Donovan."

"Fuck your easy. This is the second time you've interfered with us burying our dead. I'm sick of it." Frankie tossed his cigarette into the grass and got real close. "I don't know how you were raised but in my family we respect the dead, and the ones grieving. Now get the fuck out of here before I kick your ass."

"I'll go, Frankie, but the questions won't go away. I got a case to solve."

"Solve it another time."

"All right. I'm leaving." Jimmy walked down the sidewalk, got into his car and left, Frankie watching him the whole time.

***

THE WAKE DIDN'T LAST long; not many people showed up for Bobby. When it was over everyone went back to Frankie's mother's house for the second time in as many days. Nicky and Angela dropped off food, but didn't stay because of Donna, and there were trays of food from Mrs. Robino's, the restaurant that had served more funerals, wakes and weddings than all the priests at St. Anthony's and St. Elizabeth's combined. Lining the dining room table were trays of baked ziti, ravioli, manicotti, meatballs, sausage, and pastries that were just this side of the devil himself. In the kitchen was more wine than beer, and more than a few bottles of limoncello, the magic elixir that served happiness and sorrow in the same frozen glass.

Frankie got his mother and Donna situated and fed, then headed to the kitchen where he downed two glasses of limoncello before ducking out to the back porch with a glass of wine. He punched Nicky's number into the cell phone and waited for him to pick up.

"Hello."

"Nicky, it's Bugs."

There was a slight pause. "How's it going, Bugs?"

Frankie lit a smoke, sucked on it, then filled Nicky in. "Listen, the reason I'm calling is Borelli. He's pressing hard on Bobby, but also on Marty Ferris. You know anything about where he is, or why he's missing?"

"I barely know Marty."

"Word is you talked to him at the bar the other night."

"I did, but we didn't say much before I left."

"So what does 'didn't say much' consist of?"

Nicky didn't speak for a moment, then, "I told him Rosa didn't want him around anymore. Something like that."

"Don't tell Borelli you said that. He'd take it the wrong way."

"I know the drill."

"I know you *know the drill*. I'm telling you because Borelli seems intent on pinning this on you or me."

"He got any reason? Did you do it?"

"You *are* nuts, aren't you? I'm a cop. Of course I didn't kill him."

"As if cops don't kill people. I heard what you said, Bugs, but no shit this time. Did you kill him or not?"

"Fuck no, I didn't kill him. I already told you."

"Okay. Then we've got to go with Sister Thomas' rules. Since *you* didn't kill Bobby, and I didn't, we've got to figure out who did."

"That easy, huh?"

"Probably so," Nicky said, "but figuring out who did it and proving who did it are two different things, so let's go through the questions. Who had motive? Who wanted him dead? Or, just as importantly, who wants you framed?"

"There was money in a bank account. Fifty grand."

"There's the ticket. He didn't get fifty grand from nowhere. I'll check with Doggs and the guys, but Bobby didn't win it gambling. He wasn't that good or that lucky."

"Tell me more about Sister Thomas' rules," Frankie said. "I must have missed class those days."

"Grab a couple of Angie's meatball sandwiches and meet me at the park. We'll talk."

Frankie laughed. "The meatballs are gone, believe it or not."

"Then meet me at Casapulla's, and we'll grab a couple of subs. Make it fast, though. They're getting ready to close."

"You know I can't refuse a sub from Casapulla's. See you there."

***

I KNEW BUGS COULDN'T refuse a sub from Casapulla's, not after being gone for so long. There were a lot of places that made subs in this country, but none even came close to the ones in Wilmington.

I headed down Union Street, across the Elsemere Bridge and turned right, then took a quick left and another right onto Casapulla Avenue. I laughed every time I went to Casapulla's; where else was a street named after a sub shop. I parked in the lot across the street and waited five minutes before Bugs pulled into the lot next to me. He already looked five years older, and he'd only been home a few days. I got out of the car and walked toward him, a smile on my face.

"I wish I could be at the house with you."

Bugs made a face I knew from thirty years ago, a no-fucking-way type face, and shook his head. "Trust me, you don't want to be there. Not with Donna and Mom both in full gear."

I laughed with him, knowing he was right. Donna had taken a dislike to me, probably rubbed off from being married to Bobby all these years, but in any case, it wouldn't be good for me to be there. "How's your mom holding up?"

"Better than I thought. But shit, you won't believe…" He brushed his hand in the air. "Never mind."

"What?"

"Never mind. It's nothing," he said, and quickly changed the subject. "What are you getting?"

"Same as always. Large Italian, sweet and hot, with extra provolone."

Bugs laughed. "You never change. That's what I'm putting in your coffin, all of your favorite foods."

"No way you'll be around to put anything in my coffin, you half-Mick bastard."

Bugs winced. When he didn't come back with some smart-ass dago comment, I knew something was wrong, but I let it go. "What about you? Italian with extra hot peppers and no pickles?"

He burst into laughter. "I guess I'm predictable too."

"Ain't that the truth," I said, and grabbed his arm. "Let's get the subs. I'm starved."

We walked into Casapulla's with hunger in our stomachs and in our eyes. The smell of the place nearly knocked me out it was so good. There was nothing except Mamma Rosa's meatballs and sauce that smelled as good as a great sub shop.

Paula greeted us from her position behind the counter. "Hey, Nicky." She'd been working here so long she seemed like a fixture.

"How's it going, Paula?"

"Same as always," she said, then stretched to get a closer look at Bugs. "Jesus Christ, tell me that ain't Bugs Donovan."

"The one and only," I said. Frankie flashed his famous smile, the one he kept in reserve just for the girls. Paula wasn't a girl anymore—she was a little older than we were—and married, but she looked great, with her dark hair tied back in a bun, and her arms muscular from running the meat slicer every day for almost thirty years. I thought about Paula a lot, always did like her. In fact, if I didn't have Angie, she'd be the one I'd go after, if for no other reason than I'd like to smell her when she came home from the sub shop. There'd be nothing better than making love when your wife smelled like an Italian sub.

"It's been a long time," Bugs said.

"Long time?" Paula said. "Been ten, maybe twelve years. Where the hell you been?"

"Brooklyn. I'm a cop now."

Paula stopped slicing meat and rested her hand on the counter. "Holy shit, girls, you hear that. Bugs Donovan is a cop. In Brooklyn no less."

A few of Paula's sisters smiled at Frankie and nodded. One of them blew him a kiss.

"All right, what'll it be, guys?"

"Same as always for me," I said.

"Large Italian, extra hot and no pickles," Frankie said.

"You got it. Be ready in a few. Grab some chips while you're waiting."

I got a few bags of Herr's potato chips—a local brand—one barbecue and one regular, then picked up two bottles of water and set them on the counter. Frankie reached for money to pay, but I smacked him. "No way your money's good in this town."

Paula had our sandwiches in a few minutes and we took them across the street to a small park bench under an old oak tree. It was torture just waiting to unwrap the subs.

"So what's got you worried, Bugs?"

"Borelli. Something's not right. He started out good enough, but now he seems to be focusing on you, or me. I know how cops work. If they think they know who did it, they'll focus on that person only and try to make a case."

"I don't see the problem. Neither of us did it."

"Okay, so we didn't do it, but guess what, I hit the Bobby with a mug of beer and kicked the shit out of him in front of maybe twenty witnesses. Then I proclaimed, and very loudly I might add, that I'd kill him if he ever said anything like that again, or some such nonsense."

"Okay, so that could be a problem." I took the biggest bite I could from the sub and relished every damn bit of flavor.

"Tell me you've got some brilliant ideas, Nicky, because we need them."

"That bad? For real?"

Bugs put his head in his hands. "Nicky, I can't even begin to tell you…"

"You can always tell me anything, you know that."

He shook his head. "Some things even friends can't share."

I thought for a minute he was going to cry. I hoped not because that was something I'd never seen Bugs do, and I didn't know if I could handle it.

"Sometimes I wish we were kids again. Running the streets, getting into trouble, and dreaming of Patti McDermott."

"Those were the good old days weren't they."

He looked off toward the trees and sighed. Actually sighed. "And we can't get them back. They're gone forever."

I knew something was wrong, but I also knew Bugs was even worse than me about telling people his problems. "You ever think about going to confession?"

I expected a quick and firm denial, but he hesitated, as if thinking. Then he shocked the shit out of me by seeming to consider it.

"I don't know. I've been thinking about it lately."

"You should do it. It's good for you."

That must have touched a nerve, because he looked at me as if I was a lunatic. "What, you telling me you go to confession? I haven't read about any of the priests having a heart attack, and the church is still standing, so I don't think so."

"I go. Not the traditional way, but I do it the way I've always done."

"I know, by yourself, on Saturday afternoon."

"You know about that?" I always thought my Saturday confessionals were private. "Hey, it's better than nothing."

"Bullshit is what it is."

Before I could protest Bugs started up again. "I can't pretend to know what you've been through. I'm a cop, and I've never killed a person, so I don't know the guilt or the pain…but I also can't go in for that confessional stuff. I never could."

"I know. Just thought it might help you, that's all. If you want to talk to me about it, I'm available."

"You a priest now? Father Nicky Fusco?"

I laughed along with him. "You're an asshole," I said, and took the last few bites of my sub, then tossed the paper in the trashcan. "I could eat another one right now."

Bugs finished a few seconds later. "No shit. I forgot how good they were. I wish we had them in New York. All we got is those stupid fuckin' hoagies and they taste like shit."

I patted him on the back as we walked toward the cars. "Don't worry. We'll figure this all out."

Bugs turned to me. "Nicky, I am worried. Something's wrong. First

Bobby gets killed, and sure as I'm standing here, I'm telling you, I don't think it was what I did to him, but then, from what Borelli tells me, Marty Ferris is missing too. Something's up."

I opened his car door and let him get inside. "Don't worry, Bugs. I'm sure there's an explanation for everything."

"I hope so," Frankie said, but he knew from experience that he couldn't trust Nicky's explanations.

CHAPTER 16

BORELLI DIGS DEEPER

Wilmington, Delaware

Frankie got a call from Borelli the next morning, asking him to come to the station. Frankie didn't want to go, but he knew Borelli wasn't going away anytime soon. He parked the car, walked across the street and up the steps, making his way to the front desk.

"I'm here to see Jimmy Borelli."

Ed Mrozinski followed Bugs in, and came up behind him. "Hey, Frankie," he said and patted him on the back.

"Good to see you again, Mrozinski." Frankie looked around. "You know where Borelli is?"

"Probably in his office. Follow me."

Frankie followed him around the corner then down a hall with a worn-out linoleum floor, to what looked to be a small interrogation room. Mrozinski opened the door and pointed inside. "I'll tell him you're here."

Frankie looked around while he waited. It was obvious the Wilmington Police Department didn't have an interior decorator on staff, or even someone with taste to offer suggestions. Maybe that's the way they wanted it—soften up the suspects by subjecting them to this. Frankie noticed the handle on the door was loose when he came in, and the legs of the table wobbled when he leaned on it. As far as the artwork—he'd seen better in Sister Leona's fourth grade art fest.

After fifteen minutes of waiting, Borelli came in carrying two cups of coffee. He sat in a chair across from Frankie. The chairs weren't much, a plastic molded seat and back screwed into four metal tubes not much thicker than a crayon, and each one waiting for a fat man to put it out of its misery. If they ever brought Patsy 'The Whale' Moresco in for questioning, he'd destroy the department's entire furniture budget.

Frankie accepted the coffee, scowling as he tasted it. "What the hell, you make this yesterday?"

"This ain't Brooklyn."

"I didn't say it had to be gourmet coffee, but hot would be nice." Frankie set the cup on the table and pushed it to the side.

"Sorry again about—"

"No need for pleasantries. Let's get this over with, because I've got way too much to do."

Jimmy sipped his coffee, set it down, then took out his notepad. "Fine by me. I was just trying to be civil."

"Yeah."

"Let's start with your friend."

"Leave Nicky out of this. He's clean."

"Look, I know you guys are friends, but don't dig yourself a hole trying to protect him. The guy is bad news."

"Nicky served his time."

"I'm not talking about the time he did here. I'm talking about the rumors from New York. And—"

"Bullshit!"

Borelli put his hand up. "Let me finish. I'll forget the Woodside incident, and I'll even forget what I heard about New York, but that still leaves me with a problem."

"What kind of problem?"

"I don't buy the coincidence that six months after Nicky shows up in

Wilmington, Bobby Campisi, his old arch-enemy, gets killed. And then Marty Ferris, Angela's ex-husband, disappears. And I have reliable reports that put Nicky near Marty's house a few days earlier."

"I heard Marty was an asshole," Frankie said. "He probably figured he couldn't beat on the little girl anymore, so he left town."

Borelli's head was shaking before Frankie finished. "His apartment's still full. He has money in the bank and his car has been in front of his house for two days. Nobody leaves that way. Not on their own."

"Nicky's clean. Married with a kid, and he has a good job."

"People like him are never clean, Frankie. You know that."

Frankie stood, tossed his cup into the trash. "If that's all you got, you wasted your time and mine. I'm outta here."

"I'm not done with you, either. I've got questions regarding Bobby."

"What's keeping you? Ask away."

Jimmy smiled. "Just waiting on DNA. It shouldn't be long."

Frankie stormed out, slamming the door.

Jimmy got up and opened the door, yelling down the hall after Frankie. "You know the old saying, Donovan—don't leave town."

* * *

ED MROZINSKI CAME IN after Frankie left. "Jimmy, I don't get it. There's no way he killed Bobby, and you know it."

"That's not what the evidence says."

Ed shook his head. "He's a cop. He's not going to a bar, beat his brother-in-law's ass, and then go kill him. Especially knowing his DNA is going to be all over the place."

"We'll see," Jimmy said.

"I don't understand you. You can't believe he did it."

"He's guilty," Jimmy said. "End of subject."

* * *

HALF AN HOUR LATER, Borelli and Mrozinski showed up at Nicky's workplace. Borelli flashed a badge at the receptionist and asked for Nicky Fusco.

"May I ask what this is about?"

"Police business," Jimmy said.

When she left to get Nicky, Mrozinski leaned and whispered to Jimmy. "We don't have to be pricks about it. The guy could get in trouble. Remember, he was in prison."

"Fuck him."

It only took Nicky a few minutes to come out. He looked at both of them with narrowed eyes, and then nodded. "Borelli, how are you?"

"I'm great. You know my partner, Ed Mrozinski?"

Nicky shook his hand. "I knew your older brother."

Mrozinski smiled. "I remember you, Nicky. You stopped those Harrison Street guys from kicking my ass one time."

"Does that mean I have a friend on the force?" Nicky smiled along with him.

Before Mrozinski could answer, Jimmy spoke up. "I know you've been back a while. Seems odd you haven't seen much of the old gang."

"I don't hang out much. I mostly work and go home."

Jimmy nodded. "That's probably good. Everything's changed now. Drugs change it all."

"How's that?"

Jimmy stared at the wall as if in a trance. "Fuckin' drugs. They're everywhere, and they change the game. Instead of a robbery, we now get a robbery where they shoot the people. Instead of a mugging, someone's beaten to death. Three weeks ago, we had four bodies in a parking lot on Front Street. We didn't find anything but I know it was connected to drugs."

Nicky waited for more, but Jimmy didn't say anything else, just stared at the wall. "What do you need, Detective? I've got work to do."

"Oh yeah, I forgot, you're a respectable man now. Husband, father, ex-killer."

Nicky tensed. "Is there a question in that?"

"I've got a witness that saw you with Marty Ferris the night he died."

Nicky looked at him. "I didn't know Marty was dead."

"He's dead, all right. We might be the only ones who know it, but Marty Ferris is definitely dead, and *you* know where the body is."

Nicky held out his hands. "So lock me up. You've got a witness, I presume."

"Where were you the night Bobby was killed?"

"Now you're trying to pin Bobby on me? I thought you had Bugs pegged for that one?"

Borelli paced. "You probably killed Bobby for the money, but you didn't figure on Donovan getting into a fight with him at the bar. That fucked things up, didn't it? Put the heat on him."

"Are we talking about Marty Ferris, or Bobby? Or are you trying to pin both murders on me. That is, if Marty is really dead."

"I *know* Marty is dead, and I'll let you know when I can pin anything on you. It won't be long."

"I don't know what the hell you're talking about. But then again, you never had many smarts."

"You shouldn't have come back here, Fusco. You don't belong down here with decent people."

Nicky paused, seemed to compose himself. "Get used to me, Jimmy. I'm here to stay. And I don't want any trouble."

"Ever since you came back people are dying. I've heard the rumors. I know what you do, but I ain't no Bugs Donovan. I don't let killers go."

Nicky clenched his fists and gritted his teeth. "You said one thing right. You ain't no Bugs Donovan." With that, he turned and walked back to his office.

Borelli stormed out of the building and across the parking lot, Mrozinski close behind him. When they got to the car, he stopped to light a smoke.

"What the fuck was that about?" Mrozinski asked. "Ferris isn't dead, not that we know of, and how can you suspect Fusco for Bobby? I thought you already pegged Donovan for that?"

"I wanted to stir things up, see what happens."

"You might want to let me in on things before you do them. I *am* your partner."

"I really don't care which one of them goes down for it. They're in this together. I know it. Get in the car. We're going to find some evidence."

CHAPTER 17

SECOND THOUGHTS

Wilmington, Delaware

I went to bed that night in an agitated state. Borelli shook me up, not because I thought he could catch me—he wasn't that smart—but he gave me reason to think about what I'd done. What was wrong with me? I had a new life and I was risking it for a piece of shit like Marty Ferris. Suppose it hadn't been Borelli? Suppose it was a good cop investigating, like Bugs. As I stared at the ceiling with my hands under the pillow, I made up my mind. I'd let Marty go. With that resolved, I prayed that Marty was still alive.

I got up at five and started water brewing for espresso while I took a quick shower. I didn't like missing my morning run, but I figured a day or two here and there wouldn't hurt. Angie popped into the bathroom while I was drying, a curious look on her face.

"You're up early?"

"Got a lot to do today."

"Don't forget, we're going to the movies tonight."

I leaned over and kissed her. "How could I forget a date with you?"

She smacked my ass, took off her clothes and stepped into the shower. "Make me some coffee before you go. Regular, not espresso. And don't make it so strong."

"You got it, babe. See you tonight."

On my way down Front Street I called the office and left a message, telling them I'd be late, and then I headed down Route #13 toward the canal banks. Part of me wanted Marty to be dead—it would make things easier—but deep inside, I hoped he was still alive. I promised Angie and Rosa that I wouldn't hurt him, and I'd broken that promise. I empathized with Marty on one front—losing Angie and Rosa would be tough for any man—but it was his own fault. I still couldn't understand how any man could hit a woman, let alone a girl.

Traffic was hell, the normal against-the-flow drive backed up for some unknown reason. Instead of half an hour it took me nearly forty-five minutes to get there, but there wasn't a single car on the back road leading to the canal banks, and the gates were open. I drove around, checking for other cars or signs of caretakers or maintenance men. After a second pass, I pulled up to where I'd left Marty and got out then walked around for a final check. Nothing had been disturbed. I got my shovel and uncovered the box. I could hear Marty as I dug, making low moans, like a sick animal. When I got the box open, the stench was unbearable, like the time Mamma Rosa's freezer full of meat went bad.

It was a sunny day and the light must have blinded Marty at first. He called out as if he'd been saved.

"Thank God," he said, his voice weak and desperate. He sounded like someone in a movie on a life raft seeing a rescue boat coming for them. It was heartwarming, but I'm sure he didn't recognize me when he said it. When I spoke, my voice brought him back to reality.

"Glad to see you're alive, Marty."

He started crying. "Jesus Christ. Don't hurt me. Please?"

Now I *did* feel sorry for him. He was pitiful. "I came to get you out."

"You're letting me go? For real?"

"I said I'm getting you out. Whether I let you go depends on you."

"Anything. Just tell me what you want."

I reached down and grabbed his hand, helping him out of the box. He looked as bad as he smelled, and I thanked God I'd come when I did; he wouldn't have made it much longer. "Let's get you cleaned up, then we'll talk." I had prepared by putting heavy plastic in the trunk, which I got out and placed over the car seat so he didn't get it wet or stinking. I made a mental note to come back later to get rid of the box and fill in the hole later. I had to take care of Marty.

He was silent as we rode to a job site that I knew that had running water, and most importantly, no one working. The silence was probably half distrust and half fear. I can't say I blamed him, and it was fine with me because I didn't want to talk either. I checked the job out, made sure no one was there, then instructed Marty to clean up, to wash his clothes and body.

When he finished, he looked around, as if searching for an escape route.

"Don't think about it, Marty. I'll put you back in the box."

He almost teleported to the car and got in the front seat. "What are you going to do with me?"

I threw him some old clothes I brought with me. They'd be a little small for him, but I felt sure he wouldn't mind. "I told you, it depends on you."

"Depends on what?"

"I can't trust you, Marty. You'll have to leave town."

"Sure, Nicky. I'll leave. Where you want me to go?"

I sighed. "You don't understand. I need you to leave for good. Go somewhere. I don't care where. And don't come back. Ever."

Marty looked at me with a confused expression. "Ever?"

"Not ever. And that means you can't call Rosa. You don't write, or visit."

He leaned forward. "Where am I supposed to go? How am I gonna live?"

I turned to face him, not blinking as I held his gaze. "I'll give you time to get your shit straightened out. I'll even give you enough money for a couple of months rent on an apartment. After that, it's up to you."

"Up to me? I got—"

"You got shit, Marty, and we both know it. What you *do* have is a skill. You're a butcher which means you can get a job anywhere, and you'll be making more than I do, so don't give me any shit."

He looked as if he wanted to say something, but didn't. I started the car and turned around.

"Where are we going?" he finally asked.

"First to the bank. Then I'll take you home. You can sell your house, settle debts, do whatever you have to do, but I expect that within a month—two at most—you'll be packing your clothes to get out of town."

"Where should I go?"

"I already told you, I don't give a shit where you go."

I drove back using route Route #13 again, forsaking Delaware's lone interstate. Interstates had no flavor, no personality. Bugs would argue that, but then again, he was always in a hurry to get somewhere, and the worst part was that he didn't know where. It took me maybe five or ten minutes longer to get back this way, but the drive calmed my nerves so it was worth it. I stopped at the bank, withdrew some money—more than we could afford—then went back to the car. I knew Marty would be there. The shock of what I'd done was still with him. He wouldn't dare risk running. A week from now, maybe, but not today.

Ten minutes later, we pulled up to his house. I reminded him not to call Rosa. "If she calls you—ignore her. If you see her, turn the other way. You're dead as far as Rosa is concerned. Remember that. And once you get your composure, make sure you talk to Borelli. Call him and say you heard he was looking for you."

"That's it, just—"

"I'm not done talking."

"Sorry, Nicky."

"Here's the deal. Listen close." I waited until I had his complete attention. "Don't ever think you can get free of this. If you tell Borelli what happened, I'll find you. And the next time it will be worse."

"I know how to keep quiet. Don't worry about that." Marty started to get out of the car, then turned back to face me. "Can't we work this out? Why are you doing this?"

I almost hit him. Almost took him back and shoved him in that box. "Rosa." That's all I said. From the look in his eyes, I knew it was enough.

He nodded, then got out of the car. I got out with him and gave him the money. "Remember everything I told you. If I have to do this again, there will be no reprieve. You'll wither away and die in that box."

"Don't worry. You'll never see me again."

"One last thing."

He looked frightened. "What?"

"You know anything about who killed Bobby Campisi, or what he was into?"

He started to say no, but must have thought better of it. "Ask Jack McDermott," he said, and headed into his house.

Jack McDermott? What the fuck? That one threw me for a loop. And the problem was that I believed him. No way was Marty lying to me today. As I drove off toward the office, I wondered what could Jack possibly have to do with Bobby? Jack had a grudge against Bobby—a big one—but I didn't picture Jack killing him.

Guess I need to do some talking.

CHAPTER 18

CALL FROM NEW YORK

Brooklyn, New York

By the time Lou and Sherri got to the scene, a half a dozen reporters had gathered outside the building. A young female with an independent news group shoved a mic toward Lou's face.

"What can you tell us, Detective Mazzetti?"

"It's hot out," Lou said, and pushed the mic aside. He wanted to shove the mic up her ass; instead, he grabbed hold of Sherri as they made their way through the crowd and inside to the elevator.

"I imagine things are gonna get bad now," Sherri said.

"When somebody gets killed in a public place, there's no stopping the reporters. They're worse than vultures after they smell a dead body."

Lou and Sherri got in the elevator with a patrolman. He pushed the button for the sixth floor, and they rode in silence until the doors opened. Two uniformed patrolmen, known as *unis*, guarded the hallway.

"What have we got?" Lou asked a young patrolwoman.

"A damn mess is what we got," she said.

"Where?"

"Bathroom."

"In the *bathroom*?" Sherri asked.

"At least it's the men's room," the uni said.

Lou walked in first. A stall door was open with a note taped to it, and a pair of ass cheeks stared at him. The victim's head was in the toilet.

"What's the note say?" Lou asked.

Sherri got close. "'This is #2. I thought I'd leave a little more flesh for you to work with this time, but don't worry, there *will* be more.'"

Lou moved up next to Sherri. "We get all the sick ones," he said, then looked down to the body. "What's carved on his ass?"

"'*Mea culpa, mea culpa,*'" Sherri said. It flowed off her tongue as if she spoke Latin.

"Sounds like you're familiar with that phrase. Catholic?"

"All my life," she said. "So someone is sorry for something…but is it the killer who's saying it's *his* fault or is the killer saying the *victim* had something to be sorry for?"

"We didn't see this on the first vic, did we?" Lou asked.

"No. I'd have remembered something like this. My brother was an altar boy. He recited that stuff all the time when he practiced his prayers."

"Remember, there might be two killers," Lou said. "I wonder which one did this."

"Whoever did this wasn't as angry," Sherri said, and turned to the uniform at the door. "Has the M.E. been here yet?"

"They said she's on her way. She should be here soon."

"Ah, Jesus Christ." Lou shook his head and turned away. "I hope he was dead before they did that."

"Yeah, that must have hurt like hell, carving all that in his ass."

"I'm not talking about his ass, I'm talking about shoving his head in the toilet. The prick didn't even flush it first."

Sherri was silent for a moment, looking around the scene. "You know, Lou, maybe that was on purpose. Maybe he wanted to humiliate the guy."

"He did a good job of that," Lou said. "And from the little bit of blood on his ass, he was probably dead when he did the carving. My bet is drowning in the toilet." Lou shook his head again. "Bad way to die."

"There's a good way?" one of the uniforms asked.

"A better way than this," Lou said, turning to the cop who'd asked. "Tell me what we've got so far."

The uniform described the scenario as he flipped open his notepad. "The cones in the hall had been there since somewhere around lunchtime. After a couple of hours, somebody risked it and came in to take a leak. That's when they saw the body and called us." The uni pointed to his notes. "Vic's name is Ben Davidoff, at least according to his license. From what we gathered on preliminary talks, he works down the hall, some kind of investment analyst."

"So either this was random, which I don't think, or the killer waited for him to use the bathroom." Sherri took notes as she spoke. "We need to think about this, Lou. He might have been watching this guy."

Lou looked at Sherri. "I wonder what the other guy did, the John Doe. Maybe this is about somebody's investments gone bad, and whoever did it is taking revenge."

"Could be," Sherri said. "I wish we knew who John Doe was."

Kate Burns, the M.E., pushed through the door into the men's room, and whistled. "Just what I've always dreamed of—meeting Lou Mazzetti in a men's room. If only we were alone."

Lou thought of something smart to say, but he was laughing too hard. "Okay, you got me on that one." He walked over and shook her hand. "Good to see you again, Kate, though I didn't want it to be so soon."

"This guy—or these guys—aren't wasting any time are they?"

"You still think it's two of them?"

"No question in my mind." She turned to Sherri and held out her hand. "Kate Burns. I figured I had to introduce myself since your partner lacks manners."

"Here comes that prejudice you warned me about, Mazzetti. Next she's gonna be saying we all look alike."

Lou and Sherri started laughing just as Lieutenant Morreau walked in.

"I hope somebody fills me in on the humor, because when the Chief of D's sees the news tonight, I don't think he'll find it funny."

Morreau nodded at Kate, then focused his anger on Sherri and Lou. "Reporters are already talking about a serial killer, a butcher, a maniac on the loose, and those are only the headlines leading up to the live news at six."

Sherri stared at Morreau. "I'm sorry to say, Lieu, but they're not wrong. And until we figure out why these people are being killed, nobody's safe. As far as we know these could still be random."

"Don't let me hear that quoted on the news, Miller."

"Yes, sir."

"What have we got?" Morreau asked, but then he must have looked at the body. "Don't tell me we've got some kind of Catholic connection."

"Not saying we do, Lieu, but 'mea culpa' does indicate at least a rudimentary knowledge of Latin prayers."

"Who made you an expert, Miller?"

"My brother was an altar boy."

"You think he had anything to do with it?" Morreau asked.

"We're looking into it," Lou said.

Sherri held back a chuckle.

Morreau looked around the men's room. "Nobody saw anything I guess."

"Not that we know of. Unis did some prelim work, but we'll go through it again. Once we have Kate's report, we'll know for sure if it's the same people, but with that note on the stall door we gotta figure it's him—or them."

"People?" Morreau said. "Did I hear 'people,' as in plural?"

"We told you before," Mazzetti said. "Kate thinks the first vic was done by two people."

Morreau slammed his hand into one of the closed stalls. "Damnit. Don't tell the reporters that, either; in fact, don't tell them anything."

"I have my 'no comment' line down pat," Lou said.

"Me too," Sherri said. "And I'm good at it."

Morreau started to leave, then popped his head back into the bathroom. "Where the hell is Donovan? Hasn't he been gone long enough to bury his father?"

"I'll call him tonight," Lou said.

"Do that. And tell him to get his ass back up here." Once again Morreau started to leave, and once again he came back. "That's no reflection on you, Miller. Don't think I'm being biased or anything."

"Yes, sir. I know."

Kate waited a few seconds, making sure Morreau was gone before speaking. "Lou, have you heard from Frankie?"

"He hasn't called. I planned on calling him tonight." Lou pulled Kate aside. "I'm sure he'd love to hear from you instead of me."

Kate nodded. "Maybe so. I'll see."

"You damn Irish people! You know how to fight but not make up. Just call him, for God's sake."

"Thanks, Lou," Kate said, and turned as Sherri approached.

"Kate, please tell me this killer carved his name and address alongside the mea culpa's."

"If he did, I haven't found them yet. But I *did* find some interesting coincidences."

Lou moved in beside her. "Like what?"

"Like there is once again no DNA evidence that I can see. There might be some when we process everything, but this guy is careful, if nothing else."

"You're a barrel of laughs, Kate." Lou headed for the door. "We're going to ask questions. Call me if you get anything interesting."

Lou and Sherri made the rounds all afternoon, questioning the victim's coworkers and anyone else who could give them a clue as to who might want the guy dead. Sherri got his address and particulars from human resources. From his secretary they found out that he was divorced, but not seeing anyone.

"You want to check his place out tonight?" Sherri asked. "He lived in White Plains."

"No way I'm going up there tonight. Give me the address and I'll meet you there in the morning."

"What time?"

Lou frowned. "You an early bird, or a sleeper?"

"I like to get it done, boy."

He laughed. "See you at seven. How's that?"

"That's good. It'll give me time to get a workout in."

Lou waved his hand and walked away, muttering. "Goddamn young kids."

LOU PARKED HIS CAR at the house, and dragged his feet across the few feet of sidewalk to his apartment. "Buona sera, baby, I'm home."

A practiced response came from the kitchen. "Buona sera, Luigi. Did you have a good day?"

"One less citizen in the great state of New York. You tell me, good day or not." He walked across the kitchen and kissed his wife.

She continued working at the stove. "I guess it depends on who the citizen was."

Lou dipped his finger into her sauce and tasted it. "Investment analyst."

She smacked him with a spoon. "It was a good day."

"How long before dinner?"

"Half an hour."

"I've got to call Frankie. Shouldn't take long."

"You want coffee?"

Lou had his cell phone out and was already dialing. "I could use it."

***

FRANKIE'S PHONE RANG FIVE times before he picked up, and when he did, his tone was an impatient one.

"Donovan."

"Donovan, it's Mazzetti. How's it going down there?"

A big sigh followed. "Hey, Lou. Sorry about how I answered. Got a lot of shit going on."

"How's the family?"

"Not good. My sister's husband got killed the night of my father's wake. Murdered."

"What the fuck! Did you piss off the angels or something?"

"I'm sure I did. And you know what's worse, these asshole cops down here like *me* for it."

"How did *that* happen?"

"Long story, and one I don't want to go into right now." Frankie waited but when Lou didn't say anything, he spoke up. "So what's up? Why'd you call?"

"Hate to give you more to worry over but Morreau is raising holy hell and wants you back. We got a second one, and I don't think it's stopping with two."

"I assume the reporters are having a field day?"

"You got it." Lou paused to light a smoke. "I understand what you're going through, but if I were you, I'd do what I could to get back."

"Yeah, well you ain't me, so tell Morreau I need more time."

"All I'm saying is he's not going to like it."

"Fuck him. I've got people to bury down here."

Lou took a while before responding. "I know you've got people to bury, and I'm not saying drive back tonight. Take a couple of days, do what you've got to do, but then get up here before Morreau loses it. I'll cover for you as long as I can."

"How are you going to cover? What the hell can you do?"

"I don't know, I guess I'll just tell him that you're stuck in Wilmington, or whatever piss-hole-in-the-snow city you're in, and they got you pegged for a murder. That ought to shut him up for a while. Besides, I got a new partner, and she's a whole lot better than you. A lot prettier, too."

Frankie laughed. "Now I know you're shitting me. She might be better but no way she's prettier than me."

"All right, I'm hanging up. I've had all I can stand. Get your ass home before they put you in jail."

"I need to work on that. How about asking Morreau to call down here and make sure I don't get any grief about leaving?"

"I'll do it. And by the way, Kate was asking for you."

"Kate? She was?"

"Yeah, I saw her at the scene today. Give her a call. You two micks deserve each other."

"Maybe I will. See you soon, Lou. And thanks, I appreciate what you're doing." As Lou hung up, Frankie slammed his phone on the table. "Goddamnit, everything's happening at once."

CHAPTER 19

FOLLOW THE LEADS

Brooklyn, New York

Lou got to Ben's place at quarter to seven. Sherri was already there, running up and down the block at a fast clip. He got out of the car, lit a smoke, and watched her, waiting until she got close. "Hey, Miller, if you've got that much energy come to my place after work; it needs cleaning."

"You don't want me at your place, Mazzetti. I might end up telling your wife how you hit on me all day."

Lou laughed. "She wouldn't believe you. I can barely climb into bed, let alone do anything once I get there."

"Remember that little blue pill…"

"Forget that. I'm not taking anything that's going to give me a hard-on for four hours. That's just plain wrong."

"All right, I'm not arguing with you. Let's check this place out." Sherri headed up the walk a few steps ahead of Lou. The house was a small bungalow on a nice street in a nice neighborhood. Nothing fancy about it, but it was clean and tidy. Lawn mowed, edges trimmed, walk swept clean, trees groomed.

"What the hell?" Lou said. "You're not even breathing hard after all that running."

"That's the way it's supposed to be. Most people don't get out of breath from bending down to tie their shoes."

Lou tossed his cigarette butt on the grass. "Yeah, I remember those days, but it was cruel of you to remind me."

Sherri continued looking around as she climbed the three steps to his stoop, then she used the key to unlock the door. "It looks like he kept it up pretty well."

"He own this or rent it?"

She looked at the papers in her hand. "Rented it. It says here his ex got their old house, somewhere up near Tarrytown."

"I'm guessing she got the better part of that settlement," Lou said.

"We'll have to find out why. It might mean something."

The door opened into a small rectangular living room with carpet that looked as if it had just been vacuumed, and a sofa flanked by end tables and two chairs. Opposite that was a television on a small stand and a makeshift liquor cabinet. Sherri opened it up. "Empty. I guess he didn't drink much."

"Or a lot," Lou said.

Sherri moved into the dining room, noting the pictures of a woman and two kids above the china cabinet. "Must be the ex."

"I can't believe a divorced guy has a china cabinet," Lou said, as he leaned down to open it and peer inside. "Christ, it's full of fucking china."

"That's what you're supposed to keep in there."

"Only women do that, and…"

"Don't go there, Mazzetti."

"Well, you wouldn't catch me with a goddamn china cabinet if *my* wife left."

"I can't figure out why she hasn't. I'm not going to read about you in the paper someday am I. 'NYPD detective kept wife locked in house for thirty years.' Or some such shit."

"Keep going, Miller, you're giving me ideas." Lou moved to the kitchen, opening the fridge and the pantry. "No beer. No junk food. Christ, there's no coffee! No wonder somebody killed him; this guy lived a miserable life."

Sherri opened a few cabinets, checked the drawers, then headed toward the bedroom. "Let's go where all the secrets are kept."

Lou followed her in. She was staring at a picture in a small frame on his dresser. Sherri nodded to it. "It's not the same woman as the picture out there."

Lou got closer, squinted. "Not even close. This one looks far too hot for him."

"Sister?"

"No way our vic and that woman came out of the same parents," Lou said. "We better take that with us. See if we can find out who she is."

Lou spent another forty-five minutes looking around, but there wasn't much to see. He checked the garbage, the other bedrooms, the backyard, and the basement. The only item of interest turned out to be the picture of the girl. When he came back upstairs, Sherri was still checking the computer in a bedroom the guy converted into an office.

"Anything on there?"

"Nothing. I mean nothing. Whatever he had with that girl, it's over. No emails to anyone but his ex and a few to work. No appointments on his calendar; in fact, nothing on his calendar but birthdays for his ex and his kids and a sister that looks like she lives in Jersey."

"God forgive her," Lou said.

"Yeah. Anyway this guy's only got a couple of dozen songs in his iTunes. How's that for sad?"

"In his what?"

"Forget it."

"You got an address for the ex?"

"I've got it right here," Sherri said. "We might as well get up there."

IT TOOK ABOUT FIFTEEN minutes to get to Tarrytown, and another ten minutes to find the right house. Sherri parked across the street, turned the car off, but didn't get out.

Lou opened the door. "Let's go."

She hesitated. "Lou, I've never done this before."

He started to say something but stopped and looked over to her. "Don't worry, I'll handle it. Besides, it might not be as bad with an ex. I've seen some of them almost laugh. Not quite, but almost. In any case, it's not usually as bad as if they're still married." He patted her arm. "I'm not going to lie though, it's no fun."

"What should I do?"

He paused. "You're a good person, Miller. Just do what comes naturally."

Lou led the way up the sidewalk to a large two-story colonial surrounded by a manicured lawn and gardens. "My house would fit in here twice," Lou said. "Maybe three times."

"You were right. She got the better end of the deal."

"Now let's find out why." Lou used the brass knocker to rap on the door, forsaking the doorbell. "I always wanted to use one of these."

Sherri stifled a smile, trying to get herself in the right frame of mind for what they had to do.

Footsteps sounded a moment later and the door opened. The woman standing there was a slightly older version of the picture hanging in Ben Davidoff's house, her hair a little grayer and her face bearing a few more wrinkles.

"Mrs. Davidoff?" Lou asked.

"Ms. Markham," she answered. Her voice was warm, but a bit of haughtiness tainted the words. "How may I help you?"

Lou held out his badge. "I'm Detective Lou Mazzetti." He removed his hat. "And this is my partner, Detective Sherri Miller."

A guarded look came to Ms. Markham's face. "Detectives? Is something wrong with Susan?" When she said it, she stepped out onto the stoop.

"No, nothing's wrong with Susan." Lou looked around. "Ms. Markham, may we go inside?"

With that statement, her face went blank. "What's wrong? Is my daughter all right?"

Sherri stepped forward, her face all compassion. "Ms. Markham, I'm so sorry to have to tell you this, but your husband, Mr. Davidoff, has suffered a terrible accident. He's gone."

Her hands flew to her mouth, covering a gasp. "Oh my God! Dear God. Ben? Ben is gone?" She looked as if she might stumble.

Sherri stepped in to support her. "Why don't we go inside?"

She nodded and led them to a sitting room just off the foyer. "What happened? How…"

"He was murdered, Ms. Markham. We don't know much more than that yet."

She nearly fell from the chair. "Murdered? My God! How? Who would do that?"

Before Sherri or Lou could answer, she started up again. "What will I tell the girls?" she spoke, as if to herself, and then she cried. "I'm sorry. I just…"

Sherri knelt on the floor beside her and held her hand. "It's all right to cry, Ms. Markham. We understand." She looked at Lou, who nodded. "Is there someone we could call—a relative or friend you'd like to be with you?"

The sobbing stopped after a moment and she stood. "My sister. I'll get her number, if you don't mind calling." She walked toward the kitchen, then looked back. "And my neighbor, next door to the right. She's probably home now. If you could possibly ask her to come over. The girls like her."

"I'll get her," Lou said.

When Ms. Markham returned with the number Sherri took it and went outside to make the call. She was still talking when Lou returned with the neighbor, the woman several steps ahead of him, almost running. The neighbor went inside. Sherri motioned for Lou to wait as she hung up with the sister. "She's coming over right away."

"You did good in there," Lou said. "Damn good. I still get flustered dealing with things like that."

"Thanks. It just kicked in when she started crying. I think this lady was still in love. If not, she sure can act."

"Let's give her a minute, and then see if she's up to talking. I hate to do it now, but we need to get a head start on this." Lou took out a smoke and reached for his lighter.

Sherri looked at him with a scowl on her face. "You should give that up, you know. You're already panting and puffing whenever you do anything."

"Yeah, yeah. Heard it all before."

"I'm worried about you, Lou. My grandmother died from cancer, and it wasn't very nice."

Lou put the smoke away. "All right, for Christ's sake," he said, and paced the sidewalk. After three or four walks from the street to the stoop, he reached for the door. "Let's see what we can do." He turned at the last minute and whispered to Sherri. "You do the talking."

Ms. Markham got up when they came back in, and she warmly took the hug Sherri offered.

"I know this isn't a good time, Ms. Markham, but we need to get a few questions answered."

The neighbor rose from her chair. "I'll meet the girls at school and bring them home."

"Thanks, Joan," she said, but before her friend went out the door, called to her. "Don't tell them."

"I won't."

Ms. Markham sat in the chair. "How did Ben die? What happened?"

Sherri looked to Lou. He nodded. "He was killed at his office. There's still a lot we don't know, but we'll inform you when we do."

Ms. Markham wiped her eyes, sat up straight, then folded her hands on her lap. "What can I do to help?"

"Do you know of anyone who might want to harm Ben? Did he have any enemies? Owe money? Gamble?"

Markham shook her head. "Nothing. Everybody liked Ben. He never hurt anyone. He didn't gamble or do drugs. He didn't even gossip."

"If it's not too much to ask, why did you get divorced?"

She wiped a few tears from her cheeks. "An affair. Several years ago. He got caught up with some young girl and…" Markham sat up straight and took a long slow breath. "This girl controlled him. He was like a puppet for her and she had him doing things he would have never done otherwise. When I found out, I gave him an ultimatum but he chose her. The girls and I decided and asked Ben to leave."

"We found a picture in his house. Do you mind if I show it to you?"

She held out her hand and Sherri showed her the photo.

Markham nodded. "That's her. How he ever thought she wanted anything but his money, I'll never know." She seemed lost in thought for a moment, then mumbled, "Men and their egos."

"Do you know her?"

She shook her head again. "Not personally. I know that she worked in the same building as Ben, but I don't think she worked at his firm. He called her Kitty, but I don't know if that's her real name." Markham took a drink of water from a glass on the table next to her. "It was over with them, though. It has been for a long time. Ben and I are…*were* going to get back together and give it another try." Tears came again. "He loved our girls."

"All right, I appreciate your cooperation in this," Sherri said. "If we have any more questions, we'll call."

Markham started to get up, but Sherri stopped her. "We'll let ourselves out," she said, and held her hand. "Take care of yourself."

As they walked down the sidewalk, Lou said, "Sounds like a model citizen." He opened the car door and climbed in. "We'll have to see about that, though. There aren't many people that don't have dirt hidden somewhere."

"That's why I like you, Lou, that eternal optimism."

He rolled down the window and grunted. "Wait till you meet Donovan."

Sherri drove a few blocks, turning onto the ramp leading toward the interstate. "Where will that leave me, when Donovan comes back?"

"Right where you are now. We can use Frankie's help, but I'm not letting you go anywhere. As it is Morreau is probably going to assign us another team. Hell, I *know* he will once the news breaks tonight."

"I want to get the son of a bitch doing this."

"We need to before he does it again," Lou said. "And don't forget, it might be two sons of bitches." Lou scrunched his eyebrows up. "Did I say that right? Is it sons of bitches, or is it son of a bitches?"

"It's sons of bitches. If you're gonna curse, do it right." Sherri got in the left lane and hit the gas. "You think this girl, Kitty, had anything to do with it?"

"I don't know if she had anything to do with the murder, but sure as hell the ex was right; from the looks of Kitty, she had her sights on Davidoff's wallet."

"First thing tomorrow, we'll check her out," Sherri said.

CHAPTER 20

BACK TO NEW YORK

Wilmington, Delaware

Frankie spent the rest of the day pissed off. As if it wasn't bad enough having two funerals to deal with, now he had Borelli crawling up his ass trying to pin Bobby's murder on him.

I should have never come home. Should have sent a fucking card and flowers.

Donna walked around the house wailing as if she really loved Bobby—and maybe she did—hell, who was Frankie to judge. His marriage lasted all of a year, and he hadn't been in a relationship since then that was worth a damn. Good or bad, love or not, Donna made her marriage last ten years. Something to be said for that. A touch of pity shook him, and for a moment he wanted to stay and find out who did this to Bobby. He wanted to do it for Donna if nothing else. Maybe answers would give her peace. Maybe not. But Frankie had to get back to New York and find that maniac before Morreau went nuts. He just hoped Morreau cleared it with Borelli's boss.

Frankie spent the rest of the night mending hurt feelings. In the morning he packed and prepared for the emotional outburst he knew would come when he tried to leave. He said goodbye to Donna first, wishing her the best.

"Keep me informed, Donna. Don't let them do anything without asking me, especially if it concerns the money. I'm sure they're going to take it, but it's worth fighting over."

"I wish you didn't have to go, Frankie. Despite the circumstances, it was nice having you around again."

He hugged her. "I'll be back soon. I promised Mom I'd visit more often."

She squeezed tight and kissed him. "Please do. Mom needs that."

After that, he said goodbye to his other sisters, then went to face his mother. She was still a mess from the funeral and Frankie feared she'd break down. He sat next to her on the sofa and took her hand in his. He patted it for a moment, then stroked her hair. "You still have shiny hair, Mom. Dad always loved that."

She nodded, but said nothing, then, after a few seconds she leaned against Frankie's shoulder. Soon, she had the handkerchief to her face, crying. "He was a good man. Better than you know."

"I know, Mom. I know."

"I didn't deserve him. But he was good to me." She sobbed, her chest heaving and her head bouncing off Frankie's chest.

"It's okay, Mom. Everything will be okay."

He let her cry for a few minutes, holding her and whispering to her. Finally she stopped and turned to him. "I know you have to go, but come back soon. Will you?"

Frankie kissed her on the cheek. "I will. I'll come back real soon. Promise."

She kissed him, then sat back on the sofa. "Drive safe, Frankie."

"I will. I'll call when I get there."

She nodded but didn't look up. Frankie took that as his cue. He waved goodbye to the others and walked to his car. As he pulled away from the curb he called Borelli.

"Just informing you that I'm leaving, Borelli. Got called back to New York on a case."

"Bullshit. I told you—"

"Take it up with your captain. I'm sure my boss called and cleared it. Either way, I'm out of here." Bugs hung up the phone before he said anything to get himself in trouble. He had planned on leaving straight for New York, but he decided to see Nicky first. He called him as he drove up Clayton Street.

"Fusco."

"Nicky, where are you?"

"Down by the riverfront. Right off Market."

"I'll be there in ten." Frankie turned right on Front Street and drove toward Market, pulling into the lot when he saw Nicky's car.

***

I SAW BUGS' CAR pull into the lot, and walked over to meet him. "I thought you were leaving today."

"I'm on my way. Wanted to see you first."

"What, kiss me goodbye?"

"Asshole." Bugs took out a smoke, cupped his hand to block the wind and lit it. He didn't say anything for a minute, just looked around, sucked on his smoke, and walked a few steps. "You know, Nicky, this is your chance. You've been clean for a while and you've got the perfect opportunity to start fresh."

I looked at him with a cocked head. "Are you preaching to me? Besides, is anyone ever clean? Isn't there always something that needs to be taken care of? Let me tell you—"

"Don't tell me anything. I'm still a cop."

"Don't try that shit on me."

Bugs nodded. "Maybe you're right, but I've got a badge, and more times than not I honor the oath to uphold the law."

"So what are you here for? You didn't come to tell me I can start a new life."

Frankie kicked some gravel, scuffing the tip of his Moreschi shoes. "Fuck! Look at that." He licked his fingers, reached down and rubbed the mark. "Can't believe I did that."

"Still waiting, Bugs."

"Borelli's got me pegged for this murder, and I don't know why. I can't believe he really thinks it's me, but there's no doubt that he wants to pin it on me."

"It won't stick."

Bugs crushed the cigarette out. "That's the thing. It might. He'll have DNA from the fight at the bar, he's got me coming back late to the house with no alibi, and he's got me saying in front of a dozen witnesses that I'd kill Bobby."

"I still don't know where you're going with this."

Bugs looked like he was in pain. "Where were you that night?"

I didn't answer.

"I went by your house after I left the bar. No one was home."

"I was—"

Bugs held up his hand. "Don't tell me you were at Doggs' playing cards, because I went there. I needed someone to talk to. You weren't there."

I decided to stay silent again.

Bugs lit another smoke. "Look, I don't even want to know if you did it, just remember I stuck my neck out for you. I can't go down this road again."

I stared at him in disbelief. I felt like hitting him, but I didn't; instead, I lowered my head and turned away. "I'm sorry for what I put you through, Mario Francis Donovan. Truly, I am."

He ran up behind me and grabbed my shoulder. "Nicky, I'm sorry for that, but…I need help."

I turned. "What?"

It was Bugs' turn to lower his head. "I need help. I know it's a lot to ask, but maybe you could check around with some of the old guys and see if anybody's heard anything. They're not going to talk to me but they might talk to you."

"What do you think they know?"

Bugs looked anxious, like he was losing it. "Shit, I don't know. Maybe nothing, maybe a lot. I know I didn't kill Bobby, and Borelli is trying to pin it on me. And I know that there isn't a snowball's chance in hell that Bobby Campisi saved fifty grand. That means the money's the key."

"You still haven't said what you expect me to do."

He fidgeted, as if he didn't want to say it. "I want you to act like a cop. I need you to investigate this case for me and find out who the fuck killed Bobby."

I heard him, but didn't believe what I was hearing. Then I laughed. Loud. "You want *me* to be a cop?"

Bugs didn't say anything, but when I laughed, he did too. "I guess that sounds stupid, huh?"

I looked at him, the best friend I had in this world, and made up my mind. It didn't take long. "I'll do it only if I can deputize Sister Thomas."

"Done," he said.

I stared, and then I held my hand out to him with a closed fist like we did so many years ago. "Friendship and honor, Bugs."

He joined me, and I swear I thought I saw tears in his eyes. "Friendship and honor, Nicky."

I punched him in the arm. "Go on, get out of here."

As he walked to the car, he called back to me. "Follow the money, Nicky. Follow that money."

CHAPTER 21

FINDING KITTY

Brooklyn, New York

Lou got to the station early—by his standards—but Sherri was already there and, more importantly, she had coffee made. She handed Lou a cup as he walked into the coffee room. "Here you go, lucky."

"Lucky? I haven't been lucky since I married my wife, thirty years ago."

Sherri stopped and stared at him. "That's so sweet."

"That's what the girls call me—Luigi 'Sweet Lou' Mazzetti."

"If you keep up your smart talk, I won't make you coffee any more."

"You've already spoiled me. I told my wife she's got competition now."

"And what did she say, to let me have you?"

Lou sipped the coffee, set the cup on the table as if thinking. "Not exactly in those words, but close."

"Close?"

"She wasn't quite so nice with her language, is what I mean."

"That's what I figured. You ready to head down to the building?"

"As soon as I'm done with the coffee," Lou said, and he took out a pad to write notes on. "What do we know so far?"

"We've got that picture. Nothing else except he called her 'Kitty,' according to the ex. So that could be what—Kathy, Kate, Catherine, Kathleen? It has to be something like that."

"Or it could be just a nickname." Lou gulped the last sip of coffee and tossed it toward the trash, missing it by at least a few inches.

"Mazzetti, when are you gonna learn that you can't play basketball?"

Lou picked up his cup and dunked it. "Hey, there were a lot of great Italian basketball players."

"Name one."

Lou looked up to the left, thinking. "There were plenty."

"Name just one."

"Jerry...or Ernie...I forget his last name, but he was good."

"I know. I forget them too, mostly because there weren't any."

Lou headed out the door, Sherri close behind him. "Yeah, well, name me a good black hockey player."

"Okay, we're even. Now can we get to work?"

Lou laughed as he walked down the steps. "Have I told you lately that I like you, Miller?"

"Keep reminding me."

"As long as you keep driving."

"I'll keep driving just to stay alive, but okay, you've got a deal." Sherri walked out the front door and headed toward the parking lot. "Stay here. I'll pick you up."

As she walked away Mazzetti hollered, "You're beautiful, Miller."

She pulled to the curb a few minutes later, and he got in, tossing his half-smoked cigarette to the gutter. "I hope we find something today. I'm tired of hearing Morreau's shit."

THEY GOT TO THE building in about forty minutes and went inside. Two people were manning a reception desk by the front door. Sherri approached first, showing them the picture of the girl along with her badge. "Detectives Miller and Mazzetti. Have either of you seen this woman before?"

The first guy, a young, twenty-something guy with pierced ears and a cheap suit shook his head. "Not me, but I've only been here a month." He handed the picture to his partner who took a good look at it. He stared at it, shook his head, then stared some more.

"I maybe saw her. Check Pierson and Riddle, second floor."

Sherri's eyes lit up. "Thanks. You don't happen to know her name do you?"

"Can't even swear it's the same girl."

"Is it Mr. Riddle?" she asked.

"And Mr. Pierson," the guard said.

Sherri handed him her card. "If you think of anything else…"

"Yeah, I know, call you. Just like in the movies."

"That's it, just like the movies," she said, and headed toward the elevators with Lou.

"Maybe we got lucky," she said and increased her pace.

Lou fell a few steps behind her. "Fat chance."

Pierson and Riddle's offices were at the end of the corridor, left of the elevator exit on the second floor. Wide, double doors were the gateway to the executives with "Pierson and Riddle" etched into fine glass—one name for each door.

Sherri pushed a door open and stepped inside onto plush carpeting. The receptionist desk sat high, making Sherri feel like a third grader going to the teacher's desk. She showed her badge. "Detectives Miller and Mazzetti here to see Mr. Riddle or Pierson."

"Have a seat, please."

The lobby chairs were big and stuffy. Sherri took a deep sigh as she sat next to Lou. Even the air seemed stuffy.

Lou leaned toward her and whispered. "Like the ex said, 'way out of his league.'"

"Maybe so. We'll see."

After a fifteen minute wait, a man in a charcoal suit that looked as if it had been pressed ten times burst through a side door, his hand extended as soon as he entered the foyer. His pant cuffs dusted the tops of oxford shoes—purchased this morning from the looks of them—and barely concealed black silk socks.

"John Mason," he said. "I'm Mr. Riddle's assistant."

Lou and Sherri stood, expecting to be led to an office or a conference room, but Mason didn't budge.

"How may I help you?"

Sherri handed him a card. "Detectives Miller and Mazzetti. We're here on an investigation, and we need to ask Mr. Riddle or Mr. Pierson a few questions."

Mason smiled, the kind of smile that intimated what a ridiculous request she'd made. "I'm afraid that would be impossible; however, I would be more than happy to answer your questions. What would you like to know?"

Sherri's eyes narrowed and her lips pursed.

Lou stepped forward before she let loose on the guy. "Show him the picture, Detective Miller."

She shot Lou a glance like his wife did when he'd had three or four too many beers, but Sherri pulled out the photo and showed it to Mason. "Do you know her? I understand she works here."

Mason's eyebrows pitched skyward. "I've never seen her before, but that doesn't mean she doesn't work here. Have you shown this to Anna?" he asked, indicating the receptionist.

"Not yet."

He walked to the desk and laid the picture atop it. "Do you know her, Anna?"

She immediately shook her head. "She doesn't work here, Mr. Mason. I'm certain."

"Do you have anyone named Katherine or Kathleen here? Anyone who goes by Kitty?"

"I'll check," Anna said, and punched a few keys to bring up a database. "I've sorted by first name, checking Katherine and Kathleen with both a 'c' and a 'k' and nothing comes up. Sorry."

Mason turned back to Sherri and Lou with a manufactured smile. "There you go. If she worked here, Anna would surely know. I'm sorry we couldn't help you." He started to turn, then did an about-face. "Anything else, detectives?"

Sherri looked like she wanted to smack him, but instead she smiled. "Nothing, Mr. Mason, thank you."

Lou opened the door and led the way down the corridor toward the elevator. "You know, if it's really been a while since she and Davidoff saw each other, she could be long gone."

"Yeah, but right now it's the only lead we've got."

Lou punched the elevator button and popped a dry cigarette in his mouth as they waited for it to open.

"Let's look at it this way, Mazzetti. The only thing this guy ever did wrong was have an affair. We might as well start with that."

"I'll have Morreau get a few uniforms down here. If 'Kitty' still works here, we'll find her."

***

LISA JACKSON DRESSED FOR work, wearing what Tom had picked out for her—a tight-fitting skirt that he said massaged her ass every time she moved, and a blouse that showed the outline of a sexy bra. She tried to convince him that it was inappropriate for her office, but he would hear nothing of it, said if she was going to act like a whore she might as well dress like one. Maybe Tom was right. Maybe she was just a whore.

She hated dressing this way, but she did like the way the men turned their heads and eyed her, and the way it brought smiles to their faces and made them go out of their way to do things for her. Already this morning, two guys nearly got into a fight offering their seat to her, and another one, sitting across from her, strained his neck trying to get a peek up her skirt.

Lisa was yanked back to reality by a sharp pain in between her legs, from where Tom abused her. She *had* to get away from him.

But how? He has Mom.

As much as Lisa fought with her mother, she couldn't let her die. Lisa had brought her mother to New York from Texas, convinced her to move when she didn't want to. And no matter what, Lisa had no doubt about whether Tom would kill her mother. He never liked her to begin with.

Lisa worked on plans during the ride to work, but when her stop came up, she still had nothing. She got off the subway and headed into work, getting on a crowded elevator. An older guy in a light brown suit turned away when she caught him looking at her.

Lisa worked on getting into a different frame of mind. She had to be convincing or her mother would die. She smiled at the gentleman next to her. "Nice day, isn't it?"

He turned back, the look on his face complete surprise. "Yes it is," he managed to get out in a feeble attempt at making conversation.

A woman about her age moved aside, as if Lisa had a disease. When the door opened on the third floor, Lisa inched closer to the man. "I haven't seen you before. New to the building?"

"In fact, I am, yes. I just moved to Starks and Company. I came down from the Boston office."

"Well, good luck, New York takes a lot of getting used to." She let her arm brush his, sure that it sent a jolt through his body. Just as he was about to say something the door opened for the fourth floor. "This is me," she said, and waited for the people in front of her to exit.

"What a coincidence. This is my floor, too."

As she stepped out she almost gasped. A cop stood in the corridor and appeared to be looking over everyone who came out. Lisa took him in with a glance. It didn't take her long to figure out what to do. The cop looked to be in his thirties and he wore a wedding ring. She could make his dick hard in three seconds, and once his dick was hard his brain would cease to work. She continued her conversation with the older guy, walking out alongside him, and she made sure to swing her hips a little more than usual. If that cop was like most men, he'd be looking at her ass. Lisa felt certain that wouldn't be on a police snapshot.

Thankfully Starks and Company was the first door in the corridor. Lisa lost her companion and ducked into the restroom in a panic.

What is a cop doing here? Are they looking for me? How did they find me? She had to call Tom. No, she couldn't do that. What if they were tracing her calls? If Tom so much as saw a cop, he'd kill both her and her mother. Lisa knew one thing for sure: she had to get out of this building.

CHAPTER 22

BARSTOOLS AND SECRETS

Wilmington, Delaware

I thought about Bugs and the burden he put on me. More than once it pissed me off, him leaving town and expecting me to pick up the pieces and put them back together. It wasn't *my* brother-in-law that got killed, and it wasn't my ass on the hook for it.

I measured the last wall for the new condos, checked it against the blueprint, then confirmed the height of the building for a final estimate. As much as I cursed what Bugs asked me to do, I had to admit that somewhere inside me, maybe deep inside, some primal emotion wanted to do it. I'd always been a puzzle solver as a kid, and I loved figuring things out. What was murder but a big puzzle, the most challenging one of all. After checking the job one last time, I headed back to the office to work on the bid. Every now and then, I'd get an idea and write it on a separate notepad I designated for my detective work. I laughed. How about that shit—detective work, me, Nicky Fusco. If only the guys at the smoke shop could see me.

The afternoon passed slowly. Eagerness to do something else seemed to make time stand still, or at least that's what Sister Thomas always said, and I had come to learn that most of what she said was either true, or had so much truth in it that it wasn't worth arguing over the differences. There were a lot of truths like that in this world. People just had to take the time to realize it. I remembered a line by one of the old plumbers I used to play cards with. I was looking for a job when I came back to Wilmington, and I asked what it would take to be a plumber.

He looked at me, and, as serious as a heart attack said, "All you need to know is water and shit both flow downhill. Understand that, and you can be a plumber."

I knew plumbing was a little more complicated than that, but in essence he had it right. Like most things, once they're broken down they tend to be simple. That's the way I looked at this case. I laughed. *Case.* As if I were a real detective. Anyway, I figured to attack it like Sister Thomas always said, from the beginning. Bobby Campisi was last seen getting his ass kicked in Teddy's bar—so Teddy's bar was where I'd start.

Angie made *polpettone* for dinner, a Neapolitan meatloaf that tasted no more like an American meatloaf than a filet did a flank steak. She made her *polpettone* with veal and ground beef, and stuffed it with prosciutto and mozzarella, then sprinkled a healthy dose of Parmigiano on it as she cooked. Angie had learned all of Mamma Rosa's secrets and made *everything* taste good. She served the polpettone with a side dish of sliced tomatoes, onions, and cucumbers, mixed with olive oil and garlic, and sprinkled with pepper. Pencil-thin asparagus topped with orange *Agrumato* topped off the meal. It tasted so good I didn't want to quit eating.

Rosa excused herself as soon as dinner was over and went to her room, swearing it was for homework, though both Angie and I knew it was to talk on the phone.

Angie looked at me as Rosa went up the stairs. "Did we talk as much as these kids?"

"We didn't have cell phones, remember?"

"Things were sure different then."

I grabbed my plate, and Rosa's, and took them to the sink, rinsing them with hot water. Then I grabbed the scrub brush and started washing. "You dry tonight, Angie."

"I can wash," she said. "I don't mind."

"Yeah, but I do. You're too slow."

She smacked me with that damn wooden spoon which seemed to appear out of nowhere. "That's because I actually *clean* the dishes. I don't just rinse them."

I handed her the brush and the dishcloth while I grabbed her towel. "Okay, I surrender."

About halfway through the dishes, I stopped. "I've got to go out tonight. I hope you don't mind."

She looked at me, not with suspicious eyes, but questioning ones. "Where?"

"I'm doing a favor for Bugs. Trying to help him figure out who killed Bobby. He had to go back to New York, and Borelli seems set on blaming Bugs for this."

"What can *you* do?" Irritation had entered her voice.

"Not much. Maybe ask a few questions, see what I can find out."

She turned off the water and placed her hand on her hip. I knew I was in trouble as soon as that happened, so I prepared for it. "Angie, I *owe* Bugs. He'd do it for me; besides, I won't be long. I'm going to Teddy's to ask some of the regulars what they saw that night."

Her eyes got hard. "And that's all? Nowhere else?"

"Nowhere else."

She turned the water back on hot and swatted at me. "All right, get out of here, and don't wake me when you get back. I've got to get up early."

I leaned over and kissed her on the cheek. "You're the best, baby."

"Remember that, Mr. Fusco."

Teddy's was more crowded than I thought it would be for a weeknight. The lot was full and half of the street on the side. I parked down the block and walked up a narrow sidewalk stained by decades of drunks puking, tossing gum, and crushing their cigarettes on it. A good pressure washing would bring it into the land of the living, but I knew Teddy wasn't paying for that, or *any* cleaning, for that matter. The light bulb in his outside lamp was burnt out, had been a week ago, I remembered now, but the neon sign in the window flashing "Teddy's Place" provided enough light to see. Ever since Bugs unofficially deputized me I realized I'd been training for a job like this. When I was a shooter my life depended on paying close attention to *everything*. Detective work wasn't much different. With that in mind, I cleared my mind of memories of the bar. I wanted to see it for the first time as I walked in.

Ten more steps had me in front of a rickety old door, maybe oak, and it looked as if it was from the original construction many years ago. A good hard kick from any Polack worth his salt would have busted it, and that made me wonder if it was original; surely that had happened once or twice if not more. I opened the door and walked in, the smoke overpowering me as soon as I entered. The fire marshal might have something to say about that, with the no-smoking ordinance and all, but I thought I saw him slumped over a chair in the corner, so there was no sense calling in a report. Most of the bars enforced the smoking ban, but Teddy's seemed to be immune to it.

Five feet in, a pool table blocked the way, and on either side of it, old wooden stiff-backed chairs for people to sit on while they waited for a game. I didn't ever remember coming into Teddy's when the pool table wasn't occupied with at least two or three people waiting. Some things never changed.

"Hey, Nicky," somebody called.

I nodded, not recognizing the face, then I waved to another guy who said hi as I made my way toward the long bar that sat on the far wall to the right. Left of that were all of the tables. "All of the tables" sounds like a lot, but there were probably only ten of them. The tables seated four each—if Teddy had chairs to accommodate four each—but he didn't, so chairs were always shuffled around between whoever claimed a table first.

I walked up to the bar, squeezing between two guys I didn't know and plopped onto a worn barstool. It had some fluff and maybe other things protruding from one side of the seat. I scooted to the opposite side and looked down the bar to Jerry Simpson, the bartender. He seemed busy. Jerry was a handsome guy, except for the whiskey nose, and it was a bad one. The cops used to say they could tell how much Jerry had to drink just by looking at his nose. He never argued with them so I guess they were right, or close to it.

Jerry meandered down, nodding when he recognized me.

"Haven't seen you in a while, Nicky."

"Angie keeps me home. Tough to get out."

He laughed. "Don't I know that. If I didn't work here, I'd never get a drink."

Everyone within hearing distance laughed. We all knew that Jerry would find a drink in church, or on the moon.

"When's Fred coming in?" I asked.

"He won't be in till tomorrow night."

I nodded. "How about a beer? Whatever you got on tap is good."

"Coming up. Stay put."

I spied Millie, an old-timer who was such a regular the mailman delivered her mail here. She'd been a blonde once, but gray had won the fight for dominance long ago, just like wrinkles had won over make-up, and sadness over the sparkle that once lit her big blue eyes. Her face used to catch a man's eye, now those features had dwindled to old skin stretched over strong protruding bones. "Bring it down the end for me, Jerry. And get me a drink for Millie."

I took the empty chair next to Millie—there was always an empty chair next to her—and pushed the drink her way. "I'm Nicky Fusco, Millie. You might not—"

"I know who you are. I knew your father when he was a young man. Of course, I was young back then. Young and…" She looked at herself, and I could almost hear her finish the sentence. "Pretty." That's what she wanted to say, but I think she was too embarrassed.

"My father mentioned you. He said you were a looker."

She lit up. Even her shoulders seemed to straighten. "He did?"

For a moment, I saw doubt in her eyes, and a look like she was going to sink back into despair. I wouldn't let that happen. "He did. I always remember that. He said, 'That Millie sure is a looker.' Those were his words, 'a looker,' he said."

She pulled a cigarette from her case and held it in her long slender fingers, as if waiting for a gentleman to light it. For a moment she was Rita Hayworth or Lauren Bacall. I didn't disappoint her. I grabbed a pack of matches from the bar and offered her the light, bringing a smile to an old woman's face, and some lightness to her heart.

She took a long, slow drag and exhaled it in a thin stream, as classy an exhale as any movie dame ever did. Remnants of smoke leaked from the corners of her mouth as she said, "Nicky, what can I do for you?"

"I'm trying to find out what happened the night Bobby Campisi was here."

"You mean the night he was killed?"

I nodded. "You were here, right?"

She leaned forward and tapped her cigarette on the ashtray, dropping a long ash with class, then she took another long drag. "Right at this same chair. And with a good view of what went on."

I wanted to light a cigarette of my own; instead, I pulled one out of Millie's pack and put in in my mouth but I didn't light it. "Go on."

Millie had shifty eyes, the kind that could take in an entire ballroom in a few glances, and unless someone was watching they wouldn't even know. She did that now, checking to see who was watching her as she talked to me. It was a cautious glance, almost as if she was afraid.

She took another drag, blew it out quickly, took a sip of her drink, then whispered, "Bobby called Frankie's mother a whore." Millie cast those surreptitious glances around again, then focused on me. "Actually, he called Frankie's sister a whore, then said, 'Just like her mother.'"

"What happened after that?"

"Frankie almost killed him. He smashed Bobby's head with a mug of beer, then beat him to the floor and kicked him. After that, he left."

"And Bobby?"

"He stumbled around, got another beer from a friend, and then he left." Millie nodded to the door. "Walked out that front door on his own two feet. If you ask me it wasn't Frankie who killed him."

This was exciting. I was getting somewhere. "Why do you say that?" I had my own opinion but I wanted hers.

"You know Frankie. He's got a temper. If he wanted to kill Bobby, he'd have done it right then, when he beat him. Frankie isn't the type to wait outside for him. It's not his style."

I smiled. Millie was my kind of girl. "Who else was here that night? Anybody that's here now?"

She nodded to the other end of the bar. I followed her gaze and saw Jack McDermott.

Goddamn. How's that for coincidence? Jack is in the same seat as he was the night Bobby died.

I stood, leaned in and kissed her cheek, a good kiss. "Here's looking at you, kid."

Millie held me with her eyes and smiled. For a moment I thought I saw a tear, but if it was there she kept it in check. "Thanks, Nicky. You're as much a gentleman as your father was."

As I walked toward Jack, I signaled Jerry to get Millie another drink on me. I passed by half a dozen guys, wondering if any of them were there that night, but I couldn't be concerned about them right now. I knew Jack was here, and he was only a few feet from me, hunched over the bar like a good Irishman, with a shot and a beer sitting before him. Surely not his first.

He lifted his head as I approached. "Hey, Nicky, how about them fuckin' Phillies?"

I laughed. If I told him, or anybody else for that matter, that I didn't watch the Phillies, or the Eagles, or the Flyers, or whatever team played basketball for Philadelphia, they'd not only not believe me, they'd hang me from the nearest tree when they discovered the truth. "How about 'em, Jack? Good to see you." I learned long ago that you didn't really have to know anything about sports to converse with sports people, especially in bars. You just had to repeat what they said with more enthusiasm. It worked almost every time, and if it didn't you just ordered another round of drinks. That *always* worked.

I asked the guy next to Jack if he minded moving over a seat. Surprisingly, he didn't even want to fight me over it; he simply moved. I sat next to Jack and ordered another beer from Jerry, offering one to Jack as well. I never liked Jack much, but that might have been because he was always busting our asses as kids. He was the Mick's older brother, and never cut us a break. Of course he did suspect we stole his cigarette heist from the train one night. If he had ever proved it we probably wouldn't have reached puberty. When the beers came, I lifted mine, tapped his mug, and said, "Jack, here's to you."

He tipped his glass. "I see you're asking around about Campisi."

I liked that he got right to it. "Got a few questions about that night if you know anything."

"Anything I tell you is gonna be tainted. I hated that fucker."

"Right there with you on that. He cost me ten years." I regretted open-ing my mouth as soon as the words came out. Jack didn't waste any time making me feel like an idiot.

"Ten years? It cost my brother his fuckin' *life!*"

I looked the other way, but nodded. "I know. It was stupid of me to say that. I don't know what it's like to lose a brother, but Mick was one of my best friends."

We sat quiet for a while, then Jack said he had to piss and asked me to order another beer. On his way back from the bathroom I noticed he limped. "Where'd you pick that up?"

"Prison," he said, "along with a few other treasures."

I nodded. We all brought mementos out with us, usually not ones we cared to remember. I kept silent, letting him drink. He started up after his second beer.

"I was here that night. Not long after you left, I saw Bugs give Bobby an ass-whipping, bad. Might be what killed the fucker."

"That bad?"

"It was worse than bad." Jack slugged down the rest of his beer, then wiped his mouth. "I don't know what they say killed him, but that mug to the head could've done it."

I nodded. I could see Bugs getting that pissed, and he *did* have a temper. "What happened after that?"

"Not much. Bugs kicked his ass, told him he'd kill him if he ever said anything about his mother again, then he left. Campisi took a while getting up, scarfed a beer from some guy, then *he* left. That's all I know."

"Who else was here? You remember?"

He nodded toward the end of the bar. "Millie, Fred, you, and Marty were here earlier that night." He pointed to a corner table. "Two couples over there. I didn't know them, though. And Johnny Deuce was playing pool. I do remember that."

The last one took me by surprise. "The Deuce was here? I thought he didn't drink."

"I don't know about that," Jack said, "But he was shooting pool with a guy I don't know."

I nodded again, making a mental note. The Deuce was a local legend, a great pool hustler and a character to boot. Everything he did was in twos: he wore shirts with two pockets; carried two packs of cigarettes and two lighters; and he had two guns tucked into the back of his waistband. "And you haven't heard anything, I mean since then, on the streets?"

Jack shook his head. "Nothing."

I looked around, made sure no one was listening. "So when did you get out, Jack?"

"Two years."

"Different, huh? Lot of adapting you have to do."

"Different going in," he said. "And maybe worse coming out."

"You working?"

He shook his head. "Labor here and there. Puts a little change in my pocket, lets me stop here two or three nights a week."

I handed him a card. "Not promising anything, but if you want work, call me. I'll see what I can do."

He looked at the card. "Estimator, huh? I can't—"

"It won't be an estimating job, but something with the crews. They've got a lot of work. You ought to call."

Jack smiled and tapped me on the shoulder. "Thanks, Nicky. I always said you were okay."

I finished my beer, plopped a few bills on the counter and told Jack to have another on me. "And don't forget—call if you hear anything about Bobby."

"I will, man. Thanks."

I started to leave but turned around. "You know anything about Bobby having a bunch of money?"

"I don't know *anything* about him."

"But you never heard anything? Like where he might get fifty large?"

Jack laughed. "Fifty large? Bobby Campisi? Come on, Nicky, that's bullshit."

I laughed too. "Yeah, that's what I figured." I leaned in closer. "But tell me, Jack, who would know about where a loser like Bobby would get his hands on fifty large?"

Jack backed up a notch, his posture straightening, his mind clearing. "How the hell would I know?"

I stared at him for a long time. "Just checking, that's all." I patted him on the back. "See you around, Jack. Take care."

"Yeah, see you."

As I walked out of the bar, I tried to process what I'd learned. Millie and Jack both said Bugs kicked Bobby's ass, and their stories were almost identical. That matched what Borelli was tossing around, but—and this was a big one—Jack McDermott got scared shitless when I questioned him about the money.

He knows something, and I intend to find out what.

CHAPTER 23

THREE'S COMPANY

Brooklyn, New York

Lou did a fast walk/shuffle over to where Sherri stood, near the cafeteria. It was as close as he got to a run, at least for the past fifteen years. "We might have something up on four."

Sherri came alert. "What?"

"Uni at the elevator said he may have spotted her."

"Let's go," Sherri said.

When the elevator stopped they were greeted by the officer who called it in.

He nodded. "Detectives."

"Let's have it," Lou said.

"I can't be certain, but I think she passed by here a few minutes ago. It sure looked like her."

"And you didn't detain her?" Sherri asked.

"I wasn't sure if it was her. If I stop the wrong person, and it turns out to be some stock broker, it's my ass, and you know it."

Sherri pulled out the photo of the girl. "Take a good look. Was it her or not?"

He shrugged, hesitated. "I'm still not sure, but she went that way," he said, pointing down the corridor to the left.

"Thanks," Lou said and started off in that direction.

Sherri caught up in a few strides. "How can he not be sure?"

"Because he was looking at her ass, not her face."

Sherri wrinkled her brow. "Are you shitting me? With a job to do, he's getting distracted by that?"

Lou half-laughed, half-coughed. "You are a rookie, Miller. Let me fill you in on a secret. If you've got a pretty girl with a nice ass, a cop will get his head blown off while he's watching her."

"Men!"

"Now you're learning."

Lou stopped at the first office, pushing the doors open. He and Sherri showed their badges then the picture of Kitty, but the receptionist didn't recognize her. They had her look for her name, but no luck there, either. They stopped at each office on the fourth floor, showing her picture and having them look for anyone named Kathleen or Katherine who worked there. Near the end of the corridor, with three offices to go, they hit gold.

The receptionist took one look at the picture and nodded. "She works here, but her name's not Kathy; that's Lisa Jackson."

"I'll be damned," Lou said. "I thought we'd strike out."

"Please tell her we'd like to see her," Sherri said.

The receptionist called Lisa, but got no answer. She tried again and when no one answered that time she buzzed the admin responsible for that area. "Vera, is Lisa Jackson around?"

She listened a moment then looked up at Sherri and Lou. "She never came in today."

Sherri looked at Lou, then the receptionist. "Are you sure? She was seen in the building."

"That's what Vera said. She never came in, and she didn't call."

"I assume that's unusual," Lou said.

"Very."

"Do you have her home address?" Sherri asked.

The receptionist looked nervous. "I don't know…that's private infor-mation. We're not allowed to give that out."

Lou flashed his badge. "This is a murder investigation. Ms. Jackson could be in danger."

"Oh God. Wait a minute," she said, and got up, walked back to a closed office and knocked on the door. She returned a few seconds later. "You'll have to speak to human resources about this. I'm not allowed to release that information."

Lou slammed his hand on the desk, causing the woman to jump. "Goddamn asshole rules." He got close to the receptionist. "Get me a name in human resources."

She fumbled with a few keys, then printed out a paper which she handed to Lou. "We're just a branch office. Human resources is in—"

"Figures," Lou said. He turned to Miller. "Let's go, kid. I've had enough of this shit."

***

LISA JACKSON STAYED IN the restroom for fifteen minutes composing herself, then went to the stairs and walked down to the first floor, peeking through a crack in the door before exiting. She forced herself to move casually through the lobby, looking straight ahead and making certain she didn't appear to be in a hurry. At one point she realized she'd been holding her breath, so she made a concentrated effort to release it, then slowly resume a natural breathing pattern. Soon she was outside, mingling with crowds and heading toward the subway. There was safety in numbers.

All the way home she worried about what had gone wrong. The cops were almost certainly there for *her*, but how had they found her?

She worried during the ride on the subway and for the ten minutes it took her to walk home. By the time she got to the apartment she was in complete panic. She burst through the door, tears flowing before she reached the kitchen. God only knew what this maniac would do to her, and her mother.

"Tom, where are you?"

A sound from the bedroom drew her in that direction. She flung open the door. "Tom, something terrible happ—" She stopped cold with a gasp.

A young girl lay on the bed. She looked to be no more than a teenager, with the nothing-but-ribs figure a lot of young girls had nowadays.

"What are you doing?" she screamed at Tom.

The girl looked as if she might scream too, but Tom glared at the girl, and she went mute. Then he got off her and approached Lisa, walking to her slowly from the bed to where she was. He was naked, as was the girl, and she didn't move to cover up.

Tom smacked Lisa, hard, across the cheek. "Don't you knock? Doesn't a man have privacy in his own home?"

Lisa recovered from the hit and straightened herself. "What are you doing to her? Who is she?" Lisa walked closer to the bed, staring. "For God's sake, she's just a kid."

He smacked at Lisa again, but she raised her hands to protect her face. "She's twenty," Tom said, "but what difference does it make? How many men did you fuck in this bed while I was gone? Huh?" Tom raised his hand, and Lisa cringed.

"Go make us coffee—and be quick about it."

Lisa stood in the doorway, watching as Tom started back to the bed. The girl was up and getting dressed. Tom grabbed her by the hair and yanked her toward him. "Did I tell you to leave? Did I?"

The girl shook her head, eyes wide.

"Then do what you're best at," Tom said.

Lisa left the room, slamming the door.

I have got to get out of here.

CHAPTER 24

BUGS RETURNS

Brooklyn, New York

Frankie jumped on the interstate and headed east across the Delaware Memorial Bridge, then north on #295 to the Jersey Turnpike. It wouldn't take long to get back to Brooklyn, less than three hours even if he hit traffic. That should give him plenty of time to figure things out, maybe decide how to get rid of the baggage in his life and get back to the happy person he used to be.

One thing that made Frankie happy was Nicky agreeing to take on his case. Not that Nicky would solve it, but the fact that he agreed to try told Frankie that Nicky really was innocent—at least of killing Bobby. No way Nicky would leave Frankie out to hang if he'd done it. That, at least, was something.

Happiness was a funny thing. People were either born to it, or not. Nicky was happy, yet if anyone had a legitimate reason not to be it would be him. A black cloud had followed Nicky all his life, but he kept a good attitude, always found a silver lining.

He learned that from Mamma Rosa, Frankie thought, and wondered why her own son never did. Tony had everything a kid could want in life, yet he was miserable. It killed him in the end, his misery did. Frankie laughed when he thought about Paulie Perlano; he'd been happy too. Damn near exuberant. Far happier than Frankie would have been growing up in a row house with eleven kids.

As Frankie drove up the interstate he had an urge to veer off and meander through the Pine Barrens, forget about murders and funerals, and family problems…but, he had things to do, and Lieutenant Morreau would be throwing a fit by now.

Mazzetti, too. He's probably cursing me right now.

Frankie got onto the Jersey Turnpike and continued north, fighting the ever-present traffic and trying not to be pissed.

Images from fun times as kids flashed through his mind, like when he and Nicky were running from the cops and ducked into the church to hide. Once inside, they walked as fast as they could to the stairs, ran down the steps and out the back door, then hid in the bushes by the convent. Escaping the cop made their whole day worthwhile, even worth the beating from Sister Theresa when she caught them in her garden.

Frankie tapped the brakes, slowing to what seemed like a crawl but it was only down to about fifty, and that was good for the turnpike. He took his time, thinking about everything but his family. The past week had worn on him, and not just because his dad died. Learning more about his mother and her past sins seemed more of an issue than his dad's death. It was horrible to think that, but it was true. No matter what he tried, he couldn't shake this feeling of…shame…now that he *knew* about his mother.

A car in front of him stopped suddenly. Frankie swerved to avoid hitting it. "Goddamn idiot." Frankie pulled onto the shoulder, then turned back into traffic as it picked up. He slammed his hand into the steering wheel. "Focus, Frankie. Goddamnit, focus."

If there was anything he should be worrying about, it was the mess he left behind in Wilmington. Borelli sure as shit wanted him for Bobby's murder, and the evidence supported that, at least the evidence Frankie knew of. Anything else they'd found, he wasn't privy to.

I sure as hell hope Nicky finds something.

FRANKIE DIALED KATE'S NUMBER, letting it ring through to voice mail.

"This is Kate Burns. If you got this message it means I'm out looking at cadavers. Leave a number, and I'll call you back."

Frankie laughed. Kate was one-of-a-kind. "Kate, it's Frankie, and I got a body you can look at. I'm on my way back. How about dinner? Call me."

He hung up and called Lou, but got his voicemail.

"You've reached Detective Lou Mazzetti. Leave a message. I'll get back to you right away. Maybe."

"Lou, it's me. Call."

Frankie drove for ten or fifteen more minutes, and decided to call Shawna. He owed her an apology for rushing out without telling her anything. He dialed her cell.

"Shawna Pavic."

"Shawna, it's Frankie. How's it going?"

"Where are you?"

"On my way back…and sorry for the quick exit and no communication, but my dad passed away and—"

"No need to explain." She let a pause build. "You up for dinner?"

He almost jumped on the invitation and said yes, thoughts of what might happen after dinner racing through his mind. Images of Shawna naked on his bed and her pert little ass… but then he thought of Kate.

What if she calls?

"I'd like to, but I'm just getting back, and Lou tells me this case is a mess. I've got a lot of catching up to do." He breathed deep, glad he managed to get that out. "Sorry. We'll make it another night."

"Don't worry about it." She seemed to switch gears then, from Shawna the horny ex-wife of a banker to Shawna the reporter. "So what is going on with this case? Any news for me?"

"Nothing I can share. You'll get yours along with everyone else. Don't worry."

"Come on, Donovan. I need help here. I'm fighting Channel five with their cutesy little Cindy Ellis."

"What's so special about her?"

"Didn't Mazzetti fill you in? She got a call from the killer, or at least what we assume is the killer, telling her there will be a lot more bodies."

"What? When?"

"Few days ago."

She waited through the silence, then, "Come on, Frankie."

"I feel sorry for you, kid, but I can't help. Gotta go now. I need to call Lou." Frankie punched in Lou's number. "C'mon, Mazzetti, where are you?"

"Mazzetti."

"Lou, it's Frankie."

"Donovan? I hope you're on the Brooklyn Bridge or Flatbush Avenue."

"Close enough. What's up?"

"Trying to figure out who killed the second guy, and we still don't even know who the first guy is."

"Have you done *anything* since I left?"

"I've got mixed company here, or else I'd tell you what I really think about you and your detective skills."

Frankie laughed. "All right. Tell Morreau I'm on my way in. Be there in half an hour barring a traffic jam."

"Welcome home, Donovan."

"You know what, Mazzetti? This is the first time it really feels like home to me, and I don't even know why."

"Yeah, Brooklyn does that to you. Eats you up, but makes you fall in love with it. Sort of like a sexy broad."

Frankie laughed. "If I *ever* start saying shit like that, pull out your .38 and shoot me. Promise?"

"You got it," Lou said.

Before he could hang up, Frankie said, "Have you seen Kate?"

"Getting horny?"

"Cut the shit. Have you seen her or not?"

"Talked to her earlier," Lou said, "And my *partner* spoke with her not long ago."

Frankie hit the brakes, beeping at the driver in front of him. "Yeah, well tell that temporary partner that the boss is back in town."

"She's not here. I sent her on an errand, personal kind, and besides, she's not temporary. This one's a keeper."

Frankie's interest was piqued. "A keeper, huh? Does your wife know?"

"I tell her every night."

"I'm sure you do," Frankie said. "See you soon. I'm hanging up."

It took about forty minutes to get to the station. Frankie went straight to Morreau's office, where he spent thirty minutes filling Morreau in on the situation in Wilmington.

"Don't worry," Morreau said. "I already had the captain call. Besides, I'm sure they'll clear this up soon." He offered Frankie some tea from a pitcher on his desk, but Frankie refused. "You meet Miller yet?"

"Miller? You mean Lou's partner? No."

Morreau took a big swig from his glass. "She's good. I think you'll like her."

"So I'm gonna get a chance to like her? Is she staying on the case?"

"We need all the help we can on this one, and she's been in on it from the beginning." Morreau set the glass back on a coaster next to his phone. "Don't bust her balls, Donovan. I'm warning you."

"Does she have balls?"

Morreau laughed. "Bigger than yours I'd bet."

"Guess I won't bust 'em then," Frankie said, and stood to leave. "I'm heading home. See you tomorrow."

Frankie made his rounds, saying hi to Carol and some of the others in the station, but then he headed out, driving slow to his apartment. It felt good to be home. He pulled onto the street to his apartment and began the search for a parking space. Even the end of the block wasn't too early to start looking. All the spaces were taken, and he gave up hope as he approached his stoop, but then he saw an empty spot maybe fifty or sixty feet ahead. Alex and Keisha were standing guard, manning two construction cones. They raced to pull them aside.

"Hey, FD. Good to see you home." Alex was a neighbor, the son of a drug addict/whore on the floor below Frankie. He was a good kid, though, and he loved Frankie. Always called him FD.

Frankie pulled into the spot and put the car in park, then got out with a smile on his face. "Hey, guys, I didn't bring anything for you today so I guess you'll have to settle for a few bucks." He reached for his money clip.

"Put that shit away, old man." Keisha was a soon-to-be gorgeous young black girl who had a sassy but sweet attitude. "Today's a gift, but starting tomorrow you gotta pay like everybody else."

"Deal," Frankie said, and hugged both of them. "What happened to your pigtails?"

"Thought I'd get sexy for you," she said.

Frankie got a serious look on his face. "Don't start that talk so young. You've got plenty of time. Say that around the wrong people and…"

Keisha frowned. "Yeah, I know. I'm screwed."

"Screwed for real." Frankie leaned down and kissed her forehead, then rubbed Alex's head. Both of them walked with him toward the apartment.

Alex looked up at him with big dark eyes. "How was it, FD?"

"How was what?"

"The funeral?"

Jesus Christ, how did they know?

"Not good, Alex, but thanks for asking." When they hit the stoop, Frankie sat on the top step, reliving his fun times with the two of them. "You guys been keeping a watch for me?"

"Ronnie's still dealing dope out of his Lincoln, and Wilma's still doing tricks every time her mom leaves for work. What else you want to know?"

Frankie shook his head. Why did he think things would change while he was away, and how the hell did these kids know so much. "I guess that's enough for today." He stood. "I'm tired. How about we talk tomorrow."

"Fine by me," Alex said. "Starting tomorrow, you'll be on the clock."

"Send me a bill," Frankie said, and started up the steps into the building.

He made it up the stairs with some degree of effort, opened the door to his apartment, and plopped onto the sofa after getting a bottle of water from the fridge. The remote control lay within his reach so he got it and turned on the TV, flipping instinctively to the channel where Shawna worked. The news would be on in a few minutes.

Sometime during the endless stream of commercials, Frankie fell asleep, his head resting against the back of the sofa. He lay there oblivious to the droning of the anchors until Shawna's voice woke him. Something about her voice always aroused him, even from sleep.

"This is a Channel 3 exclusive," she said.

Frankie sat up, staring at her and wishing he'd taken her up on the dinner invitation. Dinner with Shawna always led to bed with Shawna and he could use that right now. Her big white teeth seemed to take up half the screen.

"We have it from the best sources that Detective Frankie Donovan is back in the city and will be assuming the lead on the brutal murders committed by the one known as the 'chop shop' killer. If you remember, Frankie was…"

Frankie popped up, fully alert. "What the fuck?"

He turned up the volume and lit a smoke, all the sleep gone from his eyes. He hadn't taken two drags when his cell phone rang. Instinctively, he answered. "Donovan."

It was Morreau. "What the fuck is this? Have you seen the news?"

"Lieu, I don't know—"

"You don't know? How is it that we go a whole fucking week with no leaks, and you're back in town a few hours and the case is all over the news? And what's this about a 'chop shop' killer? Where the fuck did that come from?"

Frankie stood, pacing while he talked. "Lieutenant, *I don't know*. Not from me."

"If I find out you had anything to do with this, it's your ass, Donovan."

"Yes, sir," Frankie said, and hung up.

He slammed his fist on the table. "Goddamnit, Shawna."

* * *

TOM JACKSON SURFED THE channels, looking for something interesting to watch, eager to see if his exploits were being reported. He stopped at Channel 3 to watch their older, but still cute, answer to Channel 5's Cindy Ellis.

"We have it from the best sources that Detective Frankie Donovan is back in the city and will be assuming the lead on the brutal murders committed by the one known as the 'chop shop' killer."

Tom paused the TV, calling Lisa and the little imp into the room with him. Lisa sat next to him while the girl stood. "Who the fuck is this Donovan guy?" Tom asked, and pushed "play" again.

Shawna Pavic came back on, her cutesy smile irritating him already. "With Frankie Donovan on the case it shouldn't be long before the 'chop shop' killer is behind bars."

"Or dead," her co-anchor said.

She laughed. "Right—or dead. Detective Donovan takes no prisoners."

Tom muted the television and turned to Lisa. "Who is Frankie Donovan?"

Lisa shrugged. "Some hero cop. Got famous a while back when there were a bunch of murders in the city. I think he busted some big Mafia guy."

"Big fucking deal, a Mafia guy."

"It *was* a big deal," Lisa said. "This guy—"

The jolt from Tom's blow knocked her to the floor. She screamed, hand going to her face, fear filling her eyes.

"I didn't mean it. I—"

Tom got on top of her and shoved his hand over her mouth. "How many times do I have to tell you, if you make noise it only gets worse." He slapped her across the face then hit her with his fist, making sure his knuckles caught the side of her head where her hair would hide the bruise.

She whimpered, just like old Beau had done years ago, but she didn't wail, and she didn't make any noise.

Guess I taught her a lesson.

Tom got back on the sofa and stared at the image of Frankie Donovan they had splashed across the screen.

Now I might have to teach one to him.

CHAPTER 25

TROUBLE WITH KIDS

Wilmington, Delaware

I got home from Teddy's, later than I wanted to, and crept into bed so I wouldn't disturb Angie. She was in a deep sleep, breathing calmly. I slid my hands under my pillow and stared at the ceiling. It was so quiet I felt as if I should be able to listen to her heart beat, but all I could hear was her breathing and the click of the clock when the minute hand moved.

The next thing I knew, Angie was calling me for breakfast. I got up, threw on some shorts, and went to have the morning meal with her and Rosa. "Good morning, ladies. How goes it today?"

Angie set a plate of eggs and sausage on the table while I poured coffee for the two of us and then took a seat next to her. "Do any good last night?" she asked.

"I talked to a few people, but they didn't tell me much more than I already knew." I looked to Rosa. "Pass the toast, please."

"Who could have done it?" Angie asked. "Think it was a random mugging or something?"

"That happens all the time down in the President's District," Rosa said. "There were two more shootings on Harrison Street last night."

I looked at the counter. "You get the paper already?"

Rosa sighed. "*Google news*, Dad. Nobody reads the paper anymore; besides, paper kills trees."

"Good coffee, Angie. And no, I don't think it was random. Somebody planned this."

"Are you ignoring me, Dad?"

"I would *never* ignore you, sweetheart. I'm just allowing time for your wisdom to sink in."

Rosa laughed. "So you're saying that whoever did it planned to make it look like Bugs?"

"*I* call him 'Bugs.' He's Mr. Donovan or Uncle Frankie to you."

"I like 'Uncle Mario' better."

"If Bugs hears you call him Mario he might kick your ass." I sipped more coffee and shook my head. "Besides, the whole thing could have been coincidence, with Bobby being killed the night he and Frankie fought."

Rosa finished her meal and took the plate to the sink, where she rinsed it. "I thought you didn't believe in coincidences."

"I don't, but sometimes they happen."

Rosa washed her plate, dried it, and put it away. "I went to Casapulla's the other night and Marty wasn't there."

"I thought you weren't seeing your stepfather anymore."

"Don't try to change the subject, Dad. You know I met him on Thursday nights and he *always* showed." She turned her head to look at Angie, then back at me. "And he doesn't answer his phone, and yesterday I called his work." Tears came now. "They said he hasn't been to work all week." She looked as if she was going to break down. "Did you...do something to him? Did you..."

"What, kill him? Is that what you want to ask me?" I was pissed. "No, Rosa, as much as I wanted to, I didn't."

"Where is he? Or is this another *coincidence*—you show up and Marty disappears?"

I took my plate to the sink to clean it, but I really wanted to smash it.

"No coincidence. I *suggested* that Marty leave town. And I suggested he never come back."

"Who gave you the right—"

Angie slammed both hands on the counter. "That's enough! This conversation is over."

"Mom—"

Angie spun toward Rosa. Her face carried all her anger. "*Over*. Do you hear me? This conversation is over."

Rosa lowered her head. "Sorry."

"Tell your father that, not me."

Rosa turned to me, her head still lowered. "Sorry, Dad. I didn't mean it."

I pulled her to me and we hugged. "I'm sorry too. I should have told you first." I held her tightly. "Get ready for school. We'll talk later."

Angie looked at the clock and panicked. "My God, look what time it is." She undid her apron and tossed it on the counter. "I can't afford to be late, not the way they're cutting people down at the plant."

She grabbed her purse and ran for the door. "You, too, Nicky, you better get going."

"I'll drive Rosa."

She ran back and pecked my cheek. "Thanks. I love you."

"Love you too, babe. See you tonight."

I drove Rosa to school, apologizing again to her, then kissed her goodbye. "Have a great day. See you tonight."

"You too, Dad. Bye."

After that, I hit the job on Front Street, another one on South Market, then back to the office to finish a few bids. I was in a groove and the numbers were all working. I got done far earlier than I expected. I told the boss I'd catch some measurements on a site we had just started, then I headed out, stopping at Teddy's on the way. Fred was there, and three of the regulars who had been there the night in question.

I left with a frown on my face. Everyone told me the same story—Bobby insulted Frankie's sister and mom, then Frankie kicked his ass and threatened to kill him. Things didn't look good for Bugs.

From Teddy's I went to the site. The work went quickly, and I had almost two hours before the end of the day. I decided to surprise Rosa by taking her to Casapulla's. Maybe she and I could start a tradition like she had with Marty. I turned down Union Street, then left on Front Street, right on Dupont, and headed home to Beech.

I got out of the car whistling a happy tune, then bounced up the steps to the door and into the house, eager to see Rosa. As I opened the door I nearly fell over. Rosa was on the sofa, a boy on top of her with his hand under her blouse, groping her. I bolted across the room, yanked him up by his hair and reared my fist back.

Rosa jumped up, screaming. "No, Dad. Please don't hurt him. Please?" Tears were already flowing.

The boy was trembling. I wanted nothing more than to beat his fucking brains out, but all I could hear was Rosa's pleading.

"*Please*, Dad?"

I looked at the boy. He was maybe fifteen, and scared shitless. "I'm sorry, Mr. Fusco. Really, *really* sorry."

"Shut the hell up."

He grabbed his stuff to go, but I stopped him. "Sit the fuck down."

"Dad!"

She never heard me say that in front of her, though I knew she'd heard it many times from others, probably even said it herself. I pointed my finger at her. "You sit down too."

I paced the room, mumbling. "Goddamn idiots. You're nothing but kids."

"Dad, you and Mom—"

I moved to stand in front of her. "You don't know *shit* about your mother and me, so don't bring it up. In fact, don't say a *goddamn* word until I tell you to."

The boy hadn't breathed since I came in. I'm sure I was a scary sight. I know what I *wanted* to do to him, and I'm certain it showed. "What's your name?"

He stood, as if he were in class being called on. "Mike Riley, sir."

"Mike Riley? A goddamn mick."

He looked at me, confused.

Rosa managed a straight face, though she looked as if she was restraining a laugh. "I don't think he knows what a mick is."

Now *I* was confused. "What do you mean? He's Irish."

"Kids nowadays don't know that stuff. Nobody says things like that anymore."

Jesus Christ, no wonder the world is falling apart. "All right, Mike Riley, I'm not going to kill you today…"

He let out a deep breath.

"But don't get excited," I said. "I might kill you tomorrow when this all sinks in."

He smiled. "Yes, sir." Then he stared me in the eyes. "Sir, I really love Rosa. I didn't mean any disrespect."

I still wanted to smack this kid, but now I wanted to hug him too. It took guts for him to say that. I opted for the hug, pulling him close. "Okay, kid. What you just did saved your ass. And it might even buy you a sub sometime in the future."

His face lit up. "Yes, sir. Thank you."

I got serious again. "But right now, you need to get out of my house because I don't trust my temper with you here."

His eyes went wide and he gulped. "Yes, sir." He bolted for the door in what I called a controlled panic, not even bothering to say goodbye to Rosa.

I closed the door and turned to Rosa, but she had vanished—to her room, I felt sure—and it would likely be at least a day until I saw her again. That was okay. I was too pissed off to be rational. I might say things I didn't mean, and I'd done enough of that in my life.

As I worked on calming down, I decided to go ahead and get subs for dinner after all. Angie would be tired, so it would be a nice break for her;

besides, once you've got your mind set on eating subs it's tough as hell to move on to something else. I got in the car and drove to Casapulla's, not more than ten minutes away, and ordered three large Italians with sweet and hot peppers, and extra provolone on mine. I grabbed some chips, a few drinks, paid, and headed home.

In the first thirty seconds of the ten minutes it took me to get home, I decided I wouldn't tell Angie about this afternoon with Rosa and her friend. No sense in giving her more to worry about. That left my mind free to think about Frankie's situation, and who killed Bobby. Bugs said to focus on the money, and the more I thought about that, the more I realized that if anyone had gotten fifty grand illegally—and this was definitely illegal—then Doggs Caputo either had something to do with it, or he'd know something about it. I smiled. Now I had a link to follow. After dinner, I'd go see Doggs. He knew something; I just had to convince him to talk.

CHAPTER 26

FAVORS AND OLD FRIENDS

Wilmington, Delaware

I walked to the smoke shop. It wasn't that far and I needed the exercise. That large sub weighed heavy on me and Angie was making mushroom ravioli tomorrow. Despite my vow to lose a few pounds, there was no way I wasn't going to stuff my gut when she made mushroom ravioli. Sometimes I swore that Mamma Rosa left a little piece of her inside Angie when she died, and nothing pleased me more.

After a few blocks I hit Union Street and headed north, watching the drivers, impatient as they endured the traffic. I never understood that. They knew there'd be traffic every day to and from work, so why did they let it bother them? Another mystery for what had become life for a lot of people. As I crossed Front Street I thought about the days when this place was crowded with people, and everybody walking. Back then a lot of families only had one car and people walked more. I'm sure that's what kept some of the pounds off.

Another couple of minutes and I was at the smoke shop. Jimmy the Gem was watching the front.

"Hey, Jimmy. I need to see Doggs. He around?"

He looked at me funny, but he nodded and headed for the back room. "Watch the front for me. Be right back."

I waited for Doggs to come out. It only took about half a minute. He was grumpy as usual, cursing at anything that moved—or didn't move.

He lowered his head and stared over the top of his thick glasses."What the fuck do you want, Rat? I'm a busy man."

"I figured if anyone knew the answers to what I need, it would be you, Doggs."

He looked around the shop, a ten-by-ten hole with a not-so-secret door at the back, and spread his hands in amazement. "What the fuck, I'm a fuckin' mind reader now? Answers to what?"

I knew a barrage of 'F's' would soon be flying from Doggs' mouth. Some things never change. He still used the 'f' word as punctuation. "I needed to talk in private. That's why I asked you out here." I turned toward the door. "Can we step outside a minute?"

He threw his hands up in the air. "What the fuck. I got a fuckin' game going on. This better be good." He followed me out the door and immediately lit a smoke.

I knew I had little time so spit it right out. "What can you tell me about Bobby Campisi?"

Doggs tossed his newly-lit cigarette into the street and got right in my face. "Bobby Campisi? He's fuckin' dead. How's that for news?"

As we were talking, Charlie Knuckles came up. He stopped to listen. It was too late for me to worry about privacy, so I continued. "I know he's dead. I need to know what got him killed. Who wanted him dead, and where did he get all that money?"

"What the fuck? You a fuckin' cop now? First Bugs and now you? The only fuckin' one of you who was any good got killed." He nodded his head. "Tony was a good man. Good earner."

I was pissed off and ready to hit Doggs, but I held my temper. "So that's how it's going to be? All these years—"

"Fuck you and your years, and fuck you and your friend Bugs." He pushed past Knuckles and went back inside. "No need for you to come back here, Nicky. You're not welcome."

Knuckles looked at me. "Yeah, who the fuck are you?" But as the door shut, Knuckles leaned close and whispered, "See me tomorrow night, late."

I turned and walked back down Union Street, discouraged and upset. All of these years I assumed Doggs was a friend. Now I realized he used me like he did everyone else. Funny how that happens. I saw him using the other people, but always thought I was the exception. Stupid fuck is what I was.

After a few more blocks of bashing myself, and thinking what a waste of time this was, I realized I learned something important. When I mentioned "all the money," Doggs hadn't raised an eyebrow. And if anything raised his bushy eyebrows, it was talk of money. That meant he knew Bobby had money, which told me Doggs was involved. All I had to do was find out how.

Maybe Knuckles will know.

THE NEXT DAY SEEMED longer than usual, but I got off work on time and hurried home. The smell of red sauce hit me as I opened the door. "I'm home."

I heard dishes rattling in the kitchen. "I didn't get a chance to talk to you last night. How did it go with Doggs?"

I hugged Angie from behind, careful not to disturb her cooking. "Like shit. He was a prick."

"It's about time you realized that. He's always been that way."

I pecked her cheek and stepped back, opening the fridge to get some water. "How is it you know all of these things, and I don't?"

"Because I'm smarter than you," she said. Then, "Why don't you set the table."

I grabbed plates and silverware and placed them in the appropriate places, knowing it would be my ass if I didn't, then got napkins and glasses. "No wine?"

"We're out," Angie said. "And we don't have the money to get more until Friday. You'll have to suffer."

I stared at the cabinet, trying to figure out how Jesus did that trick with the water, then opted for going next door instead. "I'll see if Pete has any. I can't have ravioli without wine."

"If you're going to ask Pete for wine, at least invite them for dinner."

Pete and Rita joined us for dinner, then we played pinochle until about nine, although Rosa retired to her room as soon as she finished the dishes. When the neighbors left, Angie yawned and said she was going to bed.

"Are you coming up?"

"I gotta see someone tonight."

Her eyes narrowed and her stance changed. "See someone?" She looked at the clock. "At this time of night? Who, and for what?"

At first I didn't say anything, but then I owned up. "Knuckles. It's about—"

"Nicky, don't be doing something to get in trouble."

"He might have some leads about Bugs."

"How long are you going to keep this up? We've got a life to live."

I got a little pissed at that, and I'm sure my tone reflected that. "It's not like Bugs didn't risk his career to save my ass." I stood up to face her. "Remember what I told you."

She didn't say anything, just looked at me, but I stared right back at her. "No way I'm leaving him on a limb. *No way.*"

She stood there for what seemed like an hour, but it was probably only a few seconds before she went to bed, her feet hitting the stairs a little harder than usual. "I'll be asleep when you get home." Her tone carried a warning.

I sat in my chair in the living room and read a little, waiting for the right time. Knuckles said "late," and I knew late meant at least midnight. I had to work the next day, but I figured I could suffer through a day of estimating with sleep in my eyes. I just hoped the numbers weren't off or

I'd get my ass fired. Besides, this information would likely be valuable; Knuckles wouldn't have me come by for nothing.

About 11:45, I got up and went outside. I pulled out the keys and hit the remote, unlocking the door to the car. As I went down the few steps to the sidewalk, then down the next set to the street, I decided to walk instead of driving. It was a nice night with the breeze kicking the trees around a little. I always liked that sound.

I headed up Beech Street to Clayton, reminded of the old days when Bugs and Paulie and Tony and I would come this way after working the games. We'd be pumped with money, and high on energy and the thrill of being out late. There wasn't much more exciting when you were a kid than roaming the streets at night, and the later the better. I smiled at the memories. Back then we *owned* this neighborhood, and we knew every shortcut and every hiding place within a square mile or more.

Within fifteen minutes I got to Knuckles' house and tapped on the door. When he answered he checked the street both ways, as if I might have been followed. I thought that was strange, but said nothing. "Hey, Knucks, how's it going?"

"Good, Rat. How about you?" He stepped aside and invited me in. "Want a drink?"

"Too late for that. I'm a working man."

He laughed. "So I heard. Estimator, right? How's that going?"

"It keeps me out of jail."

Another laugh, but this one was fake. "Ain't it the truth." He grabbed a beer for himself and sat in a big recliner. He grabbed the remote and turned off the TV. "So what else you been doing? Any other work besides estimating?"

"Just helping Angie with things." I was starting to wonder why he asked me here, so I pushed the conversation my way. "What's up? You got information for me?"

"Information? Yeah, I got information, but if I'm doing you this favor, maybe you could help me out some." Knuckles offered me a seat on the sofa, which I took, then he pushed an ottoman aside and plopped into a chair next to me.

"Sure. What do you need?" I asked.

"I got a little problem up in Philly with a guy."

The hair on the back of my neck rose, tickled my skin. "What kind of problem?"

He shrugged as if it were nothing. "Some guy up there is into me pretty deep and it's causing me trouble."

I let his words hang in the air. Knuckles never asked me to do anything like this before. He obviously heard rumors about what happened in New York. "I don't do shit like that. I'm an estimator. I don't collect."

Knuckles brought the recliner up to a straight position, and then handed me a smoke, which I refused, but as he lit his, he stared at me through the top of his glasses. "I'm not asking you to collect. I need an example made of this fucker. If I don't do something, everybody up there will think they can stiff me."

I stood and held up my hands. "Whoa, Knucks. You've got me wrong. That's not me."

He stood when I did, then walked right up to me, almost touching me. "Don't play that shit with me. I know what you did up north. What, you don't think we heard about that down here? What the fuck's wrong with you? You stupid?"

Charlie walked to a bookcase and pulled out a book which had a false cover. He opened it and brought out a wad of hundreds, riffling them in front of me like a deck of cards. "In case you were thinking I'm asking for nothin'—I'm not. I got four large here. You get four more when it's done."

I almost laughed. Back in Brooklyn, I wouldn't have broken a guy's legs for eight grand, and Knuckles was asking me to take somebody out for that much. Still, it was tempting under the circumstances. Angie and I *did* need money.

He handed me the wad. It felt warm in my hands. Instinct had me reaching for my pocket to tuck that money away but, as my hand moved,

Angie's voice chided me. I could hear her telling me "*no*" and in no uncertain terms. And I could almost see Mamma Rosa's wooden spoon wagging in her hand.

I handed it back. "I'm sorry, Knucks. That's not me anymore."

Charlie started to say something but I shook my head and turned to go. "Hey, I'm not being disrespectful, but I gotta go. Get somebody else."

The walk home wasn't nearly as refreshing as the walk there had been. I had counted on Knuckles for help, and all he did was piss me off. I guess all the old guys were users. All of them—just like Doggs.

As I thought about where to go with this "investigation," the money Borelli said Bobby had in the bank kept popping into my head, and I knew what I had to do. Since Doggs and his crew wouldn't tell me what I needed to know, I had to go to the next logical choice, even though I dreaded the thought of it. Donna hated me for reasons I didn't understand, but hate me she did. Regardless, I had to see her. I owed it to Bugs.

CHAPTER 27

SOMEONE'S WATCHING

Wilmington, Delaware

We had eggplant parmigiana for dinner the next night, not my favorite, but the way Angie fixed it made it more than edible. Once everyone had been seated, I started the blessing.

"In nomine Patris, et Filii, et Spiritus—"

"Dad, this is America. Even the priests don't use Latin anymore."

"Maybe they should," I said, and continued, "…et Spiritus Sancti. Amen."

"Let's eat before it gets cold," Angie said.

We ate the meal in virtual silence, and after dinner, I took a seat in my favorite chair, a stiff-backed, wide-seated behemoth with an ottoman sitting in front of it. I kicked my feet up to rest and opened a book to where I had left off. Rosa stood beside me.

"Do you want a glass of wine, Dad?" She seemed more cordial than she had at dinner.

"I thought we were out of wine."

"Mom got some on her way home. You want any?"

"No, but thanks for asking."

I went back to reading, but Rosa still stood there, silent. After a few seconds I put the book down. "Do you need to talk with me?"

Nervousness showed on her. I waited, and after a few more seconds her expression went from nervous to angry.

"Do you have someone following me?"

It came out as an accusation, not a question. I looked up and focused on Rosa.

"What do you mean? Tell me about it."

She didn't budge. "Answer the question. Do you have someone following me?"

Her tone irritated the hell out of me. I stood and faced her. "No, I *don't* have someone following you, so if you think someone is, you better tell me what this is about."

With one hand planted on her hip, she cocked her head and glared. "You swear you don't have anybody following me?"

Anger was setting in now. "I already told you I don't."

Rosa sighed, but her face lost its tension. "I've seen a car for the last two days, the *same* car, with the same two men in it."

She had my attention. "Where?"

The first time when I was coming home from school, walking up Clayton Street. Then today as I came down Beech."

"And you're sure it was the same car."

She scoffed. "DVK0943."

"What is that?"

"License plate. Same on both days. Pennsylvania tags."

I hugged her but grimaced at the same time. She *was* her father's daughter at times, and it ate at my gut whenever I saw that side of her. Tony had a memory like a steel trap, and she seemed to have inherited it. "Write it down for me. I'll check it out."

Her expression changed to fear. "So this isn't you? For real? You don't have someone following me?"

"Rosa, I already told you. But this could be a coincidence, nothing else. Don't worry, okay?"

"For someone who doesn't believe in coincidences there have been an awful lot of them lately."

I patted her back. "Don't worry. It's nothing. But just to be sure, I'll check out these plates."

"How are you going to check out the plates? Are you a cop now?"

"I just need to make a few calls."

Rosa went to her room after that, and Angie visited a neighbor, coming back about nine o'clock. We read together then went to bed.

As we lay there, she turned to me, her voice soft, but worried.

"Do you think someone really *is* following her?"

"I don't know, but I'll find out."

"If this has anything to do with Bobby's murder, you need to quit. It's not your responsibility. It's not worth risking your job, and I won't have my daughter's life put in danger."

I put the book on the nightstand and turned to her. "Suddenly she's *your* daughter?"

Angie closed her eyes, and she seemed to bite her tongue. "I'm sorry. I didn't mean for it to come out that way."

I got out of bed, went downstairs and sat in the dark. This was the kind of thing I feared most when I agreed to marry Angie.

It didn't take her long to come down. She pulled up a chair and sat in front of me, making sure I couldn't ignore her.

"Nicky, listen to me. I know Bugs is your best friend, and I know how you feel about that oath you guys made together. But when is it going to be his turn? It seems like you are always the one giving."

I closed my eyes and shook my head. "You don't understand. It's not about taking turns. It's about who's in trouble. If Bugs is in trouble, I've got to help. *Got to.*" I stood and walked toward the dining room.

"Nicky."

I stopped, then I felt her hands on my shoulders. She came around and kissed my head. "You're right. I don't understand, but I'll trust you." She kissed me again. "And I'm *so* sorry for what I said about Rosa being *my* daughter. You know I didn't mean it that way. Forgive me?"

My heart melted. I kissed her on the forehead, and then on the lips. "I'd never risk her safety, Angie. No way in hell."

"I know."

In the morning, we had breakfast, as usual, and then Rosa got ready for school. I thought about driving her, but figured she'd be okay because she walked to school with three other girls. Before leaving I called up to her. "Don't forget to walk home with someone. Not by yourself."

"I know, Dad. Bye."

On the way to work I called Bugs and asked him to run the plates. When I got to the office, I parked and hustled inside. Several bids had a deadline of tomorrow. All day, though, I worried about Rosa, and I watched the clock like a kid during last class on Friday. About 3:00, I packed the prints in my briefcase and headed for the door. As I walked down the hall, I heard my name called. It was Joe Tomkins, the boss.

"Nicky, hold on a minute."

Shit. I turned, knowing I was about to catch hell. "What's up, Joe?"

"Leaving early?"

"I have to pick up my daughter today. She's—"

"I'm not an unreasonable man, but lately you've missed a lot of work. Too much. I understand normal difficulties, but I've got a business to run." He eyed me. "I can't have you missing any more time. Understand?"

I lowered my head. "I understand, sir. And don't worry, I'll have these bids done on time."

"Done and accurate, I hope."

I noticed the tone of his voice. "Yes, sir. Accurate, too."

He nodded. "All right. You can go today, but I expect to see the lights on pretty late around here for a while."

"Yes, sir. You can count on it."

I left the building with a restrained walk, but the whole time I felt like racing. When I got to the car, I punched it into gear and took off, praying I wasn't too late. If anything happened to Rosa, I'd never forgive myself. And surely, Angie would never forgive me.

I pulled into a spot on Oak Street and waited. I had been worried that I'd be late, but fortunately I still had a few minutes. Looking around, I saw no sign of the car, but it might show up. School let out, and hordes of kids filled the streets, a sweeping mass going in all directions. By the time they reached Oak and Clayton, they had formed small groups, a few couples here and there, but mostly clusters of guys or girls, walking each other home. I ducked, not wanting Rosa to see that I was watching her, but she wasn't paying attention.

It wasn't until after she passed Oak Street that I saw them, two guys in a blue Ford with Pennsylvania license plates—DVK0943.

"Son of a bitch."

They crept up slowly, as if waiting on the traffic of kids, but they had definitely been stalking Rosa from behind the church. Now they followed her slowly up Clayton Street. I'd packed my gun this morning, and as I sat there, I checked to make sure the clip was loaded. Just as I opened the door, a patrol car came up the street behind them, forcing them to move faster. As they passed Rosa, the guy in the passenger side stretched to watch her.

"Mother fucker," I said.

On the way home I thought about what to do, and say. I decided not to tell Rosa or Angie about it. No sense in worrying them more than necessary. But even as I thought that, I grew worried. Who were these guys? And why were they following Rosa? Did it have something to do with the case? There were a lot of questions I needed answers to, and quickly.

CHAPTER 28

SPECIAL DELIVERY

Brooklyn, New York

Lisa got out of bed and prepared to go to work. She studied her reflection as she applied makeup, covering the bruises on her face. No one would see the bruises between her legs. She gritted her teeth and vowed to get even with Tom. Kill him. She had to figure out how to get away. She had to find out where he was keeping her mother first, though, or he'd kill her.

Lisa dreamed of killing Tom, drew strength from those thoughts alone. Once she killed him, she'd kill that whore he had in the bedroom. As soon as those thoughts entered her mind, Lisa wondered what had become of her. It wasn't the girl's fault.

***

AFTER LISA LEFT FOR work, Tom Jackson tied up the girl, gagged her, and left her sitting in front of the couch, television tuned to her favorite channel—VH1. He made her wear a diaper in case she pissed or shit herself while he was gone, but he doubted she would; she'd done that once and hated cleaning it up. He thought about leaving her in the bathroom, but there was no sense being cruel. She'd do fine where she was.

"I'm leaving now, girl. You be good while I'm gone." He left, locking the door, including the deadbolt from the hall, then walked down the stairs to the first floor. He didn't like the elevator; it felt too closed in. Fighting in Afghanistan taught him to like open spaces, and there'd been plenty of that. Too much even. Made it difficult to find the ones he had to kill. He imagined a scenario where he was a sniper in a crowded city, like New York or London, though he couldn't picture London as he'd never been there. He'd sit atop one of the skyscrapers, his rifle resting on a ledge and his scope sighted in on the crowds below.

"Blam, blam, blam," he said, stomping his foot on a new step with each utterance. The first smile of the day came to Tom's face, the first real one, as he thought of the damage he could do. But he knew it would be suicide to go on a sniper shoot. What he was doing now was safer.

Tom exited the building and turned left, walking the six blocks to a storage facility, where he had rented a locker. He checked to make sure no one was watching, then opened the locker and removed the cooler. Inside was dry ice, packed around the hands, and other parts, from the first victim. One hand had a carving on it. He removed it and put it into a plastic garbage bag, tied it, and put the cooler back into the locker. Pretty soon he'd need to put more ice in there. That or let it rot. Guess it didn't matter much now. He left the storage facility and took his time going home, stopping to get more coffee at a small shop near the house on his way.

When he returned, the girl was just where he'd left her—not that he expected different, but it was nice to know that things were as you expect them to be. She bounced up and down, mumbled a lot through her gag, but Tom ignored her. She probably had to piss.

He sat at the table and, using plain paper he ripped from a notebook in a store, and a pen he got at the corner market, he printed a note, laughing about his cleverness. When he was done, he tucked the note into an envelope, also stolen, but from a different store, and put it in the bag with the hand. Once again Tom left, this time taking a right when he exited the building. He took the subway, switching trains several times, then exited in Manhattan near a delivery service that did same-day local deliveries. He told a homeless man he'd pay him fifty bucks to take the bag into the building and mail it. It only took a few minutes.

When the man returned, Tom paid him and left, a smile as big as Texas on his face.

I can't wait until Cindy Ellis gets that.

✳✳✳

FRANKIE GOT TO THE station early, knowing he had a long day ahead of him. He'd made up his mind last night that from this day forward, he'd be a new man. The old Frankie Donovan, the one who was happy all the time, was coming back. After parking the car, and going through a round of condolences from friends on the first floor, he took the steps to the second floor two at a time, as if he had to race to make up for the delay.

Carol sat at her desk, guarding the gates of Hades. "Morning, Donovan," she said without looking up. "Sorry about your dad."

Frankie leaned down and kissed her cheek. "Thanks, Carol. You're a sweetie."

Carol *did* look up now, and she stopped what she was doing, too. "What the hell was that? No sarcasm, no innuendo, just a plain old flat out compliment? Don't do that to me." She shook her head as she returned to typing. "Give me a damn heart attack."

"It's the new me," Frankie said, and turned toward the coffee room. "Seen Lou?"

"He's in there, but you better let me warn him first. His heart's not as strong as mine."

"Go to hell."

She smiled. "There's the Frankie Donovan I know and love."

Lou had a coffee in hand when Frankie came through the door. "Don't start on me, Donovan. I heard that banter between you and Carol. If you think to throw me off by being nice, it's not going to work." He took a sip of his own coffee when Frankie grabbed his cup. "By the way, this gorgeous thing behind me is Sherri Miller. Say hi, Sherri."

She stood and stretched out her hand to greet him, long slim fingers wrapping around his. "*Buon giorno, Francesco. Come va?*"

Frankie damn near fell over. "Pretty good. No wonder you're not getting shit done on this case; it must have taken Lou all week to teach you that."

"Are you dogging Lou's teaching or my learning?"

Frankie took a seat next to Lou. "This is the new Frankie Donovan. I wouldn't do either."

Sherri said, "I'm just kidding, Frankie. *Mi dispiace per tuo padre.*"

Frankie looked at her with new respect. "I *know* he didn't teach you that because he doesn't know that much."

Lou laughed like hell. "She's half Italian, Donovan. Imagine that. Just like you."

Frankie stared at Sherri with a blank look. "Imagine that."

Sherri lost her smile, and got a serious face. "Listen, Frankie, all kidding aside. I know this is your case, so I can bow out now that you're back."

"If I knew how to say bullshit in Italian, I'd tell you." He pointed his finger at her. "This is your case and Lou's. I'm just here to help."

"Not according to Shawna Pavic, Channel 3 news."

Frankie shook his head. "Yeah, that's another story. I'm gonna kick her *goddamn* ass."

From the other room, Carol shouted. "That's my boy, Donovan. I knew this nice guy shit wouldn't last."

"Pay her no mind," Frankie said to Sherri. "Tell me about your Italian heritage."

"My grandparents came from Sicily, and my mother was actually born there. She met my father in college and they fell in love. That was it."

"I'll bet that caused a stir when she brought him home to dinner."

Sherri laughed. "To hear them tell it, it did. I think he said it took two years for them to accept him, but once it was over you couldn't tell the difference; in fact, I'm closer to most of my Italian relatives than those on my dad's side." She sighed. "They loved my dad."

Sherri laughed again, and couldn't stop.

"Must have brought up a good memory," Frankie said.

"It did—end of summer cookouts. Every year before school started we had a big family cookout and there was always a who's-got-the-best-tan competition. Guess who won."

Frankie and Sherri laughed, and while they were talking, Lou's phone rang. He stepped out to talk, coming back in a moment later. "Let's go. The lady we want is in the house."

"Who?" Frankie asked.

"The receptionist lady from the place where Lisa works, the one who was having the affair with our last vic. She's at work today."

"Let's go have a chat with her," Sherri said.

Frankie stood up and tossed his coffee cup into the trash can. "Hurry up, Mazzetti."

"I gotta piss first. I'll be a minute or two."

Sherri raised her eyebrows. "A minute or two? How long does it take you to piss?"

Lou laughed. "Give me a break, Miller; it's got a long way to travel."

Frankie shook his head while Miller laughed. "You fell for that one, rookie."

"Guess I haven't heard all of the old-timer jokes yet. But I'm getting there."

"Keep working with him and you will."

While Lou was in the bathroom, Sherri grabbed a bottle of water from the fridge. "So I guess you know about me, right? I mean about what happened before I became a cop."

Frankie looked at her strangely. "I don't run checks on people I work

with, if that's what you're getting at. And unless it has something to do
with your performance, I don't need to know."

Sherri looked at him, then cast a quick glance at Lou, who was just
returning, and shook her head. "No, nothing with performance."

"Then let's get moving."

"Take your own car," Lou said. "I'm riding with Miller."

***

SHERRI GOT INTO HER car, started it and headed out. Lou reached over
and turned off the radio, looking at Sherri. "What, you thought I'd tell
him about you?"

"He's your partner, I assumed—"

"I told you, it was between you and me. That doesn't mean you and me
and Donovan. When I give my word, it's good."

She blushed. "I guess I'm not used to that."

"Yeah, well, all I got is this old fedora I wear, a wife I haven't been able
to get rid of in thirty years, and my word."

At the next red light, Sherri looked at Lou through narrowed eyes, but
with a smile. "You're all right for a grumpy old guy. And tell that wife of
yours she better watch out. She might have competition after all."

"Better take out life insurance if you plan to seduce me."

"Why? She the jealous type?"

"I didn't mean on you, I meant on me. If I get in bed with you, I'm
afraid I won't make it."

"You're a card, Mazzetti. A damn card."

"Yeah, that's me. Always an ace."

"So what's Donovan like to work with? He seems nice enough."

Lou stared straight ahead for a moment. "Frankie's a tough nut. He
doesn't cut anybody slack, but he's fun to work with. And a damn good cop."

"Honest?" Sherri winced when she said it, afraid it might offend Lou.

"Don't believe what you hear in the hallways, Miller. Or the shit you hear in the bathrooms about him and women. I've been working with him a while now and I can tell you he's a good guy."

"So those stories about him letting a killer go are just that—stories?"

"I worked that case with him. If you think he did something wrong, you'll have to think it of me, too."

They rode in silence for a few blocks, then Lou said, "I don't mind, you know. You asking about it, I mean. I expected you to at some point. All I'm saying is, you can trust Frankie with your life."

"Fair enough. Case closed."

Sherri pulled into the parking garage and they got out and walked toward the building. Donovan was standing outside the front door, smoking. "About time," he said, sucking hard on a cigarette then crushing it out.

Lou walked right past him, holding the door open for Sherri. He looked at Donovan as if he'd been holding up the operation. "No sense wasting time, Donovan. Let's get you back in the saddle."

"How are we handling this?" Sherri asked.

"You take the lead," Frankie said, pushing the button for the elevator. "We should line up several people to be interviewed to make it look as if we're not singling her out, so for all she knows, we might be interviewing everyone."

"Why go to the trouble?" Sherri asked.

The elevator opened and Frankie stepped aside, holding the door for her. "If she thinks she's just one of a group, she'll lie."

"But don't we want her telling the truth?"

"We'll get the truth—don't worry. But first we have to catch her in a lie. Once we do that, it's easier to get her to tell the truth."

They got off on the fourth floor and started down the corridor. About halfway there, Frankie's phone rang. He kept walking while he answered. "Donovan."

"Detective Donovan, this is Cindy Ellis, Channel 5."

"I remember you, Cindy. Long time."

"This isn't a social call. A package was just delivered to me. It's a person's hand."

Frankie stopped, signaling Lou and Sherri to wait. "Goddamn! Don't touch it."

"Do you think we're nuts? I'm not getting near that thing."

"Did you tell anyone else? Who's seen it?"

"Just my assistant and my boss."

"Keep it that way. We're on our way."

"What was that about?" Lou asked.

"The affair lady will have to wait. That was Cindy Ellis. Someone delivered her a hand."

"Damn," Sherri said, and started for the elevator.

"Who'd the bastard kill now?" Lou asked.

"I don't know," Sherri said, "But I'm sure we're gonna find out." She turned to Frankie. "Should we call Kate Burns?"

The mention of her name excited Frankie. "I'll call her. You know the way there?"

"By heart. See you in a few."

CHAPTER 29

NOTHING LASTS FOREVER

Wilmington, Delaware

I was still worried about the guys following Rosa, and I figured the sooner I saw Donna, the faster I'd find out what was going on. I still had a few hours before Angie got home, time enough to chat with Donna. I made a turn going south on Clayton Street, turned right on Banning and then south on Coyne. Her house was a few blocks down.

I parked, walked up and tapped on the door, but no one answered. I tried again, but again got no answer. On the third attempt, I knocked a little louder, making a neighbor pop her head out of the door and holler at me. "Donna's at her mother's house. Up on—"

I waved. "Thanks, I know where she lives."

I got back in the car and despite not wanting to, I drove to her mother's house. I had waited as long as I could before going to see Donna, knowing it wouldn't be pleasant, but it was something that had to be done. The money was not only a big issue; it had to be the central issue. No way Bobby got that much cash legally. The bad thing was that she still blamed me for his death; hell, she probably blamed me for her father's death.

I parked with my right wheels on the sidewalk, like we used to in the old days, and got out of the car, wishing for the millionth time that I had a cigarette to calm me. Six concrete steps led up the hill. Gripping the old wrought-iron railing brought back a flood of memories from childhood when we raced up these steps to get each other up in the mornings, or crept up them to call each other out late at night. A smile covered my face as I tapped on the door.

Donna opened it a few seconds later and stood there, staring at me with hatred in her eyes. "What the fuck do you want?"

"I'm not here for the conversation, if that's what's worrying you. But I do have a few questions."

She started to shut the door. I jammed my foot in and held it open. "Not so fast, Donna. I'm trying to help Bugs."

"Since when have you tried helping anyone but yourself?"

I pushed the door open and stepped inside. A baby cried from the other room, and I could hear music playing softly, an old Janet Jackson song I thought. "Look, I know you don't want to, but we need to talk. Bugs is in trouble."

"I don't—"

She never finished the sentence. I looked past her to see Mrs. Donovan, looking ten years older than she had a week ago.

"Come in, Nicky. Please?" She turned to Donna. "Get our guest some coffee. We'll talk in the dining room."

I followed them in and sat in the chair at the end of the table, but felt like running out of there. I hadn't planned on asking these questions in front of Mrs. Donovan.

Donna brought coffee for me and her mother. Donna sat at the other end of the table, the farthest seat from me. She had poured iced tea for herself.

"What do you need to know?" Her tone was as cold as her drink.

I looked at her, hoping to read her reaction. "How did Bobby get so much money?"

"What money?" her mother asked.

Damn. That threw me off, but it was interesting that Donna hadn't told her. "Mrs. Donovan, Bobby had fifty thousand dollars in a bank account."

She sat up straight. "Fifty thousand! Where did he get that kind of money?" She leaned across the table toward Donna. "Did you know about this?"

Donna looked at me, as if pleading for me not to say anything. I nodded. "I got no idea where he got that money, Mom. How would I know?"

Mrs. Donovan turned to me. "Where would Bobby get that money? You don't think he stole it, do you?"

I sighed. There was no easy way to do this. "I think it had something to do with drugs. It almost had to. No one gets that kind of cash unless it has something to do with drugs."

"Maybe he won it playing cards," she said.

I shook my head. "We all know Bobby wasn't that good at cards; besides, if he won it at cards, he'd have been bragging all over town about it."

Donna nodded. "Nicky's right. Bobby couldn't keep his mouth shut if he beat me at gin."

"Who will get that money now?" Mrs. Donovan asked.

"That's for the cops to decide, or a judge. For now, it's evidence. Besides, even if by some chance you get to keep it, you'll have to explain it to the IRS."

Donna took a sip of her drink and looked at me, perhaps for the first time with warmth in her eyes. "I'm sorry for the way I've been acting."

That took me by surprise, but I felt sure she was putting on an act for her mother. Donna was interested in the money. Nothing else mattered. Despite that, I was grateful for the relief of tension.

For the next half an hour or so, I asked her everything I could think of—did Bobby have any enemies, had he been going out more often at nights, mention any new people he'd been hanging around with, any increase in late-night calls? I asked for a list of his cell-phone bills so I could see who he called and who called him the past few months, and I was surprised when Donna told me that Detective Borelli hadn't bothered getting that information. In fact, she said, he hadn't asked much at all about Bobby, mostly about the money.

I finished my coffee, made small talk with her mother, then said my goodbyes, once again offering condolences to both of them for their loss. Donna walked me to the door. I was curious when she followed me out onto the stoop.

She handed me a key. "I found this in his drawer, but I have no idea what it fits. Nothing in our house, for sure."

It looked like a key to a locker. A number was written on the attached key ring. "You tell anyone else about this?"

"Nobody. Not even Frankie."

"Let's keep it that way," I said, and started to walk away.

"I meant what I said about being sorry."

I turned back and smiled. "It's nice of you to say that, but I don't believe you. It doesn't matter, though; this is all about Bugs right now. I've got to find a way to help him."

Her smile turned sour, and instead of waving goodbye, she shot me the finger. I smiled again. It was good to know things were right in the world.

I took the six steps down to the street and got in the car to head home. It was a nice day, and Angie had the windows open. As I climbed the steps, the aroma of garlic and red sauce hung in the air like the scent of pine needles on a winter night. I upped my pace a little, taking the final steps two at a time. "Hey, babe, what are you cooking?"

"I think you know," she hollered from the kitchen.

I set my briefcase on the chair by the front door, then went to the kitchen. As I turned the corner from the dining room, I saw her standing there with her sauce-stained apron. She held Mamma Rosa's old wooden spoon in her hand.

"Did I miss my birthday or something?" I walked over and kissed her, dipping my finger into the sauce for a quick taste. It earned me the mandatory admonishment, but it was worth it. No way could I pass up a pot of meatballs without tasting the sauce. "What are you doing cooking my favorite meal?"

I checked to make sure Rosa wasn't around, then smiled at her. "You horny or something? Because if you are, we could close these blinds and—"

Angie hit me with the spoon, then quickly rinsed it off. "Open some wine and set the table. We're eating in the dining room tonight."

I whistled. "Fancy tonight. We got company, or what?"

"Just set the table," she said. "Rosa is at Abbie's house."

Now I knew something was wrong, but I wasn't going to say anything. I'd wait until she told me herself. After putting the plates and silverware on the table, I grabbed a few candles and lit them, opened a bottle of wine and poured two glasses. She was almost ready to serve the meal anyway.

Throughout the first part of the meal, she let me talk about my day, but I could tell she wasn't listening. She was judging when she should tell me whatever it was she had to say. Finally, I leaned back in the chair, wiped my face with the napkin and did my usual. "Damn, that was good. Just like Mamma Rosa's."

Angie smiled, but it was fake. I put my napkin on the table, got up from the chair, and went over to her. I rubbed her shoulders, massaged her head, then leaned over and kissed the back of her neck. "What's the matter?"

She issued a few denials, but it didn't take long for her tears to flow. "I got laid off." She turned and stared up at me, her eyes as big and soft as a baby deer's.

I hugged her, bringing her head to my chest. "Don't worry. We'll be all right."

She cried. "How? We're barely making it now with both of us working. And you spent all the money you had on the house."

"Did they give you any severance?"

"Nothing," she managed between fits of crying.

I rubbed her head. "I'll talk to Fred down at the bank. I'm sure we can take out a loan on the house."

Her crying went from bawling to sobbing. "I don't know. With the economy so bad…"

I hugged her, but something told me there was more. "Angie, this isn't like you. What else is bothering you?"

She kept crying, then stood and turned to look at me. "Nicky…oh God, Nicky, I'm pregnant." When she said that, she fell into my arms.

At first I didn't know what to say. I didn't understand why she was crying. I pushed her back and stared. "Angie, that's *great* news. What's wrong with being pregnant?"

"It's a bad time. The economy, me getting laid off…"

"Who cares? That's all little stuff. We don't need to worry about that." I sat her back down in the chair. "The important thing is we're going to have another baby."

"You're not upset? What about the expense?"

"We'll get by. I'll find things to do."

Suddenly she jerked back and stood, staring at me with a look that could kill. "Don't even think about doing anything illegal. You hear me? I don't care if we have to lose this house and move into an apartment." She wagged her finger at me. "I'd rather die than lose you again."

I kissed her lips, softly. A tingle ran through me, an electric jolt that lifted my heart. It made me feel…*special*…I guess is the word, like I didn't deserve this life. Or her.

I hugged Angie tight. "You'll never lose me again. I promise." Even as I said it, though, I wondered where we'd get the money to pay for a baby, especially with her not working. As I thought more on it, all I could see in my mind was the wad of hundreds Knuckles had offered. Even the sound of the trees blowing outside reminded me of the way he riffled them in front of me.

Eight large for taking out a scum. What would it hurt?

CHAPTER 30

THE IRISHMAN RETURNS

Wilmington, Delaware

I got up early and even passed on breakfast so I could get to work before the boss. I hugged Angie for an extra long time. "Don't worry about anything," I whispered so Rosa didn't hear. "And take care of that precious cargo. I'll see you tonight."

"I can't believe you're not eating, Dad. You never go to work without breakfast."

I kissed Rosa goodbye and grabbed my briefcase. "Got a lot to do," I said and headed out. Before leaving I reminded Rosa to walk home in a group and not to split up until she was at the house. On the way to work, Bugs called with information on the plates.

"The car was registered to Mike Ferrieri from Avondale, PA."

"Ferrieri? Don't we know him?"

"Yeah, he's from the neighborhood. Got a brother named Tim."

"You got anything on him?" I asked.

"He's clean, Nicky. No record."

"All right. Thanks, Bugs. I'll let you know if anything comes of it."

"Be careful," Bugs said.

ALL MORNING I WORKED on the bids, making certain the details were covered before submitting them to the boss. No way I was risking a mistake after Joe chewed my ass out. About 11:30 I organized the prints and bids and took them out to Sheila. "Will you make sure Joe gets these? I'm grabbing lunch."

"I'll put them on his desk," she said.

"Want me to bring you back anything?"

"No thanks."

I headed down to French Street and the train station, with the key Donna had given me in my hand as I drove. If someone wanted an anonymous locker in Wilmington, the train station was a logical place for it. I parked the car and went inside, locating the locker in a couple of minutes. When I slipped the key in, it fit perfectly, clicking open. I smiled when I saw a gym bag. I pulled it out and opened it. "Fuck me!"

Two keys of coke stared up at me. *What the hell was Bobby into?* One thing for sure, this wasn't the leftovers from a deal. This is what got Bobby killed. No doubt about it. This is where the fifty large came from.

And he put it in the bank!

The way I figured it, Bobby Campisi deserved to be killed for being so stupid. I shut the bag, shoved it back into the locker and closed it up. No way I was getting caught with that on my person.

I drove to a nearby sandwich shop, picked up a roast-beef sub, then thought about what I learned. I now knew what got Bobby killed, but what I had to figure out was whose junk he stole, because sure as shit they wouldn't stop looking. Donna would likely be next.

And she'll tell them she gave me the key. Fuck me twice.

After finishing my meal, I went back to work. Some new bids were coming up, and if I could get a head start on them, it would look good. As I copied the prints I heard Joe arguing on the phone with someone in the next room. Pretty soon he came into the copy room, a smoke dangling from his mouth. I knew he was pissed; he never smoked in the building.

"What's up, boss? Somebody giving you trouble?"

He waved his hand. "Nothing," he said. "Just some asshole blocking our bid on that new state project."

I didn't say anything, just kept copying.

"I looked at those bids Sheila turned in," he said. "How did we come in so low on the warehouse?"

"I looked at the supplies. We were paying too much for rods, so I called a guy I knew and made a deal."

"A deal?"

I heard the suspicion in his voice. "Nothing illegal, if that's what you're thinking. Just old friends doing each other favors."

He nodded. "Okay, I like it." Joe started to leave and then turned. "You don't know anybody who could help with this other thing, do you?"

"You dealing with Moresco?"

Joe lit up. "Yeah, Johnny Moresco. You know him?"

I shrugged. "I know him, but I don't know if I can do us any good. I'll check if you want."

Joe smiled. "Do that, Nicky." As he left he said, "And I'm sorry about yesterday. I was in a bad mood."

"No problem. You were right." I finished up the day worrying the whole time about Rosa, so I drove faster than I should have to get home. A contributing factor being that neither Rosa nor Angie were answering their cell phones. What were phones for if not to answer? Did they wear them as jewelry? Lose them in their purses? An image of their purses came to mind, and I realized I must have just solved the mystery. That's where both of the phones were.

Now that I felt better about that, I focused on Johnny Moresco and what I'd say to get us in the door. I settled for relying on the friendship I had with his father, Teddy the Tank, and his uncle, Patsy the Whale.

Angie and Rosa were home, both in the kitchen cooking dinner and singing. The two of them had a great relationship and they were two of the happiest people I knew.

"What's for dinner tonight?" I hollered as I came through the dining room.

"Leftovers," Rosa said, and gave me a big hug.

I sniffed the air. "Leftovers, my ass. That smells like homemade ricotta, and that—" He pointed and spoke to Rosa. "Looks like ravioli that your mother is making."

I dipped my finger in the sauce and tasted it. "Needs a pinch of sugar."

She got a defiant look, put one hand on her right hip, and cocked her legs. I laughed. It was the exact same look Angie used to give me when we were teenagers. Normally just before she swung the spoon at me.

"Do what you want," I said to Rosa, "But I'm telling you it needs a little sugar."

Angie glanced over as she finished stuffing ravioli. "If your father says it needs sugar, you better put some in."

"Mom…"

"Trust me, Rosa. He can't cook, but he's a good taster. Every cook needs a good taster. Even Mamma Rosa used your father."

Rosa rolled her eyes, but she grabbed the sugar, and turned back to me. "How much, Chef Niccolo?"

"One tablespoon should do, smart ass."

Rosa laughed, added the sugar, and handed me the spoon. "If you can stir the sauce, I'll pour the wine," she said.

"Anybody follow you today?"

She shook her head. "I didn't see them."

"Good. Now I can eat in peace."

I took the glass of wine Rosa poured and went to the living room to turn some music on. Just then the doorbell rang. A quick detour had me staring at a young, pale-faced kid with a big smile. It hadn't taken Mike Riley long to get his courage back, though I suspected that hormones had a lot to do with it. A fifteen-year-old boy who thinks he's in love will jump in front of a train for the chance at copping a feel, or worse. And though I dreaded to think *that* was going on yet, I was a realist. Despite those thoughts, I smiled.

"Well, if it isn't Mike Riley, the mick who doesn't know he's a mick."

He let out a bashful laugh.

"Come in, Mr. Riley."

As he stepped through the door, I leaned down and whispered, "Mrs. Fusco doesn't know what happened."

His face lit up. "Yes, sir. Thank you."

"Who was at the door?" Angie hollered from the kitchen.

"It's Rosa's friend Mike Riley. You remember him."

Angie came out of the kitchen wiping her hands on the apron that was always wrapped around her while she cooked. It was like a magical apron, as if she couldn't cook without it. She smiled and stretched her hand out to greet him. "It's so good to see you again, Mike. How are you? Are you hungry?"

I watched as she spoke—the way she smiled, the warmth in her voice, her genuine niceness. All the reasons why I loved this woman so much. "Don't fatten him up too much, Angie."

"Oh no, Mr. Fusco. I love Mrs. Fusco's cooking. I don't get things like this at my house."

I jabbed him in the shoulder. "I got news for you, kid. I'm not trying to get rid of her yet, but Rosa is just as good a cook as her mother." From the corner of my eye I saw Rosa whisper to him.

"Better."

"Sit down, Mike. Tell me about yourself." I turned to Rosa. "Pour Mike a glass of wine."

She came and sat on my lap, while she sipped her wine. "Dad, Mike isn't allowed to drink. I told you before, most parents don't give their kids wine."

I shrugged. "All right, you better not then. But tell me about yourself anyway."

Just as Mike started to talk, my phone rang. I flipped it open. "Hello."

It was Johnny Moresco. I had called him on the way home. "Hang on, Johnny, I'm going to step outside."

"Tell me this ain't the same Nicky Fusco I visited in prison when my dad was there."

"Same one, Johnny. And I still owe him one. Tell him I'll drop a few cartons off like I used to in the old days."

There was silence. Then I detected sorrow in Johnny's voice. "Yeah, well, you might have dropped off a few too many, Nicky. Guess you didn't know, but Pops got cancer. He's not doin' too great."

"I didn't know. I'm sorry to hear that."

"Yeah, so anyway, what did you call for?"

"I feel bad for even bringing this up now."

"Go on. This is old times. Tell me."

I breathed in deep. "I work for Joe Tomkins and I know he was trying to bid on the—"

"Say no more. Tell that asshole as long as you're handling the project, he can submit a bid."

I let out a *huge* silent sigh. "Thanks, Johnny. That means a lot."

"Nicky, this isn't a gimme. It's a shot at a bid, that's all. This ain't the old days."

"I know. The old days are long gone, and not for the better." I paused. "Thanks again. My prayers are with your dad."

Angie had dinner on the table when I went back in. It looked and smelled great. I sat between Rosa and Angie, opposite Mike. I said grace—in Latin—despite Rosa's warning glare, and then we talked about the Bobby Campisi case while we ate. I almost laughed at Mike, who seemed to be engrossed with eating, though I couldn't blame him for that. After dinner, he got up and helped with the dishes. He didn't just offer like most people; he jumped in and *did it*. Another plus for the kid. As much as I didn't want to, I liked Mike Riley. A lot.

I grabbed Angie by the arm. "Grab your wine. Let's go out front and talk."

Angie hollered to Rosa. "We're leaving the dishes to you guys."

We sat on the stoop, sipping wine and chatting. I patted her belly. "I meant to ask, should you be drinking wine in your…condition?"

"I checked. A glass or two won't hurt." She kissed me on the cheek. "But thanks for thinking about it."

I kissed her back. "Now there will be a lot more to love."

She beamed. "I was afraid to tell you. I thought—"

I leaned over and kissed her again. "How could I not be happy."

"I meant to ask you earlier," Angie said. "If you're saying someone was after Bobby, how did it happen to take place the same night Frankie kicked his ass?"

I nodded. "Been thinking about that myself. No one could have known Bugs was going there, especially the night of his father's wake."

Angie rubbed my arm. "So that means either it was a God-awful coincidence or—"

"Or the someone who was after Bobby happened to be at the bar that night and took advantage of a situation."

"So who was there?" Angie asked, and took another sip of wine.

"That's what I intend to clarify." I kissed her again. "By the way, did I tell you that you'd make a great detective?"

Her brow furrowed. "Nicky, why isn't Detective Borelli following leads like this?"

"I've been wondering that too. Something's not right."

***

ROSA WASHED THE DISHES and handed them to Mike to dry. "You're slow."

"I'm not used to this. We use a dishwasher at my house."

"They're even slower," Rosa said. "Look, we're almost done."

Mike looked around, making sure they were alone. "We need to tell your dad."

Daggers came out of Rosa's eyes. "Don't you dare say anything."

"I don't like this. We owe him."

"I don't know what your problem is," Rosa said. "He wanted to kill you the day he caught us."

"But he didn't, and I like your dad. He's scary, but he's nice."

Rosa glared at Mike. "If you tell him one thing, you can forget seeing me again." She shoved a pot at him. "Hurry up and dry."

CHAPTER 31

INTERROGATION

Brooklyn, New York

Donovan arrived at the Channel 5 news building at almost the same time as Lou and Sherri. Cindy Ellis met them at the elevator, then set a quick pace down a long hallway.

"I can't believe this is happening," Cindy said. "First the nut leaves me a message telling me there will be more bodies, now he sends me a hand. A hand!"

She turned to Frankie, walking close behind her. "You don't think I'm in any danger do you?"

"He wouldn't dare assault a member of the press," Lou said, and managed to refrain from smiling.

"I hope not." Cindy opened a set of double doors that led to an even longer hallway. About halfway down the corridor, she turned left through a door with an empty nameplate on it. "They had me put it in here," she said, and waited for everyone to enter before closing the door.

A small box sat on a table near the center of the room. She pointed to it. "It's in there."

"We should wait for Kate," Lou said.

"I want to see it," Frankie said. "I'm not touching anything." He opened the lid, peering inside. Sherri Miller stood beside him.

"It's a hand, all right," she said, and leaned back.

"It's got something written on it," Frankie said.

Lou got closer. "What?"

"I can't tell, but something is definitely written in the skin." Frankie closed the lid. "Where is Kate?" He grabbed his cell phone and dialed her number.

"Hello, Donovan. Looking for me?"

"Where are you?"

"About half a dozen floors below you, waiting for an elevator."

"Okay, see you in a few." Frankie turned to Sherri and Lou. "She's on her way up."

Kate arrived a few minutes later with less than a full complement of aides, although her trusted photographer did accompany her. He took photos of the inside of the box, then Kate pulled the hand out and set it on the table, again taking photos of it from all angles. After that, she unwrapped it, removed the clear plastic and examined it. "Looks like you got yourself a real human hand, Donovan."

"I got that far," he said. "What else?"

"By the way, I'm sorry about your father." She never took her eyes from the body part. "I got your message, and I wasn't ignoring you, just busy."

Frankie put his hand on Kate's arm. A tingle raced through him, forcing a shiver. It had been a long time since he'd felt something so good. She turned to him and held his gaze, then got back to work. It was only an instant, but Frankie thought he saw something in her eyes. Enough to bring a smile to his face.

Kate brought the hand closer and narrowed her eyes. "Uh oh."

Frankie moved closer. "What?"

"We got us a religious wacko."

"Are you talking the—"

She nodded. "Yep. Mea culpa," she said. "It's scratched in here real small, but with damn good writing. I'd say this gentleman had good pen-manship."

Lou and Sherri looked at each other at the same time. "Catholic school," they both said.

"Another thing," Kate said. "This isn't a fresh cut. This hand was removed days ago, at best. Maybe more. I won't be able to tell until I get it back to the lab, but it's definitely been a few days." She reached her hand into the box and brought out something else. "Hold on, we've got more. A note."

"What's it say?" Frankie asked, moving closer.

Kate held him off. "Hold on a minute. I'll get it to you as soon as I can." She turned to her assistant. He took a photo of it as she laid it on the table. "Okay, you can take a look. Just don't touch anything."

"What's it say?" Lou asked. "My eyes aren't that good anymore."

Sherri looked close. "Says 'this one belongs on the fifth floor. One more piece to the puzzle.'" She turned to Lou. "You think he means fifth floor of the building where we found the other one?"

"Got to be," Lou said.

Frankie leaned over Kate's shoulder, inhaling her scent. It had been a long time. A very long time. "Anything else?"

Kate shook her head. "That's it. And if you guys are finished with this, I'm taking it with me." Kate put her gear away and leaned in close to Frankie. "I'm busy tonight, but I'll see you later this week."

Frankie smiled. "You got a deal."

"If you two are through having fun," Lou said. "We need to interview a suspect."

Frankie nodded. "You're right about that. Something fishy about this whole thing. And what does that mean, 'one more piece to the puzzle'? You think this asshole is playing some kind of game with us?"

"We're not going to find out standing here," Sherri said.

***

THEY STOPPED OUTSIDE OF the building where Lisa worked. Frankie assumed command despite what he said to Sherri earlier, about her taking the lead.

He lit a cigarette, talking as the smoke poured from his mouth. "We need to check every office on the fifth floor. See if anyone is missing, or has been missing. Kate said that thing was old. Not fresh cut."

"I'll handle that," Sherri said.

"No way. I need you with us. Call it in and have Morreau send a team down here. If he gives you any shit, tell him I said so."

Sherri looked at him as if he were nuts. Tell the lieutenant that? "You want *me* to do that?" Her voice was meek.

"No time like the present to learn, and one thing you'll learn quickly in homicide is if you don't fight for resources, you're screwed."

They walked quickly down the corridor to the office where Lisa worked, flashing badges as soon as they entered the door.

"We need to speak with Lisa Jackson," Frankie said.

"May I ask—"

"No," Lou said, and shoved his badge in front of her again. "Just call her."

Lisa Jackson was not anything like what Sherri expected. She had seen the photo of her, but that must have been a few years ago, and she must have been fifteen or twenty pounds heavier then. And not nearly as gorgeous. She approached them with a confidence not unlike a movie actress, and a smile that any woman would envy. Her eyes were penetrating, and she focused on Sherri as she extended her hand.

"Hi, I'm Lisa Jackson. You must be the detectives they said wanted to see me."

Sherri took her hand. "Detective Sherri Miller," she said and handed her a card, then introduced the others. "This is Detective Lou Mazzetti and Detective Frankie Donovan."

Lisa looked at each of them as she shook their hands, then flashed a smile that was both warm and inviting. From what Sherri could tell from their reactions, it was as if Lisa had undressed. This was going to be a tough interview.

"Is there someplace private we can go?" Sherri asked.

"There's a conference room down the hall. May I get you some coffee, or water?"

"Coffee would be great," Frankie said. "Black."

Sherri frowned, but went along with it. "I'll have some too, please. No sugar and a little cream."

Lisa had someone run for the coffee then led them to a conference room large enough to seat twenty people. She closed the door after Lou straggled in. "What's this about? I assume it has something to do with Ben Davidoff."

Lou looked at Sherri, but she didn't return the look. "Part of it, yes. Did you know Mr. Davidoff?"

Lisa leaned forward and smiled. "I think we both know I did. I had an affair with him for two years."

Sherri didn't move back when Lisa leaned forward; instead, she leaned closer. "Why don't you tell me about it."

Lisa shrugged. "There's not much to tell, Detective. We had an affair. We went to dinner, to movies, to plays, and we slept together. All pretty standard stuff."

If she meant to put Sherri off with her candor it wasn't working. "Wasn't he a little old for you?" Sherri was trying to bust her, but so far she seemed to be telling the truth, and Sherri trusted her truth meter, a built-in one that had worked all of her life.

Lisa looked at Frankie, then at Lou, smiled at each of them, then focused on Sherri. "Have you ever slept with anyone you shouldn't have, Detective? If not, you've lived a pretty dull life."

It took all the willpower Sherri had not to jump across the table and smack Lisa. "Not for two years straight, no. Did it have anything to do with his money?"

Lisa didn't answer, just sat back and looked at her hands, folded in her lap. The runner bringing the coffee provided an interruption. It also gave Lisa something to do with her hands, which she wrapped around the Styrofoam cup as if it were a life jacket. "I'd be lying if I said the money didn't matter. It mattered a lot. Ben's company, and his money, came at a time when I desperately needed both."

Sherri stared for a long time, analyzing the vibes she was getting. She wanted to hang this girl, but the problem was she felt that was the truth too. "When was the last time you saw him?" This would be the answer to trip her.

"Saw him? As in had sex with him? Or saw him as in physically seeing him with my eyes? There's a difference."

"I know the difference, Ms. Jackson. Why don't you answer both?"

Lisa sipped her coffee. "The last time we made love, if you could call it that, was almost two years ago, but I had lunch with him last week, and I saw him two or three times a week on the way up to work in the elevator."

Sherri was disappointed, hoping to catch her in a lie. "Why did you have lunch last week?"

"He called me and said he wanted to talk."

"About what?"

Lisa thought for a moment. "That's the funny thing. He never said. We ate, chatted about some good times we had, and he talked about how he and his wife were going to try to get back together." She seemed to be searching for memories. "Then he thanked me for meeting him and said goodbye. The next thing I heard, he was dead."

Sherri was getting pissed; she couldn't nail this little snot on anything. "So tell me, Ms. Jackson, did you have affairs with anyone else in this building?"

"No," she said, but she said it too quickly, and without the same conviction as her other answers.

I got her now, Sherri thought.

"No? You never had affairs with *anyone* else in this building?"

Lisa hesitated, then lowered her head, tears welling in her eyes. "My husband was in the army in Afghanistan." She pulled a tissue from her purse and wiped her eye. "He was killed, and after that, for a while—too long a while—I had a few flings. Most of them were just one or two nights."

"Who with?"

"I don't know." Once again she cast a sorrowful glance to Frankie and Lou.

"Who?"

"I can't remember."

Sherri pressed hard. "Are you trying to tell me you don't remember the men you had sex with?"

Lisa jumped up from her seat, sending Sherri back. "There were a *lot* of them, okay? A *lot*!" She sat back down. Crying now. "I don't feel good about it. I'm embarrassed, but that's behind me. I don't do that stuff anymore."

The sobbing got worse and she ran out of tissues.

Lou handed her his handkerchief as Lisa cried like a grieving widow.

Finally Sherri gave up. "All right, Ms. Jackson, that will be all for now. If we have any other questions, we'll call."

"Thank you," Lisa said, and shook Sherri's hand. Then she took Frankie's hand, but she held his a lot longer, and squeezed it tighter. She did the same to Lou, but not quite so passionately. "Call me if you need anything else," Lisa said, and walked toward her office.

***

LISA JACKSON BREATHED DEEPLY as she walked down the hall. She had been torn between telling the detectives the truth—that she was being held captive by her lunatic husband—or steering them off course. At the last minute she opted for "off course," and felt she'd handled it well. Detective Miller didn't like her, but Donovan was the one who was watching her for lies. Lisa had done her best with him; if he was like most men—and after seeing him she felt sure he was—he stopped thinking soon after he met her. Stopped thinking of anything productive that is, and focused only on how to get in her pants. Lisa sighed. Now all she had to do was figure out how to kill Tom and save her mother.

CHAPTER 32

PUZZLES AND PRAYERS

Brooklyn, New York

It took twenty minutes to get back to the station, Frankie arriving just before Sherri and Lou. She climbed the steps, staying behind Lou all the way to the second floor. "You want anything to drink, Mazzetti?"

"Water."

"I'll get it. Tell Donovan I'm getting him a coffee." Sherri returned a minute later, shaking her head as she sat at her desk, next to Lou. "Jackson's lying. I don't know about what yet, but something."

"I don't think she had anything to do with it," Lou said.

Sherri pulled out her desk drawer, took out a tablet and pen, poised to write. "Is that your dick talking? Because I thought that little bitch did nothing but lie. I can't point to anything specific, but she lied." Sherri turned to Frankie. "And you, I'm ashamed of you. That girl did everything but reach over and unzip you, and you ate it up."

"You've got to admit, Miller, she was cute."

"Cute? Since when does cute have anything to do with an investigation? She—"

Lou and Frankie laughed loud enough to draw Morreau from his office and Carol from her post.

Carol stood a few feet away, hands positioned on her hips as if she were a teacher ready to dish out a scolding. "What did you guys do to her?"

Frankie managed to bring his laughter under control. "Just an old interview gag. We needed to get her going."

Sherri looked at him, eyebrows raised. "You mean…"

Lou nodded. "We knew she was lying, but it helps if you let them think they fooled you."

Sherri looked at Lou, then Frankie. "You rotten sons of bitches. That wasn't right."

"Rookie jokes are over," Frankie said. "I'm sorry, it's just that—"

Morreau came up behind Frankie. "Rookie jokes better be over, Donovan, because you need this rookie. You and Mazzetti don't have shit. Maybe you better let her call the shots."

"You got it, Lieu."

"What have you got on the hand? Anything yet?"

"We're waiting on Kate to call. Her first take on it was that it's at least several days old, probably more."

"We're guessing it could be the hand of the first vic," Sherri said. "Remember, it was missing hands and feet, and…"

Morreau cringed and his hand instinctively went to his crotch. "Yeah, I remember. All right, push Kate on this one. We need something before the papers go nuts." Morreau left to go to his office and Frankie put his arm around Miller.

"Sorry about the stunt we pulled. It was all in fun."

"I'm glad it *was* a stunt. I was beginning to think I was hooked up with a couple of horny old men."

"You are," hollered Carol from the other room. "Don't let them fool you on that one."

Frankie pulled a chair up next to Sherri and Lou. "All right, let's go over what we've got. And by the way, Miller, for the record, I *know* she was lying. It was all over her face. We couldn't let her know we were on to her, though."

"Yeah, and Frankie called in someone to follow her home tonight."

"What for? We have her address."

"We want to see if she stops anywhere, talks to anyone, does anything different after we saw her. Maybe we'll scare something out of her."

"Okay, good," Sherri said. "Let's get back to what we've got."

Frankie took a notepad from his pocket and flipped the page. "From what you guys told me, and from what we saw today, we got a guy, or guys—"

"Or guy and girl," Lou added.

"Okay, or guy and girl, who kill people and then carve 'mea culpa' into the body."

"He carved up the first one, too. Don't forget that. So why not the second?"

Lou sipped his water. "First one was killed and brought to an apartment house. Second one killed in his office building in the middle of the day." His cell phone rang.

"Mazzetti."

He listened for a second then handed it to Frankie. "Kate."

"You got anything for us?" he asked Kate.

"I can assure you that hand is at least a week old."

"How do you know?"

"Because it matches the rest of the body on the first victim."

"Okay, thanks. I'll call you later."

Frankie handed the phone to Lou. "Hand was from the first vic."

"So why did he wait until now to send it to us?" Sherri asked.

"What was it he said in the note?" Lou asked.

Frankie flipped a page on his notepad. "'This one belongs on the fifth floor. One more piece to the puzzle.'"

Sherri wrinkled her brow. "What does that mean, 'one more piece to the puzzle?'"

Frankie drained the coffee from his cup. "I'm assuming the fifth floor is a reference to the same building. Did we get any results yet on the canvas?"

Lou leaned toward the hall. "Hey, Carol, can you—"

"Already on it," Carol shouted back.

Mazzetti looked at Frankie and Sherri, whispering. "Does she listen to everything we say?"

"Everything," Carol said.

"So we assume that this is the same building and it's on the fifth floor." Sherri stood and paced. "If that's the case, why? Is it coincidence? Does he have something against the owners of the building? What's the connection?"

"Lisa must have something to do with it?" Lou said.

"Or she's next," Frankie added. "She *is* on the fourth floor."

"Son of a bitch," Sherri said. "I didn't think of that."

Frankie stood. "I'm getting more coffee. You want any?"

"I'll take some," Sherri said. "Little bit—"

"I know, no sugar and a little cream."

"Damn, Frankie, you're good. Keep it up and you might make a good waitress."

"You know, that's the first time you called me Frankie."

"Keep getting me coffee, and I'll call you anything you want."

"Lou, how about you?" Frankie asked.

"I'm cutting back," Lou said. "Get me another water, though."

When Frankie returned he handed the water to Lou and the coffee to Sherri. "I've been thinking about it, and I'm of the mind we need to focus on the religious aspect."

"You mean the mea culpas?" Sherri asked.

"Got to be. Everything else could be coincidence or explained some other way, but not the killer carving that into the bodies."

"So let's look at that," Lou said. "We've got mea culpa on the hand, which we now know is the first vic, and mea culpa, mea culpa carved onto the second vic's ass."

Sherri wrote a note on her tablet. "Why, though?"

Frankie thought about it. "Guy has got to be Catholic to even know that term. Possibly an altar boy."

"Or a priest," Lou said.

"Oh shit."

"Yeah. Suppose this is some fuckin' priest who did something really wrong. Wouldn't that justify a mea culpa?"

"Or two?" Sherri said.

Frankie nodded. "When we identify the first vic, we'll see if they went to the same church? Or if not, if the churches they did go to had any of the same priests."

There was a moment of silence, then, "I didn't even ask, Lou, but was the first guy Catholic? The first one we found, not the first one that was killed."

"I don't know." He turned to Sherri, who was already digging in her file.

"He was," hollered Carol.

"Fuck me," Lou said.

"No thanks," Carol answered, and then walked into the room. "And by the way, we have confirmation on the first vic, the one with the hand. His name was Kevin Mercer, and he worked on the fifth floor. They didn't report him missing because he was on vacation." She started to leave then turned back. "And yes, he was Catholic."

Sherri whistled. "That doesn't mean shit by itself, but tie in the Latin stuff and we might have something."

"I don't like it," Frankie said, "but you're right. We just might."

Lou opened the bottled water Frankie brought him. "I'm going to be pissing like a wizard this afternoon."

"Just how do wizards piss?" Sherri asked.

"I don't know. It just sounded good to say that."

Sherri shook her head. "Mea culpa means 'my fault,' right?"

"To get technical, I think in the Confiteor it is translated as 'through my fault, through my fault, through my most grievous fault.'" Frankie stood and bowed. "Altar boy."

"Don't get cocky. Remember, we're thinking of one of them as a possible suspect."

"Screw you, Miller," Frankie said.

Sherri paced again. "Through my fault… So this guy, whoever he is, thinks he's done something wrong."

"Or he's saying the vic did something wrong, and this is the payment," Lou said.

Carol chimed in from her desk. "Or he's a wacko and using the recent rush on blaming the Catholics to cover his sick deeds."

Lou looked out at Carol. "Is there another detective assigned to this case, or is that our smart-ass guard dog?"

"Eat shit, Mazzetti."

"That's my girl," Frankie said.

Sherri raised her brows for about the fifth time today. "I guess it's good I have tough skin. Looks like you need it around here."

Frankie stared at the desktop, saying nothing.

"What's up, Donovan? Not like you to be silent."

He chewed on a pencil for a moment then stood. "Okay, the way I see it is this. We all agree that religion has something to do with it, but we don't have a clue as to what, and we can't go tracking all the priests and altar boys in the city, so we put that on the back burner." He paced, tapping the pencil on the back of his hand. "And we all agree that Lisa Jackson has something to do with it, but we don't have a clue as to what. She could be the killer, the killer's accomplice, or the next victim. We can, however, track her, and fairly easily. So I say we keep our tail on her and when she shows up at the office tomorrow, we take the opportunity to search her apartment."

"We don't have a warrant," Sherri said.

Lou slam dunked his water bottle into the trash. "Maybe you shouldn't come with us, Miller."

She looked at Frankie, then at Lou. "Bullshit. I'm in."

"If you're not comfortable…" Frankie said.

"I'm in," she said.

Lou nodded to her. "Pick me up at seven."

Frankie nodded. "I'll see you guys at the cafe by her work. Seven thirty, maybe eight."

As Sherri said goodbye, Carol nodded, then whispered, "You did good, girl. Don't let them get to you."

CHAPTER 33

TRAPPING THE TRAPPERS

Wilmington, Delaware

I slept very little, thinking all night about the "coincidence" of Bobby's killer striking the very night Frankie and Bobby had a fight. The way I figured it, the killer *had* to have been at the bar. He must have been stalking Bobby, and when he saw what happened with Frankie, he decided to do it that night. It was the only thing that made sense. That still left the question of why Borelli hadn't thought of it. He was the goddamn detective. And of course, it left the bigger question of *who* wanted Bobby dead.

As I dressed for work, I heard the sweet sound of Angie's humming from the kitchen. I think she inherited that habit from Mamma Rosa. Few things in life made me happier than that. She had a way of making my day brighter just by listening to her hum. I bounced down the steps, probably with a little too much vigor. "Morning, babe," I said, and kissed her. "How's my favorite pregnant wife today?"

"What?" I heard from behind me, and froze. I forgot we hadn't told Rosa, though we were planning on it tonight.

When I turned to Rosa, she was racing to embrace Angie, the both of them laughing like silly kids. "I'm going to finally get a baby sister. I can't wait." She then turned to hug me.

"Could be a baby brother," I said.

She hugged me real tight. "I'm so happy for you, Dad. I know this means a lot."

She was right about that. I almost teared up. "We were going to tell you last night, but Mike came by, so we figured we'd do it tonight. My big mouth let it slip."

I kissed them both goodbye, and reminded Rosa not to walk alone. "Maybe we'll get subs tonight," I said as I headed out the door.

JOE TOMKINS WAS IN his office when I got to work. I grabbed a coffee and knocked on his door.

He looked up from the computer and waved me in. "Have a seat."

I shook my head. "I've got a lot to do, Mr. Tomkins. I just wanted to tell you that we can bid that state job for Moresco—"

He jumped up. "How did you arrange that? No, never mind. I don't want to know." He came around the desk to shake my hand. "That's great."

I held up my hand. "Wait. Before you get all excited, there are a few catches." When I said that Joe got a look on his face like I was going to ask for a bribe or something. "Johnny wanted to make it clear that this is a shot at a bid only. There's no fix in on this."

Joe seemed relieved when I said that. "And?"

"And he said he wants me to handle the project." I didn't like saying that, and I hoped he didn't think I put that stipulation in.

Joe hugged me, patting my back. "Nicky, that's all we need is a shot. And I'd be pleased as hell if you handled the project. Tell Johnny we got a deal."

I started to leave, but he called me back, looking me square in the eye. "I misjudged you. Thanks."

"No problem, Mr. Tomkins. It's part of my job."

"Well, from now on your job is going to pay better, and I might even put you in sales when the estimating is slow. You could make good money in sales."

"I like what I do fine, Mr. Tomkins, but I'm willing to try anything." I headed to my office with a *huge* smile on my face. The raise came at just the right time. I started on the day's work but found it difficult to focus; all I wanted to do was tell Angie about the raise. It would ease her worries. Before long Sheila came to the door.

"You have a visitor," she said, but she was leaning over and she whispered it, as if it were a secret.

"Who?"

She leaned in even closer. "A nun. She said her name is Sister Mary Thomas."

I smiled and got up from my desk. "That's okay. She's a friend of mine from way back."

Sister Thomas came in and I hugged her. "A cloudy day just got brighter."

"I could say you're full of something, Mr. Fusco, but I'd have to go to confession."

I laughed as I offered her a seat, then pulled up another chair and sat opposite her. A serious look crossed my face. I knew if Sister Thomas was here it was something important.

"There are two children who have come to me with something they want to get off their chests, but they need secrecy. No one must know."

"This about Bobby Campisi?"

She nodded. "They saw something that night."

"When do I meet them?"

"I'll let you know. Maybe tonight, maybe tomorrow. But you must assure me—"

I nodded. "No problem, Sister. You know me."

"Good. Then I must be going. I'll call you."

"Wait, I'll walk you out. I've got to see about leaving early anyway." I went down the hall to Joe's office, figuring he couldn't be too upset about me leaving a little early after getting the bid. I poked my head inside. "Mr. Tomkins?"

He got up and came over, surprised, I think, to see a nun with me.

"Joe, I was wondering if I could take off the rest of the day. I know it's not a good time, but my wife just told me we're going to have a baby, and I wanted to celebrate."

Sister Thomas hugged me, her face all excitement. "Niccolo, you didn't tell me! That is wonderful. I know Angela must be excited."

Joe smiled too. "By all means, Nicky, for God's sake…" He bowed to Sister Thomas. "Forgive me, Sister, I didn't mean…"

"Don't be silly."

"Joe, I forgot, this is Sister Mary Thomas," I turned to her and said, "Sister, this is—"

She reached out her hand. "Joe and I know each other," she said, "but by his look of confusion, I can tell he doesn't remember me." She smiled. "You would have known me back in school as Concetta Panelli. We spent a few years under Sister Gertrude's tutelage."

His eyes lit up. "Concetta!" he said, and that started the conversation rolling. I left while it was in progress.

As I drove home, I decided to watch for Rosa's mysterious followers. I parked off to the side of the church and watched as she walked home with her friends. I spotted them right away, and they didn't waste time. They drove slowly past her, then parked about a block up the street under a big sycamore. I figured out the rest of the drill; they'd wait for her to pass, and one of them would jump out and grab her.

My gut churned and my heart raced a million miles an hour. *What the hell is going on?* Once they got situated, I got out of the car and walked at a strong pace up the other side of the street, my head lowered, watching Rosa the whole time. I had my baseball cap on and a small derringer underneath it. Not a powerful weapon but it would do the job at close range, though if I got in that close I probably didn't need a gun.

I was halfway up the block when they got out of the car and approached her. They were moving fast. My heart raced faster. I moved quick and silent. One of them reached for her, his hand on her shoulder.

"Why don't you come with me?"

I was almost to him when he touched her. I closed the remaining distance with lightning speed, then struck. Spreading my arms wide, I grabbed their heads, smashing them together like they used to in the *Three Stooges* shows. It sounds stupid, but I don't know a quicker way to disable and disorient two people. One of them fell. I grabbed the other in a chokehold. I fought, forcing calm so I didn't kill him.

"Why are you following my daughter?"

He gasped, unable to speak. I let off some on the hold. The other guy stirred. I kicked him in the gut, knocking him over.

"We're cops," the guy I had in a chokehold said. "We're goddamn cops."

The fear in my gut grew worse, but I wasn't buying it without proof. "Show me."

He opened his jacket and I saw the badge. When I let go, he spun around, looking like he wanted to hit me. I stood firm. He helped the other guy up. "You okay, Tim?"

Tim rubbed his head. "I'm all right," he said, then glared. "Who the fuck are you?"

"I'm her father, and watch your mouth."

Rosa had tears in her eyes. "What's going on, Dad?"

I hugged her. "You and your friends go home. I'll take care of this."

Tim started to say something but the other guy stopped him. "I could arrest you for assaulting an officer."

I shook my head. "No jury in the world is buying that. I'm her father, and she tells me she's being followed, then I see two guys come out of a car and lay their hands on her." I shook my head again. "No way in hell." I poked my finger in the one guy's chest. "Why are you following her?"

"We got orders."

"Orders? You're driving a car with PA tags. Whose orders?"

Tim got a confused look on his face, but it cleared. "This was my brother Mike's car. I just bought it off him and haven't changed the tags yet."

"You didn't tell me who ordered you to follow Rosa," I said.

"You'll have to ask Borelli about that."

"Borelli?" I wanted to hit this guy. If Borelli had been there I would have hit him. "Tell him to see me if he wants something. This girl is a minor and I forbid any questioning of her without me being present." I stared from one to the other. "Got that, boys?"

"Borelli will be pissed."

"Good, because I'm more than pissed. And you can tell him that."

Tim laughed. "I don't think Detective Borelli will care whether you're pissed."

I moved real close to Tim, within inches of his face. "He'll care, *Tim*. Believe me. And you can tell him Nicky the Rat told you to say so."

CHAPTER 34

SETTING TRAPS

Brooklyn, New York

All the way home Lisa thought about how to handle Tom. She couldn't just kill him. She had to find a way to get her mother safe first. Lisa got off the elevator, and took her time getting to the door, making sure to wear a frown as she entered.

"What's the matter with you?" Tom asked.

She dropped her purse in the chair by the door. "They came to the office today. They *interrogated* me."

"Who did?"

"The cops. Three of them." She ran to the kitchen and grabbed a glass of water. "I'm scared."

"Don't worry about it," Tom said. "They question everyone when something like this happens."

The girl came out of the bedroom, naked, and looking puzzled. "When something like what happens? What happened?"

"Go back to the room," Tom said. "You come out when I tell you."

She disappeared behind the door, but Lisa felt sure she was standing there listening. It's what she would have done. "We've got to get out of here. We can't stay."

Tom muted the TV and put his head down. "I've got to think," he said. "Give me time to think."

"I need to see my mom."

"Bullshit," said Tom.

"I just need to see that she's all right," Lisa said.

Tom grabbed her hair and yanked it. "I'll worry about that old hag. You worry about those detectives."

"Okay, Tom. Let go."

Tom released her hair, walked to the window, and peeked through the blinds.

"What are you looking for?" Lisa asked.

"I'm sure they followed you. They'd have to be pretty stupid not to."

"I checked. No one followed me."

He laughed. "You couldn't check shit," he said, then looked up and down the street. "Oh, yeah. There they are."

She ran beside him, peering out. "Where?"

"See that woman waiting by the bus stop? The Latina?"

"She's waiting for a bus."

"No, she's not. Look at how she's looking around at everything, everything but over here." Tom pulled Lisa closer. "Take a close look and tell me she's not a cop. Go on."

"I'm sorry."

"I just wanted you to see how stupid you were. I swear, I don't know why I ever married you." He closed the blinds and went back to sitting on the sofa.

In the morning, Lisa made coffee and then headed to work. She decided during the night, while Tom was fucking that *girl*, that she would talk to Donovan today. Maybe.

***

FRANKIE WAS AT THE cafe long before Sherri and Lou arrived. He had a lot of thinking to do, especially about what was going on in Wilmington. Nicky called last night and the news wasn't good. Not a single lead that would clear him or point to another person in Bobby's death. And Frankie wasn't faring much better in Brooklyn. They had nothing, unless you counted the one interview of the lady from the office building. But an affair with the deceased didn't point to a murder suspect, especially when the lady's husband is dead. Still, they might find something at her house.

Frankie got another coffee, a cappuccino this time, and sat at the table, opening the paper to the business section. Not like he had investments to keep track of, he just liked reading the business news. As he scanned the technology section he heard Sherri's friendly greeting.

"Good morning, Frankie."

Frankie set the paper down. "How's it going, Miller? Surprised you could be so chipper after riding in with the grump."

"Mazzetti? He's a prince. I heard you were the nasty one."

"Yeah, you know how it works…first one to the well, and all that."

Sherri shook her head. "I don't know what you're talking about."

"He doesn't either," Mazzetti said, returning with two coffees. "He picks up sayings now and then from other cultures and tries to use them, but he usually gets it wrong." Lou grabbed a chair from an empty table next to them. "That one comes from some desert race. You know how they talk about water and wells and thirst."

"I guess in—"

Lou waved his hand as if to brush her comment away. "Nah, means nothing. They just like to sound philosophical."

Sherri stood. "I'm starting to rethink what Frankie said about who the grump in the morning is."

Lou tossed his half-filled coffee cup into the trash and stood with her. "I knew you'd side with the handsome one. Haven't you learned from the movies yet that the good looking guy is always mean and the old grumpy guy is nice."

"I don't have time to scratch through all that, Lou."

"Then I guess we better get going?" Lou said, and turned to Frankie. "How do you want to do this?"

"Might as well ride together," Frankie said. "We can all fit in my car."

They drove for about twenty minutes through medium traffic. Sherri pointed to the street coming up and said, "Turn right here. It's just up the block."

"You know this area?" Frankie asked.

"It's a lot like the rest of Brooklyn. Everybody minds their own business, so we probably can't count on any help from neighbors."

"Do we know she's at work?" Frankie asked. "Anybody check yet?"

"I did," Sherri said. "Monica said Lisa came in a few minutes late, but she's still there."

"Then all we have to do is wait."

Sherri looked over at him. "For what? I thought you said we were going in?"

"We are, but we have to wait for someone to come into the building. I'm not breaking down the front door."

"But you'll break into her apartment?"

Lou looked at Frankie, who turned to her. "I guess you could put it that way."

"Everybody got their phones off?" Lou asked. "Can't afford a goddamn ring tone going off while we're sneaking inside."

"Mine's off," Sherri said.

"How are things going in Wilmington?" Mazzetti asked.

"Shit, that reminds me," Frankie said. "I've got to call Nicky."

Lou looked at him with narrowed eyes, then turned to Sherri. "Give us a minute, will you, Miller?"

Sherri cocked her head to Frankie, then back to Lou, but she stepped away. When she was out of earshot, Mazzetti said, "Don't tell me you're still hanging out with that damn Rat guy? *Please* don't tell me that."

"Forget about it, Lou."

"Forget about it?" Lou paced. "You might have fooled the rest of them with your bullshit, but I know who killed all those people, and it wasn't Tito Martelli."

"You don't know anything about him," Frankie said. "He…never mind."

"I know you risked your career for him. You better ask yourself what he's ever done for you. That's all I'm saying."

Frankie tensed, jaw tightening. "I said *forget about it*."

"Yeah, I'll forget all right. I'll forget I ever fuckin' knew you when they come to put the cuffs on."

Frankie looked over to Sherri and waved her to come back. She didn't ask what that was all about, but the question was on her face.

About fifteen minutes later a lady carrying a bag of groceries walked up the sidewalk toward the apartment.

"That's us," Frankie said, and approached her. Sherri and Lou followed him.

He got to the door just ahead of her and flashed his badge. "We need to get inside, and we'd like to keep this quiet." He leaned close to her. "Undercover operation."

She raised her eyebrows. "Oh my. All right. Follow me in." She opened the door with her key then stepped aside. "Drugs?"

Lou held his finger to his lips. "Can't say."

She nodded as if she were in on the whole thing.

Frankie and Sherri waited at the elevator for Lou, then pushed the button for the fourth floor.

"Good thing they've got elevators," Lou said. "Otherwise you'd be doing this yourselves. Me and steps parted ways."

Frankie tapped Sherri on the shoulder as they rode up in the elevator. "I know this is all new to you, so listen up. We're going in on the sly, as they say. That means no warrant, no record of us going in. It also means no clues left. No fingerprints, no DNA, nothing. Got that?"

"Sounds illegal to me."

"Never thought of it that way," Lou said.

"We play fair," Frankie said. "If we find something connected to the murders we use it to nab her somehow. But if we find drugs or anything else, we leave it be."

She looked at him with a doubtful stare. "Really?"

"No shit," Lou said. "For real."

"All right, I can buy into that. Let's go."

About then the elevator stopped and they got off, making their way to #412. Frankie held up his fingers, signaling them to keep quiet, then leaned his head in and listened at the door. He signaled Sherri over, cautioning her to be quiet, and whispered real low. "You hear that? TV is on."

"Could be she just left it on," Sherri said.

"Let's go in," Lou said.

Frankie listened closely then looked at Lou and Sherri. "I think somebody's in there."

***

LISA JACKSON WALKED UP and down the hall outside her office. She knew what she *should* do was call Donovan, but every time she pulled out her phone, she thought about her mother and what would happen to her if Donovan couldn't get Tom to talk.

The hell with it, she finally said, and dialed the number Donovan had given her. It rang twice then went to voicemail. Lisa almost hung up, but decided to leave a message. "Detective Donovan, this is Lisa Jackson. I need to talk with you right away. It's important. Very important." Before she hung up, she said, "Oh, and *do not* call back on this number. I'll call you later."

***

TOM JACKSON HEARD A noise outside the door. He was tempted to mute the TV, but if they had heard it, then they'd know someone was in here.

He grabbed the girl, pulled her onto the sofa and pressed his knife against her throat. He leaned in close and whispered in her ear, "Quiet, girl. Very quiet or I'll bleed you."

She nodded, not saying a word.

He got up from the sofa and, with her neck under his arms, walked slowly toward the door, his knife still pressed against her neck. When he reached the wall he leaned close, listening. The girl was good, he had to admit. She never made noise, not even a gasp when the lock seemed to move. The cops were out there. Tom thought about what he'd do if they came in. Not much he could do. *Guess I'll have to kill them.*

He planned it out, moving a little farther behind where the door would open. He'd leave them just enough room to open the door and get inside, then he'd spring from behind it and take them one at a time, each one with a swift cut to the neck, or a jab into the lungs. He felt the girl tremble. Her fear gave him comfort. She'd be no trouble.

***

SHERRI PUT HER EAR to the door and listened. She nodded to Frankie then stepped back into the hall, motioning for them to come to her.

"What's up?" Lou asked.

"I'm with Frankie. Somebody's in that apartment."

"Are you sure it's not just the TV?" Lou asked.

"I'm pretty sure," Sherri said. "I think I heard footsteps."

"We have to break it off," Frankie said. "We can't risk blowing this whole case because we don't have a warrant."

"Then we need to post some uniforms outside, and we need to keep tabs on Lisa."

Sherri nodded. "I'll call as soon as we're outside."

***

LISA JACKSON GOT OFF the subway and ran most of the way home. Her pulse raced, and she felt short of breath even though this was nothing compared to her normal workouts. She raced up the steps from the subway, weaving in and out of people, then darted across the street, dodging cars and cabs while trying to stay focused.

A bit of calm returned after she entered her building, and more after she got in the elevator, a sense of safety coming with each floor. She exited on the fourth floor and turned toward her apartment, stopping halfway to make sure of what she was doing. Her life, and her mother's life, might hinge on what she decided to do next. She closed her eyes, thought about it, and then pulled out her cell. She pounded out a text.

> *Detective Donovan, I tried reaching you today. I won't be able to talk later, so meet me at the cafe by my house at 8:30 tomorrow morning. And do not try to contact me.*

Lisa deleted the message from the sent list, put the phone back in her purse, took a deep breath and headed for the door. Forgive me, Mom, if I'm wrong.

"Tom?" she called as she entered. When he didn't answer, she called again. "Tom?"

She made her way quickly to the bedroom to ask the girl where he was, but she was gone too. "What the hell?"

In the kitchen was a note.

> *'I want you to go to the Monterrey Motel, room #213. Don't tell anyone. Don't call anyone. I decided you were right about getting out of town. I've got the old hag with me, but you only got two hours to see her, then she goes back. Better hurry. I have Buster.'*

Lisa closed her eyes and said a prayer. She *had* done the right thing. She grabbed the note, and her purse then headed out. She could be at the Monterrey Motel in half an hour.

CHAPTER 35

MEA MAXIMA CULPA

Brooklyn, New York

Lisa got off the subway and walked the four blocks to the motel in record time. She climbed the stairs to the second level and headed down the concrete walkway toward #213. Her heart beat fast in anticipation of seeing her mother.

As she passed room #205, the door opened. Tom reached out and grabbed her, yanking her inside. His hand covered her mouth before she had a chance to scream. Once inside, he held a knife to her throat.

"Are you alone?"

Lisa nodded. "Yes! I did just what you said. Where's Mom?" She looked around the room, heart racing. "Where's Mom? And where's Buster?"

Tom pointed toward the bathroom. "Buster's in there, but your mother's not here. I have her across the street. I wasn't going to trust you."

"Is that why you said 213?"

Tom smiled. "In case your detective friends came with you." He took Lisa by the arm. "Get Buster and then we'll go see your mother."

***

Frankie got in early, got coffee, and went looking for Lou. "Mazzetti, where are you?"

"He's in the pisser," Carol said. "What do you need?"

Sherri Miller came around the corner just then. "What's up?"

"Do we have backup arranged?" he asked.

"We got it," Sherri said. "You think this is real?"

"Hell no, it ain't real," Lou said as he exited the men's room, zipping up his pants. "She's either trying to get into Frankie's pants, or she's plotting something."

"What could she be plotting?" Sherri asked.

Frankie's expression said it all. "It could be anything. I don't trust her." He looked at Sherri. "Who do we have watching her apartment?"

"Fernandez and Troy," Sherri said, "And I just spoke to them a few minutes ago. Nothing of interest."

"Where are you meeting her?" Lou asked.

"Cafe by her house, at 8:30."

"Backup is supposed to be there by 8:00, so they can see anybody setting up in advance."

"And we'll be set up across the street," Sherri said.

Frankie thought about it and nodded. "All right, sounds good. Let's get it rolling."

FRANKIE SHOWED UP AT 8:15, ordered a coffee and a biscotto and took a seat at a sidewalk table farthest from the front door. From there he could see anyone coming, and, more importantly, so could the backup and Lou and Sherri. At 8:30 Frankie went to the men's room to relieve himself. When he came out he got a cappuccino, then walked to his table, all the while eyeing the booths and tables inside the cafe. Lisa Jackson was nowhere to be found.

He looked at his watch three times between 8:30 and 8:45, but it didn't make matters any easier. She still hadn't shown and he was still waiting. His cell phone chirped and he picked it up. "Donovan."

"What do you think? She coming or not?"

"Mazzetti, you've been watching me. Have I had any communications with anyone besides you?"

"You realize you're a prick, right, Donovan?"

"I know. Now if you want to do something worthwhile, see if she's at work. Maybe she got held up."

A few minutes later, Frankie's cell phone rang. He picked it up. "What do you want?"

A female voice, or what sounded vaguely like one, came over the receiver. It was Carol.

"I just had a call from Cindy Ellis. The nut called her again and said we should check out the Monterrey Motel, room #213."

"Are you shitting me?"

Carol sighed. "Yeah, Donovan. I'm shitting you. I waited all day to call you up and pull this on you. Now how about you get your ass over to the Monterrey Motel, huh?"

"Tell your husband he'll be in my prayers tonight, Carol. And every night thereafter." Frankie hung up and dialed Mazzetti. "Change of plans. Cindy Ellis got a call about the Monterrey Motel. Pick me up, and let backup know. We'll want them with us."

Twenty minutes later they were in the motel parking lot. Once backup arrived, Frankie deployed them and then he and Lou and Sherri went to the front desk, flashing badges. "Need the key to room #213," Frankie said. "And we want to go in quiet."

The clerk handed him the key, and went back to his business as if this was a daily routine. Frankie started up the steps, but stopped about half-way up, turning toward Lou. "Mazzetti, why don't you stay here. Sherri and I can take this."

Lou didn't hesitate. "You won't get an argument from me. Go get 'em, Miller."

They finished climbing the stairs and moved quickly to the room. Frankie and Sherri drew guns, and Frankie knocked on the door. When no one answered he knocked again.

"This the right room?" Sherri asked.

"That's what Carol said. Room #213."

"I don't like it. We should go in."

"Yeah, I thought I heard something in there anyway, maybe someone in trouble." Frankie looked at Miller. "Just in case a judge asks."

Frankie handed the key to Sherri and held the gun in firing position. He nodded to her and she turned the key, kicking it open.

"Son of a bitch!" Frankie said, and stopped dead about four feet in. A young girl lay naked on the bed, covered in blood. He swept the room, then headed toward the bathroom. "Cover me."

"Right behind you."

When he cleared the bathroom, Sherri stepped outside and called Lou and the others up while Frankie called Kate. Sherri leaned on the railing and took deep breaths of fresh air. "This is my third homicide but this one's the worst. Sick son of a bitch is what this guy is."

Frankie put a hand on her shoulder, causing her to jump, but then she looked at him. "Who does shit like this?"

"Try to remember they're gone now. It doesn't hurt them anymore. And these sick bastards do it just as much to hurt the living as they do the dead. They know it's shocking."

"They're right."

"Yeah," Frankie said. "I know."

Just then Lou made the final climb and started the journey down the walkway. "I'm going to presume that we've got another stiff or you wouldn't have dragged my ass all the way up here."

Frankie headed back to the room. "Take a look."

The body lay on the bed, face up and naked. A note was pinned to her face.

'Guess I won't be talking too much today, Mr. Donovan.'

And beneath it, on her chest was carved 'mea maxima culpa,' ending at a spot just above her vagina.

"That's not her," Lou said.

"Right. It's not," Frankie said. "So who is it?"

Sherri shook her head. "Can't be more than seventeen or eighteen. My God, her life was just starting."

Sherri shook her head while she stared at the body. She thought about her own life and how she'd been lost and alone at seventeen, on drugs, damn near a prostitute. She'd have ended up like this one if not for one caring cop, but that was just luck. Not everybody got those breaks.

She looked at the body again. *This girl sure didn't.* Sherri said a silent prayer and tried to control the anger rising in her, but she wasn't very successful. This anger was too deep rooted. "You know what I'm going to do, Mazzetti? I'm gonna kill this fucker, that's what I'm gonna do."

CHAPTER 36

MONROE

Wilmington, Delaware

I didn't like what was happening to me. All of this time, since getting out of prison, I managed to stay out of trouble and keep my temper under control. Suddenly things were getting away from me. Three times today I thought about calling Knuckles and telling him "yes," then have him give me the name of that scum in Philly. And though I managed to fight off the feeling, I worried whether I could do it again tomorrow and the next day.

A passing thought came to me about something Rosa said the other day, about another shooting on Harrison Street, in the Presidents' District. That made me think of Monroe. I hadn't seen him since prison, and though the relationship we had there had endured for more than a few years it was still a tentative one, founded on mistrust and glued together by connections and smuggling cigarettes. I wondered what his reaction would be to seeing me now.

Despite my reservations, I decided I had to see Monroe. From what I remembered he usually kept to his part of town, but Bobby had fifty large in the bank. To me that screamed drugs. If drugs were involved Monroe might know something. It was worth a shot. That night after supper I prepared for my venture to the dark side—the President's District was the meanest, most dangerous part of town. I put a Beretta in my waistband and another Beretta behind my back. I also wore my special hat, rigged to hold a derringer. A long gray shirt draped over my jeans and the cap said "Phillies."

I got in the car and headed out, carefully plotting how to do this. It had to be just right, or I'd never see my new baby. Monroe was not the kind of guy who played games. He'd either shoot me as I stood, or we'd do business. It was a risk, but one worth taking.

MONROE WASN'T HIS REAL name; it was the street he grew up on, the south side of it just below Seventh. Willie Parker was the name his mamma had given him at birth, but by the time he was six, kids were calling him Monroe, mostly because he ran up and down that street as if he owned it. He would race down the hill to Fourth Street and then back up again to Seventh, though he never ventured farther than that either way.

All cities had territories, and there were always bigger kids, and meaner ones, on the other side of the boundaries. Sometimes those territories had noticeable boundaries—a four-lane busy street, a city park, a creek or river. Monroe Street had numbered cross streets, and the area between Fourth and Seventh belonged to Monroe even at that young age.

Willie "Monroe" Parker never got very big, and he was cursed with a face that made him look as if he hadn't matured. He had a smile that complemented that look, but underneath it lurked a vicious man. He'd cut half a dozen boys with knives before he was ten, and had taken a slice or two of his own—two of them still shining white against his ebony skin—one on the left side of his neck and one across his lip. The lip-one gave him a funny way of talking, and that whole package—youthful looks, funny voice, and friendly smile—could be deceiving as hell. Many a tough guy had gone to the hospital after mistaking him for an easy mark. A few went straight to the morgue. At times he reminded me of Don Cheadle in that movie with Denzel Washington, *Devil in a Blue Dress*, laughing one minute and cutting you or blowing your head off the next.

Prison is supposed to rehabilitate a person, give them a fresh start on life. When Monroe got out he started fresh, forced to reclaim his old territory. By the time he was done with it, the boundaries had expanded. And from what I heard, he now controlled from Third to Eighth on Monroe Street, and all of the cross streets from Washington to Harrison. He had all the presidents locked up, which is why it was now called the President's District, and Monroe owned all of it.

In prison, Monroe ran the black gang, and I'd needed to make deals, so I approached him first, offering the sweetest deal on smuggling smokes into the prison. It was a smart move for me. I had the best connections and could guarantee the smokes got past the guards, but I left the distribution to Monroe, letting him make any deal he wanted with the other inmates. I took very little of a cut too. Money wasn't that important, but staying safe was. And making connections. This did both for me. Nobody wanted to fuck with the dude bringing the smokes in.

I pulled into a space by St. Francis' Hospital, parking on the Dupont Street side, at the edge of Little Italy. I walked down Seventh Street, past Tilton Park, planning out what I'd say when the time came. It didn't take long to attract attention. Before I got halfway down the next block, three young toughs were following me. At the corner of Seventh and Franklin, I turned around, hands in my pockets.

"Here to see Monroe."

They stopped about twenty feet from me. "What's a white boy got to see Monroe about?"

"He'll want to see me. Why don't you let him decide?"

One of them lifted his shirt, showing me he was packing. "How about you move on down, and take your hands out."

I opened my coat, lifting my shirt to let them see. "Easy, guys. I'm showing you my gun, so don't get nervous. Like I said, I'm here to see Monroe."

The guy in front took my gun, a sneer on his face. "What the fuck's a white boy like you want with Monroe?"

"Already told you, he'll want to see me. We're old friends." I fixed him with the hawk eyes I inherited from my father.

The man stared at me for a few seconds before turning away. "You follow me, bitch, and don't even think of trying anything."

I slowly let my hands drop, then turned and walked even slower, taking a right on Monroe Street. Music blared from a stereo about halfway down the block. From the sound I could tell it was a good stereo. I could almost feel the street vibrate from the heavy bass. One of the guys behind me was talking on his cell, audible even over the beat of the music. Just before we got to the house where all the music was, Monroe came out to the sidewalk, thin leather coat over jeans and sporting the newest fashion in shades.

He removed the shades, then laughed, heading toward me with his hand extended. "If it ain't my white brother. I thought you'd be dead by now."

I smiled and took his hand. It was the reaction I'd hoped for, but I wasn't sure I'd get it; it had been a long time. "Been a while, Monroe."

"That ain't no shit, brother. Come on in." He waved to his boys behind me. "It's all right. Go on about your business."

The man who had taken my gun handed it to Monroe, who smiled real wide. "My man, Nicky. What are you here for?"

"Here to talk."

"Let's go talk then." He grabbed my shoulder and led me toward the door where music blared from the windows. "Let's find us a place to relax."

I stopped. "Before we go, I need to tell you—I have two more guns on me. One in the back and one under my hat."

Monroe turned quickly, and stared at me.

I stared back. "Didn't know what I'd find."

"Same old fuckin' Nicky. What, you were gonna come in here and shoot up my whole place?"

"Didn't want to."

Monroe's face lost all expression. He still held my gun. Quick as lightning, he jammed it against his man's head, shoving him into the brick wall. "I ought to goddamn kill you, nigger. Lettin' a man in here with three fuckin' guns. You tryin' to get me killed, nigger? Are you?" Monroe yanked the man's head back and slammed it into the wall, then prepared to shoot him.

I watched but said nothing.

"Please, Monroe? Man, I didn't check him 'cause I thought you knew him."

Monroe looked to me. "What do you think? Should I kill him?"

"I'd keep him. From what I hear, you're going to need all the soldiers you can get."

Monroe handed the gun to me, but kept staring at the guy against the wall. "Better thank this white boy, Dupree. He *owns* your ass now."

He smacked Dupree on the side of the face, then walked up the steps into the house. He had taken three of the row houses and knocked out walls to make it all one unit, and he had redone the entire inside. We sat in a living room three times the size of the original.

"What brings you here?" Monroe lit a smoke and offered me one.

I brushed it off. "Still don't smoke."

"You still running?"

"When I can. Five miles a day on nice days. No rain or shit."

"My man," he said and flashed his gold. "You been back a while and just now come to see me. I'm guessing it has to do with Bobby Campisi."

"I was hoping you'd be connected like that. I need to know what happened, what got him killed, who he dealt with, and, of course, the ultimate, who killed him?"

Monroe's laugh was genuine, and loud, and contagious. I almost found myself laughing along with him. "And you expect me to give you all this? For what?"

"Old times, I guess. I've got no money."

Monroe got up and came back with a few beers, tossing one to me. We talked about Campisi, about the state of the world, about old times, and we generally had fun. I liked this guy, despite what he did. Before I knew it, a couple of hours had gone by. He looked at his watch and stood. "I'll tell you what. I'll put the word out, see what I can do for you. I ain't making no promises, but...I'd bet I can find out something."

I hugged him, thanked him for the beers, and made my way out.

"You need an escort?" he asked as I walked out the door.

It was my turn to laugh. I was still laughing halfway up the block.

***

DuPree looked out the window at Nicky through cracked blinds. "What the fuck's that white dude laughing about. I should have shut his fucking mouth when I saw him."

Monroe laughed so loud, the others joined him and didn't even know why. Then Monroe leaned toward DuPree and stared at him. "Nigger, let me tell you something. You ever try to kill *that* white dude, he'll take you out before your thoughts are clear. You know who the fuck that was?"

DuPree said nothing, his face as hard as steel.

Monroe smiled. "That was Nicky 'the Rat' Fusco. And there's only one thing you need to know about Rat—he don't care if you're white or black or orange; he'll kill you just the same. And when *The Rat* kills somebody, it ain't fun."

DuPree swallowed hard. His eyes showed he recognized the name, or at least the reputation.

Monroe nodded. "Yeah, that's right, nigger. The Rat."

CHAPTER 37

DREAMS OF DYING

Brooklyn, New York

Tom Jackson watched from across the street, checking to see who came and what they brought for backup. He saw the SWAT team and the other detectives, the old man and that young sexy black thing. Maybe he'd fuck her when this was all done with. Tie her up and show her what a real man was.

He looked over at Lisa. "What do you think? Should I fuck the black bitch?"

"I think you better tell me where my mother is, goddamnit."

Tom laughed. "You didn't like me fucking the girl, did you?" Lisa didn't answer. "I know you didn't. But it serves you right for what you did. Maybe that'll teach you a lesson."

"Where's Mom?"

Tom closed the blinds and turned toward Lisa. "I killed her."

Lisa narrowed her eyes. "Killed who?"

"The old hag. Your mother."

Lisa's head started shaking side to side, slow at first, then faster. Then she exploded toward Tom, hands outstretched, nails scratching at his face. "Noooo!"

Tom grabbed one of her hands and twisted it behind her back. He kicked her legs out from under her, toppling her to the floor. She landed with a thud, and then he kicked her in the back. "If you rouse the neighbors, I'll kill you."

A scream erupted from Lisa, but Tom silenced her by stomping on her stomach, taking all the wind from her lungs. He picked her up, dragged her to the bed, and gagged her. Afterwards he tied her hands and feet. "Guess you used up all your luck, old girl."

***

FRANKIE LEANED ON THE railing, smoking his third cigarette since they arrived, and wondering what was taking Kate so long. "What do you think, Miller? What do the mea culpas mean?"

"More importantly, where is Lisa Jackson? And who is this?" Sherri nodded back to the room. "That's a young kid. No way she fits in with the other two."

Lou grabbed Frankie's cigarette and took a drag then handed it back to him. "And did Jackson do it, or was she part of it."

Frankie looked at Lou as if he were nuts. "Did you just take my smoke?"

"I think I did, yeah. I'm trying to save you, for Christ's sake. Make you smoke a little less."

"She had to at least be part of it," Sherri said. "The big question is how much a part."

The sound of footsteps brought their attention to the end of the walk. Kate Burns and a few of her lab techs were coming up.

Kate waved. "Good to see you again, Frankie. You, too, Sherri." Kate frowned. "And even you, Mazzetti."

"I get the picture now," Lou said. "It's Frankie and Sherri on a first name basis, but then it's Mazzetti."

Kate smiled and smacked him on the arm. "What have we got today?"

"Same killer. Different type of vic. This one's a young girl."

"Messages?"

"Mea maxima culpa," Lou said.

"So, our Latin is expanding. If he keeps going, we'll run out of body parts."

"This one was stretching it," Sherri said. "She was still a teenager from the looks of it, and as skinny as they all are nowadays."

Kate walked into the room and shook her head. "Damn shame is what it is. I hate to see the young ones."

Sherri studied the body, then looked to Kate. "Could a woman be doing this?"

Kate cocked her head, her eyebrows raised. "I want to say no, but it's possible. It would be a first for me to see a woman doing such brutal killing, but it's happened before." She removed her gloves and put them in a bag. "She could be the accomplice, though. I'm still convinced it's two killers, although the second vic didn't show signs of that."

"You really think a woman could be the accomplice?" Frankie asked.

"As I told Lou before, it looks to me like two people are doing this. I'd almost bet on one of them being a woman. Or…"

"Or what?" Lou asked.

"Or it could be the male lover of the other."

"Tell me about it," Frankie said.

"The wounds are tentative, as if the second person doesn't want to do it. So either they aren't into it, or they're being controlled by the other person."

Frankie turned to Sherri. "Suddenly I'm feeling like a stupid ass. We need to get into Jackson's apartment."

Lou put a smoke in his mouth but kept it unlit. "I already called for a warrant. Morreau said he'd have it hand-delivered to the judge. No problem getting one now, not with Lisa being either a suspect or a potential vic."

Frankie cracked his knuckles while he thought. "Okay, Lou. Tell them to meet us at her place with a warrant. We're going over now." He turned to Kate. "If you get anything exciting, call me."

Kate made eyes at him. "Could I just whistle, Detective? I *do* know how to whistle."

Frankie's laughter echoed as he raced down the steps. "That's why I love you, Kate Burns. You're the only M.E. I know who can recite old movie dialogue."

CHAPTER 38

EYEWITNESSES

Wilmington, Delaware

J immy Borelli stopped by our house around dinner time the next day. People always seemed to stop by our house at dinner. I wondered if it was because of Angie's reputation for great cooking, and of inviting everyone in to eat. Angie greeted him as if he were a long lost friend.

"Jimmy Borelli, what a surprise. Come in, please." Angie opened the door and stepped aside. "We're just getting ready to eat. You must be hungry." Angie wiped her hands on her apron and steered him to a chair at the head of the table, opposite me.

"Mrs. Fusco, I—"

Angie shot him a look that said everything, one of those "don't you dare call me Mrs. Fusco" looks. Nothing else was required. "Rosa, get Mr. Borelli a glass of wine, please." She emphasized the *mister*, so Jimmy got the point quickly, settling into his chair with no more objections.

Rosa held back a chuckle. "Sure, Mom. Hi, Detective Borelli. How are you?"

Jimmy shifted in his chair, looking uncomfortable. "Fine, Rosa. Thanks."

He looked to me. I shrugged and raised my eyebrows—one of those universal signs that men have to let the other guy know things were now beyond his control. "So what brings you, Jimmy?"

Angie was just setting the last of the dishes on the table as I said this, and it earned me a smack on the arm. "Time enough for that after supper," Angie said.

She sat and folded her hands, another silent signal that it was time for me to say grace. I didn't know if the girls had special classes after school that we didn't know about, or if it was something their mothers taught them, but somewhere, somehow, they learned their signals. And they were all good at making them. I made up my mind that in a later life, I'd find out. For now, though, I folded my hands to say the blessing.

"In nomine Patris, et Filii, et Spiritus Sancti…"

We started eating after grace and Jimmy dug in as if it were his first meal of the day, stuffing ravioli in his mouth one after the other. "I swear, Angela, these are fantastic."

"Thanks," Angie said, "but Rosa actually cooked these. She helps me all the time."

I smiled at Angie. These were leftovers, which most women would have been embarrassed to serve to begin with, offering apologies, and excuses, but Angie never was that type. She offered a guest what we had and never looked back. I checked off another reason I loved her.

Jimmy turned to Rosa. "I can't believe you cooked this. My kids—" He stopped suddenly and seemed uneasy, then he regrouped and continued. "Let's just say they can't cook like this."

"Detective Borelli, how is Pete?" Rosa asked. "The kids at school said he was sick."

Jimmy swallowed hard, and looked away from Rosa, sipping his wine. "He's doing better. Thanks for asking. But tell me, how did you make this ravioli? I need to tell Cindy about it."

As we finished the meal, Rosa made us coffee and brought two cups to the table. "Would you like some grappa in it, Mr. Borelli?"

Jimmy's eyes lit up. "That would be great, Rosa. Thanks."

We made idle chat for a few more minutes, and then, when Angie fin-ished, she got Rosa to help her with the dishes. After we finished the cof-fee, I poured more wine and invited Jimmy out front to talk. Play time was over. As we stepped onto the stoop and closed the door, I turned to him. "What the fuck is going on?"

He held up his hands. "Hold on. You—"

"All I know is you had a couple of fucking imbeciles following Rosa around and scaring her half to death." I was shaking I was so pissed. "They're goddamn lucky I didn't kill them."

Borelli raised his own voice, going into protective mode on his men. "They made a mistake. I know that and I chewed their asses out."

That settled me down a bit, but there was still a lot more to answer for. "So why were you following her?"

Jimmy gulped, again, like he had at dinner. "Rumors are that Rosa knows something about Bobby's killer, that—"

"Bullshit. And you know it."

He held up his hands in surrender. "I'm just telling you what's on the street. You don't believe me, check it out. You've got contacts."

Borelli handed me his wine glass. "Tell Angie and Rosa thanks for the dinner. I've got to go. And by the way, I heard from Marty Ferris. I guess you didn't kill him after all."

"So that's it? No apology?"

I watched him go down the walk and wondered if there was even a shred of truth to what he said. I hated to question Rosa on something that would get her angry; we'd had enough trouble of late, but I couldn't leave this alone, either. After taking the wine glasses to the kitchen, I turned to Rosa. "We need to talk."

Angie looked at me, surprised, but Rosa didn't seem surprised at all. That told me a lot. We went to the living room, where Rosa sat on the sofa opposite my chair. Her mother sat next to her. I leaned forward, hands folded and resting on my legs. "Rosa, Detective Borelli said the reason those officers were following you is because you know something about Bobby Campisi's murder."

She sighed and turned her head while Angie denied that Rosa could have any involvement.

"Angela Fusco," I said, commanding her attention. "I'm not an interrogator for the Nazi regime. I'm Rosa's father, and I'm asking her a question. No need for your protection."

I turned to Rosa, waiting for an answer.

"Maybe he means because I've been asking around the school a lot."

"Why have you been asking around school about it?"

She still wouldn't look at me. "Just because."

"Just because is not good enough. I need answers."

Tears formed in her eyes, and she fought to hold them back, but they came out, mixed with her words. "I'm trying to clear your name."

It was my turn for confusion. "Clear *my* name? What are you talking about?"

"Oh, God." Frustration had risen to the surface now. "People talk, Dad. They say you killed Bobby."

"That's bullshit, and you know it." I stood, pacing.

Anger replaced her frustration. Rosa stood, facing me. "Bullshit or not, that's what they're saying. Some of the kids can't even hang out with me."

"Do you know something or not?"

She hesitated, cooking up a lie is what I figured. "I heard some kids might have seen something by the railroad tracks that night."

I perked up at that. "Who?"

"I can't tell you."

"What do you mean, you can't tell me? This is serious."

"These are my friends. I rat them out, and I'm shit from then on."

Angie jumped up. "Rosa, watch your mouth."

She turned to Angie. "It's true, Mom."

I was ready to hit the wall. "So you'd take sides against family? If that's the way you want to be, fine. From now until I say differently, you can't see your friends and you can't see Mike Riley. You'll learn. These kids are only your friends; *we* are your family."

Rosa's laugh cut deep. "Is that a joke? Mom worries and prays every day, and people say you're a killer."

I moved quickly to her, almost slapped her, but stopped myself.

"Go ahead, slap me," Rosa said.

"I've never been convicted—"

"I know, Dad. Never been convicted of murder. So deny it." She glared at me. "I dare you to swear on the Bible and deny it."

"Get the Bible."

She started for the dining room, where her mother kept it in a drawer. Angie's cry stopped her.

"*Enough!* I won't have this in my house. There will be no swearing on Bibles in *this* house. Not now. Not *ever*."

Rosa was not placated. "Forget the Bible. Swear to it on Mamma Rosa's soul. Go ahead."

Angie smacked her *so* hard and *so* fast, it knocked Rosa to the side. Then she advanced on Rosa with death in her eyes. "You want someone to swear. *I'll swear.* I'll swear that if you ever say anything like that again I'll make you wish you were…"

Rosa was holding her cheek and crying. She reached over and hugged her mother, laying her head on Angie's shoulders. "I'm sorry, Mom. I didn't mean it."

"You need to tell your father that."

Rosa turned to me and bawled even more. She was at that stage where emotions were all over the place, the teenage rollercoaster ride. "I didn't mean it, Dad. Promise I didn't. You know I love you."

I hugged her back and buried my face in her hair, mostly to hide my own tears. "I know. I didn't mean it either. Sometimes we just get carried away and say things we don't mean." I hugged her some more then said, "I love you, Rosa. More than you could know."

The rest of the evening was tense. We had a lot of forced conversation and fake laughter, but by the time we went to bed, things had gotten better. As I lay in bed that night, I thought about quitting on Frankie, calling him up and saying I couldn't do it anymore. This case was tearing my family apart and that was something I couldn't allow.

CHAPTER 39

EVERYONE TRUSTS A NUN

Wilmington, Delaware

At breakfast Rosa told me that Jimmy Borelli's kid hadn't been to school in almost two weeks. *Strange to be out sick so long,* I thought, and made a note to ask around. Last night, I noticed something wasn't right when Rosa asked him how his kid was doing. Too many things weren't adding up, and they were all connected to this case.

Sister Thomas called while I was at work and said the kids who witnessed what happened wanted to meet me. I told her I couldn't make it until after work, so we agreed to meet then. I parked the car at my house, deciding to walk since it was such a nice day. I grabbed a small notepad and pen before heading out the door. I walked up Beech Street to Clayton and took a right toward the school. A smile popped on my face as I passed Canby Park. What fun we had there as kids, climbing rocks that seemed as big as mountains. I looked down toward the old pool; the rocks were still there, looming above the sidewalk in front of the swimming pool, but as I looked at them I realized they were no more than three or four feet high. An insurmountable climb for a little kid.

The small stone wall was there too, the one we used as the judgment for a home run when we played step ball. Hitting the wall was a double, and going over was a home run, just like in the majors. A far cry from the fields kids played on nowadays. I shook my head as I thought about it. We were happier then, playing on a sidewalk or in the street with sticks, than the kids now with all the equipment money can buy.

I looked to the left, at the church standing tall atop the hill, and blessed myself. It held many memories too, not all of them fond. Taking advantage of a lapse in traffic, I crossed the street at a leisurely pace, then walked up the steps into the school. I felt ten years old again, walking into that building again, going to see Sister Thomas. I smiled at the thought of her. She'd be sitting at her desk, working on papers, or, she'd be cleaning the room, even at her age. I wondered if that was what kept nuns so alive and healthy—their penchant for keeping busy, both physically and mentally. Mamma Rosa used to say so, and I put a lot of faith in what she said.

As I entered the room, Sister Thomas put down her broom and greeted me with a smile. "It's good to see you again. Have a seat. The children haven't shown yet."

As we waited on the kids, there was a moment of silence, then Sister Thomas said. "You never mentioned your father's letter."

I looked at her. "If you mean, did he mention about you and him...yes." She nodded. "I see."

"Nothing inappropriate, of course, but it shocked me, made me think back to all of those times you beat my...knuckles." I laughed. "Not like I didn't deserve it."

Sister Thomas smiled too. "Yes, not like you didn't." She got up and hugged me.

I stood a good six inches taller than she did, but I had no doubt she'd whack me with something—anything—if I said the wrong thing, so I hugged her back.

As I stood there with Sister Thomas I figured it was as good a time as any to get advice. I had been praying to God, seeking advice on what to do about all of this, but so far he hadn't answered, but I had to clear Frankie; I had promised him. Yet to do that meant breaking my word to

Angie. Someone was going to get hurt, sure as shit. And likely someone was going to get killed.

"Sister, what is God's take on doing something bad for a good reason?"

"You mean like running a red light to get to a hospital?"

Good old Sister Thomas. "I was thinking of something a little more sinister. Like someone killing a person to protect his family."

"God doesn't condone killing."

"Didn't God kill a lot of people? I mean, for good reasons, but didn't he?"

She looked at me with her probing eyes. "Only God has the right to take a life, Niccolo." The gaze she was famous for had lost none of its power in the years since I'd sat in her class. Today it carried an admonishment *and* a warning.

I nodded, knowing I had started a discussion I couldn't win. I looked around the room then walked to the window and peeked through the blinds. "So where are these kids?"

She looked at the clock on the wall. "Stay here. I'll find out."

Sister Thomas returned a moment later. "They will be here shortly. A little bout of fear overtook them momentarily."

"Who is it? Do I know them?"

Sister Thomas hesitated, then nodded, as if to herself, as she sat on her desk. "Since they'll be here any minute, I see no harm in telling you. It's Abbie Enders and her boyfriend, Ben."

"Abbie." I gritted my teeth. "That damn Rosa. I should—"

"You should watch your mouth is what you should do."

"Sorry, Sister."

"Good, now as far as Rosa is concerned..." Sister Thomas patted the desk beside hers. "I seem to remember a story about three kids who stole from a grocery store—cigarettes, I believe it was. The cops caught one of them but, try as they might, they couldn't get that boy to talk."

Embarrassment really had a hold on me now. "You knew about that?"

"There wasn't much I didn't know about back then. I'm slipping in my old age, though."

"Must not be slipping too much if you heard about this."

Sister Thomas patted my arm. "It wasn't me who heard. Rosa and Emily—Abbie's older sister—convinced Abbie to talk to me."

"Rosa and Emily did? Really?"

Sister Thomas nodded. "Really, Nicky. You should be proud; Rosa is a wonderful girl."

I was thinking about what she said when the door opened. Abbie and Ben walked in with their heads hung low.

I got up and walked to them, offering my hand to Ben. "It's good to see you again. We met when you came home with Rosa one night."

"Yes, sir. I remember."

I hugged Abbie, pulling her to me. "There's no reason to be upset or ashamed," I told her.

She wouldn't look at me.

"No one is going to know about this outside this room." I pulled her chin up with my finger and stared at her. "I promise."

"For real?"

Sister Thomas stepped over and led Ben to a seat, then grabbed Abbie by the shoulder. Then she did something I never expected. "I know you kids hear rumors, and there are plenty of them that go around about my dearest friend Mr. Fusco. You shouldn't listen to most of them, but *one* of the rumors is true. If Nicky 'the Rat' Fusco gives you his word that he won't say anything, you can take that as gospel."

We all stared at her as if she had transformed into a vampire or something. *Where did that come from?*

Sister Thomas stared back at all three of us. "Well, I had to get this nonsense over with didn't I? Now let's get on with it. Abbie, Ben, tell us what happened."

Abbie was the one who started. "It was the night of Mr. Donovan's wake. Ben and I were down at a place called Lover's Loop, it's a—"

She seemed to be nervous telling this so I interrupted. "If it makes you feel any better, Abbie, Rosa's mother and I know that spot well."

"You do?" She seemed incredulous by the idea, and I suddenly found myself wondering just how old these kids thought we were.

"And if it makes both of you feel better," Sister Thomas said, "*I* know that spot as well."

We all turned. "Sister?" I said.

It was her turn to look incredulous. "I haven't been a nun all of my life." She straightened her posture, if that was possible, and told Abbie to continue.

As Abbie started up again, I realized that on the night in question, Rosa had asked me to drop her off at Abbie's house when I left Frankie's. Now I was left to wonder what Rosa was doing that night. *Probably with Mike Riley.*

"Ben and I were…well…you know, and then we heard the train coming. We were laying in a clear spot by a couple of big trees, but we could see the train. We watched it come around the bend when all of a sudden something fell out of one of the cars. Before we realized it, a man jumped out right behind it."

Ben broke in to tell some of the story, caught up in it now. "As soon as the guy jumped from the train, I knew he'd shoved or pushed out a body. The body rolled down the hill, and the guy followed. We hid in the bushes and watched."

"What did he do?" I asked.

"He rolled the body to the creek, turned it over, took some things from the pants of the guy, then left."

"What, back up the tracks?"

"Yeah, up the hill and down the tracks."

"So he didn't go over the hill; he went down the tracks?"

"Down toward Elsemere," Abbie said.

This was good stuff they were giving me. Definitely cleared Bugs. "What did the guy look like?"

Abbie looked at Ben, who shrugged. "I don't know."

Oh shit. "Try to think."

They sat there for maybe five seconds, a lifetime to them I'm sure. "I don't know," Abbie said. "All I picture is a blur."

"Me, too," Ben said.

"How tall? Was he fat, skinny? White, black?"

"He was white, for sure," Ben said. "Not fat. And not too tall, but... probably taller than you by maybe a couple of inches."

Okay, we were getting somewhere. "Do you remember what he was wearing?"

They both shook their heads.

"How about hair color, or style?"

Another pair of head shakes.

Sister Thomas tapped me on the shoulder and stood. I let her have the floor. "In my writing class, I ask the students to imagine things to write about. When we do it, we always close our eyes. I have found that imagination and memory are closely tied, so why don't we start by closing our eyes?" When they didn't respond, she prodded them. "Go on, close your eyes."

They closed their eyes and sat still.

Sister Thomas walked the floor. "Don't open them until I tell you. Just listen. Go back to that night and imagine, yes imagine, that you are there all over again. Think of what you were doing, but for the sake of all of us, let's not dwell too much on that."

They laughed, but didn't open their eyes.

"All right, now *hear* the train coming up the tracks. *Feel* it, as it rumbles and shakes the ground. I know you could feel it because you were on the ground. I remember what that felt like."

They nodded.

"Now picture that body falling out, but quickly, and this is important, quickly shift to the man who jumps from the train. What did he look like? How far did he jump? Did he stumble, then pick himself up? Did he say anything—anything at all? When he rolled the body toward the creek did he do it with his feet? What did his shoes look like? When he turned the body over and took the man's wallet—look hard, were his hands big? Scarred?"

Sister Thomas left them thinking for a moment, then said, "And when he walked back up that hill, the one with the rocks along the banks, what did he look like from the backside?"

"He wore construction boots!" Abbie called out. "Just like Uncle Jerry's."

I made notes. This was good.

"And his hands were big," Abbie said, now proud of her recall. "I remember him taking the wallet from the body. He had big hands."

"He had a limp," Ben said, and almost yelled it. "His right leg. He was limping when he went back up the hill."

They thought of a few more things. When we were done I thanked them for their help and once again assured them it was our secret. They walked out of the classroom holding hands and smiling. I thanked Sister Thomas, not only for arranging this meeting, but for reminding me of those things in life I tended to forget. And for reminding me what a wonderful daughter I had. As I exited the school, though, only one thing was on my mind, and had been ever since Ben said, 'he had a limp.'

Had a limp.

Everything else went blank. All I could think about was the image in my mind of Jack McDermott limping across that bar toward his seat; Jack McDermott, who used to heist cigarettes from the train yard and knew the railroad tracks like the back of his hand; Jack McDermott, who hated Bobby Campisi perhaps more than anyone.

It was time to have another talk with Jack McDermott.

CHAPTER 40

MESSAGE IN BLOOD

Brooklyn, New York

Frankie made plans and backup plans as they raced to Lisa's apartment, not knowing what they'd find.

"Anybody call a bus?" Frankie asked.

Sherri looked at him. "You think she's dead?"

"Good guess, don't you think?"

"I called the ambulance," Lou said.

"So you think she's gone?"

"I didn't say that, but if I have to go up one more flight of stairs, I'm going to need one, so I called them."

Frankie screeched around a corner and turned onto the street where Lisa lived. "Miller, now do you see why I wanted a new partner?"

"I'm starting to," Sherri said. "Lou had me fooled for a while."

Frankie double-parked and they all rushed to the apartment door. He had to buzz a neighbor to let them in, and then they took the elevator to the fourth floor. Lou and Sherri had their guns drawn while Frankie used his skills to pick the lock and let them in.

Lou entered first, crouched low, with Sherri beside him, standing. She swept right, him left.

Frankie drew his gun as he entered, turning slowly to cover the room. He moved through the living room and toward the kitchen one step at a time. "Kitchen cleared."

The words must have jolted Sherri to her senses. She got in line behind Frankie, then took the lead advancing toward the bedrooms. A bathroom door sat on the left. She kicked it open with her foot and swept it. "Bathroom clear."

Frankie moved to the bedroom door on the right, turning the knob and pushing it open. He ducked low as he went in. "Clear," he said as he stood.

The only room left sat at the end of the hall. Sherri tapped the door with her foot, but it didn't budge, so she crouched and twisted the knob. When she pushed it open, she and Bugs both went in, her low, him standing. She swept right, him left.

"Clear," she said, and breathed a huge sigh.

"All right," Frankie said, "we need to dig through this place and see what we can find."

"Might as well start here," Sherri said, and went to the closet in the bedroom. "Looks like they didn't take much."

"Nothing in the hamper," Lou said.

"And the drawers in here are neatly stacked with freshly done laundry. Somebody went to a lot of trouble to clean up before they left." Frankie looked around. "And check this out, no sheets on the bed, no dirty towels in the bathroom…"

Frankie went to the kitchen but found more of the same—nothing in the dishwasher or the sink, nothing in the other bathroom. The place was immaculate.

In the bedroom, Sherri got down and looked under the bed, hollering out to Frankie. "Why go to so much trouble to clean it up? We know who lived here."

"I think it's to cover up who we don't know about. Kate said there were likely two of them, right?"

"That's what she thinks," Lou said.

Frankie nodded. "The other one was living here with her. That's what they're hiding."

"Husband?" Lou thought aloud.

Sherri shook her head. "He's dead, remember?"

"Who said he's dead?" This from Frankie.

"She did, when we interviewed her."

As soon as Sherri said it, alarm bells went off in Frankie's head. "Exactly. *She* said he's dead, but what if he isn't?"

Lou was already dialing his phone. "Carol, we need you to check on Lisa Jackson's husband. Anything you can find on him." Lou put his hand over the phone. "We know a name? Anything?"

Sherri shook her head. "Nothing."

"We've got nothing here, Carol. You're going to have to run this one yourself." Lou nodded. "Call me when you get something."

"So whoever this guy is, husband or not, he could be forcing her to go with him," Frankie said. "Goddamn! I can't believe we just bought her 'dead husband' tale. We should have checked it out."

Lou lifted the edge of the mattress and looked under it. "Hey, Donovan, something's under here. Help me lift it."

He and Frankie lifted the mattress while Miller grabbed an envelope lying between the mattress and box spring. She opened it.

Hi, Detectives. I knew you would find this, but I didn't want it to be conspicuous. Don't worry, though. I'm not done yet. Not by a long shot. Sleep tight, and don't forget your prayers, especially the Latin ones. But by now you've probably figured out that the prayers don't mean anything. It was fun for a while though.

"There's something written on the back," Frankie said.

Sherri turned the letter over, handling it carefully even though she wore gloves. She gasped when she read it, then her face tightened and her eyes narrowed.

"What?" Lou asked.

She handed it to Lou, and he read it.

Oh, Frankie, one more thing. Tell your little black bitch friend, the cute one, that I'm going to fuck her. Real hard. And when I'm done fucking her, I'll make her do other things. Tell her that for me, will you?

"This guy is a genuine wacko," Lou said. "Certifiable."

Sherri's jaw was still clenched and Frankie was pacing, cracking his knuckles.

"What do you think he meant about the prayers thing?" Lou asked.

"Just what he said, that he was messing with us. I think this is all nothing but a jealous nut bag on a vengeance kick about his wife having affairs."

"Assuming the *he* we're talking about is her husband," Sherri added.

"I'd bet on it," Lou said. "I'm with Frankie on that."

"One thing for sure," Frankie said. "He sure as shit knows who we are, so we better watch our asses from now on. Crazy as this bastard is, I wouldn't put it past him to kill a cop."

CHAPTER 41

FREIGHT TRAINS AND HOBOS

Wilmington, Delaware

As a kid, I was scared of Jack McDermott. Maybe not scared, but he'd given all of us our fair share of beatings, especially his brother, "The Mick." That was all behind me, though, and had been for some time. Jack and I had shared prison time, and he knew me and my reputation. There was no way Jack McDermott would fuck with me now. But there was no way he'd roll over either. I knew before I confronted Jack, I'd need a lot more evidence than a guy with a limp, especially if that guy had just jumped from a moving train onto a hill covered with a bed of rocks.

It reminded me of when we used to hop trains, waiting at the bend of the tracks where they had to slow down. As soon as the engine was around the turn—so the conductor couldn't see us—we'd jump out of the bushes and race alongside the train, reaching for the ladders on the end of the box cars. Then we'd pull ourselves up and hang on for the ride. It was always a trick to stay on the right length of time, because if you stayed on too long and waited for it to hit the straight stretch of track by Elsemere, it got going too fast. Then we'd have to jump off onto the damn rocks at high speed. Many of us ended up with sprained ankles in those days, until we got to be pros at it.

Getting my mind back on things, I decided I'd better talk to Millie again, and Fred. And see if I could find Johnny Deuce. Between the three of them I should get a morsel or two, maybe enough to fry Jack's Irish ass.

It took about ten minutes to get to Teddy's. Lucky for me Fred was tending bar. I took a seat near the end of the bar and signaled for a beer.

"Nicky, you're making yourself a regular," Fred said.

"Don't get too concerned. I've got a two-beer limit set by the boss."

He plopped a mug in front of me and laughed. "Boss limits are the best kind. The limits I set myself I always break."

"Before you go, tell me again about that night Bobby got killed."

Fred sighed. "Jesus Christ, you want my blood or what?"

I stared him down. "I want the fucking truth. And I swear, Fred, I better get it tonight. Don't make me come back here."

"What's this all about? I told you—"

I leaned forward a little. "You lied last time. Or was it your short memory that forgot to mention that Johnny Deuce was here that night, playing pool with one of his buddies?"

He took his towel and wiped the counter in front of me. "It must have slipped my mind."

"Slipped your mind? A guy who remembers what a person drinks even if they haven't been here in years? And *this* slipped your mind?"

He slapped the bar and looked around. "Fuck, Nicky, what do you want?"

"I already told you: the truth."

He did another quick scan of the place, then got close to me, whispering. "So Johnny Deuce was here hustling people, and he had a guy with him, guy named Pepe, I think. But I swear, there's no way they had anything to do with Bobby. They were here a good half an hour, maybe more after Bobby left."

I sipped my beer. "Who left right after Bobby? Anybody?"

He wiped the counter more, though it didn't need it. "Ah shit, Nicky. Is this between me and you? For real?"

"Tell me, Fred."

"Jack McDermott."

"What about Jack?"

"He left five, maybe ten minutes after Bobby."

I took a big gulp of beer and set the mug down. "You're sure?"

Fred nodded.

I left him money for the beer and a tip, then I moved to the end of the bar to see Millie. "How's it going, beautiful? I assume that seat's for me?"

"It's been waiting here every night since you left." She patted the stool beside her. "How are you, Nicky?"

"Be better if I knew who left here within a few minutes of Bobby Campisi the night he was killed."

Millie held an unlit cigarette between her fingers, waiting for a gentleman to light it. I obliged. "If I were a snoop, which I'm not," she said. "I'd have to say that Johnny Deuce's pool partner is a prime suspect. He quit the game early and damn near trailed Bobby out the door."

Goddamn lying Fred! "And the other?"

"Who said there was another?"

"Come on, Millie, I don't need to be Philip Marlowe to know that."

She took a long, slow drag on her smoke and flipped the ash into the ashtray. "Your friend and mine—Jack McDermott."

"So Jack followed him out?"

"I wouldn't he say followed Bobby out, but he didn't wait long, either. Maybe ten minutes. Could have been less."

Even at a little less than ten minutes, that put it too late. No way Bobby waited around in a parking lot for someone to come get him. I was still missing something, unless I had it wrong; maybe Jack wasn't the guilty one after all. "So why am I hearing this for the first time?"

She shrugged. "Don't get me wrong; you're a charmer, Nicky, but Johnny Deuce gave me a c-note to keep quiet."

I cocked my head, surprised again. "Johnny Deuce did? Gave you a hundred?"

She nodded as she flicked another long ash.

"But now you're telling me anyway?"

"I saw Fred spill his guts and figured you got what you came for."

"No way you heard what Fred and I talked about. Not from here."

A long throaty laugh tainted by forty years of cigarettes and whiskey rumbled from Millie, trailed by a nasty cough that carried something with it. "I've been on this barstool for the better part of ten years. I know when Fred has to piss by the way he walks, and I know when his wife's been holding out on him by how grumpy he is. I sure as hell can tell when he gives up a secret."

I leaned in and kissed her on the cheek. "You're a princess, Millie. Thanks."

"Remember that when Johnny Deuce kills me."

I patted her hand and winked. "Don't worry about that. You're going to die at a nice old age like you should."

"You mean of cancer or liver disease?"

"Probably, yeah."

She crushed out her smoke in the ashtray and blew me a kiss. "Thanks, Nicky."

I left the bar, thinking I'd rather go via Johnny Deuce than by cancer, but to each his own. I had more to worry about than how Millie might pass into eternity. The clues from this case played over in my mind, confusing the hell out of me. I made a mental note to give Bugs more respect for what he did. Once again I went through things. Bobby's car was found by the old tracks and his body by the Den. That gives an edge to Jack; he knew the tracks and everything that went with them. But Jack didn't leave the bar until at least five, maybe ten minutes after Bobby. No matter how you played that one, he couldn't have counted on Bobby still being there. And, Deuce's man, Pepe, left hot on Bobby's trail. That edge went to the Deuce. Tack on the fact that Bobby owed Deuce money, and that put a lot more weight to it.

I got in the car and headed home. It had been another long day. As I turned down Dupont Street, more thoughts came. If Johnny Deuce did this because Bobby owed him money, why did he kill him without getting the money. Bobby sure as shit wasn't one to withstand torture. Jack, on the other hand, had reason to kill Bobby that had nothing to do with money. Jack flat out hated Bobby. As I pulled into the parking spot in front of my house, I realized I had resolved only one thing.

I had to get back to Sister Thomas' rules of deduction—when you have more than one possible answer, rule something out. So what did I know? I knew that if Deuce had anything to do with it, Doggs would know. That's where I needed to go. And this time he better have some answers.

CHAPTER 42

STREET TALK

Wilmington, Delaware

I was tired when I got home, and I faced a horrific outlook for the night. Angie would be ticked off that I was out so late working on the "so-called case" as she called it, and even worse, dinner was long over and I was damn hungry. I opened the door and stepped inside, tossing my briefcase on the chair. "Hey, Angie, I finally made it."

She and Rosa were at the dining room table, working on what looked like homework. Both of them were twirling their hair behind their ears and humming. *Just like Mamma Rosa.* It was one of the many things I loved so much about both of them. Maybe I had made out okay after all.

Rosa jumped up and ran to me, excited. She wrapped her arms around me and hugged.

"Good to have you home, Dad."

Her greeting was a sure sign that Abbie had talked to her and must have told her that I was okay. Kids never know if their parents are okay until their friends grant approval. I kissed her cheek then made my way to Angie, leaning down and giving her a peck. "Hi, babe. How much did you miss me?"

"Not a bit. And unless you plan on helping with Rosa's schoolwork, keep yourself busy and quiet."

Rosa walked by with raised eyebrows.

"I saw that," Angie said.

"Be careful, Rosa. Your mother spent too much time with the nuns. Don't be surprised if you get an eraser in the head at any minute."

"Or a yardstick on your ass," Angie said, but she couldn't keep from laughing. She seldom cursed—even hell or ass—and on the occasions she did, she couldn't help laughing. "Get out of here, Nicky, and let me get this done."

I grabbed some crackers and cheese, and the glass of wine Rosa had ready for me on the table beside my chair. I picked up my book and started to read, but then Rosa came and sat beside me.

"So what's going on with the case?"

I set my book down and looked at her. "If you really want to know, I could use some help."

Her eyes lit up and she bounced off the chair. "Help? With what?"

"The other night when Detective Borelli was here, I noticed he reacted strangely when you asked about his son."

"He's been out sick a long time."

"I'm sure there's nothing to it, but if you could find out more about it for me—without anyone knowing."

"I'll check it out. I can't wait. And don't worry, nobody will know anything. I'm the best snoop in school."

I looked at her and nodded, but quietly wondered if being the best snoop was something to be proud of. Perhaps nowadays it was.

Angie came in from the dining room, where she had switched to working on bills, trying to figure out how to pay what we owed with one less paycheck. My raise would help, but not enough to stop her from worrying. The scowl on her face was as wide as Bancroft Parkway. "Niccolo Fusco, what are you having your daughter do?"

Rosa tried sneaking up the stairs, but a firm command from Angie stopped her. "Rosa! Back down here."

Rosa stepped back into the living room. "Mom, it's not like I'm doing anything illegal. I'm just asking a few questions for Dad."

Angie poked her finger at me, then at Rosa. "I don't know how to tell the two of you this, but your father *is not* a detective. He's an estimator. At least he was when this so called case started, but if he doesn't get back to work, he probably won't be much longer."

"Don't worry," I assured her. "She's not doing anything wrong, and you know I wouldn't cause her trouble."

Angie huffed. "She's already had cops following her, scaring the life out of us. I don't want…"

I got up and hugged her. "Don't worry. I promise it's nothing."

She gave a reluctant nod, enough of a signal for Rosa to dart up the steps before minds were changed.

"You need help with the bills?" I asked.

"Only if you can turn our silverware into gold. Then I'd go sell it and pay things off."

"That was Mamma Rosa's silverware. No way you'd sell it even if it were gold."

Angie started to say something but my cell phone rang. I stepped into the other room to answer it. "Fusco."

"My man Rat. How's it going?"

It was Monroe. "You got something for me?"

"Got something but we gotta meet."

"When?"

"Now, Rat. Got news, but I don't trust cells. You know how it goes."

I felt Angie's glare burning holes through my back, so I decided I better turn to face her. She wore a frown to accompany the glare. Pretty soon, I knew, the finger would start wagging. "I can leave in five minutes. Where are you?"

"Same place. And you won't have any trouble this time."

The finger was wagging now, and her look had grown threatening. "Do you see what time it is? This is no example for your daughter. Bad enough when you go out playing cards with those…those…"

"Hoodlums?" I asked, supplying her favorite word for the guys at the smoke shop.

"Get out!"

I got a cold kiss before leaving, then got in the car and headed to Monroe Street, parking up the hill near Tilton Park. DuPree, the ever-present guard on the west end, nodded to me as I passed. I smiled and nodded back. It was likely he still hated me for showing him up last time, but that couldn't be helped. Someone had to be the fall guy. About half-way down Seventh Street, Monroe greeted me then signaled for his guys to step back. We stood on the side of the street talking, leaning against the old brick homes like we did as kids.

"What's so important that you couldn't trust cells?"

Monroe sucked on a joint while we talked. "Word is that Bobby was into drugs. Started off real small, and moved up a little. He got lucky about six months ago with a deal that got him noticed."

Bobby being into drugs didn't shock me, especially after finding the dope in the locker. "Noticed by which people?"

"Doggs' crew."

That news *did* shock me. "You telling me Doggs Caputo deals in drugs?"

Monroe looked at me as if I had just landed from another planet. "Shit, man, *everybody* deals drugs. That's where the money is."

Just like Borelli said. Drugs change everything. "You, too?"

Monroe looked around, tapped my shirt, checking for a wire, but only half-heartedly. "Got to if I want to be part of the game. That's what it's come to. You don't do drugs, you lose your crew. If you don't have a crew, somebody's going to pop you. That simple."

"Sort of like the old days in the joint?"

"No different, Rat. Except out here, it's worse. No bulls there to break things up when the shit goes down. Dude rides by in a car, window drops, and all of a sudden—wham—lead's flying and people are going down." Monroe shook his head. "I'd trade it all for the old days when fists, a club, or even a knife settled things."

I sighed, knowing exactly how he felt. "Back then it was really the toughest who ruled things."

"Fuckin' drugs," Monroe said, and took the last hit on his joint.

I didn't know who controlled what in this city as far as drugs went, and I wasn't going to ask Monroe who he worked for—that would be breaking the rules—but maybe he'd tell me about Bobby. "So Bobby worked for Doggs?"

"Not worked for so much as drove for. Shit man, you knew Bobby. He was as stupid as a brick. No way Doggs was gonna let him handle real money."

"So he did what?"

"Drove for him, kept a lookout when a deal was going down. That kind of stuff."

"Who were they dealing with? You?"

A shake of his head said no. "Don't even know the dude, but he moved in here big time in the last year or so. Got runners and dealers popping up all over. Nasty motherfucker, too."

"Another Mafia crew? Russian?"

Another shake of the head. "Mexican, but man, none of this shit better surface with my name attached to it."

I was shocked by the tone in his voice. Monroe was afraid of whoever this was. Now I wondered if he really didn't know who it was or if he just wouldn't say.

"You know your name won't come up." I thought for a minute, trying to piece it together. I knew I didn't have much time left for questions. "So, Doggs is distributing for the Italians, you've got your own sources, and you mean to tell me Bobby, stupid Bobby somehow got caught up in this and ended up with fifty large?" That part of the murder was common knowledge now so I had no problem letting it out. I kept the drugs part to myself.

"You're not alone wondering that. Everybody's been asking the same question and the only one with the answer is probably your old buddy."

"My old buddy?"

"Remember that whitey in prison you knew. Jack?"

"McDermott?"

"That's him. He's one of Doggs' crew, but there was bad blood between Jack and Bobby. About two months ago a deal went bad and four guys ended up dead."

"What's that got to do with anything?"

"Bobby was the driver for Doggs' crew that day, and that guy from down on Harrison Street, the one who used to run smokes up and down the coast…"

"Vasquez?"

Monroe nodded. "Vasquez, yeah. He was supposed to be the lookout for the Mexicans. Anyway, four guys end up dead and Bobby and Vasquez don't get a scratch. To top it off, a hundred large and four keys go missing."

"And they think Bobby and Vasquez took it?"

"Doesn't matter. They were dead as soon as they left the scene. Only way to save their asses would have been for each one of them to go back with their share of the deal."

"So somebody gets trigger happy, these two survive, scoop up the prizes and beat it."

"That's the way everybody figured it. Vasquez bolted. Nobody heard from him again. Bobby stayed around and kept to his story. Trouble is nobody believed him. I think Doggs was only waiting to find out where Bobby hid his shit, then he'd have killed him. Might be what happened."

"And this Mexican, he's that good?"

"I told you, this guy's got shit covered. And he's playing it different. You fuck with him and somebody's dying. That's why I keep to my territory."

"You telling me this Mexican guy is moving in on your territory?"

"You haven't been listening to me. He's taking from everyone, even your old dago buddies."

"And they're putting up with it?"

Monroe shook his head. "Not so much putting up with it as trying to figure out what to do. I'm telling you, Rat, this fucker's crazy."

I thought about what Monroe said. "Your territory won't last long if this guy's moving that fast."

"I'm waiting for one or the other of them to knock each other off. That's all."

"That wait-and-see ploy isn't a good strategy," I said, and tapped him on the back. "But thanks, Monroe. I appreciate it."

"That's one you owe me, Rat. Don't forget."

"You know I don't forget. See you around."

As I walked up the hill to my car, I was seething. I was more convinced than ever it was Jack McDermott, and I intended to pay him a visit. Not tonight, though, tonight I had to get my ass home and stealthily crawl into bed or I wouldn't be seeing tomorrow.

CHAPTER 43

THE FINAL NAME

Brooklyn, New York

Frankie sat at the table with Sherri and Lou, discussing the case and where to go with it. "He's got to be hiding somewhere in the city," Frankie said. "I don't see him leaving us a warning, or a promise, whatever you want to call it, then leaving."

"Unless he was trying to get us thinking that way," Sherri said.

"We know who that girl was yet?" Lou asked.

Sherri shook her head. "Not a clue. No matches and nothing on missing persons."

Carol popped her head in the door, a printout in her hand. "We do know about Mr. Thomas Jackson, though. And the news ain't good, as they say in Tyler, Texas."

Sherri jumped up and took the report. "Thanks, Carol."

"Share the news," Frankie said.

"Whew! Army Special Forces, and even worse, special assignment. Left one month ago with a dishonorable discharge."

"What does 'special assignment' mean?" Lou asked. "Does it say?"

Frankie chewed on a cigarette he couldn't light in the office. "It probably means they can't, or won't, say. But if he was in Special Forces and he was on special assignment, that's not good."

"Were they divorced?" Lou asked.

"Not according to this," Sherri said, then leaned back in her chair. "So let's imagine this. Tom Jackson comes home, finds out she's screwing half the building where she works and starts taking them out like they're members of the Taliban or something."

"Sounds good," Lou said, "But where does the girl fit in? I doubt Lisa was screwing her, and if she was, I doubt her husband would care."

Frankie tossed his smoke away and stood. "Get Carol to run all her credit cards, see if any of them have been used. Check all relatives. Send some unis out to see them, but warn them about this guy. They should go wearing vests and with plenty of help. Send a pair down to her building to see if she had any friends who might know where she'd go in a pinch."

"You know this won't do any good," Lou said.

"Yeah, I know, but we've got to do it anyway."

"So what do we do now?" Sherri asked.

Frankie cracked his knuckles and stared at the wall. "We wait for him to make a mistake. Or kill someone else."

***

LISA JACKSON LAY ON the bed naked, hands and feet tied, gagged, and waiting for Tom to return from getting ice. She played the events of the past few days over and over in her mind, knowing that before long it would be her turn to be found by the cops with something carved into her chest or ass, or somewhere.

No one ever accused her of being smart, but she always had a sense for survival. She had used it to latch on to Tom Jackson and get out of that hick town she lived in, and then, when he went into the army, she used the other men for her needs. With men around, she seldom had to buy dinner and never had to buy jewelry or clothes. All she had to do was whisper the right things at the right times. Now, though, she felt as if she would need all of her skills just to stay alive. Dealing with Tom Jackson *now* was a bit different than dealing with him before. The army had changed him.

The sound of the door opening interrupted her thoughts and brought her focus to the present. Tom came in, checked the room with a glance, and sat on the edge of the bed next to her.

"Ready, girl?"

She nodded.

Tom untied her, then removed the gag and sat on the bed next to her.

Lisa reached for a bottle of water on the end table. After taking a long drink, she wiped her mouth and punched him. "I told you *never* to call me that again. I swear, I'll be the one doing the killing if you call me *girl* again."

Tom laughed and smacked the side of her ass cheeks. "I like that spirit, *girl*. I was thinking of killing you, but maybe I won't."

He popped the lid on a beer, took a big gulp, then took off his clothes. "I've been thinking about what to do. If I don't kill you, it might be better if we head out. Maybe we'll go back to Texas."

Lisa curled up and tucked her hands between her legs. Tom mentioning a place to settle down frightened her more than anything. He might have forgotten he told her, but she knew there was a lot more than Beau buried on that farm. A lot more. And unless she missed her guess, he aimed to expand the graveyard by at least one more. Something had to be done. *But what?*

Lisa thought about it all night while Tom drank and watched TV. She even thought about it while he fucked her. An idea came to her as he was finishing up. She waited until he lay beside her, flat on his back. Lisa turned to him and wrapped her arms around his neck. "Tom, if we're going to leave I want to start a brand new life."

He looked at her. "I already told you, I'm thinking of going back to Texas, to the farm."

"I know, but I want to clear the air between us. I don't ever want to have to lie to you again."

He raised himself up on his elbows and got that mean look in his eyes. "You been lying to me, girl?"

She cowered. "There is one more name…"

"Who?"

"I don't want to say. Can't we just leave it at that?"

"Who is it?"

"I'm afraid to say."

"You better tell me now. I won't hit you if you do."

"No. I'm afraid for you."

He laughed. "Afraid for me? Now that is heartwarming, but I don't think you need to worry about that." He grabbed her by the throat. "Who is it?"

She put her hands over her face and mumbled. "That cop, Donovan."

"What?" He smacked her when he said it, then he smacked her again, and again. He didn't stop until she lay still, blood dripping from her nose and lips and ears. Tom paced the room, cursing and muttering to himself. He finished two more beers before he said another word, then he looked at her and shook his finger. "I don't know if you're going to make it to Texas, girl. It'll be a coin flip at best. But one thing's for sure, your boyfriend ain't gonna make it. No, sir. He won't last the week."

CHAPTER 44

ANOTHER INTERROGATION

Wilmington, Delaware

I had to find out about Jack McDermott and his involvement in Bobby's murder, but more importantly, I had to go to work. All day I thought about how to get him to talk to me, and finally, before leaving to go to Teddy's bar, I figured I'd take the head-on approach. Confront him and see how he reacted. The bottom line was I had enough to convince me he had something to do with it, but as far as real evidence goes, I had nothing.

By the time I got to Teddy's I had a plan, a stupid one, but a plan none-theless. I waited down the block until I saw Jack pull in, like he did almost every night, then I gave him a few minutes before I entered. Jerry was the bartender. I sat one seat away from Jack, but on the corner so I faced the front. I ordered a beer for me and another for Jack.

He nodded in my direction. "Thanks, Nicky. I could use it tonight."

"Why's that, Jack, you need to kill someone?"

He chuckled and sipped his beer. "Yeah, that's what I got going. How about you?"

"I'm serious. I've been busting my ass looking for Bobby's killer, and all this time, you've been sitting right here."

Jack pulled a smoke from a pack of Marlboro Lights on the counter, struck a match and lit it. I wondered what these people were going to do if anyone ever enforced the law banning smoking in bars, at least in Teddy's. *Probably keep smoking.*

Jack squinted and closed his right eye as smoke from the cigarette curled around it. "I don't know what fucking game you're playing, but I didn't kill Bobby Campisi. Not that I didn't want to…"

"Yeah, that's a good defense. The way you always let people know that you hated him or wanted him dead. I've got to tell you, it worked for a while. Threw suspicion off right away. At least, for me, it did. I don't know about Borelli, but then again, he hasn't been doing much investigating, has he?" I stared at Jack trying to pick up a read. "Is he in on it? What's Borelli got to do with this? Is he getting a cut?"

Jack scoffed. "You don't know shit."

"I know you got Bobby down to that parking lot on Maryland Avenue. I know you killed him and put him on the train, then dumped him at the Den. The way I figure it is you either walked or caught another train to Elsemere and came back up Union Street to get your car." I leveled my gaze at him. "That close enough?"

"You got no proof. And no jury—"

"I've got two kids who saw you dump him at the Den, then saw you take his wallet and climb back up that hill and over the tracks."

He shook his head, but with less vigor than before. "Won't hold up."

I stuck the tip of my gun into his gut and pushed a little. "You feel that, Jack? It's the barrel of a Beretta. I know I don't have proof, but I also know I'm right. So we're going outside, going somewhere very quiet. When I'm done with you, trust me—you'll tell me everything."

"I ain't telling you shit!"

I laughed while I stood and tossed a ten onto the bar. "Let's go."

"I ain't going nowhere, you crazy fuck. What are you going to do, kill me in front of everyone?"

I looked around. Millie was here, and Billy Finn, and of course, Jerry.

"Not here, Jack, but I'll get you, even if I have to wait outside until the joint closes. It'll just be worse on you."

Jack lit another smoke, took two drags and crushed it out with a vengeance. "Ah, fuck it!" He turned to me and looked me square in the eye. "What do you want to know? I'm tired of this shit anyway."

He looked, and sounded, like a tired, broken man. It shocked me, but I wasn't about to let the opportunity slip by. "I want to know what happened. All of it."

He signaled Jerry for another beer. "You want one?"

"I'm good. Keep talking."

Jerry delivered the beer and Jack took a quick sip. "Why don't we get a table? Then—"

"I like it where we are. I can see the front door from here." I pushed the ashtray his way, the smoke from his cigarette drifting into my face. "Go on. You were saying?"

"I hated Campisi. I'd been waiting to kill him all these years, but we both worked for Doggs, and you know how he is about that. It would have been too risky."

"So what changed?" I knew Monroe's story. I wanted to see if Jack's matched.

Jack sipped his beer, looked around the bar, lit yet another smoke, and started his story. "Bobby was never too bright, you know that. But he stole money and dope from Doggs and this guy named Carlos, a Mexican drug dealer, a mean motherfucker. Anyway, he ends up with a price on his head. Not a big one, but enough to give me incentive to kill him." Jack chuckled again. "Like I said, I'd have done it for nothing.

"So I follow him for a week or two, waiting for the right time and then that shit happens here with Frankie, and I figured, okay, right time. I followed Bobby to the parking lot and found him by his car. He was pissed at Bugs and he didn't want to go home so I invited him to have another drink but said he'd need to drive. We left the lot, and as he drove down Fourth Street, I stuck a gun in his gut. 'What the fuck is this?' he asked. And I told

him, 'This is where you take a right and head down Maryland Avenue.'
So I took him to the parking lot by the railroad tracks. You remember it,
Nicky, halfway down the hill on the way to the old creek?"

"Sure I remember. Used to be an old Acme Supermarket at the bottom
of that hill, the one we stole cartons of cigarettes from all the time."

"Yeah. There was a lot of fun between cigarettes and trains back then."

"You bet. Lot of action."

Jack looked lost in the past, and once again I felt a twinge of pity for
him.

"Anyway, we parked his car in the back of the lot and we drank some.
I had a couple of quart bottles of Pabst—didn't want to waste the good
shit on him. While he was drinking, I whacked him alongside the head,
right where Frankie hit him. Figured it would at least take them a while to
distinguish my beer-bottle glass from the mug Frankie used."

"How'd you get him into the box car? Bobby was a heavy guy."

"It took me almost half an hour to get his fat ass in there, but I did it."

I sat and thought a minute. "Why'd you get off the train? Why not just
dump him?"

"Shit, I was half lit and forgot to get his wallet. Stupid of me, I know, but
Christ, he could have had some good cash in there. Know what I mean?"

"What did Johnny Deuce and Pepe have to do with it?"

Jack shook his head. "Not a damn thing that I know of. He might have
owed Deuce some money. Hell, Bobby owed everybody, but it couldn't
have been big, or Johnny would have gotten to him long ago."

"You're trying to tell me that it's just a coincidence that Pepe, Johnny
Deuce's man, leaves the bar as soon as Bobby does, and he's got nothing
to do with it?"

Jack lit a smoke and looked to the sky. "Must be."

"And it's another coincidence that Bobby is waiting in the parking lot
for you to come get him and take him to the slaughter like that lamb in
the Bible."

Jack took another long drag, very slow, but his hand was shaking.

When he spoke his voice quivered. "Hey, Nicky. It is what it is, man. What the fuck? Why are you busting my balls? I already told you."

"You told me you did it because you think I'm not going to do anything. Because we're old prison buddies, and your brother was a friend. You're thinking because I hated Bobby Campisi, I won't follow through with this." I stared him down, made him turn away. "You're wrong, Jack. Wrong on all counts. You won't be able to protect Pepe or the Deuce, and you won't be able to protect your Mexican buddies, either. And you won't get your dope or your money."

Jack slipped a notch, showing the surprise I figured I'd generate with that comment. "Yeah, I know about that. I think I have a good picture, but why don't you fill in the details?"

"You're really not getting off this, are you?"

"I'm not getting off this for one reason. This is for Bugs. Because I promised him I'd find out who killed Bobby and clear his name."

"I ain't going back inside. No fuckin' way."

"Then call the Maldonaddos and order some coffins. One each for Pepe, the Deuce, whatever Mexicans are involved, and one for yourself, Jack."

He looked like he was going to reach for a gun, or something. I shifted in my seat and shoved the gun in his gut again. "Don't do it. When we were kids you kicked my ass, but that was a *very* long time ago." I paused to let it sink in. "If you try something, I'll do things to you that will make you remember that limp with affection, like your first piece of pussy."

His hand moved back up to the counter and he stared at the ceiling. "Fuck, Nicky. This is complicated, man. You don't want to know this shit. Back off and go home to Angela."

"Talk."

He slammed his hand on the counter. "Jerry! Get me another goddamn beer."

Jerry purposefully took his time bringing it, and spilled a little when he set it down, again, on purpose, I was sure. Jack waited for him to leave before picking up the story.

"All right, here's the short and sweet. Bobby took the money like I said. Doggs was looking for it. He had Deuce and Pepe trailing Bobby. I knew that Carlos had a tag on Bobby, so I go to Doggs and offer to get his money for five large. The Mexican was willing to pay me another five large if I whacked him, but I had to get the dope. I figured what the fuck, I'm getting ten grand and I get to whack Bobby Campisi besides. What a fucking deal. It was like Christmas."

"Where did it go wrong? Sounds like you had it figured out."

"Went wrong because I fucked it up…like I do everything. You had it close to right. Pepe followed Bobby out and held him until I got there, then I took Bobby down to Maryland Avenue. But I guess I had too much to drink that night. All I wanted to do was make him talk, tell me where the money and dope were, so I could get my payday. When he wouldn't say, I hit him with the bottle, and…Jesus Christ, don't you know the fucker goes and dies on me." Jack slammed the counter again. "One fucking whack, and he dies."

I let him sit there in silence for a while. "That messed up everything."

"Tell me about it," Jack said. "I can't claim I did the job or the Mexican and Doggs would think I took their goods, so I've got to hope it goes unsolved, all the while telling Doggs I had nothing to do with it."

"How did you clear that with Pepe?"

"Me and Pepe go way back, and Deuce is my cousin by marriage. When I told them the situation, they went along with it, but I had to promise to cut them in on the money if I ever found it."

"And it didn't bother you that Bugs might go down for this?"

"I never counted on that, but then again, I didn't figure on Borelli buying into this. I mean, who taught this fucker how to investigate? He barely asked me any questions. I figured he'd clear Bugs in no time. Next thing I know, Bugs is suspect number one."

Jack took a while before talking again. "I'm telling you this for old times, but don't expect me to sing for the cops. Like I said, I *ain't* going back inside."

I nodded along with him on that; besides, something was up with Borelli and I had to find out if I was going to get to the bottom of this. I finished my beer with a gulp and turned to Jack. "I don't know what I'll do yet, but one way or another this case is getting solved, and I really don't care if there are a few lies involved as long as Bugs is cleared." I pointed my finger at him, like Angie always did to me. "Come up with something, Jack. I'm going to talk to a few people, but I'll be back to see you."

CHAPTER 45

CONVERSATION WITH A COP

Wilmington, Delaware

I left the bar with my mind racing, trying to figure out which way to turn. I had Jack as Bobby's killer, but it would be another thing to prove it. I shook my head, not even believing what I was thinking. Who was *I* to prove anything? The best I could do was get the information to Borelli and hope he did his job.

That's what I'll do, I thought, but I had a funny feeling about it. On the way home I decided to call Bugs and see what he thought. He picked up immediately.

"Donovan."

His voice sounded stressed, as if he expected bad news, like somebody waiting for a hospital call or something.

"Bugs, it's me."

A short pause, then, "Nicky, damn it's good to hear your voice. How are things? You okay?"

"I'm fine. Just busting my balls trying to clear some dumb half-ass Irishman of a murder charge."

"What's up with that?"

"I can tell you that Donna hates me."

"Who doesn't she hate?"

"Okay, Bugs, here's the rundown. The way I got it figured, Jack McDermott is the one who did Bobby in."

"You know what? I swear to God I had him pegged in my top three suspects. Swear to God."

"Yeah, well if you were still here, the list would have been longer."

"What do you mean?"

"Bobby was into drugs, working for Doggs and—"

"Whoa. Holy shit, back up. Bobby into drugs? You mean selling?"

Before I could answer, he went on. "And with Doggs? You telling me Doggs is dealing?"

I empathized with the surprise in his voice. I felt the same way when I learned of it. "You heard right. Doggs is dealing and he had Bobby working. Nothing more than a scout, but working it."

"So what happened?"

I filled him in on the details as I'd heard them from Jack then told him what Jack had said about the Mexicans. Told him the vibes I got from Monroe, too.

"Nicky, I know there are a lot of guys named Carlos, but if this is the one I'm thinking of, you need to watch your ass. Hang it up. Give the cops what you've got, and let them handle it."

I listened silently.

"Are you hearing me, Nicky? I don't want you involved in this anymore."

"Why? What's changed?"

"*Carlos.* This guy killed two cops up here, and more in Houston. He's ruthless and he has an endless supply of money. Give what you've got to Borelli and let it go." Another short pause, then, "You know I appreciate what you've done for me. I owe you, man. Big time."

I smiled. "Friendship and honor, right Bugs?"

"Friendship and honor. Forever."

After hanging up, I felt relieved. I didn't want to kill anybody, had promised Angie I wouldn't, and sure as shit, if I had continued with this *someone* was going to die—maybe me—and that was the last thing I wanted. At least I had a plan: gather up all my facts, take them to Borelli and wash my hands of the whole mess. Best of all, I had Frankie's blessing.

I had been parked in front of my house for the last few minutes of the call, so I put the cell in my pocket and got out of the car then bounded up the steps. Rosa was waiting for me at the door.

"Dad, you're not going to believe what I found out." She was like a kid with a good report card.

"Then you better tell me," I said as I walked over to give Angie a hug.

"Pete Borelli has been out of school for over two weeks, right? So Abbie's sister, Emily, went to visit Pete's sister last week, and guess what?" She stared at me, almost unable to restrain herself.

"I give up."

"Pete is nowhere in the house. She passed by his room and he wasn't there. He wasn't in the basement or anywhere."

I was about to say *that's it*, but Rosa continued.

"And I found out from Monica that Pete hasn't turned in homework since he's been out, and, are you ready for this? He hasn't posted to Facebook in two weeks! Either he's in the hospital, or…I don't know, but something's strange."

I nodded, forced to agree with her. Something *was* strange. I reached over and patted her on the back. "If all else fails, you'll make a good detective." I kissed her cheek. "Thanks. I appreciate it."

"Did it help? I mean with your case?"

Angie's scoff carried through the house. I looked over to catch the last of her head shakes. The mumbling I didn't hear, but I could pretty much guess what it was, or the general idea of it, anyway. "You bet it helped. Now we better change the subject before your mother gets the spoon."

I spent what little time I had left playing word games with Angie and Rosa, who both beat the pants off of me almost every time, but we had fun. It was one of the things I looked forward to. We designated one night a week as game night, and we played Boggle, Scrabble, and anagram games until somebody got too tired, usually Angie.

After they went to bed, I sat down to read, but soon closed the book. All I could think of was how to resolve this "so-called case."

The news Rosa had given me wasn't good. I made a note to check it out, but from the sounds of it, I couldn't see a happy ending. Something was up. It could be as simple as Borelli's wife leaving him, or it could be a lot worse. As of yet, I didn't know what that could be. As I pondered the situation, the phone rang. I looked at the time—11:30—*who the fuck is calling now?* Caller ID was blocked.

"Fusco."

"It's Jack."

I didn't bother asking him if he knew what time it was; Jack wouldn't care. "What have you got for me?"

"I know what's wrong with Borelli."

"Don't make me guess, Jack. It's late."

"That fuckin' Mexican got his kid."

The news hit me hard, but as soon as Jack said it everything fit: the way Borelli acted when Rosa asked about his son, the way he was dogging this investigation, his hostility, all of it. "You sure?"

"Sure as shit. And what we talked about earlier—if you're game, I'm in. I don't give a shit about anything else. I'll help you take this fuckin' Mexican down."

"From what I heard of this Carlos guy, it could get dangerous."

Jack laughed. "You don't know the half of it. It'll be way past dangerous. Way past."

"How am I supposed to trust you?"

"Because I hate these fucking Mexicans more than anything." Jack lit a smoke and sucked on it hard, the way Bugs used to, the way he still did. I could hear it through the phone. "I'm tired, Nicky. Might as well go out with a bang."

I thought fast, trying to determine what my next move was. It came to me more from instinct than anything else. "We'll have to get the boy out, Jack."

"We won't get in without arranging a buy. These guys keep a tight watch."

"That means we'll need money."

"A *lot* of money," I said.

"Doggs has money."

I heard Jack suck on that smoke again. "Doggs won't give you a fucking nickel."

I made up my mind about something else right then. "Doggs will give me whatever I want. Count on it."

"All right, assuming you get the money, we still have to worry about Borelli."

"What about him?"

"He'll do anything so they don't kill his boy. I think that wouldn't stop at killing us."

"Let me take care of Borelli. Your job is to figure out where the Mexicans are keeping his boy and how we can get in there."

It was almost midnight before we hung up, and while not a late night for me, I *did* have to work tomorrow. As I climbed the stairs to the bedroom, my mind started racing again.

Why did it have to be his kid? Anything but a kid.

I thought about it for a long time. What could I do? I thought about calling Bugs back, but I already knew what he'd say—go to Borelli's superior. But that would likely get his kid killed. After more deliberation, I realized my initial thoughts had been right—I had to see Borelli and find out what he knew. Maybe there was a way.

Not without killing someone.

CHAPTER 46

LISA'S CHANCE

Brooklyn, New York

Lisa knew Tom was spiraling out of control and she was the only one left for him to vent his rage on. She had played her last card by giving him the detective's name, hoping Tom would go after him and get caught, preferably killed. She figured if anyone could kill Tom, it would be Donovan. He had a dangerous sense about him.

Tom was busy watching porn on the TV, trying to get himself aroused again. Lisa quietly got out of bed and began dressing. She didn't even have her panties on before he noticed.

"What do you think you're doing?"

"Getting dressed."

"Stay like you are," he said, and tapped his hand on the bed beside him. "Sit next to me."

Lisa cringed, but she did as he said, taking the spot on the bed next to him. No sooner had she sat down than he put his hand between her legs and rubbed her. She closed her eyes, tried pretending she wasn't there, but it didn't work. All she could think of were the people he'd killed, and what he'd likely do to her once he got to Texas.

"Let's have some fun," Tom said.

Lisa smiled and lay back on the bed.

They screwed for a long time, him getting almost to climax then holding off, and her pushing him to the limit. "This is just like the old days,"
she said. "I'm glad you got rid of that girl."

"You didn't seem glad at the time."

"I was scared. That's all."

"You should have been. I had a hard time choosing which one of you
to kill."

"What? You had to even think about it?"

Tom got off of her and stood beside the bed. "I think about a lot of
things. Like right now...you want to know what I'm thinking?"

Lisa smiled. "Sure, what are you thinking?"

Tom's cruel smile returned. He leaned close and whispered. "I'm thinking that you made up all that about screwing that detective, hoping he'd
kill me."

"You're crazy. He made me—"

Tom yanked her to her feet, then he hit her in the stomach so hard
she fell to the floor gasping for breath. Tears welled in her eyes when his
foot caught the side of her head, laying her out flat. "Don't lie to me, girl.
Hear me?"

Still fighting for breath, all Lisa could do was nod. He kicked her again,
in the stomach, then on the side of her face. Blood poured from her
mouth.

"Tom...don't. Tom..."

He stood over her and raised his right foot, then stomped on her throat.
He used a pillow to finish her off, then, just in case, he slit her throat
before sitting back down to watch the movie. As he satisfied himself, he
thought about Detective Frankie Donovan and how he'd have to kill him.
After all, she might not have been lying. Tom couldn't live with that.

CHAPTER 47

LET'S BUY SOME DRUGS

Wilmington, Delaware

I called Jimmy Borelli on my way to work and left him a message, marking it urgent. "Call me, Jimmy. We need to talk."

Somewhere around three or four, Borelli called and we made plans to meet after work at Mrs. Robino's. I thought it odd that he didn't press for what I wanted, but he'd find out soon enough. The rest of the day went by fast and before I knew it I was turning on Union Street and parking the car. I was early, so I grabbed a quick water ice and nursed it while I waited for Jimmy. As I thought about how to play this, I decided I'd take it slow, see where it led.

Jimmy pulled up a few minutes later, got out of his car and tossed a smoke to the street. "What's so important?"

I tossed what was left of my drink into a trash can and walked toward Mrs. Robino's. "We can talk over dinner. I'm starved."

I got us the table closest to the back and asked the hostess to hold off seating others by us as long as they could. "Cop business," I said. "We don't want to be disturbed."

The waitress, who I now knew to be Tammy, brought us a bottle of wine and some bread. I asked for a few minutes before ordering. I tapped my glass to Jimmy's. "*Cent' anni.*"

"I don't want to live a hundred years. Thirty-five, and I'm already wishing I were dead." Despite what he said, he tapped my glass and drank.

I checked to be sure no one was listening, then leaned close. "Why are you so insistent on pinning Bobby's murder on Frankie? You know he didn't do it."

"I happen to think differently."

"What about the witnesses I told you about? The ones who saw somebody dump Bobby off the train? They'll swear it wasn't Bugs."

He was silent, so I continued. "How about the money Bobby had in his account? You get anywhere with that?"

He shook his head. "Nothing yet, but I'm working on it."

"And the people who say he owed money to the wrong crowd?"

"Didn't pan out."

"All right. Just checking." I put a smoke in my mouth, twirling it, but never lit it. It felt good just being in there. One hell of a temptation though. "Before I forget, Rosa said to ask about your boy…Pete, isn't it? Said she hadn't seen him in a while."

I noticed a sharp reaction, not a nice one. "She asked that the other night. Tell her Pete's fine."

"Yeah, I'll tell her. So where's he been? She said he hadn't been in school for weeks."

Borelli gritted his teeth and glared at me. "What's with the questions about my kid? I said he's fine."

"So you said, but I don't think you're telling me everything."

He got up from the table. From his posturing it looked as if he was ready to fight. "Lay off my kid, Fusco."

Borelli was trembling. This was fear. Not anger—fear. "Jimmy, do they have your kid?"

"Fuck you. Don't breathe a word."

I put my hand on his arm and got him to sit. He was shaking. Tammy came by, but I signaled her away. I looked at Jimmy and felt a swell of pity; he looked like a beaten man. "Jimmy, if these fuckers have your boy, I can help."

"Don't even try it; they'll kill him. Promise me you won't try anything stupid. Think if it were Rosa."

"I *am* thinking like that." I leaned in close to him. "Trust me, when people like this take your kids, there can be no good outcome. You've got to take the initiative."

He breathed deep, looked as if he would cry. "I promised his mother I wouldn't put him in danger. I've got to trust that they'll keep their word."

"I'm going after him."

"Don't do it, Nicky. Promise me."

I got up to leave, tossing a fifty on the table. "Eat some dinner, Jimmy. I'll see you around."

"Where are you going? Goddamnit, you better tell me."

"I'm going to buy some drugs."

I WAS MORE PISSED than ever now. I guess I'd known they had his kid going in, but to get the verification from Borelli sent me over the edge. I thought about the rules Johnny Muck had taught me. Rule number two, in particular: *Murder has consequences.* Johnny said to never let it get personal or it would have dire consequences.

It seemed like it took me a lifetime to decide, but it wasn't. The decision had been made when Jack told me the Mexican had Borelli's kid. There was no way I was letting that boy go to the slaughter; he was Rosa's age. I nodded to no one, maybe just telling myself the choice was made. I had passed the point of no return. Now I *knew* people were getting killed, probably a *lot* of people, and I didn't want to do that again.

Goddamnit, I promised Angie.

I turned left, went down Fourth Street then up to Monroe Street, parking where white people didn't, but what the hell, I was here to make a statement and it was critical to get Monroe's help. No way Jack and I could do it ourselves. As I got out of the car I saw DuPree and two of his henchmen waiting, wearing identical sneers.

"Good evening, gentlemen. I believe I have an appointment with the king."

DuPree didn't like me, but even he laughed at that. "You got guns on you, Rat? Don't make me search you, because this time—"

"Not carrying today. I promise."

He started to search me then said "Fuck it. If he shoots me, I'll shoot you before I die."

When we reached him, Monroe greeted me with suspicion. "What's up, Rat? Something must be or you wouldn't be back so soon."

"You need help, Monroe, and I'm here to give it to you. It's going to cost you, though."

After a moment of looking me up and down, he nodded. "I got your dago buddies holding the line at Dupont Street, and the PR's at Second and Harrison—fuckin' Ricans must have fifty people in one house—then I got Marx and his boys on the Prinz badgering my east side." He tossed a beer can into a pile of them in a large container near the corner of the room. "So tell me, how's Nicky the Rat going to help me?"

"Life's tough, but there are always solutions."

"Tough like you don't know, 'cause there's also that Mexican trying to take over from everybody."

"That's what I came to help you with."

Monroe looked at me and laughed. "The Mexican?" When my expression didn't change, he laughed some more. "You're one crazy fucker, Rat."

"A couple of people have told me that." I shot Monroe a look. "Can't wait until Armageddon to decide. If you're not in I'll find somebody else."

"You won't get any muscle from your dago buddies, and the Puerto Ricans won't go against them—"

"But Marx will. He's eager to expand and I know he's had his sights set on Washington Street for a long time."

Monroe popped another beer. "Tell me what you got in mind. If I see it clear, I'm in."

I filled Monroe in on the plan, telling him it had to go down the next night. "I'll need three of your best guys. Make DuPree one of them."

"I thought you didn't like DuPree."

I shook my head. "Don't care one way or the other, but I know he's eager to prove himself. He'll do good."

We went over the details one more time before I headed out. It was getting late, but I had one more stop to make.

I pulled into a parking spot about a block from Doggs' place, rehearsing my plan before I went inside. The Whale greeted me when I went in. Patsy seemed to grow bigger every time I saw him.

"Hey, Nicky. I thought you were gone for good."

"Tell Doggs I'm here to see him, Patsy."

"He ain't gonna like that shit."

"Tell him anyway."

Patsy disappeared behind a door, which seemed like a trick right out of a magician's bag, like hiding an elephant or something, but he returned in less than a minute. "He said to tell you to go fuck yourself."

I nodded, expecting as much. "Tell him one more thing, Patsy. Tell him if he doesn't come out here, I'm going to the cops, and I'm telling them he had the Deuce following Bobby Campisi to try to collect on the drugs and money from that bust that went bad."

Patsy shook his head, and when he did, his whole body shook. "Don't do it, Nicky. You don't want to even say shit like that."

"*Tell* him." I put as much command in that statement as I could.

Patsy was still shaking his head when he disappeared through the door. This time, it only took about half a minute. Doggs burst through the door, a string of 'F's' preceding his entrance.

"...fuck did he say. I'll kill that motherfucker."

Just hearing that upset me. I preferred to remember Doggs as the crazy, lovable character with a mouthful of 'F's' but a heart of gold. Guess drugs changed that, too. In the old days Doggs never dealt drugs, sticking to gambling and dabbling a little in loansharking. And he used us kids all the time to carry bags and even to collect. Hell, nobody would hit a kid Doggs sent to collect. That was double bad. Seeing Doggs as he was now made me sick. He was just another dope dealing prick. He got right up in my face, those thick glasses steamed from the change in temperature between rooms.

"Did I hear right? You threaten to rat on me? What the fuck do you think you can do?"

I knew he expected me to back away; instead, I moved closer, our faces only inches apart. I could smell the sausage roiling in his gut and onions riding on his breath. I stared for a long time, making him sweat. "First, Doggs, I can go to Borelli, or if he's on your payroll, I'll take it to someone else. Either way, I'll keep probing until I find someone who doesn't like your money, and I'll fill them in on the whole Deuce/Bobby/Pepe thing, prominently mentioning the drugs, of course."

"You wouldn't dare, you little fuck."

"I would, and you know it. But I'm not done, because here's the best part. If that doesn't work—the cop thing—then I'll come up here and kill you myself." I paused. "So do you want to step outside or do you want me to embarrass you right here?"

He removed his glasses, waving them in the air like a madman. "Embarrass me? You fuckin' prick. Who the fuck do you think you are? Don't think I'm fuckin' scared of you and your fuckin' reputation." He walked around me adjusting his Coke-bottle glasses so they didn't fall off his Roman nose. "Yeah, I heard about your fuckin' exploits up in New York. I heard about the scary fuckin' Nicky the Rat." He got right in my face and poked his finger into my chest. "A fuckin' estimator. Big fuckin' deal. How much you make, Fusco? Can you *estimate* that?"

I held Doggs' with my glare for a few seconds before speaking. I knew that no matter what he said, he was worried. This was Doggs' bluff, his bravado, his bullshit at full tilt. "What I make doesn't matter. And neither does anything else. I'm here to get money from you to make a buy."

"What the fuck are you talking about?"

"I'm making a buy from the Mexicans, the same ones who fucked up the deal when Bobby stole your money."

Doggs' expression went from pissed off to interested in a millisecond. Maybe he smelled what he thought was money, a cut of the profits, and nothing turned Doggs around like money. "Fuck, why didn't you say so to begin with? If you need some front money we can work things out."

"I don't need front money, and you won't be getting a cut of anything. I need fifty large to do a deal. When the deal is done, I'll give you back the money."

His beady eyes turned hard again. "You—"

"Hold on. As collateral, I'll give you two keys of coke."

"Fuck you. I can get it cheaper."

"Doesn't matter if you can or not. That's what I'm giving, and you'll take it."

That last comment did it. He tried to punch me, and when I held him back, he went ballistic.

"Patsy, kick his fuckin' ass. Who does this prick think he is." He jumped at me. "Let me tell you, Fusco, a bullet can kill you just like anyone else."

I was tired of dealing with him and had to get home. I grabbed Doggs by the throat and drew my Beretta, shoving it into Patsy's face. He'd been moving to help Doggs, but he didn't move fast. "Don't try it, Patsy. I don't want to, but I'll kill you." I shoved Doggs onto the counter, choking him. "Doggs, we can do this civil or we can do it the other way. Decide."

"Let me up. Let me the fuck up."

I looked to Patsy. "Back up, Whale. Keep your hands in front of you." I kept the gun pointed at Patsy, knowing he had a piece behind him at all times.

Doggs rubbed his throat and moaned. "Fuckin' damn near killed me, you prick."

I pulled the locker key out of my pocket and handed it to Doggs. "The dope's in a locker at the train station. If I don't come back, it's yours."

He nodded. "When do you need the money?"

"I'll pick it up tomorrow night around six. Have it ready."

"After this, we're done. Hear me? Fuckin' done."

"We've been done, Doggs. You just didn't know it." I backed out of the shop and nodded to Patsy. "No hard feelings, Whale." Then to Doggs. "See you at six."

Angie was asleep when I got home, though I knew she would be, and that worked better for me. I got a pad of paper and sat at the dining room table struggling to write down my thoughts. For the first time in my life I worried about what might happen if I died. For the first time, I had something great to live for, and I didn't want to lose it. I *couldn't* lose it.

Sometime long after midnight I folded up the two letters—one for Angie and one for Rosa—and sealed them in envelopes. I would mail them tomorrow at work, to myself. If I made it home, great, they'd be torn to shreds and discarded, and if not…I only hoped I expressed myself well.

I said prayers that night before going to sleep, praying to keep me alive, and in the event that didn't happen, to keep the family safe. When I was done, I asked God to forgive me for the people I was going to kill.

CHAPTER 48

PRAYERS AND DEATH

Brooklyn, New York

It had been five days and still Frankie had no clue where Tom Jackson or his wife were hiding out. They had found Lisa's mother in the basement of her house, throat slit. Kate said it happened weeks ago.

Frankie tapped a pencil on his desk as he thought. "Where are they?"

"They might have skipped town," Lou said.

"This is a long time between bodies," Frankie said. "And we still haven't got a clue on the young girl."

Sherri looked at some notes on her desk. "Kate said there were bruises on her that were at least a week old—a lot of bruises, so we can probably assume he had her that long, and doing God knows what to her."

Frankie continued tapping on the desk. "And we know he had her in the apartment, right? Kate confirmed the blood match on the carpet?"

Sherri flipped a page and read some. "On the carpet in front of the sofa. And more in the bedroom."

"And all we've got is his army picture to identify him?"

"Yeah, and nobody saw him at the hotel. The room was rented by the young girl. The clerk ID'd her picture." Lou looked through his set of notes, a copy of what was in Sherri's folder. "And that army picture, people probably wouldn't even recognize him from that. You know how that goes."

"So what are we going to do?" Sherri asked.

"Call Shawna," Lou said.

"Who's Shawna?"

Carol's voice rolled in from the hallway. "He has sleepovers with her. You know, pajama parties?"

Frankie brushed his hands in the air. "She's full of shit. Shawna is a reporter from Channel 3 news."

Lou nudged Sherri's arm. "She gets a lot of exclusives from Frankie. I don't know what he gets in return."

"Screw you, Mazzetti." Frankie said.

Lou laughed. "You know I'm shitting you. But really, we could get her to do a story on him and quote us."

"You might piss him off that way," Sherri said. "We need to be careful about that."

"Trust me, if Frankie goes on the air, he'll piss him off all right. He's good at pissing people off."

Frankie stopped tapping and leaned forward in his chair, staring at Lou then Sherri. "You really think I ought to do this? If we hit the wrong button with this guy he could go nuts on us."

"The trick would be to get him to come after *us*," Lou said.

"Hell of a trick."

"Give it another day," Sherri said.

"What?"

"One more day. Let's see what we can do in one more day, and if we've still got nothing we try to draw him out."

"Sounds better," Frankie said. "I'm not fond of being target practice for a Special Forces guy."

Sherri got up. "We better get to work then. I'm heading to Lisa's office. I want to talk to some more people there."

"I'll take the neighbors," Lou said.

Frankie grabbed the smokes off his desk. "Wait up, Miller. I'm going with you. My car's in the shop. You still live out by me, don't you?"

"For now I do, but that's about to stop with the rent going up so high."

Frankie blew Carol a kiss as he passed, and waved, then continued down the steps with Sherri. "I already told you, there's a place coming open in my building. Cheap, too."

"Cheap to you and cheap to me might be two different things."

Lou was a few steps behind them. "Don't count on it. You'll probably have enough left over to go to the movies."

"You been to the movies lately?" Sherri asked.

"I saw *Flashdance* back in…"

"Pervert," Sherri said.

"Hey, that was art…"

"Art my ass, that was…well, ass is what that was."

"Okay, maybe you're right. It wasn't all art, but it was a good movie."

Frankie stopped and looked at both of them. "Can we get off the *Flashdance* discussion and focus on the case?"

Five hours after they started questioning people, Frankie and Sherri left the office building. She got in the car, started it up and headed home. "Waste of time there."

"I'll call Shawna tonight, and we'll get her to put it on the evening news tomorrow."

Sherri glanced over at him. "I hate for you to do this. Maybe I should be the one. Remember what he said about me in the letter? I could—"

"Out of the question."

"Why? I didn't know you decided all—"

"I'm lead on this case. I decide."

"So that's the way it works with you?"

"Has nothing to do with me; that's the way it always works. Welcome to Homicide."

Sherri didn't talk much on the way home, not much more than asking directions on getting to Frankie's house. When they pulled up to his stoop, he got out and waved to Alex and Keisha, then stood with the door open talking to Sherri. "So what, see you in the morning at 7:00?"

She sighed. "Make it 7:30. I promised my little cousin I'd take him to a movie tonight, and I'm one of those people who needs sleep."

As Sherri was talking, Alex came up beside Frankie. "Hey, FD, how's it going?"

Frankie bumped fists with him. "Going good, Ace, how about you?"

Alex poked his head inside Sherri's car. "Nice ride, lady. You a hooker or something?"

Sherri's face tensed and she almost smacked him, but Alex pulled back. "Don't get so riled. I was just messin' with you."

Frankie smacked him on the back of the head, a loving pat. "This is my partner, Alex. Detective Sherri Miller."

Alex poked his head back in and held his hand out to bump. "Sorry, Detective. Didn't mean no harm."

Sherri smiled. "I'm sorry too."

"Alex, why don't you wait on the stoop? I'll be right there."

"Yeah, well the thing is, FD, I didn't come over here to say hi. Don't look, but you see that dude hanging out by the bodega?"

Frankie cast a surreptitious glance in his direction while he lit a smoke. "The one with the hood?"

"Yeah, that dude."

"What about him?"

"That white dude don't belong here. Flat out don't belong."

Frankie turned back to Sherri, as if he were talking to her. "Tell me how he doesn't belong here."

"Hey, FD, why don't you hand over one of them smokes."

Sherri glared at Frankie. "You give that boy cigarettes?"

"Time for that later, Miller." He handed Alex a smoke and a light. "Go on, Ace, finish up."

"When me and Keisha walked by he looked at her like he wanted to—"

"Whoa! I think I know how he looked at her. Okay, I'll check it out."

Frankie looked the other way down the street. "Miller, laugh or do something. Just don't look his way."

Sherri looked at Alex and then at Keisha, still sitting on the stoop. "Why don't I take the kids inside?"

"They can get inside all on their own. We might have a pervert here, so how about you drive away like you're leaving, but circle the block and come up on the other side of him. I'll sit on the stoop for a half a minute, and then stroll on down there, so give me a good two minutes."

"I don't like it. He'll see you coming. Suppose it's Jackson? If it is, you're dead."

Frankie thought for a moment, then turned to Alex. "Get inside, and make Keisha go with you."

"FD—"

"No shit on this. Get inside now." Frankie got back in the car. "All right, go to the corner, like it's any other day and take a right. We'll come around the back side and come up on him from the other direction."

Sherri drove around the block, parked on the side street, out of sight. They got out and walked toward the bodega. Before turning the corner, Frankie checked his gun, making sure he had a full clip. Sherri did the same.

"Follow my lead," Frankie said. "Let's go."

When they made the turn, the guy was gone. Frankie drew his gun. "Stay alert, Miller."

She reached for her gun. "No need to tell me that."

They hadn't taken five steps when the guy came out of a storefront 30 feet ahead of them, his gun pointed at Frankie.

"Watch out!" Miller shouted, and shoved Frankie aside. A bullet whizzed past, hitting a van parked on the street.

The guy fired two more shots. Frankie hit the ground hard, diving behind an old Buick. The guy turned on Miller. She had her weapon raised, but he fired first, his shot taking her in the gut. The impact dropped her to the curb.

Sherri tried crawling behind the car. A shot hit her leg just above the knee. "Goddamn!" She raised her gun, aiming, when another shot got her in the right shoulder.

Frankie scrambled to get into a position he could fire from. "Goddamn!" He crab-walked toward her, keeping his head low. He reached out and grabbed Miller's collar and dragged her to safety.

"Get me out of here!" she said.

"Enough of this shit." Frankie stood, gun in hand, firing.

Tom Jackson dropped to a squatted position, switching his fire. Frankie could almost feel the bullets flying by. His hands were steady, but his gut churned. Fear had a good grip on him. He didn't mind fighting anyone, no matter how big, but he hated fighting bullets. They always won.

Franke dropped below the trunk of the car, as if he were taking cover, then popped right back up, firing as soon as he had Tom Jackson in his sights. Jackson was in the process of standing after Frankie took cover. He was caught off guard. A bullet hit Jackson's left shoulder, spinning him toward the bodega. Frankie advanced, firing all the time, slowly, methodically. His next two shots missed, but the fourth one hit Jackson in the chest. That one took him down.

Frankie approached slowly, gun in hand. Jackson lay on the sidewalk, his right hand extended still clutching the gun. Frankie took it easy, one step at a time. When he got beside Jackson, he stepped on his wrist. A smile was on Tom Jackson's face.

"Guess I'm gonna have to wait to fuck that black bitch partner of yours."

Frankie took a quick glance around. "Yeah, might be a little while though." Then Frankie hollered, "Drop the gun!" and he fired three more shots into Jackson's chest. For good measure, he shot him in the neck.

Frankie picked up the gun and turned to go for Sherri. Sirens screamed as he ran to check on her. Three cop cars screeched to a stop, officers out with guns drawn.

Frankie raised his hands. "I'm a cop. Got an officer down here!"

"That's Donovan!" one of the officers yelled, and they ran to help.

"We got an ambulance coming, Detective."

Frankie was on the ground, holding her. "Come on, Miller. Don't you fucking die on me."

CHAPTER 49

A PRAYER FOR THE DYING

Wilmington, Delaware

I was a bundle of nerves all day. Not fear, at least not fear of dying, but fear of leaving Angie and Rosa and our new baby to fend for themselves. The day was unproductive as hell, most of my time spent planning for what would happen that night. Jack called and filled me in on the details, and to confirm that we had a deal for two keys. We promised the Mexicans a lot more business if this worked out. I finished up the last estimate and left, stopping by to pick up the money from Doggs. He had checked the locker and verified that the coke was there, but left it where it was.

As I drove down Union Street, I thought about what I was doing. I was in a no-win situation. If I went through with this, I'd be breaking my promise to Angie, and to God. If I quit now, which is what I wanted to do, Borelli's kid might die.

An image of Borelli's face stuck in my mind, the worry etched in his eyes when I confronted him in the restaurant. I imagined if it were Rosa they had, and then I thought of Angie, and how it would tear her up. Jimmy's wife was probably going through hell right now.

Just like Angie would.

Every time I thought about quitting and turning this over to the cops, I thought of the consequences.

What if her boy dies? What if I don't go, and he dies?

That thought made up my mind. I couldn't live with myself if Borelli's kid died, knowing I could have done something about it. I didn't like cursing God, but I felt like it now. Why did He put me in these situations? He knew what I'd do if they took the boy.

If You didn't want me killing, why did You let them take Borelli's kid?

I didn't expect God to answer, but it didn't matter. I made a decision long ago in my life: Some things were worth dying for; others worth killing for. This fell into the killing category.

I took a right on Lancaster Pike and headed west. Jack was meeting Monroe and his guys a few miles out, close to where we had to go. These Mexican guys weren't like the other drug dealers; they were setting up shop in upscale neighborhoods, using them for distribution points. Bugs had filled me in on some of this, and now Jack confirmed it. I stopped at a place on the side of the road a few miles before getting to the meeting place, gathered my thoughts, and called Angie.

"Hello?" she said, in her always-pleasant voice.

"Hey, babe. What are you doing?"

"Cooking, and you'll be sorry you missed it—baked ziti with sausage and meatballs."

"Save some, I'm gonna be hungry."

"You know I will." She paused. "Why are you calling? I thought you were playing cards."

"I just missed you, and wanted to tell you how much I love you." I knew I screwed up as soon as I said it.

"Nicky, what's going on? You're not telling me something." Her voice was laced with suspicion. "Is everything all right?"

"Everything's fine. I thought I'd call that's all. Now, take care of that ziti so you don't burn it. See you later."

"Okay, win big," she said, and hung up.

I felt like an ass, almost blowing it with Angie. Should have known better. I got back into the mode for the night's work, though, and pulled into the meeting place with about five minutes to spare. Jack was there, and so was Monroe with three of his guys, DuPree included. He had an old black van. I got out of the car and greeted everyone. "Jack fill you guys in?"

Monroe flashed one of his smiles. "From what he said, you and him go in alone. You'll call me on the cell before you enter and leave it on. We come in when we hear the signal."

"Gate might be locked." I said.

"No question it will be," Jack said. "Once we go in they'll lock it again."

Monroe tapped the van as if it were a tank or something. "Unless they got a concrete gate, we'll make it through with this."

I stared at each of Monroe's guys, wanting to make sure they got the message. "I don't know what you guys are used to, or what experience you have, but this is going to get nasty. People are going to die, maybe some of us. Maybe all of us."

Most of them nodded. One of them said it was nothing compared to the streets, and DuPree said he could handle whatever the Mexicans brought on.

"Monroe, if I'm dead you get that kid. You've got to promise me that."

He nodded, and we shook hands. I'd done my job; it was time to go. I shook hands with each of his guys then turned to Jack. "You ready?"

"I already told God I'd likely be seeing him soon."

I smiled. "If only for a minute, huh?"

Jack laughed. "That's right, Nicky—if only for a minute."

As we drove in, I checked the weapons again, a Beretta in my waistband—front and back—and a derringer under my baseball cap. Everything would depend on those two shots from the derringer, and on Jack's reaction once things started. Jack had a gun in his waistband, too.

I looked over at Jack. He seemed calm. Maybe too calm. "Let's go over this one more time," I said. It wasn't that I didn't trust Jack, but when it came down to guns and bullets you didn't get second chances. I needed to make sure.

"I got it," Jack said.

"I know you do, but remind me anyway."

"Gonna have six, maybe seven or eight guys for sure. All armed. The gate is guarded, but probably only one person. They're going to check us when we go in, and there will probably be at least three guys, maybe four. The rest of them will be throughout the house."

"And it's a two story?"

"Yeah, two story, and it's big. Got a basement, too."

"We have any idea where the kid is?"

"I don't even know if he's here. My contact said yes, but he didn't know where."

I nodded. "All right, we're going to have to watch for that."

We were almost there when I told Jack to pull over.

"What for?"

"I want to say a prayer for those about to die."

"Fuck that," Jack said. "I don't give a shit about them."

"I'm not worried about them," I said. "But it might be us who die."

Jack pulled over and blessed himself then started his prayer. When we finished, he pulled back onto the main road. "Don't forget to close your eyes, Nicky."

I laughed. It was a joke we had as kids. One of the nuns had told us that hell wasn't full of fire, like most people said, or full of ice like Dante's Ninth Circle. She said that when people died, God let everyone get a glimpse of heaven, even those who were going to hell. *That*, she said, was what hell was all about. Hell was having to live for eternity knowing what heaven looked like but never being able to experience it. Hell was an eternal longing to have what you could never have. We used to joke that all we had to do to beat the system was close our eyes.

"I won't forget, Jack, but I think I'll try to stay alive, just in case closing your eyes doesn't work."

"Yeah, me too," Jack said.

I said a quick prayer for the drug dealers, too, but I couldn't afford to start feeling sorry for them—that would take the edge off. As we drew closer I reminded myself that they were drug dealers and if we had to kill them they deserved it.

Besides, they've got Borelli's kid.

The guard at the gate looked inside the car then waved us on. He was talking to someone on a cell. A few seconds later we pulled up the driveway to the front of the house. Four of them were waiting for us.

"I was hoping it would only be three," Jack said.

"Got our work cut out for us, Jack. Stay cool, man. Stay cool."

I got out of the car, my right hand held in the air and the left holding the bag of money. Jack got out the driver's side and held his hands up.

"*Buenas noches, señores.*" Jack had a definite American accent to his Spanish, but it wasn't too bad.

"Good evening," the one who looked to be in charge replied, without an accent. He could have passed for somebody born in Philly.

They approached slowly, the other three with guns in hand. One carried a shotgun—he'd have to go first—and the other two had what looked to be Glocks. I'm sure the guy addressing us had a gun, but he'd have to reach for it. The guy with the shotgun stood a few feet back, cautious. I'd need him closer for this to work. He was the one that *had* to go out first.

The leader nodded toward the bag I carried. "The money?"

I nodded back. "It's all here. Where's the coke?"

"Inside. After I look at the money, we'll go have a drink."

I smiled. "Sounds good."

"Rico!" The way he said it was a command, and one of the guys holding a Beretta came forward, checking us for weapons.

"In my waistband," I said, "front and back."

He kept his eyes on me while he checked. I could tell he seemed pleased I told him about both guns. "Any more?" he asked.

"None."

He checked anyway, running his hands up and down my legs and even checking my ankles and under my arms. He didn't, however, check under my hat. Good damn thing. He moved to Jack and went through the same routine, but Jack only had the one gun and he told him so. He had put his own gun away when he checked me, then handed mine to the other guy.

The leader stepped forward and I handed him the bag. He looked inside, riffled through the stacks of money, then smiled. "Perhaps we should have a little tequila now, señor."

When he turned toward the house, so did the guy with the shotgun and one of the others. The last guy stayed behind. This was my chance. I pretended to wipe sweat from my brow, flipped the hat off and grabbed the derringer. I stepped forward to the man holding the shotgun, shoved the derringer in his ear and pulled the trigger. I shot the other guy in the face, close to his jaw. Definitely not lethal.

I sensed the guy behind me moving. I got the gun from the guy I just shot, spun and fired. I missed with the first shot but hit his neck with the second. He was aiming his gun, so I jumped on him, sending us both to the ground. I hoped Jack was taking care of the other guy and that Monroe heard the shots.

Two more rang out behind me as I struggled with the guy on the ground, holding his gun hand away from me. I head-butted him twice, and I heard Jack yell.

"Got him, Nicky."

The guy I was fighting went out. I took his gun and shot him once in the head, then moved to Jack's side. "They dead?"

He nodded. "All of them."

I grabbed both of my guns and checked the clips while Jack got the shotgun. "Let's go."

As we moved into the house, Monroe's van busted through the gate, simultaneous with two more gunshots, and DuPree's cackle. I figured he got his first guy.

I waited. No sense in going in light. A moment later, Monroe and his guys joined us, DuPree joining me and Jack to check upstairs, while Monroe and the others took the first floor. Jack took the lead up the steps, slowly, followed by me and DuPree. The landing opened to a long hallway with rooms on the east and west. I nodded to the west and Jack started down the hall, me behind him, and DuPree, facing backward, guarding the rear.

We hadn't taken five steps when a door opened and two guys jumped out with guns blasting. I dropped to the floor and fired, but from behind me I heard more gunshots. Jack went down with the first volley, blood splattering the walls and part of my pants. I crouched and kept firing as I moved forward. I got both the guys in front of us, then turned and flopped onto my belly just as I heard DuPree yell.

"I'm hit. Motherfucker, I'm hit!"

I crawled forward firing with both guns, taking one guy in the chest, but the other one ducked behind the door. I grabbed hold of DuPree pulling him back down the hall while keeping my eyes on that door. I figured the guy was going to come out low when he did, so I focused there. Sure enough, as I dragged DuPree toward the room, the guy popped out of the doorway close to the floor. I fired and kept firing, three of the five bullets taking him in the head or chest.

From downstairs I heard Monroe call. "Rat, you okay? DuPree?"

"Up here, Monroe. DuPree's hit. I think Jack's gone." I turned so my back was against the wall and I could easily see both ways, a gun pointing in each direction. I had already reloaded. Footsteps came up the steps along with Monroe's voice.

"Let me hear you, Rat."

"Right here," I said. "You're clear."

He came into the hallway, gun in hand, followed by two of his men. "You all right, DuPree?"

DuPree was bleeding, but not bad. "He'll be fine. Not so for Jack." I looked at his men, noted one missing. "And you?"

"Lost Tucker. Had two in the kitchen. No kid, though. You find him up here?"

I stood. "Haven't searched yet. Let's take them one at a time. Be careful."

In the first room we tried, we found him, hiding under the bed, crying. "Pete, is that you?" I asked.

He poked his head out then back in, like a turtle afraid to be picked up. "Who are you?"

"I'm a friend of your father." I got down on the floor and reached my hand out. "Come on. We're getting you out of here."

That must have hit a nerve. He flew out from under that bed. "Are you taking me home?"

"You're going home. You'll be safe now."

One of Monroe's men was helping DuPree down the stairs. Monroe and his other guy took Jack.

"Who's that?" Pete asked. "What happened to him?"

"You're better off not knowing anything. Understand?"

"Who are you?"

"As I said, you're better off not knowing." This time I put some iron in my voice. As we were leaving I noticed a bag in the closet and opened it. It was stuffed with cash. Must have been two or three hundred large in there. I grabbed it and then grabbed Pete. "Let's go."

We quickly made our way out to the cars, careful in case we'd missed any Mexicans. "Get in that car," I told Pete. "Get in the back seat and keep your head down." As he moved, I turned to Monroe. "Take Jack, will you? Hold on to him until I send someone to get him. And you need to take your man so they don't know who was involved."

The briefcase of money I had brought for the drug buy lay on the ground. I picked it up and handed it to Monroe. "For your troubles," I said.

He opened it up and grinned. "My man."

One of Monroe's men eyed me. "Man you killed them fuckers cold. I mean cold, dude."

"They're just drug dealers."

Monroe looked at me, a strange expression on his face. "That go for me too, Rat?"

I stared him down. "You deal drugs don't you?"

"Everybody does nowadays. Like I said, you got to if you want to stay in the game."

I looked around at the bodies. "You know me, Monroe. I don't judge people by what they do, all except drugs. Find a new game because the one you're in sucks."

"I thought we had more than that. Thought we were tight."

I thought about how to phrase a reply, but figured the truth was always best. He had three guys with him, and one had moved his hand toward his gun. They might decide to turn the tables on me, but I doubted it. They had just seen me kill seven or eight guys, and no one wants to die, not even drug dealers. "I like you, Monroe, but we're not tight. We never will be as long as you deal drugs. We had something to do tonight that worked for both of us. Let's leave it at that."

"And in the future?"

"Let's say I won't be hanging around Monroe Street, and I doubt you'll be wandering around Little Italy."

Monroe stared at me for a moment, then he looked at his guys. "That's why I always liked you, Rat. You speak your mind." He walked over to me, hands exposed—no threat—then reached forward to shake.

I took his hand. "This doesn't make us brothers or even friends."

"I know," Monroe said. "Let's leave it that we're not enemies."

I nodded to him, then to his guys. Most of them wouldn't look at me. "I can live with that. You know I don't like trouble."

"My man," he said, and laughed, bringing smiles to all of them. He flipped me a coin which I caught with my left hand, leaving my right free in case it was a trick. I looked down at it. It was one of those presidential coins from a set they made a few years ago. It had a picture of James Monroe on the front. He looked stern and empowered, with his long hair swept back from his forehead and a scarf around his neck. Intense eyes sat above prominent cheekbones. His name was etched into the top—James Monroe. I realized looking at this that Monroe was a lot like this man, at least from the looks of it on the coin. Not a man to be trifled with.

"Just to show no hard feelings, Rat, give that coin to your daughter."

"What for?"

"That's safe passage for her. She ever gets bothered, any time, tell her to flash that coin. It'll keep her safe. I *promise*. Even people in the other hoods respect my coin."

He used the word that we had agreed to in prison that we would never break. We seldom used it with each other, but when one of us said "promise," we agreed to stick to it. It was the one thing I insisted on when we originally made our deal. I nodded. "Thanks, Monroe."

"Now I say we get the fuck out of here before somebody comes. Be hard to explain us being here with all these bodies."

"Go on," I said. "I've got to burn it."

"What?"

"No sense leaving DNA here. I'm burning it."

They left and I stayed to set the fire. It had to be one that would sweep it all up. I got the gas from the car, spread it everywhere I wanted to, then stepped out, leaving a trail to light. I looked back to the house one last time, then blessed myself and said a short prayer. Not for the bodies I was leaving behind, but for myself, asking for forgiveness. I lit the fire, grabbed the money, and got in the car.

***

Monroe drove the speed limit all the way down Lancaster Pike, passing by half a dozen cop cars with sirens blaring. "Sure hope the Rat gets out of there in time."

DuPree turned the radio off and looked at him. "What the fuck, that wasn't the fun I thought it was going to be."

"I told you, we got a lot of work to do if we want to protect our territory. This Mexican guy isn't going to give up easy. Don't worry, though; we'll get your sorry ass patched up."

"We can't go to no hospital," DuPree said.

"Taking you to see Doc Majors. He's pulled out more slugs than an army doc."

"He's a goddamn vet!"

Monroe laughed. "I always said you was a dog, DuPree."

The guys in the back of the van laughed.

"Fuck all of you," DuPree said, and then, "I got a question for you, Monroe. I know you and this Rat guy go back a ways, but why'd you give out one of your coins for his daughter? Ain't our job to protect her."

"I'm gonna teach you if it kills me, DuPree. I want you to think about what might happen if that girl wanders anywhere by our streets and something happens to her. What do you think the Rat is going to do?"

DuPree didn't get time to answer.

"I'll tell you what he's going to do. He'll kill every motherfucker he can, and that's a lot of motherfuckers."

They rode in silence for a few miles then DuPree turned to Monroe.

"You were right."

"About what?"

"I couldn't have killed him if I had a gun pointed at his head. That's one mean motherfucker."

Monroe nodded his head as he switched lanes. "Yeah."

CHAPTER 50

THE PRODIGAL SON

Wilmington, Delaware

As I exited the gate, the glow of the fire lit up the sky. I turned the opposite way to avoid running into any cops who might be coming. There was a chance some would be heading in from the north, but I doubted it. From the back seat, Pete's meek voice struggled with a question.

"Where are we going?"

"Home, Pete. Just stay put, all right?"

"If I'm going home why can't I get up?"

"You've already seen too much of me."

"But I thought—"

"Stay put!"

When I looked in the rearview mirror, Pete's head was buried in the seat. I waited until I felt we were safe, then called Jimmy. He answered on the second ring.

"Borelli."

"Meet me at the park by St. Elizabeth's. Fifteen minutes."

"What for? You didn't do anything crazy, did you?"

"On second thought, make that twenty-five. I need to make a stop."

"Goddamnit—"

"Meet me."

I stopped and gave Doggs back his money, taking the locker key in return. "Thanks, Doggs. Consider what you did a good deed."

"And that's it? A fuckin' good deed? This is the respect I get for all the years we've known each other?"

I flashed him a smile that wasn't a smile. "The respect went out the window with the drugs. You don't deserve it anymore. And by the way, if anybody asks, I was here playing cards tonight."

"Of course you were, and what time did you leave?"

I looked at my watch. "Around two."

He flipped me the finger, perhaps practicing for when he lost his voice, then disappeared through the magical door into the back room. I went out to the car, did a quick count of the money in the trunk, then drove to meet Borelli.

Jimmy was parked alongside the curb right by the bus stop at the old bench. He was outside pacing, a smoke in his hand. I pulled up behind him.

"Stay put, Pete. Hear me? I'll only be a minute."

"Okay."

I got out and walked up to Jimmy.

"Why am I here, Fusco? This better be good." His concern had grown to anger.

"I know where your boy is. But first I need to know what part you played in Bobby's murder."

He looked at me as if I were nuts, and as if he wanted to kill me, both at the same time. "I don't know what the fuck you've been smoking, but I had nothing to do with Campisi's murder, and if you know one fucking thing about Pete, you'd better tell me."

I needed some final convincing, and Borelli's sincerity showed. I turned and walked back to my car, him screaming at me the whole way. I opened the back door and leaned inside. "Pete, get out. Your dad's here."

The kid almost jumped out of the car. When he hit the street he raced to his father. I stayed back, not wanting to interrupt this reunion.

"Petey! Jesus Christ, is that you?" Jimmy raced to meet him, wrapping his arms around the boy so tight I was afraid he'd hurt him. He kissed his cheeks and hugged him. "Goddamn, Petey. Are you all right?"

I stepped further back, giving them space until I heard Jimmy calling me by name. I didn't want his kid knowing who it was, though it was probably too late for that. "Jimmy, how about Pete gets in the car while we talk, huh?"

He nodded but before he got in his father's car he reached out to shake my hand. "Mr. Fusco, I don't know how to thank you enough. I thought they were going to kill me."

Ah shit. I didn't know the kid knew me. I shook his hand but didn't smile. "You can thank me by forgetting everything you know about tonight, especially my name."

"You got it," he said, and got in the car.

Borelli rushed over to hug me, tears flowing. "Nicky, I can't express myself. How did you do it?" Then he stepped back and looked at me. "*Why* did you do it?"

"Don't worry about how; the less you know the better. This has already cost me dearly."

"Name it, Nicky. Anything."

I shook my head. "You've still got me wrong. I don't want anything from you. What kind of fuckin' scum would want money for saving a kid? But you're going to need to pay for this, and it won't be easy. Those Mexicans will assume it was you who did this, or at least that it was you who put somebody up to it. They'll be after you."

"I'll have to go into hiding."

"First you have to clear Bugs." I pointed my finger at him. "That's your priority. Clear Bugs. And when you do those reports, my name better not be mentioned."

"Did you kill Bobby?" His voice seemed almost apologetic.

I shook my head again. "No. I didn't kill Bobby." I lowered my head. "Jack McDermott did that, but he's dead."

"You—"

"No! Jack helped me get Pete out of there, but he didn't make it. The guys guarding Pete got him."

"Oh fuck."

"Yeah, so if there's any possible way to pin Bobby's murder on the Mexicans, see if you can do that. I'd hate to see Jack's parents suffer any more than they have to."

"I'll do what I can, but I'm not staying around here long. My family has suffered enough. I don't know what I'm going to do or how to protect them. This Mexican is nuts."

Pussy. You don't know about suffering. "Yeah, well this isn't all wine and roses. You have a lot to answer for about the way you handled this case, trying to pin it on Bugs."

Borelli didn't say anything for a moment. He shook his head slowly and avoided looking at me. "You'd do the same if they had Angie or Rosa. You'd sell your soul if you had to."

I thought about it and realized he didn't think like me. Probably not many who did. I'd do exactly what I did tonight. I'd kill every motherfucker involved. "Maybe," I said, and headed for my car.

"Thanks again, Nicky."

"Stay there, I'm not leaving."

I opened the trunk and got the bag out, took it back to Borelli and handed it to him. "Take this, you might need it."

Jimmy opened it and his eyes went wide. "Jesus Christ, there must be a couple of hundred grand in here."

"Four hundred fifty roughly."

Jimmy stared at me. "And you're turning this in?"

"I'm telling you to take it. Nobody knows about it, and you'll need it to stay hidden."

He stood there shaking his head.

"One thing. I want you to give fifty to Donna, not because she deserves it but because she's stuck raising Bobby's kid with no father. She'll need it."

I almost forgot the key. I reached into my pocket and handed Borelli the locker key. "This fits a locker at the train station. Bobby's got two keys of coke in there."

Jimmy teared up. "I had you all wrong, Fusco."

"Yeah, people do that sometimes."

"What about you? He'll find out who you are. He'll be coming for you."

"Who?"

"The Mexican. His name is Carlos Cortes—El Jabato."

"Never heard of him."

"You better get educated, because now that you've done this, he *will* hear about you."

"Worry about yourself. Get your family out of the state and start a new life." I nodded toward the money. "You got enough there to do it."

"I will, and thanks again for everything, but I'm worried about you. This Carlos guy, he'll kill anyone—civilians, police—he's even killed mayors."

I looked at Borelli. "Mayors don't kill back." Maybe it was the look, or maybe what I said, but he shut up after that.

We shook hands one final time, then he got in his car. I saw him hugging Pete as I left. That felt good. I should have kept some of the money for Angie and me, but that would have tainted things. Sometimes it was better to struggle through life as an honest man.

It took me less than two minutes to get home. I checked the time, but it was too late to call Bugs. I'd do that in the morning. I climbed the stairs quietly, undressed in the hall, then crept into the room and snuck into bed. Angie was lying on her back, sound asleep. I stared at her for a minute, so beautiful with a hint of moonlight shining through the window on her face.

When I started this new life, I made promises to Angie and to God. Now I'd broken both. Breaking the promise to Angie worried me more, though; God knew what was going to happen; He could have stopped it. Angie trusted me, and I'd let her down.

I lay my head on her belly, gently, hoping to feel something, but I knew it was too early. It felt good all the same. New life was in there, and I prayed the baby was more like Angie than me. The world didn't need another Nicky Fusco.

CHAPTER 51

MIDNIGHT VIGIL

Brooklyn, New York

Sherri Miller was in intensive care, on the third floor. Mazzetti rode the elevator all the way up with a clenched fist, then stormed into the ICU waiting room. Four uniforms paced the hall. Two more occupied chairs, heads held low. Nowhere was there sign of Frankie Donovan. It was a good thing, too, because Lou was ready to kick his ass.

"Where's Donovan?" he asked, in a voice too loud.

"Right here." That from behind him.

He spun, saw Frankie and almost raced to him, eyes burning. "What the fuck is wrong with you, taking her into a situation like that? She's a goddamn rookie!" He shoved Frankie, hard.

Frankie didn't respond, keeping his head held low. "Not now, Lou. I can't think about it now."

"Fuck you and your 'can't think about it.' Tell that to Miller." He shoved Frankie again. "You should have called for backup. You should have called *me*."

Frankie shoved back. "You think I haven't been through this? I made a decision and I was wrong, okay? Let it go!"

"Let it go? Let it go!"

Lieutenant Morreau walked up behind them. "That's right, Lou. Let it go. We've got an officer in ICU, and she's going to need all the support she can get. Not a couple of assholes fighting over who did what wrong."

Lou nodded to Morreau but he still glared at Frankie. "I hate to see it happen to someone so young. She had such a great attitude."

"Hey, Mazzetti," Morreau said. "She's not dead for God's sake. Give her a shot, will you?" He shook his head. "Somebody update me."

"She's critical," Frankie said. "Three shots, one in the gut, one in the thigh and one in the shoulder. The gut one is causing most of the problems. She's lost a lot of blood. BP is low, and somebody said they had concerns about her kidney."

"What happened, Donovan? How did this go down?"

"We were checking him out, thinking it was a pervert, based on what some neighborhood kids told us." Frankie paused. "To be honest, Sherri said it might be Jackson, but I ignored her. We made a move to come up behind him, but he must have sensed something. When we came around the corner, he took us by surprise and opened fire."

Morreau waited.

"She saved my ass. Knocked me out of the line of fire and into the street. He ended up shooting her."

"Christ's sake!" Lou said.

Frankie almost turned on him but didn't. His voice lowered and he choked up. "I know, Lou. It should have been me. But I can't go back and change it. Believe me, if I could, I'd do it. She didn't deserve this."

Morreau frowned, but not in a bad way. "Put it all in the report. For now, let's get together and see what we can do to get her through this."

They took turns sitting in her room, waiting for some improvement. She had been unresponsive since she came in, and trying to get information from the doctors was like trying to learn Russian in one day. About halfway through the night, Lou came out into the waiting room.

Frankie got up when he saw him, anxious.

"She's awake."

"And?"

"Doctor said she's still not good, but he thinks she'll pull through. Gonna take some time to recover, though."

Frankie waited but Lou didn't add any more. "Will she be able to go back to the job?"

"He doesn't know. I guess we'll have to wait and see." Lou got a drink from the water fountain and came back. "Sorry about what I said."

Frankie slapped his back. "Don't worry; I'd have said the same."

After maybe another hour, the doctor came out and said she was stable, but still serious, good enough that they could go home and get some sleep, though. Frankie yawned and stood. "Sleep sounds good, Lou. I'm heading out."

"Go on," Lou said. "I'm staying for a while. We got nothing to do today anyway."

"Except find that psycho, Lisa, who was married to him."

"Yeah, except that." Lou leaned back and closed his eyes. "When you find her, try not to kill her, okay?"

Frankie went home, caught about two hours sleep, then popped up. Not that he wanted to get up; it was simply that he didn't trust leaving that woman out there alone. Besides, he owed Shawna a special scoop on this. Maybe she'd pay him back with something special of her own.

As he dressed, he realized something was wrong—the prospect of Shawna perhaps granting him sexual favors wasn't even exciting him. Was he losing it? But as he drank his coffee, he recognized the real reason— Kate. Images and thoughts of her bothered him every time he thought about being with another woman.

Just my luck.

He was in the middle of making a second cup of coffee when the phone rang. He grabbed it off the table. "Donovan."

"Detective Donovan, this is Sam down at the station. They just found a woman's body in a motel room across the street from where the other one was killed. She was naked with her throat cut. Guy at the scene says it's your girl, Lisa Johnson."

"Son of a bitch! Guess she wasn't in on it after all."

"What's that, Detective?"

"Nothing. Just talking to myself. Thanks for calling, though. Tell them I'll be down in a little while."

Frankie hung up and went back to getting that much needed second cup of coffee, but before he poured it the phone rang again. He snatched it up and answered with a bit of irritation. "Donovan."

"Still grumpy in the morning, huh, Bugs?" It was Nicky.

Frankie glanced at the clock. "What are you doing calling so early? Everything okay?"

"You're clear," Nicky said.

"What?"

"Clear. Case solved. Over. You'll have no more trouble from little old Wilmington, Delaware."

Frankie went to pour his coffee. "What the fuck? Don't leave me hanging. Tell me about it."

"Not much to tell. Borelli did all the work. Turns out Bobby was into drugs, as we knew, and he crossed the wrong guys. Seems like he had a big mouth, but we already knew that, too."

"Yeah, that we did." Frankie paused. "Does Donna know?"

"I suspect she does by now. Borelli said he was going to tell her."

"So how did it bust? How did Borelli find out? He didn't seem like he was hot on the trail of anything when I left."

"Guess he didn't share with us, but he did a good job. Hey, he cleared you, didn't he?"

Frankie sensed that Nicky wasn't telling the whole story, but he knew if Nicky Fusco didn't want to talk, there was nothing going to make him. "All right, Nicky, I owe you. I mean big time."

"Big time, huh? What's that, three large subs?"

"You got it. Next time I'm down."

Nicky laughed. "Don't make it too long or you'll have to make it four subs; Angie's pregnant."

"What? Holy shit! That's great. I'm happy for you guys."

"Yeah, me too. So get down soon. It'll be good to see you under better circumstances."

"Same here. And tell Angie I said hi, and Rosa, too. Please thank them for all the food—"

"Yeah, yeah. You know that's not necessary." Nicky paused. "Listen, I gotta go. I'll see you later."

"Thanks again."

Frankie hung up and sat quietly for a moment. Something was definitely wrong on that end. He walked around his apartment, smoking the first cigarette of the morning. Damn, that one tasted good. He looked at the clock again, six thirty. Early, but Donna should be up. He called and she answered right away.

"Frankie, is that you?"

"It's me. Are you okay?"

"I was going to call you later," she said. "They got the people who did it. It was some drug people."

"I heard. That's why I called."

There was a moment of silence, then she said, "I'm sorry for all the things I said about you. I didn't mean them."

"I know. And listen, don't worry about money. If you have to, move in with Mom."

"I'll be all right now, with the money Bobby had in the bank, and—"

Every muscle tensed in Frankie's body. "Money Bobby had? I don't think you'll get that, Donna, remember what—"

"No, I got it, and he had more too—another fifty thousand in some locker. Detective Borelli already gave it to me. He was here so early he woke me. And he gave it to me in cash, for God's sake. I swear, I've never seen so much cash. Mom and I are going to the bank today to deposit it."

Alarms went off everywhere in Frankie's head. "Hold on, Donna. Hold on. Let me think." He paced a moment. "So you're telling me Borelli gave you this money—in cash—and said it's yours to keep?"

"I swear it. He said the money in the bank I'm going to have to explain to someone. Maybe the IRS. But the other money is ours. He said not to deposit it all at once or anything, but I don't know why."

"Okay, here's what you do. Listen close because if you don't, you'll end up losing that money."

"What? Oh my God, what do you mean?"

"Listen!" Frankie hated yelling at Donna, but sometimes she just didn't listen. "Call a guy named Roscoe Jones. He's got offices up on Delaware Avenue. Give him my name and tell him what happened. *Everything* that happened. He'll tell you how to handle the money."

"Okay, but—"

"Just do it, Donna. I gotta go. I have a dead body waiting for me. I'll call later."

Frankie hung up the phone and sat on the sofa. Fifty grand cash, and Borelli delivered it in person. Something was definitely wrong, but Frankie had to get to the motel and check out Lisa and he felt sure she didn't look as good now as she did before.

As he drove over to the scene, he called Carol. "Do me a favor, Carol. I need to know anything unusual that happened in Wilmington, Delaware, over the past few days. The local paper is the News Journal."

"That's all I get—'anything unusual'?"

"It's a small town. Can't be much, and if I'm right, it will be headlines or at least page two."

"All right. I'll get on it."

"See you when I get in."

CHAPTER 52

A QUIET DINNER

Brooklyn, New York

Frankie went and saw Lisa, and he was right; she didn't look as good as she had before. He felt sorry for her, but had lingering doubts about her involvement in the murders. For some reason, he didn't see her as the innocent babe-in-the-woods image she portrayed. There was a cat in the motel room with her. Frankie convinced one of the officers to take it home with him.

He got what he needed from the scene and stopped at the hospital on the way back. Lou was still there.

"Anything new, Mazzetti?"

"She's a trooper," Lou said, then, "Why don't you come in and see for yourself?"

"She's alive and kicking?"

Mazzetti laughed. "She might kick you when she sees you."

Frankie and Lou walked into her room. A nurse was just leaving and Sherri was lying there with half a million tubes and gadgets hooked to her body.

"Miller, you ready to go back to work?" Frankie asked.

Her eyes opened, and she cracked a smile. "Almost got me killed, Donovan."

Frankie leaned down and kissed her on the cheek. "You don't know how happy I am to see you. I…"

"I'm just glad you got the son of a bitch."

"He got him all right," Lou said. "Shot him so many times, IA's going to have a field day with it."

"Screw IA," Frankie said. "The guy was going for his gun."

"I saw him," Sherri said.

"Mazzetti looked at her. "You saw him? Shot up like you were, and with your head turned the other way?"

"You bet," Sherri said. "I know how to play this game."

Frankie squeezed her hand. "You're all right, Miller. I can't wait for this old shit to retire so you can be my partner. And by the way, Lisa's dead. That sick bastard killed her too. Found her in a motel room across from the Monterrey."

"Son of a bitch!" Lou said. "Maybe I had her pegged wrong."

Lou and Frankie stayed for a half an hour more, and then Frankie said he had to get back to the station.

CAROL WAITED FOR HIM at the top of the steps, papers in her hand. "How did you know I was coming?" Frankie asked.

"Might have something to do with your big mouth. I can hear you the minute you enter the station."

"Guess I'll have to work on that," he said, then took the papers from her. "What's this?"

"The information you so rudely requested early this morning about Wilmington." As she walked with him to the coffee room, she asked, "How's Sherri?"

"I just left her. Miller's tough. She'll get better." He held up the papers she had given him. "Anything in here?"

Carol raised her brows. "For a little town, they got a lot going on."
Frankie walked to his desk and sat down to read.

A fire burned a home to the ground in a fashionable neighbor-hood west of the city. Arson is suspected, say police, who are also investigating the deaths of eleven men found among the remains of the house. Five of the men were outside the house, and it has been confirmed that they were shot. The identities of the dead have not been released; however, speculation is that drugs were involved....

In a related story, Detective Jimmy Borelli, officer in charge of ho-micide investigations has resigned, saying he and his family are going to retire to a more peaceful community, tired of the gang violence brought on by drug trafficking.

Borelli stated he believes that the shootings last night are tied to a case he had been working, the murder of Robert 'Bobby' Campisi, found dead several weeks earlier.

Also last night, the body of Jack McDermott was found near the park by his house in Cleland Heights. He was pronounced dead at the scene.

Frankie lowered his head, shaking it. He pounded his fist on the table and then buried his head in his hands. A few tears fell as he said a prayer, asking God to forgive his friend.

Jesus Christ, Nicky, you didn't have to do this. I'm sorry. I'm so fucking sorry.

Frankie didn't do much the rest of the day. Three times he picked up the phone to call Nicky, and three times he put it back down. No sense in it. There was nothing he could say that would make it right. People must have sensed he was in a pissy mood, because no one bothered him. At the end of the day, he packed up and left, driving home without even playing music.

On the way home, he thought about what Lou said to him the other day about Nicky. Lou's words echoed in Frankie's mind: 'You better ask yourself what he's ever done for you.'

What's Nicky ever done for me? He killed *for me. That's what he did.*

ALEX WAS ON THE stoop when Frankie pulled up. He beeped, but Alex barely waved and he didn't come running like he normally did. Frankie lit a smoke then sat with him. "What's up, Ace? Tough day?"

"They're all tough, FD. You know that."

Frankie laughed. "Damn cynical for such a young pup. You need to look at the bright side."

Alex reached his hand over. "Gimme a drag. I haven't had a smoke all day."

Frankie was tired of arguing with him about smoking. He handed him the smoke. "This is my last one. You're going to have to share it with me or follow me upstairs."

"I don't mind sharing, if you'd quit sucking the life out of them." Alex was quiet for a moment. "So how's that cop who got shot?"

"Not great, but doing better. I think she'll be okay."

"I knew something was wrong with that dude, just didn't know what. I thought he was just a perv."

Frankie nodded. "Me, too. Bad call on my part."

Alex took one final drag and handed it back to Frankie. "Hey, FD, why you sitting here talking to me when you got your woman waiting for you?"

"What are you talking about?"

"Your woman—Kate. She came in about half an hour ago, carrying groceries."

Frankie jumped up, smacking Alex across the back of the head playfully. "You little shit. Why didn't you tell me?"

"Just stealing a little time with you, that's all. Call me the Time Thief."

Frankie laughed, but about halfway up the first flight of stairs, he realized Alex was more down than normal. He went back out and found him with tears in his eyes. Frankie sat next to him and put his arm around Alex's shoulder. "Hey, Ace, why don't you tell me what's going on? You don't seem right today."

Alex quickly wiped the tears away. "Nothing. Go on upstairs with Kate."

"Not until you tell me what's up. Did somebody hurt you? Is your mom—"

He burst into tears and leaned against Frankie. "She's gone, FD. Fuckin' left me."

Frankie hugged him. "What do you mean, gone?"

Between sobs, he managed to get out, "Left a note saying she went away with some dude. Left me fifty bucks and said I'd have to take care of myself."

Frankie took a deep breath, then clamped his lips so he didn't say anything he'd regret. He picked Alex up in his arms. "Come on, we'll get Kate and go to dinner somewhere nice."

"No way. I'm not interrupting your night."

"That's right, you won't interrupt my night. We'll share it."

About halfway up, Frankie set Alex down. He didn't say a word as they walked upstairs, but he stuck close to Frankie. "Smell that?" Frankie asked as they neared his door. "Kate's cooking bacon. Guess we'll be eating here."

"Bacon at night?"

"I love breakfast dinners. Eggs, bacon, sausage, hash browns, toast." Frankie sighed. "Doesn't get much better."

When he opened the door he was greeted with *Walk Like a Man* by the Four Seasons, and the sight of Kate swaying to the music as she cooked. The table was set with his best china, which meant Walmart, but she had his best candles lit too. Frankie hated to break the mood, but...

"Hey, Irish, what are you doing here?"

Her back was to him, but she turned, startled when she saw Alex. Her surprise turned immediately to a warm smile. "Guess I better get one more plate."

She brought the plate and silverware then hugged Alex. "What is my most handsome friend doing? Hanging out with us tonight?"

Alex shrugged.

Frankie pulled him close. "Kate, Alex's mom left him. From now on, he'll be hanging out here permanently."

Alex looked up at him, his expression confused. "What do you mean, FD?"

"I mean you can live here with me."

"What about CPS?" Kate asked, concern showing on her face and in her voice.

"No reason they have to know. I'll work that behind the scenes."

"That might be tough, Frankie."

"Yeah, tough, but I'll get it done. He's not going to CPS."

"Are you shitting me, FD? For real? You'd really take me?"

Frankie leaned down, wiped Alex's eyes, and kissed him on the forehead. "This isn't some charity thing. I'd be proud to take you."

Alex burst into tears and wrapped his arms around Frankie's neck. "FD, I love you, man."

Frankie hugged him and let Alex's head rest on his shoulder. "I love you too. And you got a home you can count on now."

"I'm going to finish cooking," Kate said. "Who's up for a movie after dinner?"

"Me!" Alex yelled, and before she could ask what he wanted to watch, he yelled that out too. "Maltese Falcon."

"Oh God. I see Frankie has you trained."

After dinner they put in *The Maltese Falcon*, Alex and Frankie reciting half the lines before the actors did.

"How many times have you two watched this?"

"Not enough," Alex said, then turned to Kate. "'Here's lookin' at you, kid,'" he said in his best Bogart imitation. "That's from *Casablanca*."

Kate laughed and hugged him. "I know where it's from, little rascal. I've watched a few movies with Frankie too." She tickled him and he laughed hard, right from the belly, like little kids are supposed to.

During the second movie, Alex fell asleep leaning against Frankie's shoulder. After a few minutes Frankie carried him to the bedroom and laid him on the bed.

"So where are we sleeping?" Kate asked, then held up a skimpy see-through nightgown.

Frankie kissed her softly. "Thanks for being so understanding."

"Are you kidding me? That's the sweetest thing you've ever done. I brought this with me but didn't know whether I'd use it." She kissed him, and put a lot of invitation into it. "What you did with Alex convinced me. I think you finally found your heart, Frankie Donovan."

As she spoke Frankie realized he was excited. Very excited, and he thought back to what he hadn't felt when he thought of Shawna. He kissed Kate, just a little peck. "I think so, too, Kate Burns."

"So where are we sleeping, Mr. Donovan?"

"We've got that other room."

"There's no bed in it."

Frankie smiled and took her hand, leading her toward the empty room. "Guess we'll have to improvise."

ACKNOWLEDGEMENTS

THE TOUGH PART OF writing a book is not the writing, it's all the stuff that comes after that. I'll take credit for the writing. For the tough parts I am honor bound to thank the following:

My great copyeditor, Annette Lyon, from Precision Editing Group.

A fantastic graphic designer, Rank Fowler, for the book cover.

Morgana Gallaway from The Editorial Department, for the amazing layout and formatting.

And most importantly the army of beta readers who worked overtime to help me get this book into shape:

Missy, Rose, Aliza, Nick, Anthony Colline, Joe Michalcewicz, Danette Ondi, Carrie Shepherd, Shari Declet, Margaret Cyran, Marina Stevkovska, Stephanie, Kathy, Chris, Pat, and my good friend, Free Falconer.

Special thanks to my grandsons, Joey and Dante. And *grazie mille* to my niece, Emiliana, who kept me company and shared coffee with me on many late nights.

Lastly, to my wife, Mikki, the one who has put up with all of my nonsense for so many years. Without her, these books wouldn't be worth writing.

Ti amo con tutto il mio cuore.

About the Author

Giacomo grew up in a large Italian family in the Northeast. No one had money, so for entertainment he and his family played board games and told stories. He loved the city—the noise, the people—but it was the storytelling most of all that stuck with him.

Now Giacomo and his wife life in Texas, where they run an animal sanctuary with 41 loving "friends." One of them is a crazy wild boar named Dennis, who is Giacomo's best buddy. Sometimes Giacomo misses the early days, but not much. Now he enjoys the solitude and the noise of the animals.

Thanks for taking the time to read the book. I hope you enjoyed it.

Authors live and die on recommendations and reviews, so if you liked the book, please tell someone about it. And if you have a spare moment, I'd love for you to put a review wherever you can: Amazon, B&N, iBooks, Kobo, Goodreads, Linked-in, Twitter or Facebook.

If you're looking for more of Frankie Donovan and Nicky Fusco, they'll be back in *Murder Takes Patience*, the third book in the Friendship & Honor Series, scheduled for a March 2014 release. Connie and Tip will be back in *A Bullet For Dominic* late this year.

In the meantime, have a peek at *Old Wounds*, first in the Redemption Series, scheduled for early summer release.

———————————

Gino Cataldi loved three things: his wife, his son, and his job as a cop. Cancer took his wife. Drugs have his son. And Gino is pulling desk duty, suspected of killing a drug dealer.

Every night he dreams of a chance to make things right. That chance comes when a high-society woman is brutally murdered, her body parts spread all over town. The investigation quickly hits a dead-end...until a late-night caller with too much information contacts Gino. Between the mystery surrounding what she knows, and his penchant for helping women in trouble, more than Gino's curiosity is aroused. He only hopes she's not the killer.

———————————

You can read the first chapter on the website:
http://giacomogiammatteo.com

If you want to email me about this book, please use:
jim@giacomogiammatteo.com

Thanks again for your time,

Giacomo

11836704R00228

Made in the USA
San Bernardino, CA
03 June 2014